I0847124

wandering in the dark

BOOK TWO OF THE WANDERLAND SERIES

ETTA LANE

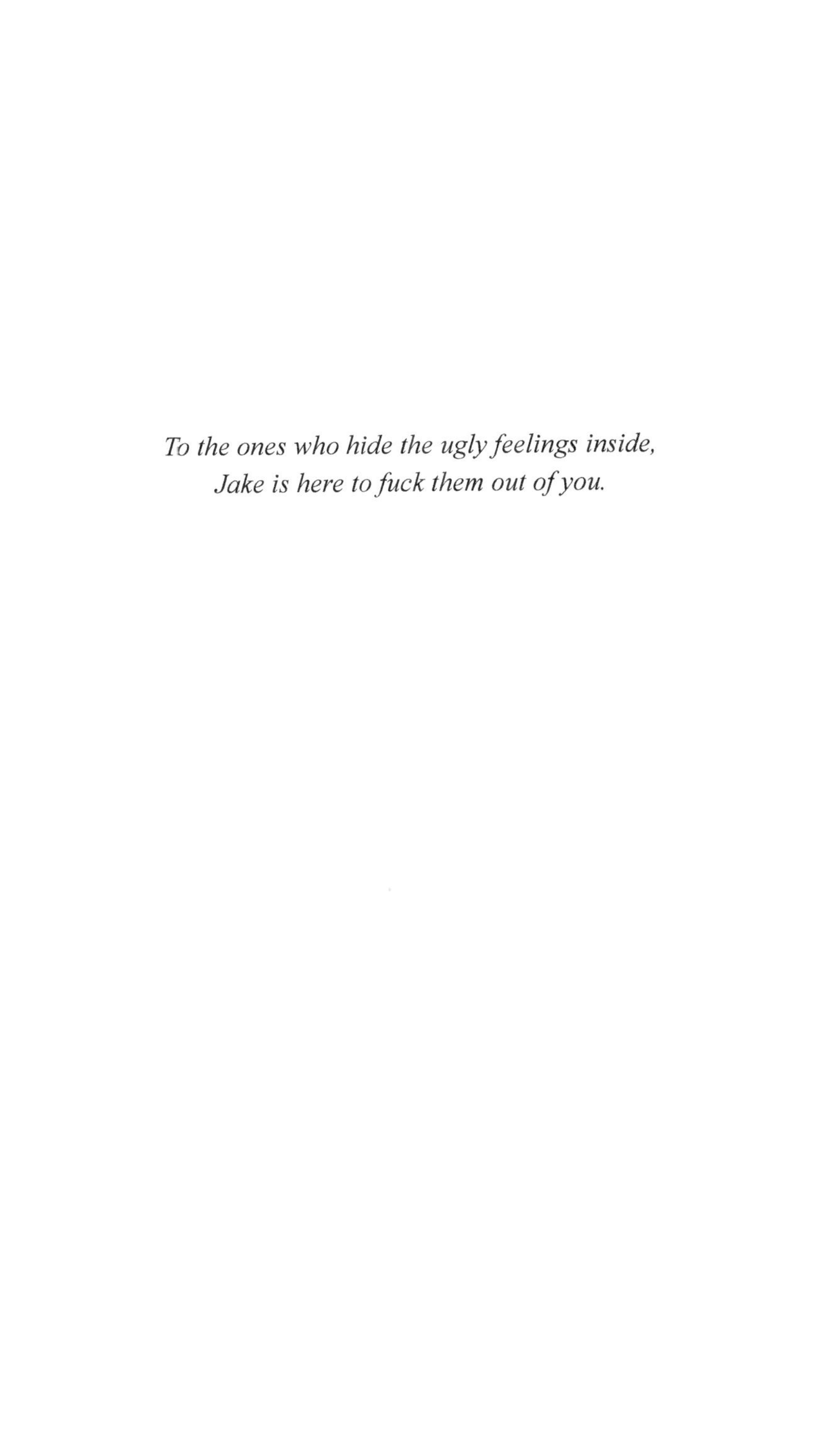

To the ones who hide the ugly feelings inside,
Jake is here to fuck them out of you.

reader considerations

Dear Reader,

In this book, a few things may be triggering or hard to read. This story takes on some heavy topics and big emotions, but I tried to handle them with care and sensitivity. Depression and dealing with the loss of a parent are the only things expressed on page. Off page, a larger range of events are covered, including parental addiction, neglect, sexual assault—not to the FMC—and the trauma that comes with those things.

If any of these things are hard for you to read, I encourage you to approach with caution or pass on this book. Your mental health and wellbeing should always be a priority.

playlist

Like Real People Do - Hozier
Jaws - Sleep Token
Broken - Seether, Amy Lee
Only Love Can Hurt Like This - Paloma Faith
Darkside - Neoni
Indigo - Sam Barber, Avery Anna
Take Me First - Bad Omens
The Death of Peace of Mind - Bad Omens
Chemicals - Dean Lewis
You Put a Spell on Me - Austin Giorgio
In Pursuit - A Tale Through Audio
Bloody Valentine - MGK
No Mercy - Austin Giorgio
Fuck Me Like You Hate Me - Jutes
I Feel Like I'm Drowning - Two Feet
Blood Sport - Sleep Token
Let The World Burn - Chris Grey
Daylight - David Kushner
Are You Really Okay - Sleep Token

CHAPTER ONE

amber

December 10th

I trace my fingers over the front row again, ensuring they're perfectly aligned and every label is evenly displayed. None of this needs to be done. It looked okay fifteen minutes ago when I started, but I've never been great at sitting still when I'm anxious. The candle display looks tacky no matter how many times I rearrange it, but I can't afford to buy fancy displays. The crates I have stacked on their sides only do so much on the foldout table.

The bell above the door chimes with Michele's arrival into Cedar and Sage. "I know, I'm late, but my Keurig chose today to give out, so I had to stop and get coffee. I got one for all of us, though."

"Please take her," Natasha quips from behind the counter. She's nineteen, and I only hired her a month ago, but she's been the best addition to the store, even if she's as snarky as me. "She's been redoing all the perfectly fine displays since she walked in here."

Michele gives me a sympathetic look, which I hate. "Do you want to step in the back for this?"

"Nope." I walk to the checkout counter and snag a pen from the mug there. "I'm ready, let's do this so we can go get Lily."

I swallow back the bile trying to make its way up, and Michele hesitantly draws a folder from her purse. It's a few signatures, no big deal. Despite knowing this is a necessity, it doesn't make it hurt any less. Jana, my aunt, has been my best friend and surrogate mother since mine died when I was eleven. She came into my life when I needed it most and quickly became my rock, no matter how much I tried pushing her away in the beginning. She's been a better mother than mine ever was, and created a safe space for me I didn't have before. When she had her stroke in July, it felt like the rug was pulled out from under me, and my world crumbled. Her house was the first and only real home I've ever known. Letting it go feels like I'm letting go of the first good thing in my life. *The only good thing in my life.*

"I marked the spots that need your signature."

Flipping through the pages, I sign all the necessary lines before gathering the papers and handing them back to her. Just like that, Jana's house is no longer hers. The money will go toward her medical bills that are stacking up, but that doesn't ease the ache in my chest. Even with her permission and being her power of attorney, letting the home go tears at my insides. For fifteen years that house has been a source of comfort, love, and understanding, and just like that, it's gone.

"Let's go. Natasha, please call if you need anything."

"I've got this, boss. Go have fun and let loose a little. You deserve it."

Michele shoves the folder back in her purse and grabs my arm, leading me out the door to her car. The cold winter air, smelling faintly of pine and snow, snatches the breath from my lungs, a grounding presence I desperately need. This day is about

Lily, and for the time being, I can shove down the pain and focus on the amazing accomplishments of my friend. We cruise through the downtown streets and out to the cabin to pick up our friend to celebrate the release of her newest novel.

Lily's an incredible romance author, and Michele and I are treating her to a spa day to celebrate, but she doesn't know Thoren, her boyfriend, set the whole thing up in preparation for a surprise party later. Thoren is everything she deserves after the hell she went through before moving here.

I spin the sleeve around the coffee Michele bought, trying to muster up a smile. She side-eyes me as we pull up to Lily's cabin, and I already know what she will say, so I beat her to it. "Let's just focus on our girl, okay? I'm okay. This is her big day, and she doesn't need to know."

After a quiet moment, she nods and grips my knee. "Okay. You have us. Please don't forget that."

I won't. I could never forget that I have them. Aside from Jana, they're all I have. Lily waltzed into my life earlier this summer, refusing to leave, and between Michele and her, they are the only reasons I keep going most days. Friends like them were a pipe dream as a kid. No one wanted to hang out with the drug addict's kid with dirty clothes. Secretly, finding out I had an aunt with a clothing store was as cool as finding out I had an aunt because I'd never had new clothes before. Now I have access to all the clothes a girl could dream of, and best friends who love me.

After a beat, Lily hops in the back seat as Michele passes her back a coffee. "Congratulations, bestie! Let's go celebrate!"

The drive to the spa in the town over is filled with laughter, but I don't register most of it. My mind is too busy thinking about how

Jana is doing today. Yesterday was a rough day for her, and she's been tired more often than not. I still see her most mornings, but it's often spent holding her hand while she rests.

"You okay up there?" Lily's soft voice breaks through my spiral.

I wipe my hands down my thighs, clearing my thoughts. "Yeah, sorry, just spacing out." Turning to the back, I paste a beaming smile on my face. "I'm so proud of you. How does it feel to have this book out in the world?"

"So good! I've loved writing all my books, but this one holds a special place in my heart. Look at all of us being girl bosses. Michele sold another house this week, you started your online store, and I published another book."

I try to hide my wince at the mention of the home sale that Lily doesn't know was Jana's, but Michele catches it and shoots me a sympathetic smile as we all head into the spa. Massages are lined up first, and by the time the three of us are sitting in cozy pedicure chairs, we're relaxed and happy—the stress of this morning not weighing so heavily anymore. We decided on a vibrant Christmas red while sipping on the complimentary champagne.

"Thank you, guys, this is everything I needed today," Lily says, leaning over to cheers our glasses.

"You deserve every good thing coming your way. We all do. Now Amber and I just need our own Thoren. Or at least a good fuck."

"If you get your own Thoren, then you will get that last part. Every. Single. Night."

Michele and I chuckle, but my mouth remains shut. They have no idea I'm still a virgin, and it's not exactly something I go around advertising. It wasn't a conscious choice, there just weren't any guys knocking down my door who enticed me, and before I knew it, I was a twenty-five-year-old virgin.

"Did you get all the new inventory yet?" Michele asks.

They've been helping with the boutique Jana owns since her stroke. With the hospital bills and rehab facility, I had to do something to make up the difference. I've been wanting to make a website for a while, and Lily convinced me this was the perfect time. I ordered double the usual inventory last month to accommodate the website sales, and sold out of half of it already.

"Most of the new things came in last week, but there are still accessories and shoes that I'm waiting on. I need a better storage and display system because they're all in boxes in the space behind the store."

"Ask Jake to make you something. I'm sure we can find you some racks online, but he can make nice display tables in the store so you can move those foldup tables to the storage area," Lily suggests.

"That's a great idea, and he'll do it for a good price. He's made a good chunk of Lily's and my furniture. I'm sure you've seen him around. Can't miss the only six-foot-four hot biker covered in tattoos around town." Michele fans herself while the girl painting her toes chuckles under her breath.

I've seen him around town, and he's exactly the type of man I fantasize over. If I still had a therapist, she would probably shake her head at the obvious daddy issues I have, but I can't help it. Growing up surrounded by darkness has made it hard to trust men. My soul has been tainted in a way few understand, and I have yet to find a man who can handle that.

amber

With our toes freshly painted, and a nice buzz flowing through Lily and me, we drive back to the cabin for the surprise party. The spa with the girls was exactly what I needed to keep my mind off everything, but this party will be hell for me. I don't love large crowds, especially when I know so few people. There's not much I won't do for Lily though, so I put on a bright smile as we pull up to the slew of cars at the cabin.

"What's going on?" Lily asks, glancing around.

"Let's go find out." Michele grins, and we lead her into the house where all of her and Thoren's friends are waiting to celebrate. I slip to the side and make my way to the kitchen while everyone takes their time talking with her. Glancing around, I see a few familiar faces, but none I know the names of until I spot Evelyn, Thoren's mom.

Evelyn has been visiting with Jana frequently in the afternoons while I'm working. She didn't know Jana before her stroke, but that hasn't stopped her from befriending her and even coming into the shop to check on me and bring meals and flowers. I don't know what we did to deserve her in our lives, but I thank God for her every single day.

Evelyn pulls me into a tight hug. "How are you doing, honey?"

"Today's a tough day," I admit. "I sold her house this morning." My eyes sting unbidden as a hot tear slips free. It doesn't matter that I haven't lived with her for two years, that house meant something to me, and Evelyn must see it. She takes my hands in hers, giving them a reassuring squeeze.

"Oh, sweetheart. Remind yourself that it's only a house and that a true home is with a person, not a place. You still have Jana, and she's what made it a home. I know that letting it go hurts, but it will take a huge financial burden off your shoulders. You aren't alone in this, and I'm here anytime you want to talk. The invite for Sunday dinners is open-ended. Please try to come."

David, her husband, comes up and places a glass of amber liquid in my hands before walking off with a smile and a shoulder squeeze. "He's one of the good ones." She winks at me. "Now, go mingle and drink your whiskey."

My hands tremble as I choke back the alcohol in one large gulp, trying not to splutter on the taste. The burn sears my throat, warming my insides as I make my way to the counter for a refill. There's too much pain lingering, and I want to feel numb. Michele and Lily are busy socializing when I spot a tall, tattooed man who has to be Jake. He stands taller than everyone in the room, his black shirt taut over his barrel chest. With messy dark hair and a slightly unkempt beard paired with tattoos spanning from the neck of his shirt down to his hands, he has the ultimate bad-boy look. It must be fate that he's here after the girls brought him up, so I make my way over to ask about working with him on some displays.

"Jake?" He turns to look at me, deep-ocean-blue eyes trailing over me with interest.

"Yes?"

"Hi, I'm Amber." I try to plaster a bright smile on my face, sticking my hand out. "Your reputation precedes you."

His face immediately sours. "Is that so?"

I leave my hand out, waiting for him to shake it. "Yeah, the girls said you're the man to come to."

"Did they?" He crosses his arms over his broad chest, glowering to the room. "You heard wrong."

I glance around the room, trying to see what has him upset. Coming up empty, I turn back to him, trying to work out what I did wrong. It can't be that there's another Jake who looks like him and I have the wrong guy … right? "Okay, well, the—"

"Excuse me," he mutters, pushing past me toward the hallway.

What a dick. I don't need new displays that bad and can certainly get them elsewhere. My night seems to be ending the way it started: complete and utter shit. The second glass of whiskey goes down smoother than the first, so I make my way back to the counter for a third.

The rest of the evening passes in a blur as I nibble on some snacks and nurse my drink. I'm going to regret this tomorrow, but at this point, I'm happy to numb the pain. With the party winding down, I take a spot on the floor near the fireplace, keeping my eyes trained anywhere but on Jake. The man avoided me the rest of the night, aside from his heated glares scorching my back. The glow of the flames reflects in the glass I'm holding as licks of heat travel up my back from the fire.

"My body is happy," Michele claims from where she's sprawled on the floor.

"Why is everyone on the floor?" Thoren asks. "I have furniture, you know?"

"Nahhh, the floor is nice. After getting a total rubdown today, then filling myself with alcohol, I am happy right where I am," Michele slurs.

"You ladies want to stay here? I make a mean hangover breakfast."

My eyes go wide with the realization Michele is my ride home. "I have to open in the morning!" Crap, I didn't even think of that when she picked me up. Lauren and Natasha can't cover tomorrow, and they're all I have.

"I'll take you home." Jake's eyes narrow as they bore into me once again. "I'm the DD, and my truck is good in the snow."

Why does it have to be this asshole who can drive me? Even if I stayed and had Michele drive me back early, I wouldn't have time to see Jana before opening the store, and I hate that. We're still short staffed, so I'll be working open to close, and evenings are closed for visiting hours at the rehab facility. Every day I get with her is a blessing, and I'm not willing to give even one up.

"Fine," I huff under my breath.

His smirk is wicked and has no right being as sexy as it is. I mutter a snarky "Thanks" and pull myself off the floor. The whiskey hits and the room spins, throwing me off balance. Jake is by my side in an instant, his large hands warm against my already overheated skin. He looks annoyed again, like my unsteady feet have offended him.

"Do you have a purse or anything?"

"I've got it all," Lily says, handing over my jacket and purse. The room still spins, so I struggle to get my hands through the sleeves. This isn't my proudest moment; tonight wasn't about me, but I needed to ease the tightening in my chest. With my snow boots back on, I stumble onto the porch.

Jake's big hands wrap around me again, leading me to his truck. Two steps into the snow, I slip, almost taking us both out. With a heavy sigh, Jake lifts me into his arms, carrying me the rest of the way to his truck.

"You're handsy," I huff, crossing my arms and refusing to hold onto him.

"And you're drunk," he snaps, opening the passenger door and plopping me into the seat. He leans over to buckle me in, and his crisp scent washes over me. His manhandling me, and the fact that he looks and smells good while doing it, really pisses me off.

He slams the door shut, stomps over to his side, and cranks the engine, then adjusts the heat. Before reversing, he leans into the back, grabbing a blanket he tosses on my lap. "It might smell like sawdust, but it's clean. My truck can take a minute to warm up."

His conflicting actions are making my head spin as much as the alcohol. What the hell is this man's problem?

"Where do you live?" His gravelly voice sends a shiver down my spine.

"Downtown, above Cedar and Sage. It's on Main Street."

He grunts in acknowledgment before carefully navigating us through the snow-covered roads back toward town. The longer we sit in silence, the more my anger over this whole day starts to fester and bubble over. Who treats someone trying to give them their business like the dirt beneath their shoes? It brings me back to the way people used to dismiss me as a child, and I'd be lying if I said that doesn't still sting.

Halfway to town, he breaks the silence. "Warm enough?"

I let out a sigh, crossing my arms over my chest. Yes, I'm acting like a petulant child, but this guy deserves it. "Like you care."

He glares over at me again but says nothing else the rest of the drive, and that's perfectly fine with me. His attitude is crap, and he hasn't apologized. I point him to the back alley where the entrance to my apartment is, and he stops right outside. It's a glass door with a small entryway with stairs leading to my apartment above my shop and the storage above the empty storefront next door.

Jake leaves the truck running but hops out to walk me the five steps to the door, fat snowflakes dusting our coats. His looming presence unnerves me as I fumble with my keys, trying to get the door unlocked. He plucks them from my fingers and unlocks the door for me. Turning to face him, I snatch back the keys and narrow my gaze on the deep scowl he's wearing on his ruggedly handsome, stupid face.

"Bye, Jake." I pull the door shut and lock it, then try not to trip up the stairs. When I unlock my apartment door and step inside, he's still standing there, waiting for me. He gives a nod when our eyes lock, then heads back to his truck while I kick off my boots and crash face-first into my bed.

CHAPTER THREE

April 25th

My suit bag hanging on the closet door is taunting me with its presence. I've only worn the stupid thing twice, and I hated it both times. Thoren's lucky I love him, because suits are the literal definition of hell. They're tight and restrictive and not made for big guys like me, along with the damn shoes that go with them. Give me a pair of Chucks and a leather apron, and I'll be a happy man. I've waited until the last possible second to walk over to his place, all to avoid putting on the monkey suit. With a sigh, I throw it over my shoulder and make the short trek, reminiscing on when I took this walk with Lily to check out her bathroom remodel. Who knew that a few short months later I would be renting her place and she would be marrying my best friend. Although, Thoren was set on making sure that last part happened.

It could be worse. At least I don't have to drive anywhere and can drink to my heart's content tonight. Another thing to thank Lily for, but I won't tell my best friend I think I'm starting to like his soon-to-be wife more than I like him. I've been renting her cabin for the last seven months, and I love the place. It's small, but most of it is newly renovated, and it's the perfect size for me. She even let me add on a garage this winter to store my bike and some tools in. The fact the cabin is on a secluded lane with only two other cabins, both owned by her and Thoren, doesn't hurt either.

There's a flurry of cars and people surrounding Thoren's cabin when I walk up, most heading to and from the large white tent on the side of the house. I trudge up to the front door and let myself in, like usual, right as Thoren and his brother River come in the back door.

"Happy wedding day, man," I say, clapping his back in a hug.

"Thanks, Jake. If you want to get changed in the guest room, I'll be right behind you. Riv will be right back to get ready too."

"Hey, my parents send their best, but they'll be leaving right after the ceremony if they can't catch you."

"Bad day?"

I nod and head up the stairs to avoid the looks of pity he and River are likely wearing. Since my dad's accident ten years ago, he's had a lot of bad days, but they've gotten more frequent. It's been rough on my mom as his sole caregiver, and even with me stopping by as often as I can to help, I know it's hard on them. Today isn't the day to worry about that. He has my mom, and he'll be okay if he takes it easy.

In the guest room, laid out on the bed, are two pink bowties and two pairs of pink socks with a note from Lily telling River and me she bought these special and it will break her heart if we don't wear them. I have to admit, even though she only uses it for good, she has emotional manipulation down to an art. River comes bounding through the door as I'm attempting to tie the bowtie, a big smile spreading across his face.

"She's a special one." He chuckles, picking up his pair of socks. "She bought Shadow a bandana that matches too."

Speaking of the devil, their dog comes trotting in wearing a pink bandana that says "Flower girl" on the front. "She's exactly what he needed. They have a love people dream about." He nods, looking wistfully across the hall to his brother's door. "Now help with this damn bowtie so I can get out of here before you strip."

"Oh, Jakey, if you wanted another look at my dick, all you had to do was ask," he tuts while practically strangling me with the pink ribbon. Thoren, River, and I lived together in college, and yeah, this wouldn't be the first time I saw the man's dick; not by a long shot.

The photographer grabs photos of us before marching back to the bride and her girls. River is their master of ceremony, and I am the unofficial best man. They decided against having any since the wedding has only thirty people attending, yet here I am, matching Lily's best friends.

Michele and Amber sit in the front row next to me in their matching pink dresses—Amber sitting first to ensure she gets the seat farthest from me. I can't help the chuckle that escapes me. She's been avoiding me since the ride home in December, but I have quite the surprise coming her way. I have to admit, as annoying as she is, she's sexy as hell with her hair curling around her heart-shaped face and the little stud in her nose glinting in the sunlight.

She looks different than the night we first met. That night, she had the same fake smile every girl in town wears when they approach me, but there was a spark in her eyes that made me want to poke at her and watch it burn. Looking at her now, though, there isn't a glow in her whiskey-colored eyes, and for some odd reason, that really irks me.

The rest of the guests take their seats as the wedding starts, and Thoren's dad walks Lily down the aisle. She looks like a vision in her white dress, the brightest smile gracing her lips. My best friend subtly wipes a tear from his eye, and a longing hits me like never before. I used to love one-night stands, giving and receiving pleasure to feel something other than numb for a night. It stopped feeling good a while ago, and loneliness overtook that emptiness in my chest. I want a partner, someone to spend my small bits of free time with, someone who sees past my looks and gruff exterior and gets to know the man I strive to be under it all.

Thoren and Lily have such a pure and beautiful love they want to cultivate and share with others and their hopefully growing family. While I love that for them, that's not what I want or need. A darkness in me calls for something more, someone I can fight with, someone I can punish and drag to the depths of my black soul, who won't balk at what they find.

I thought I saw that similar glint of pain in Amber when she stood up to me without fear, spitting her anger and hatred freely. My hand itched to spank her for her insolence, but the lifeless woman two seats down is different. A flicker of emotion appears on her face as Thoren promises to love and cherish Lily for the rest of their lives, but it's gone just as quick.

I focus back on the ceremony, as Lily whispers against Thoren's lips before he dips her in a passionate kiss and picks her up and twirls her around, burying his face in her neck. When they walk down the aisle hand in hand, his eyes trail down to her stomach more than once, and I recognize the smile on his face immediately. Thoren's been my best friend since we were kids, and we know things about each other no one else does. We've talked about our biggest goals in life, and when he talked about wanting to have children, he always got a certain look in his eyes; the same look he has now.

I can't wipe the stupid grin from my face. I may not want

kids, but I want that for him more than anything. Michele slips her arm through mine, coaxing me down the aisle to follow the happy couple.

"So, who do you think is next?" she asks, staring wistfully at our best friends.

"River, maybe? Are you dating anyone?"

"God, I hope it's not River. If he marries that twit, I don't think I can be his friend anymore. I've gone on dates, but no one is sticking. I had my great love, I'm not sure a person is lucky enough to get two."

I glance down at her, rubbing my chest with my free hand. Michele's a great friend, and an amazing and beautiful woman. The look in her eyes says she believes every word, and that breaks my heart. Ethan's a fucking idiot for not coming back for her.

"If neither of us are married in ten years, I'll marry you. It would be my honor."

She snorts out a laugh, slapping my chest. "Just because I saw what you're working with doesn't mean I want to marry you. It'll take more than a pretty dick to lock me down."

Why is everyone talking about seeing dicks today? I'm not a bad guy, and I do well for myself. I try to keep the pout off my face. I think my big dick would also aid in making me a good husband. "Fine. Your loss."

"I didn't say I wouldn't. I would be lucky to marry you. I'm just saying it's not a given because you showed me your sparkly dick a few months ago." She cackles, clearly amused with her own hilarity. It's not like I go around whipping out my cock for people, but she heard about my piercing and whined incessantly until I showed her.

I shove her arm from around mine. "You begged to see it, thank you very much. I rescind my offer."

She steps into the tent set up at the back of the house for the reception and heads straight for the bar. "That's fair. You're still stuck with me though. Papers should be ready for signature in about a week."

I nod to her and head over to River to see if he can confirm my suspicions on Lily's pregnancy. That, and I don't get to spend enough time with him. He and Thoren were the glue that held me together through college, whether they know it or not. They will always be my closest friends, and while I'm so proud of Riv's career in the MLB, I hate that he doesn't come home that often.

River is busy talking with his parents, so I veer to the bar instead to grab a drink. To my luck, a bratty little thing is waiting for a drink of her own. Her pink dress is fitted up top, flaring at her waist, the style accentuating a magnificent ass. Definitely didn't notice that at Lily's party.

"I'll get yours," I say, stepping close enough behind her that my breath fans over her hair.

"If that's your version of an apology, I'm not interested. Plus, it's an open bar, idiot." She mutters the last part, but I hear it clearly.

I chuckle under my breath as she takes a step closer to the bar and farther from me. A nicer guy would apologize, but I won't. She approached me like every other woman who wants to sleep with me because of how I look. The shallow women in town who want to claim they bagged the biker boy for a night, to see if the piercings feel as good as their friends swear they do. And yes, those are the words out of their mouths when propositioning me, but they have no real interest in me. They're scared of me, only saying what they think I want to hear, and I hate it. I like that Amber says what's on her mind, not scared of the persona I have. Even if she tried, like everyone else, to get in my pants without knowing me.

The emptiness in my chest during dull conversations with other women isn't so prevalent around her. Her anger and cutting words slice through me, and the brutality of them lights me up instead of shutting me down. This is what I've been missing. Maybe hate sex will at least make me feel something again.

"It wasn't." I order a whiskey as the bartender places one on the bar. We're the only two waiting for drinks, so I reach over her shoulder and pick hers up. "Thanks."

Her death glare is cute while she waits for the bartender to pour another for her, and I wiggle my fingers in a wave as I walk away. Playing with her is fun, like a hit of adrenaline to my thrill-seeking heart. Her snarky remarks to everything I say keep me on my toes, and I want to see what I can pull from her next. I make my way over to River and Thoren, who are watching the photographer take photos of Lily with Shadow.

"Congratulations, man. A wife and a … family all in one day. Big stuff."

Thoren turns wide-eyed, and Riv barks out a laugh, shaking his head. "She's going to kill you for letting two people know right away."

"Fuck, how did you even know? River overheard when she told me, so that's not on me."

"For starters, I saw the look in your eye. It's like you forget that I know you. But then you stared at her stomach the entire way down the aisle. Real subtle, buddy." He rocks back on his heels, looking wary but not sorry. "Really, though, congratulations. You two will make the most incredible parents."

He grins, and his eyes glaze over. They've been trying for a baby for a few months now. It's not conventional to get knocked up first, but their story is unique and filled with some bumps. I'm thrilled for them; this is what they both wanted.

"Thank you." He wraps me in a hug, gripping me tighter as he whispers, "But if you tell her you know, I will kick you out of your house so fast."

I chuckle and slap him on the back before Lily comes over

and steals Thoren for more photos. River and I walk in together and take our seats at the long table. Finally able to lose part of the suit, I discard the jacket and bowtie on my chair. Lucky for me, Amber and I are seated next to each other, so I'll have entertainment through the meal. I smirk around my glass as she sips from her whiskey, trying to ignore me. Her eyes swirl with the same amber color, fitting beautifully with her name. I wonder if that's where the name came from or if it's a happy coincidence.

"You going to get trashed again tonight? Try to sleep with everyone with a dick. Maybe find someone new to cry to."

She glares at me, not a glint or spark of life in her eyes. "I don't want to fight tonight, Jake. I'm too tired."

That resonates with me. A lot. She doesn't just look tired, she looks exhausted. Beautiful with her hair and makeup all done up, but it doesn't hide the dark bags under her eyes. I know what it's like to work yourself into the ground and feel absolutely nothing inside. Arguing with her is some of the most fun I've had in months, so I have no plans of stopping simply because she asked.

Is it also the reason I put in an offer on the workspace right next to her shop? Maybe. This blank version of her, though, isn't doing anything for me. She needs to feel something again, and I'm happy to ignite that spark.

"Too tired to try to get in my pants again? The rumors are true. I'm a great fuck. I never get off before my partner, and I'll be gentle with such a delicate flower like you." I lean closer to her, grazing her cheek with my thumb.

She white-knuckles her drink, and the anger coursing through her has a storm flickering behind her eyes. I'm half expecting her to throw her drink in my face, but she surprises me by plastering on a smile and congratulating the happy couple who are taking their seats next to us.

I watch her throughout the dinner and toasts, through the dancing and joy. She holds herself together so perfectly, smiling when she should, laughing when others do, but it all screams fake. It's so clear now that it's not the same fake persona women usually put on around me, but one I know well. It's one I wore most of my childhood while hiding the hurt others so carelessly threw my way. My fingers itch to unravel her real smile and find out what changed between December and now.

jake

After following her to the bar, I ask for another whiskey, and she switches to water. I keep my chest close to her back, heat radiating between us. Her soft curls are now messy, but her floral scent lingers. "Look at you being responsible tonight. No one to drive your drunk ass home this time?"

"Fuck off, Jake," she huffs, leaving her water and turning toward the house. I slip out of the tent behind her, following her in. My eyes are glued to the way her hips sway as she stomps inside. She spins on me when she gets to the bathroom door in the hall. "What is your problem?"

"There's the fire. I thought you might have lost it completely."

"What do you want from me? Everything I say and do makes you mad. Go away."

Her hair looks soft in this light, so I twirl one curl around my finger before tugging on it. She sucks in a sharp breath, going still. I bet she wouldn't be an empty fuck. She would make me feel a rainbow of feelings, and with loneliness at the forefront of my mind, I need that. I crave it.

"I want a lot of things from you, Whiskey. Mostly to take you into that bathroom and see what you have on under that dress. Want to proposition me again? I might go for it this time." With the back of my middle finger, I caress her jaw down to her chin and use the pad of my thumb to smear the lipstick on her plump bottom lip. My dick twitches in my slacks at the thought of those pouty pink lips wrapped around me. Her breath is shallow, pupils blown wide as she lets me touch her freely.

"What the hell are you talking about? I never propositioned you." Her voice is weak, with her eyes searching mine, but she still doesn't make a move to step away from me.

Using my free hand, I grip her thigh at the hem of her dress and take a step closer, crowding her against the wall. "Yes, you did. At Lily's party." Leaning in, I run my nose up her neck to her ear where the floral scent is stronger, wrapping tight around me.

"I was talking about your woodworking. That wasn't a proposition." I don't have time to let that confession sink in because she spreads her legs slightly and pushes her soft tits against my chest. "But this is."

I bite back a groan as she slides the hem of her dress up, exposing her lace panties. "Will I find you wet for me?"

Goosebumps erupt in the wake of my hand caressing the length of her arm. She still hasn't moved, but a small whimper leaves her lips when I clasp my fingers around hers. "Say yes." I need the confirmation, clear consent to act out every dirty thought racing through my brain.

I don't know what it is about this woman that gets me going. Why, out of all the beautiful women, she crawled under my skin after one meeting. I'll keep pushing as long as this feeling keeps buzzing through my veins.

Bright eyes meet mine, and she bites down on her bottom lip. "Yes."

Squatting, I wrap my arms around her thighs, carry her into the bathroom, and kick the door shut behind me. Her ass hits the countertop, and I lean over to flip the lock. Amber's gaze bores into mine—the fire I was looking for blazing bright.

"I've never done this before," she whispers, and a flush travels up her chest, tinting her cheeks pink.

I don't know if she means fucking in a bathroom, or with a guy she doesn't really know, but I don't care. I'll take care of her. My mouth descends onto hers as I nudge her thighs apart, stepping between them. Her ass fits perfectly in my large palms, and I drag her closer, lining her up with my aching cock.

Fuuuck, she feels so good against me. Small hands reach around my neck, curling into the hair there. Her silky dress is bunched around her thighs, and it's taking every ounce of strength not to rip it off her. I squeeze the cheeks of her ass tighter, trailing kisses down her jaw to her neck. Her body vibrates against me, a nervous energy radiating from her. "Tell me to stop, and I will," I grunt against her smooth skin.

"Please don't stop." Her shaky voice bleeds into the surrounding silence. My eyes meet hers, but the fear in her gaze is far outweighed by lust. Picking her up off the counter, I slide her down my body until she's standing against me. Our chests brush with each heavy breath as my fingers find the zipper on the back of her dress and pull it down.

The dress slinks to the floor, leaving her in a pale-blue lace bra-and-panty set. My mouth waters at the thought of tasting her, and suddenly, I don't care about her sucking my dick. I want to lick and suck every inch of her. There's no way Amber doesn't work out as much as I do, with her feminine curves blending gracefully into planes of muscle.

"Stunning," I murmur, my tattooed forearms flexing as I unclasp her bra and reveal more of her perfect, smooth skin. The striking black ink against her pale complexion takes my breath away. My gaze stays on the mirror while I slide her panties down her thick thighs, exposing each tantalizing inch of skin.

When the panties join her dress and bra on the floor, I step back, taking her in. Amber's body is perfection, every part more enticing than the last. Her chest heaves with heavy breaths, her tits sitting like perfect teardrops, tight nipples begging to be sucked. My gaze lands on the apex of her thighs, and with her need glistening in the light, a deep groan rumbles my chest.

"Fuck, Amber, you look like the perfect little toy to play with." I lift her onto the counter again, fumbling with the buttons of my shirt as her lips meet mine in a fiery kiss. "That's what you wanted from me, right? A little plaything to get you off?"

With my shirt joining the growing pile of clothes, I kneel, placing open-mouthed kisses to the inside of her thigh. The whimper escaping her has pride flowing through me as I continue my way north. Her hands grip the edge of the counter, keeping her from bucking against me, and her shoulders rest against the mirror, and God, what a sight it is.

The first lick to her sweet swollen lips threatens to tip me over the edge. My cock throbs painfully beneath my zipper when her sweet and tangy taste hits my tongue. Using my thumbs, I spread her open to lick deeper from slit to clit, then circle the small bud.

"Jake," Amber moans, and one hand spears into my hair, gripping like her life depends on it. I like the way my name sounds spilling from her lips.

I do that again, delving deep into her wet pussy, tongue-fucking it the way my cock will in a matter of minutes. "Fuck, fuck, Jake, I've never … Oh, god," she pants, and I continue my onslaught.

A guy's never gone down on her? Assholes are missing out on the sweetest pussy I've ever tasted. I add one finger, focusing my tongue on her clit. She's so damn tight with only one finger, but I have big hands. Working her gently, I sink the finger in and out of her until she's mewling on the counter, then slowly add a second.

She will need to take a lot more than that before she's ready for me.

The second finger gets worked in, and she clenches around me just as tight. My tongue circles her clit, and I unzip my pants, freeing my erection. It's painful, begging to be buried in her hot pussy.

I meet Amber's gaze as she looks down at me, and her eyes flutter shut. "You need to take one more finger. One more, then you can come and earn my cock."

A shiver racks through her, so I latch my mouth back over her clit and suck, with a third finger working into her. I keep my movements slow, stretching her around my fingers, and her slick arousal slides down my palm. Her pussy grips me as I stroke in a come-here motion, so I know she's close.

I double my efforts, circling her clit with my tongue again, and her nails dig into my scalp. "Jake, I'm coming, Jakeeee," her hoarse voice moans out, and her body tightens around me. Drawing my fingers from her, I lap up every drop of her release.

I've never been so close to coming in my boxers, but hell, I could at the sight of her coming undone for me—head thrown back against the mirror, legs spread wide on the counter, her high heels digging into my shoulders.

She's slumped against the mirror, with sex hair and panting for breath, so I pull a condom from the wallet in my back pocket and tear it open with my teeth before slipping it on. Leaving my boxers and pants around my thighs, I gaze into her eyes, notching myself at her entrance.

Her eyes go wide, and her mouth hangs open. "You're too big. I can't."

My large hand wraps in her hair, angling her head to look up at me. "You can take it," I grunt out, pushing the head inside.

Her eyes screw shut, and my head falls back because *damn*, she's so tight. Amber's body stiffens around me, so I put my thumb to her sensitive clit and swirl circles over it, coaxing her to relax.

"I'll take care of you. Relax and let me in."

She gradually loosens around me, so I push in, inch by inch. There's more resistance than I'm used to, but she hasn't said to stop, so I pull out and slowly ease back in, going a little farther each time. I feel each barbell sink into her tight heat. Sweat coats our skin as I lean forward and take a perky tit in my mouth. My tongue swirls around her nipple, drawing it into my mouth before biting down. Her moan shoots straight to my dick, and it takes everything I have not to pound into her.

"Just do it," she begs, nails marking my back. Our lips meet in a clashing of tongues, and I pull my hips back, then plunge into her in one hard thrust. My mouth muffles her scream, and I grip her hips, holding her while I drive into her. There's a sting of pain when she bites my bottom lip, drawing blood. My tongue darts out to swipe the bead of blood, and I'd be lying if I said the thought of her marking me doesn't turn me on more.

I lean back, and flickers of pain and pleasure cross her face. Her wild eyes meet mine again when I wrap my hand around her throat and squeeze. "That's a good little slut, taking my cock so well. You're going to come with me, aren't you? This pussy finally getting to claim what all the girls around here want."

I fight against the tightness of her, the flutter of her lashes, the fire behind her eyes, the way her body feels like heaven in my hands, and how I want to mark her porcelain skin. Instead, the frustration slams into me that I gave into another woman who wants to go around town bragging she fucked me.

Anger flows through me, so I take it out on her, rubbing harder against her clit as I fuck her on the counter. Heat rushes down my spine, her pussy gripping my cock like a vise. Her cries echo around the room as she shatters for a second time, setting off my orgasm. I spill into the condom, groaning out my pleasure.

My fingers release her neck, as she sucks in deep breaths and lets her head fall forward against my sweaty chest.

Matching inhales, we lean against each other until I slowly draw back and let my cock slip from her. There's red on the condom, a few streaks of blood coating it.

I look up in horror, meeting her honey eyes, ice coursing through my veins. "Amber …" My voice feels like gravel as I grit out, "Are you a virgin?"

"Not anymore."

She said it with no inflection, the look of euphoria wiped clean from her face. She slides off the counter and reaches around me to pull her clothes back on. Her fingers run through her hair as she fluffs it back out before she moves around me and leaves the bathroom without saying another word.

Now, I hate her a little bit more.

amber

I'm awake before my alarm. Again. It's happened frequently over the last three weeks since Thoren and Lily's wedding. My dreams have been filled with dark-blue eyes and rough hands skating over every inch of my body. I've never been an overly sexual person. A few toys in my nightstand make their way out sporadically, but now, they've been in frequent rotation.

The day after the wedding, I swear I was walking bowlegged, and the ache lingered for a few days. Jake commanded my body in a way I only ever dreamed of, and his degrading words mixed with the possessive way he controlled my pleasure brought out a side of me I never knew. Little did I know that the same cutting words from my mom's mouth coming from Jake's would be my undoing.

No part of me went into that day thinking I would sleep with him, or anyone. It's not like I was keeping my virginity for someone special; it just hadn't happened yet. I was a loner in middle and high school, never putting forth the effort to have friends. It wasn't until I was around sixteen and Jana forced me into therapy that I fixed my attitude. At that point, though, I had the reputation of being quiet and angry. Then along came Jake with his filthy mouth and skilled hands that are so at odds with the man I met at Lily's party.

None of that stopped the ache he left behind or the constant desire I battle since I know what sex with a man feels like. The girls don't know about it. Hell, I never even told them I'm a virgin.

Was. Was a virgin.

Shoving the blankets off my overheated body, I slip out of bed and get ready for the gym. That's been the one saving grace in this mess. With my body and emotions keyed up every morning, I've been killing it with my workouts. Rising before the sun isn't for everyone, but I love it. I've never been afraid of the dark. The quiet somber views outside my door set me at ease. It's a comfort to blend into the world around me when I'm falling apart inside.

The mostly empty gym is why I like coming at this time. This obsession is another thing I have to thank Jana for. When I moved in with her at eleven, I was angry: at her, my life, the world. She was so patient and helped me find a way to work out that pain without following in my mother's footsteps. Sucking in a deep breath of stale gym air, I try to drown out the sting in my eyes.

I set about stretching first, which only allows my mind to wander again, and of course, the first place it goes is to Jake. We haven't seen each other since I walked out of that bathroom, but it's for the best. He doesn't seem like the dating type. Though, who am I to judge. I went on one date in high school that didn't end great and a few random ones here and there. Dating apps in a small town make for … limited options. A few first dates sparked nothing, and two made it past the first date but fizzled fast after they found out I work sixty hours a week and don't do anything for fun.

Jana always tried to put me back on that horse, to get me to go out to the bars and try new things. I've been to therapy enough; I can admit I'm a little socially stunted and don't do well with that.

Without Lily and Michele randomly showing up and making me do things, I would be a hell of a lot more alone still.

With a limber body, I move to the machines. For the next ninety minutes, it will all fall away while I punish my body to within an inch of its life. It may not be healthy to use exercise as a form of grief therapy, but so far, it's working. Kind of. Most days, I feel like that angry kid again, raging because her mom died.

People told me I was lucky to have a chance to say goodbye, to know Jana's time was limited after her stroke. There's nothing lucky about losing the only person who loved me despite knowing my soul inside and out. Nothing about losing the only person I had left in this world was *lucky*. I fucking hate that word now.

Loading up the squat rack, I add on forty-five-pound plates instead of the usual forty pounds. Something needs to take the edge off this grief and pain coursing through my veins.

"Hey, Amber." Kyle nods as he sets his things by the squat rack next to me. Four of us have consistently come to the gym around this time the last few years, so we've gotten to know each other. Kyle's a decent guy, an electrician who's a few years older than me. Objectively, he's good-looking and definitely fit, but he has a preppy vibe about him that doesn't entice me.

Jake, with his tall, dark, and broody, is exactly what draws my attention … clearly. I'm pretty sure most people don't lose their virginity with two orgasms and a dick so big it felt like it was splitting me in half, but I guess I'm special. Special in the way that I'm pretty sure we hate each other even more now.

"Hey, Kyle. How are you?"

He swings his legs, stretching them before he starts. "I had a good weekend but have a busy week ahead." His eyes rake over me with an assessing gaze. "How are you holding up?"

My throat tightens at the insinuation because I know I look like crap. It's been three months since Jana passed, and I've been trying to fight the tides and keep my head above water ever since.

I can't tell that to Kyle, though. He's been a decent friend, a little flirty at times, but we aren't on a level where I can talk to him about this. Removing myself from the conversation is the easiest solution. I finish my last set of squats before answering.

"I'm doing okay, thanks. I'll see you around." Water bottle in hand, I finish my workout with a ten-minute sprint on the treadmill before heading out. The orange rays cast around the parking lot shine from the rising sun, the dew on my little Honda starting to evaporate. There's more tension in my body now than there was when I got up this morning, and a long hot shower is calling my name.

My little studio apartment is above Cedar and Sage, the boutique I now own and run. It was Jana's baby, but now it's mine. She never married or had children, choosing to instead pour all her time and love into this quaint shop. When I turned twenty-one, she surprised me by getting the small space above renovated for me. Her house was my comfort blanket of sorts, and while she loved that I was so happy there, she wanted me to have my own space. I moved in here but still had sleepovers with her a few nights a month. Just one of the many things I miss now that she's gone.

After my usual Monday morning stop following the gym, I pull into the alley behind my shop and park in my spot in the small lot back here. Aside from a shop owner at the other end, I'm the only one who uses the space above my store to live, and the buildings behind us are all storage facilities. It's a surprisingly quiet and nice place to live, but I'm worried that's all about to change.

The end unit storefront next door has sat empty for the last six months, but the for-sale signs disappeared about two weeks ago. Michele said it was purchased but the new owner wanted to keep it under wraps until they moved in. I've had my fingers crossed for a bakery or coffee shop.

After breakfast, ten minutes standing under the hot spray of the shower, and a quick cuddle session with Socks, I meander over to the storage space out back. The previous owner has allowed me to use a section of his space for free, so I house all my extra inventory in it. The website I set up has been bringing in almost triple the income that the store does, so naturally, the inventory orders have tripled. When the new owner takes over, hopefully they will let me rent out this space still. It's a warehouse with two rooms on either side, both the size of a two-car garage. I need to keep my one room here, or I'm royally screwed.

An hour of filling and packaging orders later, I head back to open the store. This is my routine most days, and I like it. Loneliness creeps in at times, but I see Lily and Michele here and there, and Evelyn stops by to check on me periodically. Bounding up the steps to my place, I rush inside to grab Socks before heading back down to the store.

This little fuzzy kitten made his way into my life last month when I found him abandoned in the alley. His little meows shot me in the gut, and we've been inseparable since. He's a spunky little thing, always scampering around, and has yet to tear up anything in the shop, so I bring him with me most days. The name fits him perfectly, with his black fur but a white belly and little white socks on his feet.

The morning ticks by with only a few customers, but Mondays are typically slow. At least I have Socks, who hangs out in a bed on the front counter while I peruse through options of what to order for my summer stock. Around noon, the bell chimes over the door, and Michele walks in with a to-go bag from the deli down the road.

"Hey girl, I brought you lunch," she says, placing the bag down next to me and scooping up my kitten.

"Thank you. Are you trying to butter me up for something?" Michele's a busy woman as one of only two realtors in town and doesn't make it into my shop nearly as often as Lily does. She's also not typically someone who shows up unexpectedly.

She puts Socks on the floor, and he scurries off. "Actually, your new neighbor moves in today, and he is open to negotiations about you renting the space you're using."

"Did the same person buy the store next door and the shop behind?"

"Yeah, he will be doing something similar to you. His storefront will be open with his furniture on display, and he's going to turn the storage unit into a workshop. And lucky for us, we know the guy and can persuade him easily."

There's the fucking word again. I feel the blood drain from my face as I start piecing two and two together. "Jake is my new neighbor?" my quiet voice squeaks out.

"Yep! How great is that? He'll be here within the hour to start renovating the store. He said he would stop in before you closed to discuss the storage situation." The more she talks, the more my hands shake, but I rub them down my legs to try to hide it. "Why aren't you more excited?"

What am I supposed to say to her? *He hates me and hasn't spoken to me since I let him take my virginity three weeks ago?* I plaster a smile on my face, trying to calm my nerves. "Just a little shocked is all. I'm not sure we got off on the best foot. Maybe a little nervous that he won't let me rent the space I need out back."

"Oh, please." She waves me off. "Jake is a teddy bear. He will be more than happy to help you out. I have to run, there's a showing I need to be at in twenty. Just wanted to bring you lunch and the good news. Dinner and drinks at my place this weekend still, right?"

I nod, unable to form words, and she blows out of here as quickly as she blew in. *What the hell have I done?*

CHAPTER SIX

The engine of my black Harley Dyna cuts through the quiet evening as I back it into a parking spot in front of my new store. *My store.* I have my work in showrooms in Seattle and Spokane, but this one here is all mine. Anderson's Fine Furnishings is becoming everything I dreamed it could be. It will showcase my work and have pieces people can buy off the floor. I've been saving for this next step since before I put my work into other showrooms, and when the previous location I used as a workshop was no longer available, it forced me to take the leap.

The storefront itself isn't exceptionally large, but it will do. I'll spend most of my time in the workshop out back anyways. This is a better setup than what I imagined, and when Michele and I did the walk-through, I knew it was the right place. Amber owning the store next door is just icing on the cake. My chest vibrates, so I pull my phone from inside my leather jacket.

DAD:

Proud of you, son.

JAKE:

Thanks, Dad. I'll get you in here as soon as it's finished.

A proud grin fills my face as I step off the bike and take in my future. While this is my dream, I also did it for my parents. To make them proud and pay back a tiny bit of the hard work they put into raising me. My mom was a homemaker while my dad worked construction. Money wasn't abysmal, but it wasn't something we had in abundance, yet they made it work. When I started asking to play sports, Dad increased his hours while Mom took on odd jobs to help pay for my equipment and fees. They never told me no, always just found a way to make it work. Ever since Dad's accident, though, I have worked my ass off to switch those roles and take care of them in the same way.

My parents deserve it, not only because of the way they raised me but for being my best friends. I struggled with friendships in school. Thoren and River have had my back since day one, but close friendships outside of them are few. It takes me time to let people in because of how I was treated by other kids. Cedar Ridge isn't an exceptionally wealthy town, but there's still a disparity between middle and lower class. Teasing started at a young age for those of us who wore second-hand clothes. Even with my mom's incredible sewing skills, it was easy to see when she repaired holes in clothes instead of buying me new ones. That bullying shut me down at such a young age.

Feeling like you don't belong and seeing others turn their nose up at you messes with a kid. It hardened me to the world and made me angry. I saw the cruelty of the people around me early on, so I vowed to be a protector. To use that anger to stand up for those who were different; less fortunate.

I let comments about me roll off my back because I had my parents' love and support. Comments about my mom, my dad, other kids, women—I didn't stand for that. It got worse as I got older, so I tried to fit in with different crowds. I was always accepted but as a kid on the edge. The jocks had a reputation for bullying and treating girls badly, neither of which I stood for. The popular kids liked that I had a reputation for fighting because they felt cool around me. Girls wanted to hang on me and liked that I filled out faster than a lot of my peers. None ever took the time to get to know me, not wanting to actually date the poor kid who liked to hang out in the woods with his best friend.

In college, I struggled with more of the same. I stopped making so much of an effort to seek friendships, but then women came to me for the same reasons. The broody guy slinging drinks at the bar, the quiet tall guy with big muscles and tattoos. I know I'm attractive, and I've used it, but I didn't want to. I wanted someone to see the real me and to make an actual effort.

I tried to protect people. To support them and help others feel like they belonged, but it all turned into more anger and more fighting as I retreated further into myself. My parents were supportive through it all. They knew I used my size to stop bullies, and they knew I struggled with our financial status, but they loved me anyway.

Several times, I tried to change people's perception of me, taking on an easygoing persona, someone always ready with a smile who could move from crowd to crowd. The kids ate it up, but still, the friendships remained surface level, outside of Thoren and River. Even with them, I struggled with feelings of not being good enough. They had things I didn't, could do things I couldn't, and life just seemed ... easier for them. To no fault of their own, it got worse in college when I saw how they hardly studied but had amazing grades. How women flocked to them, and they could so easily let them in. Them paying for my part of the rent was as humiliating as it was lifesaving.

Yet, through all my struggles, my parents were there, encouraging open communication, providing support, and lightly scolding me for my attitude and fighting problem. So yeah, this is for them as much as it is for me.

Placing my helmet on my handlebar, I run my fingers through my hair and turn toward Amber's store. Thoren and I spent the afternoon moving equipment into my workshop and setting up worktables and storage. I still have more to move and organize, but the majority is thrown in there. We separated around five so he could have dinner with his wife, and I stopped at home to grab some food and a shower.

Now it's time to pay a visit to my favorite plaything. All day I waited for her to come storming over and yell at me, but I should have known that's not her style. She put me in a fucking headspin these last few weeks. My brain felt like a pendulum going from feeling awful that I was too rough with her for her first time and furious that she didn't make it fucking clear to me. I'm not sure I would have stopped if I had known, but I would have treated her differently, been gentle and slow and took my time getting her ready. How dare she put me in that position to feel like the asshole when I didn't know.

Bells chime from above the door when I open it, drawing golden eyes to mine. Her face pales, and her breathing shallows in the tight crop top she's wearing. *That's right, Whiskey, you can't hide from me anymore.*

Michele informed me she told Amber, and the way her back straightens and she works her jaw tell me she's ready for a fight. "Jake. Let me lock up and close the store, then we can talk."

"You sure you want to be locked in here with me?" I ask, trailing my hand over a clothing rack as I walk toward her.

"Please." She rolls her eyes, letting her sass come out. "If you want to go somewhere else, be my guest. The door's right there." The smirk on her face is a challenge, one I won't back down from.

I bite the inside of my cheek to hold back my smile. Her spark is back, and it's everything I hoped for. There's a single chair in the corner of the store near two small dressing rooms, so I take a seat and put my hand out for her to continue. "Go ahead, I'll wait right here."

Looking around, I see it's a nice store. She has a plethora of items, from clothes and shoes to accessories, home decor, and even bath products. It's cute, but the shelves and displays have seen better days. I train my eyes anywhere but on her thighs being hugged by black leggings, remembering how smooth they felt beneath my palms. The last thing I need is to get hard thinking of her breathy moans and the way her nails dug into my skin when I licked her pussy. *Fuck, Jake, get your head on right.*

A jingle catches my attention before a black and white kitten jumps onto my lap. It's a fluffy little thing wearing a blue collar with a small bell. Cats aren't my thing, I'm more of a dog guy, but I have to admit it's a cute little fella. He climbs up my chest, sharp claws digging into my skin as he makes his way to my neck and settles in.

"Who is this little guy?"

Amber glances over from where she's closing the register. "That's Socks. I found him in the back alley last month, so if you find another one, it's your turn to take him home."

I scoff. That will not be happening, even if his soft fur feels nice against my scruff. I give him some pets, setting off quiet purrs, then let him snuggle into my shoulder. Amber disappears through a door in the back, only to reappear a few minutes later with a stool that she places a few feet away from me.

Her foot taps on the floor as she wipes her hands down her thighs. I make her nervous, it seems. My gaze travels from her top knot to the sliver of skin peeking between her top and leggings. There have been too many nights over the last few weeks that I wrapped my fist around my cock and stroked it to thoughts of her.

As much as she may piss me off, I can't deny that the sex was beyond compare.

"I would like to start over. Clearly, we've had some miscommunications and lapses in judgment. We're going to be neighbors now, and I really would like to rent the storage room from you."

My grunt scares the kitten, who meows in my ear. "Miscommunications? That's what you want to call it? When you told me my reputation precedes me, then told me you didn't mean in a fuckboy way, then immediately slept with me while lying about being a virgin?"

I love the glint of anger in her eyes even as she winces at my harsh tone. Taking a deep breath, she steals her spine and crosses her arms, deliciously pushing up her tits. "Yeah, Jake. All of that is on you. If you took my comment about your *business* as a comment on your sex life, then that's your problem. And I told you I had never done that before."

I bite my cheek to keep my angry words from flying out again. I'm not the only one in the wrong here. The way she came onto me at Lily's sounded like a proposition. Yeah, I might have been annoyed with her before she even spoke to me, but who wouldn't be? She was moping around crying at her best friend's celebration. That's a desperate cry for attention if I'd ever seen one. I'm not wrong on being mad she didn't tell me she's a virgin, though. She didn't make that clear at all.

I rest my elbows on the armrests, steepling my hands in front of my face, my fingers tracing over my lips. I'll wait for her to admit equal fault and apologize. We stare at each other, the tension building between us before she heaves out a heavy sigh. "What do you want me to say, Jake? I need the space. Are you going to let me have it or not?"

I pull Socks down and snuggle him into my chest. His little paws bat at my fingers, drawing a smile from me. Amber eyes me warily, but I don't have an answer for her yet. I don't need the space at the moment. One room will hold all my tools and spare wood, and the main space is plenty big for my worktables and current projects. It wouldn't hurt to have some extra money coming in from a space I'm not using anyway.

"Why should I rent to a liar?"

She stands up and moves to a table of folded shirts, reorganizing them. Even with her back turned, I can see the flush traveling up her neck. "I didn't lie. You just didn't care to clarify."

"Don't pull that shit with me. You know you weren't clear about being a virgin." After taking a breath to try to calm down, I ask the question that's been bothering me the most. "Did I hurt you?"

Her eyes cut to me over her shoulder, a scowl covering her pretty face. "Like you care. But no, you didn't. It was … better than I anticipated for my first time."

The knot in my chest loosens a little at her confession. I'd be lying if I said I didn't want to punish her with that fuck, but I'm not into pain in that way. I want my women to experience pain at my hands, but only when it's mixed with pleasure and we have talked about what they can handle.

"Look, we both got what we wanted, let's move on. Are you going to rent to me, or do I need to find a new space?"

So she wanted to lose her virginity to me? I believed her when she said she was talking about my woodworking the night we met, but maybe she lied about that too. Or maybe she just means we both received an unexpected orgasm and all is good. Either way, it doesn't matter. She clearly needs the space, and I'm not that much of an ass that I'll kick her out of it for no reason. "I'll rent to you. How does a six-month contract sound? That way if I end up needing the space we both have time to make other arrangements?" It also gives me an out if I no longer enjoy this back-and-forth between us.

"I can't afford more than four hundred a month," she mutters.

I hadn't even thought of a price, but any money is better than none. Plus, I know better than most how expensive owning and running a business can be. The money is fine, but I want something more from her; I just don't know what it is yet.

"On one condition, I want an IOU that I can call in at any time."

Her huff of annoyance is cute, as if I actually care. "Men always want something. What gives you the right to demand more after the way you've treated me?"

I bristle at her insinuation. Putting down the kitten, I step up behind her, crowding into her space. The hitch of her breath gives away how affected she is, even as she continues refolding shirts.

"My storage space means I get to make the rules." Using my pointer finger, I caress from below her ear, over her shoulder, and down her arm. I get enjoyment watching goosebumps follow the path, and she stops breathing altogether. Leaning in, I put my lips to her ear. "Those are my conditions, take it or leave it."

"Fine," she grumbles. "But I still don't like you."

It's satisfying that she refuses to turn and look at me. There's no doubt I'm under her skin the way she's under mine. I prefer an even playing field, but I wouldn't complain about having the upper hand.

Walking to the front door, I chuckle, flipping the lock. "Feeling's mutual. See you around, then. Lock the door behind me, Amber."

With that, I step out and walk back to my bike. This buzz coursing through my body can only be worked out one of two ways, so after making sure she locks her door, I head toward the gym. I have a feeling I'll be spending a lot more time there in the coming months. For the first time in almost a year, though, there's a genuine smile on my face, and I intend to make sure it stays.

jake

I've been working a minimum of ten-hour days to stay caught up with all my orders and continue making some of my best-selling pieces. Part of me thought that would slow down once I had my own shop, but it seems to be the opposite. The mornings have been spent going over plans with the construction crew that's working on my storefront. Oh, and in the afternoons and evenings, I've been organizing my shop out back while trying not to fall behind on orders.

While the store is coming together quickly and will be ready to open to the public after next week, I'm not ready. I have order slips and emails of orders strewn across my work desk, and I need to hire people to work in my store as well as a new apprentice since the last kid moved. There's one person I know who thrives on order and creating lists who would be happy to help, so I suck up my pride and dial Lily.

An hour later, her car pulls into the lot beside my workshop and parks next to Amber's. I've been keeping the two bay doors open while I work to let in the fresh spring air and help with the sawdust and stale smell. She waves, then moves to her back seat, pulling out a bag the size of her, so I rush over to snag it from her hands.

"You can't be carrying things like this," I scold her while peeking into the thing. "What the hell did you bring anyway?"

When she stops in her tracks, I realize my mistake. I've been really good at keeping her secret for the last month, but I think I just blew it. Thoren's going to kill me.

"And why exactly can't I carry things?" She scowls, hands on her hips. On someone like Amber or Michele, it might be convincing, but on sweet Lily, it just looks adorable.

My brain scrambles for any other excuse besides her pregnancy. "It's a heavy bag, and I know your laptop is in here. If that thing breaks, I know you'll be upset, and I can't risk pissing off my landlord."

Her narrowed eyes assess me for the lie as we settle into the corner I've claimed for my temporary office. When she says nothing more, I assume my lie was good enough. Lily is an incredible author, or so Thoren says. I certainly haven't read the four copies of her books she intentionally left in my cabin when she moved out … and I know her laptop is a very expensive and prized possession of hers. She looks through the messy desk while I pull out her laptop, notebooks, binders, a pack of pens, and every office supply you could imagine. I knew she was the girl for the job.

"What exactly is it you need? A calendar of projects and due dates? A way to track your orders and payments? A whole business plan?"

I scratch the back of my neck, trying not to put all my short-comings on her. These are the exact feelings I have fought to get rid of. "I took business classes in college, but technology and organization have never been my strong suit. I think I need a better way to track orders. The problem is, I get orders over email, phone, and my website, so keeping track of them and the time they came in and if they paid and such is not going well. I tried to make a spreadsheet, but I keep falling behind on filling it out. My next step is probably a business manager of some sort, I just can't afford one right now."

If this was anyone else, I would be embarrassed to admit this. It's my business, and I should know how to run it, especially since I started it in college over nine years ago. Lily doesn't look at me like I'm stupid though, she just nods and tells me to get out of her hair so she can get to work.

My mom called earlier this morning asking me to visit because she had an idea, and I have a proposition for her. Leaving Lily to her work, I hop on my Harley and make my way to my parents'. They live right outside of downtown in a quiet neighborhood. It's the same small house I grew up in, a little tattered around the edges but full of love. The rumble of my engine draws stares that I ignore as I park in their small driveway.

My boots crunch on the gravel, and my mom throws open the screen door with a wide smile. "Jacob!" She holds her arms open. "I've missed you. Do you need lunch?"

I tower over my mom's five-two frame when I hug her. At six four, I'm taller than most, even my dad at an even six foot. Sometimes, I feel like a giant who stands out no matter where I go, and sometimes, I'm grateful it gets people out of my way. "I was here this weekend for dinner, Mom. I'm going to pick up lunch for Lily and me later since she's helping me out."

She pats my arm, settling into a chair beside my dad in the living room. "That's kind, honey. Tell her we say hello. I wanted to show you my idea for your store." She pulls out a tablet while slipping on her glasses, and my dad chuckles.

"Hey, son. She's been on that dang site for days now searching for ideas." My dad's face is pale, and he makes no effort to move, so I know it's a bad day.

A few months after I left for college, he had an accident on a job site. His harness snapped when he was framing a roof, and he fell off the scaffolding to the concrete slab below. He's lucky to be alive, but with a broken hip, shattered femur and shoulder, as well as a few cracked ribs and a popped lung, he never fully recovered. My parents have been living off disability ever since, along with some help from me.

"How are you doing, Dad?" I ask, stretching my legs out in front of me.

"Hanging in there. Can't wait to come see the place when it's all set up." He could come at any time, but he hates the pitying looks he gets at limping with his cane, and on bad days, I know the pain is too much to leave the house.

"Here it is! For your walls, I was thinking you could do a mix of pictures of local landscapes and photos of your previous work. That way people can get a better idea of your skill and range of items they can ask for. Also, I was thinking of a lookbook for an extensive list of your past work with photos for the front desk." My mom scrolls through the photos she has saved of ideas. "I may have already ordered all these things," she says under her breath. "They're stacked in your old room. I haven't gotten the frames yet."

I bark out a laugh, expecting nothing less from my mom. She doesn't only offer to help, she helps, then tells you about it after. Crafting is a hobby she loves and is incredibly skilled at. She's made cushions and pillows for many benches, chairs, and couches I've made without me ever asking. It's where I came up with the idea for the shop I'm hoping she'll agree to.

"Thanks, Mom. I'll make sure to order the frames today. I'll have to come back for the photos when I have my truck."

"If you didn't have that death trap, then that wouldn't be an issue, Jacob." She eyes me over her glasses, giving her best scolding face. She knows I'm never giving up my Harley but loves to give me shit about it. *My poor baby could get so hurt. Imagine how skin grafts would look over those beautiful tattoos.* As if she loves my tattoos, which she doesn't, but does her best to hide the fact.

"I actually have a big ask for you. I need someone to work in the store for a bit until I can hire someone full-time. I was hoping you would be willing to help me out." I scratch the back of my neck, hating having to ask my parents for anything more in life. "The crew is building a little office in the back that I was thinking of setting up as a sewing room for you—if you want, that is. You can sell your pillows and such that you make to go with the furniture and work on it anytime it's slow."

Her eyes fill with unshed tears. "I would love that. We're so proud of you, and I'm happy to help whenever and wherever you need me."

We sat and chatted for another thirty minutes before I told them I needed to pick up lunch for Lily. A quick text to Thoren informed me she's been craving burritos this week, so I stopped in town to grab some. She's exactly where I left her, moving between our laptops and the mess of papers. I force her to take a break to eat, and a small smile creeps over my face at her excitement over the burritos.

"I'm updating and extending your spreadsheet, but I also bought a planner that I'm filling out with similar info. Both are color coordinated to show how they were ordered in case you need to go back and find them, and also have different markings depending on if they have been paid up front or not. In my personal opinion, you need something beyond that. When was the last time you updated your website?"

I wince, swallowing down a big bite. "It hasn't been updated since I made it … nine years ago."

She clicks her tongue at me, then sucks down her lemonade. "Figured. Websites aren't my thing. I thrive on organization and finances. Which I took a peek, sorry, but you're doing great, Jake. You need to overhaul your website. All orders should be going through there, even ones from the other showrooms. Emails and calls should only be for confirmation of details or delivery instructions. If you set the website up right, it can track everything for you like invoices and such. It will be trickier for the custom projects people want, but you can make a basic package or utilize your email for that to discuss prices and specifics."

This is all going over my head again. Scrubbing a hand down my face, I scratch my growing stubble. "Do I need to hire someone to do all that?"

She considers it for a moment, then lights up as she shakes her head. "Ask Amber. She built her website from scratch and does the majority of her sales through it. If there's anyone who knows what they're doing, it's her. She just finished an online degree in marketing too and could help you with your branding and marketing if you asked."

Of course, the one person who can't stand me is the one person I need. She owes me, but I don't want to use it on something like this. I could just hire someone to create the website, but I need someone to walk me through it all too. Huffing, I shove the last of my burrito in my mouth. Lily's help will last for a little while; it looks like she has my next month planned out and all the open orders are organized. It will give me time to figure out how to get Amber to help me.

While I get Lily's bag back in her car, she pops over to Amber's store to check on her. I should be working on the two tables I need to have done by Friday, but I decide to pop into the store instead. My crew has the wood beams on the ceiling, the back office framed and drywalled, and the cement floor painted a sleek black. All that's left is the lighting and painting the walls, then it's up to me to set the space up. I'm grateful for my mom's help in covering the walls with art because that's not my thing. I plan to build a custom desk for my mom, or whoever is working, to sit at. That also really needs to get done this weekend. Two tables and a desk in four days as well as finishing organizing my new shop, figuring out what wood I need to get ordered, and setting up the store … Easy, right?

There will be a lot more late nights in my future.

CHAPTER EIGHT

amber

I've always liked a healthy mix of routine and spontaneity. Since Jana's passing, maintaining a strict routine seems to be the only thing keeping my head above water. My mind and body staying busy allows me no time to break down and wallow in my pain. My alarm chirps at five, drawing a groan as I fumble to shut it off. This used to be when I enjoyed the peace and quiet before my day started. The quiet is something I used to take for granted. However, my new neighbor seems to have a penchant for getting on my last nerve and disrupting my serenity.

For the last four evenings, he's left the bay doors open to his workshop, so the sounds of his tools and music echo down the alleyway. Apparently, my studio has thin walls, something I never noticed before, and Jake works until ten at the earliest. Even worse, his loud motorcycle rumbles through the alley as he comes and goes, adding to the noise.

It's cutting into my sleep and relaxation time, and I'm exhausted. If I wasn't avoiding him like the plague, then I might ask him to keep his shop closed or not work so late, but that would require talking to him. Lily stopped by yesterday and mentioned he may need my help with something, and it took everything I had not to snort a laugh. I would love to see him on his knees begging for my help.

With heavy eyelids, I pull on some leggings and a sports bra for the gym. My pre-workout is no longer an aid but a necessity. I grab the rose I picked up last night and head out for the gym. My workout routine is strict, with Mondays and Thursdays being leg day and the days I stop at Jana's grave with a fresh rose. Her headstone still hasn't been delivered, so I keep the spot marked with her favorite pink flower. At some point, I'll have to change it up when these are no longer in season.

My legs fight against the heavy weights, but I push through anyway. Thankfully, no one talked to me this morning, which might have something to do with the permanent scowl on my face. If I had adequate rest, my body wouldn't protest so much. Jake's late nights need to be addressed sooner than later, but that means no longer avoiding him.

After a crap workout and a thirty-minute venting session at Jana's grave, I make my way home for a shower and breakfast. With a fresh mug of coffee in hand, I mosey over to the space out back to start organizing inventory. I have most of my summer fashion picked out and will need to place the order in the next week to get it all on time. Unfortunately, that means I need to clean out everything in here, recheck inventory, and start marking sales on the website.

Thankfully, Natasha is opening today, which gives me extra time to spend on this. Each of the side rooms in Jake's workshop has a door that leads straight to the alley and one that leads into his main workshop. I have a key to the lock on the outside door, but not one to the shop. I haven't ventured into his space, and as far as I know, he hasn't come into mine either.

Today, though, the door is cracked between our spaces, and I decide to leave it because I need to talk with him anyway when he gets in. The portable speaker in the corner plays Bad Omens while I mark off inventory and combine boxes to make extra space. It's on my list to figure out a better way to store and organize everything, but I just don't have the time right now. Natasha works twenty hours a week for me, and Lauren works a few weekends and mornings when her kids are in school, but otherwise, everything falls on my shoulders.

Jana and I used to trade off working most days, sharing the responsibilities of keeping the store running, and we had two high schoolers to help on the evenings and weekends, but both are in college now. I need to hire another person to help with online orders once I figure out a foolproof system. The downfall of a small town is there isn't an abundance of people looking for a job, but I'll figure it out.

A rumbling from Jake's shop draws my attention. I was certain the throaty sound of the Harley would alert me to his presence, but this is the bay doors opening. Worried it might be someone else, I peek my head through the door between our spaces right as Jake struts in. He looks sinfully good in scuffed work boots, dark-wash jeans, and his classic black tee stretched tight over his broad chest and shoulders. Swirls of dark ink travel down both arms to his hands, adding to the alure of the mess of dark hair on his head. It's shorter on the sides but long on top, and his beard looks like it's been growing since Thoren and Lily's wedding.

His deep chuckle is smooth as honey as he strides over to the doorway. "Did you need another glimpse of the best you've ever had, or are you trying to get a repeat?"

"Easy to be the best when you're the only." I smirk at his arrogant face. "I didn't hear your bike, so I wanted to make sure you weren't getting robbed. You're welcome."

Hot or not, I can't stand his attitude. I will never understand why all my friends love him and think he's this great guy. He's an arrogant ass who needs a reality check.

"I took my truck today. What are you doing in there? I assumed that was just storage for you."

I roll my eyes because of course he didn't care to ask previously; he's selfish through and through. "I do use it as storage. I just also use it to fulfill online orders since this is where the majority of my inventory is." I put my hands on my hips, readying myself for a fight. "Look, we need to talk about your hours. Your music and tools are keeping me up at night, so if you insist on working so late, can you at least close the doors?"

He crosses his arms and leans against the doorframe, making me step back. "Last I checked, I own this building and can do as I please. I've been gone by eleven most nights, that's not that late. Your store opens at nine, that's plenty of time to get your beauty rest."

Arrogant prick. I've had people talk down to me because I'm a young woman. It's always the same garbage: I'm too young to know what I'm doing and don't work as hard as others, the shop was handed down to me and not earned, blah, blah, blah. Most people don't know I was practically raised in this store. I was here every day after school, most weekends, and I learned how to run it inside and out.

"I'm not sure you're aware of this, but running a business means working way beyond the hours of operation. This is my third activity of the morning. I'm asking nicely, Jake. If you stay late, please close the doors and turn down the music."

A slow saccharine smile spreads over his mouth. "Activities? Now that you've been fucked, you're an addict? Found anyone who can make you come like I do yet?"

My morning with the cold hard earth beneath my knees as I sat next to the grave of the woman who held me together for over half my life flashes through my mind. I wish more than anything she was still here to talk me through all these interactions with Jake. She would have loved him with his bad-boy take-no-shit vibes. We spent so many nights watching *Sons of Anarchy* where we both drooled over Jax Teller.

I finally cracked this morning and told her I slept with him. The sun emerged at that very moment, its rays caressing my skin like a bittersweet hug, a reminder of the happy moments now lost to time. And it would have been happy, the joy on her face so clear in my mind. She was always encouraging me to put myself out there, to not let life pass me by.

My throat is thick with emotion, and I try to swallow it down. With my eyes downcast, I take a few deep breaths to keep the tears from falling. When I finally pull myself together, Jake's smug smile slips as he assesses me before he kicks off the door and heads deeper into his shop. "I'll see what I can do."

The door between us stays closed the rest of the morning, but I hear him tinkering around in there. I would like to say I don't give him another thought, but that would be a lie. There's no denying that he has an incredible talent I would have loved to use to fix up my boutique. He might even be able to build something to help with my organization. Would he even consider it if I asked him again?

My stomach grumbles around noon, so I head out the front door to check on Socks and grab some lunch. My kitten is waiting at the door for me, his little meows brightening my mood instantly. Natasha loves him, and I hate leaving him alone, so I scoop him up, grab my purse, and head down to the store.

Unsurprising, Natasha squeals with delight over having Socks being her partner in crime today. I inform her I'm going to grab food and will be back in an hour to cover her lunch break. What I don't tell her is that I'm going to get lunch for Jake and kindly ask him again to make me shelves and tables. He just bought a store, there's no way he can be turning down business, right?

With two burgers, fries, and shakes in tow, I put on my big girl panties and march into Jake's shop. He has his back to me, wiping down a table with a stinky varnish. It occurs to me that he may not be keeping the bay doors open to annoy me but to prevent the fumes from becoming too strong. I still don't feel bad about asking him to close them in the evenings.

Clearing my throat, I hold up the bag and drink carrier when he turns to look at me. "I brought a peace offering," I state. He nods to his desk in the corner and goes back to his project, ignoring me. "I was hoping we could eat together and talk. I have a job for you, if you want it."

His ocean-blue eyes find mine again, and he holds eye contact past the point of comfort, then drops his rag and stalks over to me. Pulling out the food, I set out a burger and fry box for each of us, nodding to the drinks. "One is chocolate, one strawberry, take your pick."

He surprises me when he grabs the strawberry, wrapping his lips around the straw and sucking down the shake. It's oddly erotic, so I pull my eyes away and open my wrapper.

"Thanks." His deep voice is as smooth as dripping honey. "What's the job?"

"Cedar and Sage needs a bit of a revamp. Half the shelves are chipped and worn, and the tables are a mix of thrifted items or the cheap plastic foldout ones. Would you be able to replace them all with something custom made?"

He chews his bite of the burger which is already half gone. I try not to wither under his stare, but his eyes never feel like he's just looking at me, more like they are reaching down into my soul to poke around, and it's unnerving.

"I'll do it on one condition."

I can't stop the eye roll—this man and his damn conditions. "What?"

"You help me with my website and marketing. Lily said you're a whiz at that stuff, and I don't have the time to do it. If you can make me a whole new site that people can order from and

I can track it all easily, then I'll do your shop for free. It will have to be in between other projects when I have time, though."

So this is what Lily was talking about. I think it's more he lacks the skill than doesn't have the time. Probably not smart to needle him about that though when we are forming a sort of truce. Honestly, I'm all too happy about the trade. Making websites is fun, and getting to put my degree to use is what I've been dying for. Ideas are already floating around my brain for both, a thrum of excitement buzzing through me.

"You have yourself a deal. Do I have free rein, or do you have ideas already?"

He shakes his head, slurping the last of his milkshake. "Nah, you can have access to my old one and anything you need. My mom will be working in my store starting next week, and she can show you some of my popular items and get photos for you to upload. As long as it can take orders and link to my email, I'm not picky."

His words aren't meant to hurt, but they do. One day, I will be able to listen to people talk about their parents without a pain ripping through me; today is not that day. My mom should be working at the store with me. "Okay," I mumble, packing up the rest of my food, no longer hungry.

Tossing it in the trash, I slip out and back to the store. I feel his eyes on me like a caress and almost expect him to say something, but he doesn't. When Natasha comes back from her lunch, I take Socks and retreat to my apartment instead of continuing with the inventory like I should. The rest of the day passes in slow motion as I watch *The Office* without really seeing it. I do, however, notice there is no noise from the alley after eight.

jake

Sleep last night was abysmal. After leaving the shop early, which I really couldn't afford to do with my work piling up, I went to the gym like normal after work and was even more frustrated. The crowd around ten is minimal, but at eight, it's slammed, so I cut my workout short, which led to a restless night in bed.

My whole day was thrown off when Amber showed up being nice with lunch after I have repeatedly been a dick to her. To make matters worse, I'm pretty sure I made her cry twice yesterday. That doesn't sit well with me, and the second time, I don't even know what I said to set her off. There's a beauty in her anger, a fight inside her that feels like she could face off with me and walk away unscathed. So why was she a shell of herself yesterday after our talk? It didn't escape my notice that she slunk up to her apartment and never left.

Needing to clear my mind since sleep isn't happening, I load up my gym bag and grab my helmet. The throaty rumble of my engine is like a balm to my fraying nerves. As soon as I turn off the gravel lane and onto the road, I hit the throttle and let myself fly through the quiet mountain roads. The cool morning air whips through my unzipped jacket, stinging my skin. I love the low fog on mornings like this, misting my skin as I fly. Leaning into the curves of the road, I let the rush clear every thought from my head.

When I bought this the day I left for college, my parents were horrified. Eleven years later, they still aren't thrilled that I won't give it up, but they don't understand. Aside from the fact I've put years of work into this bike, it's also the one thing that makes me feel alive. The saying that you never feel more alive than when you brush death, rings true every time the power surges between my legs.

Pulling into the gym parking lot, the predawn sky lightens, a soft, pinkish hue replacing the inky blackness, and the fresh air feels invigorating. My mind is clear when I remove my helmet and step into the bright gym. The tension slides from my body at the sight of the nearly empty gym. It's exactly what I need this morning, so I slip into the locker room to change.

With my stretching complete, I move to the free weights, and someone catches my eye in the mirrors. In the corner of the gym is none other than my new neighbor. Amber's dressed in tight little shorts and a loose top, too busy finishing her set of curls to notice my wandering gaze. This must be one of her morning activities, and suddenly, I want to align my schedule to hers.

Snagging a bench, I grab my set of weights and keep my eyes trained on her in the mirror the whole time. I knew she worked out, no one has her physique without hard work and dedication, but the weight she is throwing around is astounding. It's also a major turn-on apparently, because my dick is very interested.

Breathing heavily, I try to focus on the burn in my muscles through each set and not on how she moves effortlessly through this place. I don't know how she hasn't noticed me, but that just won't do. Dying for a hit of her fiery remarks, after this set of shoulder presses, I'll make sure she sees me.

Right as I'm putting away my weights, a douchey-looking guy approaches her. She beams a pretty smile at him, and he not so subtly lets his gaze travel down her body. My hackles rise as they make small talk, and she throws her head back in laughter. It should be beautiful, the throaty yet silky sound radiating through the gym, but it pisses me off. What did he do to earn her joy like that?

The moment she registers I'm here, her laughter dies, a scowl mars her face, and her cheeks turn red. I'm close enough to hear her whispered, "You've got to be shitting me."

Douche guy turns around, flinching as he takes me in. He's not a little man, but I still tower over them both. "What are the odds of this?"

"What are you doing here?"

"Probably the same thing as everyone else. You said no more late nights, so here I am." I'm aware how that sounds, and clearly, so do they as Amber's cheeks redden again and the guy's eyes turn hard.

Putting my hand out, I face him. "I'm Jake, and you are?"

"Kyle," he says, trying to squeeze my hand with a dominance that shows just how small his dick must be. He drops my hand, turning to Amber. "Are you okay here?"

"Yeah, thanks, Kyle." She smiles shyly at him. "I'll see you Monday."

With one more glance between us, he sulks away, and Amber turns her furious gaze to me, arms crossed under her perky tits. "What the hell is your problem? Stalking me and now trying to put some sort of claim on me? I thought we cleared the slate yesterday."

It's clear she's never been with a real man before. If she thinks that was me staking a claim, she's dead wrong. When I want it known a woman is mine, there's no question about it. It's on the tip of my tongue to tell her she became mine the moment she bled for me. How I wish I hadn't used a condom—the thought of her blood on my cock as I took her virginity makes me feral.

Adjusting my stance to hide my hardening dick, draws her attention south where it snags on my left leg that is covered in tattoos. "Thinking about how high up they go? You probably didn't get a good look in the bathroom."

She scoffs as I lean closer, pushing a stray hair behind her ear. When she opens her mouth with a, no doubt, snarky reply, I cut her off. "I don't have a problem, Whiskey, I was just preventing you from making a mistake with him. We had a clear slate until you got angry at me being polite and changing my schedule for you. Now, I'm not so sure. See you Monday." I wink, heading to the locker room to grab my stuff. Usually, I would get a little cardio in, but I'm behind on work, so I'll shower at the gym before heading to the shop.

As I'm getting dressed, Kyle walks in, his shoulders straightening. "Hey, man."

I nod in acknowledgment, pulling on my socks. He rustles around in a locker, taking out his things before turning to face me. "Can I ask what's going on between you and Amber?"

Snorting, I pull on my boots and lace them, not bothering to look up. "You can, doesn't mean I'll tell you."

I knew this was coming. His eyes were glued to her after he walked away, and his jaw tightened when I stepped in close and touched her hair. The desire for her was written all over his face.

"She's a nice girl, and she's been through a lot lately. She deserves a good man."

His insinuation I'm not, pisses me off. What makes this prick better than me? The fact he's not covered in tats and is friendly to everyone? While I wouldn't change a single thing about my appearance, I hate that everyone assumes I'm some dangerous asshole because I walk around with a scowl on my face. My fighting days are, mostly, behind me, and I can be a nice guy. I don't know why it matters, it's not like I'm pursuing Amber. It registers then what else he said.

"What's she been through?" I ask, standing and grabbing my backpack.

He huffs, shaking his head. "The fact you don't know tells me enough. Leave her alone."

Scowling, I storm from the locker room and out to my bike. Part of me wanted to step into his space and throw him against the lockers for delivering his little threat. The old me would have, but I'm trying to turn a new leaf. I'm almost thirty, and I don't need to be starting fights over nothing. Something tugs in my gut, telling me Amber is far from nothing, but I ignore it and throw on my helmet.

The entire ride to the shop, I replay all my interactions with her. First, watching her cry with Thoren's mom at Lily's party, then to the desolate and empty way she looked at the wedding before I stoked her fire. Her odd reactions to things I say sometimes. By the time I park and open my shop, I'm sure I missed something with her, I just don't know what. It bothers me I don't know what's going on with her, and even if I don't want to ask, I want to know.

Trying to clear my mind, I focus on finishing the last table I need to have ready for pickup this weekend. This is my favorite part—putting on the final touches and ensuring every inch is perfect. Seeing my hard work and designs come to life is satisfying in a way that little else is.

By the time I have the table complete and wrapped up, my mom is waiting for me in the store. It smells nice when I walk in, a candle lit on a table in the center of the space catching my attention. My mom and Evelyn are measuring the walls and marking off spots with blue tape.

"What are you ladies up to?" I ask, stepping over to the table to get a better whiff of the candle and see what scent it is.

"Do you like that?" Evelyn asks, walking closer. "I picked it up from Amber next door. It's cedar and bergamot. She thought it would be the perfect complement to all the wood furniture you'll have in here. Plus, it'll help get rid of the paint smell before you open Monday."

I have to admit it's nice. Not too sweet or overpowering, and it fits the feel of the store well. That itch under my skin I always get around Amber makes my chest feel hot. She seems to know how to affect me as well as she knows how to press my buttons. "It was a good choice." My throat suddenly feels like gravel.

"We're measuring out where to hang your pictures." My mom joins our conversation. Her and Evelyn have been friends since Thoren, River, and I were kids. While my mom is almost ten years younger, that has never stopped them from being close and helping raise all us wild boys. "We're marking where the nails need to go, but we need you to hang them. Is this all the furniture you will have in here for now?" She motions to the randomly piled tables, chairs, benches, couches, and other smaller pieces I had in storage. My crew finished painting last night and offered to move all the stuff over for me today before counting the job complete.

"Yeah, looks like it. I'll have to organize it this weekend, and hopefully, I will have a desk finished by Monday for you to use. Thanks for helping with the decorating part, it's not really my strong suit."

"Oh, we know," Michele says, winking from the front door, Lily hot on her heels. "That's why we're here."

I stare at the four of them, more than a little confused. Lily, being the soft-hearted woman she is, comes and wraps her small arms around my waist. "You're going to hang those pictures, and then you're going to leave. We are going to organize and decorate this place, and when you come in on Monday, you will have a beautiful store ready to make its mark on this town."

Emotion clogs my throat as I look between them all. For all the times I felt cast aside in the past, these women are showing me there's still good in those around me. My time in college really messed with my head and caused me to retreat into a hardened shell. In high school, I finally felt I had accepted that most friends weren't genuine but people at least pretended to care. The lack of care or even feigned emotions from my classmates back home during my dad's accident brought it all back though. I started fighting more in college, drunk fights with people who probably didn't deserve it, because I was so angry at the world. With my parents being some of the best people I know and all the shit that was talked about them because we weren't as wealthy as others. They didn't deserve the hate, so I threw that hate at everyone else. Then one major event kicked me down even further, and I've been a shell of a man ever since. I moved back to this town with a chip on my shoulder that hasn't lessened over time, and yet these four women all accept and love me anyway.

"Thanks," I croak out, clearing my throat. I get to work, hammering anchors and nails while they bring in bags of items they won't let me look at. When all the pictures are hung, I thank them again and make my escape to the shop out back.

To my surprise, Evelyn follows me out, grabbing my arm to stop me in the alley. "Hey, honey, I wanted to ask you a huge favor." I would do anything for this woman. Not only did she help raise me, but she and her husband, David, played a large part in helping my parents after my dad's accident.

"What can I do?"

She looks to the back door leading to Amber's store. "I was hoping you could keep an eye on Amber. She's hiding it well, but I know she's struggling with Jana's death. The girls are trying to spend time with her, but they can't always be around, and I hate that she has no one left. Can you pop in and say hi once in a while and call me if she seems to be having a bad day? I know I'm not her aunt and can't replace her, but I care for her deeply."

I try to hide the shock from my face that I didn't know Amber's aunt died. Is that what Kyle meant this morning? It makes sense, and I suddenly feel like even more of an ass for how I've been treating her. Does Amber have no parents or siblings? No family left at all, or just not around here?

I can't imagine losing either of my parents. For the short time my dad was in surgery, then in the medically induced coma where we weren't sure if he would pull through, it was the most agonizing pain I had ever felt. To be all alone is an excruciating feeling. I'm glad Evelyn and the girls are checking in on her, and I know their intentions are pure, but how well do they really know her? I hope they know her pain and see past the walls. As much as she might annoy me, I don't want anyone to feel the way I did for so long.

"No problem, I'll watch out for her."

"You're a good man, Jake," she says, wrapping me in a hug. "Now, no peeking until Monday, okay?"

"Yes, ma'am." I chuckle and wink, trying to hide the sea of emotions swirling around my mind.

CHAPTER TEN

amber

TRIPLE THREAT GROUP CHAT

MICHELE:

I'm making a taco bar tonight.

AMBER:

Perfect, I'm bringing tequila and margarita mix.

LILY:

I'm on antibiotics, so I'm out on the drinking. I'll
bring chips and queso.

MICHELE:

Boo! Make it the spicy queso and I'll forgive
you.

AMBER:

I'm not staying sober just because you are. I
have secrets to divulge.

MICHELE:

Oh, hell yeah. Things were getting boring
around here.

When I met Lily last July, she declared me her new friend and left no room for argument. Not that I would have argued, I kind of suck at making friends and I loved her immediately. The first time I went to dinner with her and Michele, I knew I had found friends who would last a lifetime. They have been my lifeline through everything that has happened lately. Lily helped me figure out the finances as I took over the store and took on Jana's medical debt, while Michele helped me list and sell Jana's house to pay for it all. Both checked on me constantly and were by my side as I laid her to rest.

Despite their unending kindness and support, I haven't divulged anything about myself from before they came into my life. Not for lack of trying on their part. I've just never been great at talking about my past. Jana was all I had, not just as family but also as the only person who knew what I had been through with my mom and why I was slow to let people in.

Over these last four months since her death, I have slowly pulled myself from the same dark place I went when I was eleven. A place deep in me that was numb to feelings, void of personality and happiness. The only time I feel something is when Jake brings out the anger in me. I don't love admitting it, but verbally sparring with him has helped to pull me a little further from my edge of darkness.

Jake is making me feel things again, and I have no idea what to do with those feelings. The girls are the only ones I have to talk with about the myriad of emotions swirling through me, so I've decided tonight is the night to come clean to them. I'm going to see more of him since we're helping each other out, so no time like the present.

Michele's home—an adorable two-story farmhouse with a wraparound porch—sits outside of downtown. She converted a separate garage into an office space for her real estate business that is a stunning forest green that complements her white house beautifully. Lily is already there when I pull up and let myself in through the large wood front door. "Honey, I'm home," I call out.

"Finally," Michele answers, "I need a shot and for you to spill the tea."

She's standing behind the island chopping tomatoes for home-made salsa. I learned quickly that both of these women are amazing cooks, and I've been snagging recipes from them ever since. Lily is perched in a chair on the other side, her feet resting on the stool next to her. Her bright smile greets me as she shoves another chip in her mouth. "Hey, other bestie."

After placing the bottle of tequila and mix on the counter, I maneuver around the kitchen, grabbing two shot glasses and two margarita glasses as well as her container of salt for the rims. Shots aren't my thing, so Michele raises an eyebrow, glancing between the shots I'm pouring us and me.

"Don't judge, I need Dutch courage," I quip, handing her one of the glasses. She puts her hands up in defense before grabbing her shot, clinking it with mine, and shooting it back. I wince at the burn running down my throat, and the bitter taste lingers in my mouth. A lime wedge is placed in my hand, so I suck the tangy juices down.

"You're lucky I had those cut up for the tacos. Now, make us margs and spill it."

I plop into one of the chairs next to Lily and start on our drinks. There's no good way to say this, so I keep my head down and spit it out. "I slept with Jake."

A knife clatters to the counter, and Lily chokes on her bite of queso. I pat her back as they stare at me wide-eyed. "We're going to need more information than that," Lily coughs out.

"Yeah, like when, where, and how was it?"

Heat travels up my chest at her questions. It's not like I haven't talked about sex with them. These girls are dirty as hell, even if I'm unsure if Michele is having much sex. I take part in their talks, but this is about me, and they have no idea I was a virgin until Jake.

"It was at your wedding," I admit, embarrassed. "In your downstairs bathroom, to be specific."

I'm half expecting anger, or at least disappointment. Maybe even disgust. Instead, Michele belts out a laugh as Lily pouts. "I haven't even had sex in there yet, that's not fair."

"Why are we just finding out now? That was over a month ago. Plus, you didn't answer the last question. Did he blow your mind?"

Resting my elbows on the counter, I drop my head into my hands and groan. "Yes. God, that man has a filthy mouth. He was all hot and demanding, and his dick is massive. Pretty sure my vagina was broken for a week." That also could have been because it was my first time, but I don't want to ask them if that's how they felt.

"You ain't lying, that thing needs to be registered as a deadly weapon. Especially with the barbells. How'd they feel?"

My gaze snaps to Michele's, and I try to tamp down the onslaught of emotions inside me. It feels an awful lot like rage and jealousy, but that's not fair. They are free to sleep with whoever they like. I have no claim on the man, and it's not like I didn't know he sleeps around. He insinuated as much when we first met. Still, the knowledge that Michele knows what his cock looks like sits hot and hard in my stomach.

"You've slept with him?"

Lily and Michele burst into hysterics, and Michele shakes her head. "Lord, no. He's like my brother. I mean, he's obviously hot as hell, but it's not like that between us. I'd never seen a pierced peen before, so I begged him to let me see it, and he did. Even flaccid that thing is intimidating."

The tight feeling in my chest eases with her explanation. I

don't blame her for being curious. I was buzzed when we had sex, and he had the condom on before I got a look. I couldn't even tell you what the piercings look like because I didn't know they were there, and I have nothing to compare it to.

"Oh, okay. Yeah, I think the piercing felt good. I mean, he made me come twice."

"Now that's what I'm talking about! A man that puts a woman's pleasure first. Please tell me he gave you a hand neck-lace too. He seems like the type," Michele squeals.

With heated cheeks *again*, I slowly nod. Holy hell, did his hand around my throat feel good.

"Good for you." Lily clinks her water to my margarita glass. "What's going on with you guys now? Getting it on all the time in the back offices?"

This is the part I'm worried to talk to them about. They love Jake and think he's this sweet man. I've seen the softer side to him, sure, but only when he's talking to other people. I'm not sure what it is about me, but he enters every conversation with me looking for a fight, and I seem all too happy to give it to him.

"We're kind of frenemies? Maybe just straight enemies. I'm pretty sure he's hated me since the day we met. We constantly fight, he pushes my buttons, and I might hate him back. I don't know."

They trade glances, but neither look like they want to talk. I knew this would happen. Michele has known Jake since they were kids, and Lily is married to his best friend. Of course they're going to want to defend him and think I'm crazy.

I miss Jana, she would have known what to say. Probably would have slapped me upside the head and said something like *Have you seen that man? Who cares if you fight, fighting is half the fun.* She was always a little wild like that, and it seems the only time my wild side comes out is around Jake.

Maybe I am crazy? I seem to be the only woman he treats this way. It brings up the lingering feelings I've fought hard against that I'm the problem, but he still slept with me anyway. He can't even blame his hatred on my lie because he hated me before he unknowingly took my virginity.

"You guys are oddly similar, in an opposite way. He's all dark and broody on the outside but sweet in the center, and you're all sweet on the outside with a dark and broody inside," Michele finally says.

"You think I'm broody on the inside?"

They roll their eyes in unison, and I have to bite back a laugh. I mean, I know I am, I just didn't know they saw it too.

"I've known you coming up on a year now, and this right here is the most you have ever opened up except about Jana's stroke. You told us in a freaking text that she passed. I know it's been a rough few months, hell, a rough year, but yeah, you're dark inside, and that's okay. It's what makes you strong and resilient. Our little fighter."

"Fuck yeah," Michele adds. "There's nothing wrong with your dark and broody. I think it's what you know and are comfortable with, and that's okay. For now. One day, you'll find someone to share that side of yourself with, and we will support you until that day comes."

I didn't expect my emotions to feel so heavy tonight. Blinking, I clear my blurry vision as I take in their warm expressions. It makes me want to share more of myself with them and to open up the way they do. This is the first real friendship I have ever had, but I know these girls are genuine and understanding down to their very core.

"Seriously, though. Jake needs someone that isn't intimidated by him and actually makes an effort with him. And I say this in the most loving of ways, but you keep everything so bottled up and tight to the chest that I sometimes worry you're going to explode. Maybe you need someone that pushes your buttons, someone strong that can handle getting rocked when you implode," Lily adds.

My mind whirls with their assessment. Even if they think we fit together, there's too much animosity between us. I don't need to have an extensive dating history to know that I deserve a man who is happy to see me. I'm not even asking for a man who wants to spoil me or to worship the ground I walk on. I simply want a man who's willing to look beyond the smiles and doesn't cower at what he sees. Someone who wants to be my partner in all things, that understands my long hours at work and my passion for my business.

The girls move everything to the dining room where we eat and drink, but my focus fades in and out from the conversation. My head is too busy wondering if maybe they're right. Michele said Jake is sweet in the center, but I've seen his mask slip. He's hiding pain, and the more I think about it, he seems to keep everyone at arm's length much like I do. What happened in his life to make him that way?

Life can be so vicious and cruel when it chooses to be. I've learned that the hard way over and over. Kindness despite the pain is what makes us human, what breathes hope into the world. You can't change the past, but your actions can change someone's future. Lily did that for me the day she came into my store and hugged me when she saw me upset. Without knowing me, who I was, or what was hurting me, she showed me a kindness I can never repay.

Yet, with the stormy seas life has thrown me time and time again, it has also sent me a life raft when I needed it most. In the beginning, I struggled to see it that way. I focused on the sea raging around me and the current trying to drag me under. Now, though, I look for the outstretched hand that doesn't always seem like the way out. I hated Jake's cocky attitude and the way he felt he knew me, but there was something there. A small string that tugs at my chest every time he's around. Maybe that string is the outstretched hand, drawing me out of the bleak emptiness I have inside and forcing me to feel the world around me again.

Before I leave for the night, they make me promise I'll keep an open mind with him. Working with him will definitely require that, so I agree to try. Something tells me the cocky asshole is just waiting for me to show an ounce of kindness so he can throw it back in my face.

CHAPTER ELEVEN

SAUSAGE SQUAD GROUP CHAT

RIVER 🏀:

Congrats buddy! Sorry I can't be there, but I can't wait to check it out.

THOREN 🔨:

You could at least send him flowers.

JAKE 🪜 :

Yeah, where's my care basket like Lily got?

THOREN 🔨:

Doesn't make it to your grand opening. Doesn't send a gift. What's he even good for?

RIVER 🏀:

Care basket is on its way, asshole.

RIVER 🏀:

screenshot of order of bag of gummy dicks

JAKE 🪜 :

HAHAHA Thanks man. Wish you were here.

This weekend almost killed me with all the hours I put in at the shop completing my orders and building the desk. Despite my burning desire to want to peek into my store, I forced myself to only go to and from the shop out back. I didn't even drive past the front, taking the side roads to avoid the urge to look. Even with the long days, this anxious buzz under my skin hasn't gone away. There's no expectation for my store to do magically well. Cedar Ridge is a rather small town, but having a real storefront that is all mine has always been the end goal for me. That doesn't mean I don't fear I'll have no customers and my mom will sit there alone day after day while I lose money.

Sleep evaded me for most of last night, which made it easy to drag myself out of bed this morning and head for the gym. I took my truck today so I could bring my bag of clothes I plan to keep in the store. My mom spent twenty minutes on the phone with me last night explaining how important image was and how I at least needed to have a button-up shirt or two around to slip on when I was in the store. She's lucky I love her so much.

I can't keep focusing on what might happen when I open those doors today, or I'll go crazy. My only hope is that a mouthy little blonde is at the gym this morning to distract me. After my talk with Evelyn, I did a little internet sleuthing and found the obituary for Jana Sage Wright. I felt like even more of an ass after reading about how she was a pillar of our small community and raised her niece, Amber. She was only fifty-one when she had her major stroke and passed eight months later.

Finding out about all of that should have told me to go easy on Amber, but I won't. She finds a way to piss me off every time I see her, and I doubt that's magically going to stop because I know her aunt died. I can be empathetic to her situation while still pushing her buttons. To my delight, she's posted up at a squat rack when I enter the gym. Our eyes collide in the mirror as she reracks, and I send her a wink.

The blush that creeps down her neck sends a thrill through me. Throughout my workout, my gaze finds its way to her. The douche is here again, but he seems to keep his distance despite his eyes being glued to her as well. Amber steps onto the treadmills, and I can't hide the small smile that we have a similar routine. As I make my way over to join her, Kyle beats me to it, taking the open one next to her. This guy is starting to piss me off, but I jog on one in the row behind them.

Their conversation is too low for me to hear, but there's an ease of familiarity between them. I'm dripping with sweat by the time Amber hops off and picks up her bag. She waves to Kyle before turning to me with a "See you later." That acknowledgment eases some of the tension in me, so I hop off my treadmill and make my way to the locker room to shower and change. I take my time, finger-combing my hair and taming my short beard. I listen to my mom and put on a button-up shirt but still have my jeans and boots. At least these ones are mostly scuff and stain free. The shirt feels restrictive, so I roll up the sleeves and leave the top two buttons undone.

My mom will complain when she sees me, but you can only teach an old dog so many new tricks. I promised Mom I wouldn't enter the store until she got here and could experience the opening with me and watch me take it all in. So, here I am, sitting in my truck in the back alley waiting for her to let me know when she's here. I could wait in my shop, but I'll start tinkering and ruin my nice shirt.

I've been sitting in my truck for about twenty minutes when Amber pulls up next to me. She left the gym over an hour ago, and when she steps out of her car, it's in the same sweaty outfit she had on. I try to slink into my seat, but with my tinted windows, she doesn't seem to notice I'm here. Her eyes are red-rimmed and puffy as she gathers her things and heads up to her apartment. Where has she been for the last hour?

My phone dings as I watch through the glass door as she ascends the steps. Grabbing it off the seat, I read the text from my mom saying to come to the front of the store. I straighten out my shirt and twirl my keys while walking around the building. My steps falter when I take in both my parents standing on the sidewalk waiting for me. Their eyes shine bright with pride, and my mom wraps her arms around me. Emotion sits heavy in my throat as my dad pulls me into a hug next, patting me on the back.

"I'm so proud of you, Jacob." His voice cracks, and he clears his throat to cover it.

Mom not so subtly wipes her eyes, then clasps my dad's free hand. "Well, let us in so we aren't crying out on the street. I can't wait for you both to see it!"

I hadn't even bothered looking at the store yet, too focused on the fact that my dad made it for opening day. This is why I work so hard to help support my parents. They would give anything to support me, and I don't take that for granted. When I turn to the store, there's a large banner hanging over the front window announcing the grand opening today. My mom gives me a nudge, so I unlock the front door and hold it open for her to escort my dad through.

Following them in, I'm taken aback by how amazing it looks. The sleek gray walls and black concrete floors are nothing new to me, but the navy-blue accents everywhere are. There are accent rugs under some of my furniture displays, and the dining tables are set up with dinnerware. In one corner, there's a blue velvet couch set up with one of my coffee tables, and upon closer inspection, it has my lookbook displayed on it. None of it is overdone, just set out naturally, with an open spot off to one side.

"That's where I thought we could put the front desk you made," Mom says when she sees me eyeing it. "What do you think?"

I don't have the words to tell her how grateful I am. It's so much better than I could have imagined. The fact she came together with my friends and they did all this has my eyes burning as I swallow down my emotions.

"Thank you. Just … thank you, Mom." We stand there hugging for so long that my dad clears his throat.

"Might want to get that desk and set it up. You open in thirty," he says, ambling over to the couch and slowly lowering himself on it. "I hope you don't mind me breaking this in early, I doubt I'll be moving until you close."

The smile on my face is wide. I nod to him and make my way out the back to get my dolly and the desk. With some careful maneuvering, my mom and I get it in and set up on time for opening. She chatters incessantly while I hook up the computer and card reader I bought. I will still have my mom take orders on paper until my website is set up and we figure out how to input custom orders, but at least I have this ready. She knows about Amber and our trade of services since she'll need to know how to work the new website too. My dad listened with a keen eye, chuckling when I told him this was costing me much more than it was costing her, due to all the materials.

"It's time," my mom announces. "Go do the honors, honey."

Glancing up from behind the desk, I see the small hoard of people waiting out front. All my friends are out there, as well as a few locals. For the second time this morning, I'm overcome with emotion.

Thoren rushes in first when I unlock the front door, slapping me on the back as he goes straight to the corner to talk with my dad. Lily follows close behind, wrapping me in her warm embrace. "We're so proud of you. I want to make an order, but I'll wait until the crowd leaves to do it."

One by one, the small crowd enters the store, and I greet them all. Michele whispered something about loving how our community shows up for their own as she hugged me in passing, and I couldn't agree more. Last to walk in is Amber. Her previously sad eyes hidden behind makeup, and a fake smile plastered on her face.

"I brought you a small gift. Evelyn said you liked it, so I hope you didn't lie to her. Congratulations, Jake." She hands me a small gift bag, then steps back out and heads to her store. I should talk with my customers, but my feet follow her of their own accord.

"Where are you going?"

"I have to open my own store. I'll stop in again to talk more about your website when Lauren gets in this afternoon. Good luck today," she says over her shoulder, unlocking her store.

There's a nagging feeling to follow her, but I go back to my store instead. My mom is talking to someone at the desk, and the rest of the patrons walk around looking at everything. Opening the gift bag, I see a bundle of the candles Evelyn had burning in here on Friday. Lily pops up beside me and smiles at the gift before pulling me to the side, then flicks my ear.

"Ow, what the fuck was that for?"

She scowls at me, crossing her arms. "I don't know where to start. We're supposed to be besties, and you don't even tell me you slept with my other best friend? And I cornered Thoren because you're as subtle as an ox, and I know you know about the pregnancy."

"What was I supposed to say? Hey, sorry you have a shitty friend, and she conned me into taking her virginity? That I didn't know until it was too late, and I feel like a piece of shit about it?"

The shock on Lily's face makes me feel even worse. Clearly, she didn't know about the virgin part, and my asshole status just got an upgrade. "Oh, Jake." She grips my arm tenderly. "Look, I won't tell her you told me that tidbit, and I don't know what's going on between you two. Just be easy on her for a bit, okay? She's been through more than any of us know, and she's heading for a spiral if she doesn't start talking about it soon."

Her concern is evident, and it makes Evelyn's words float through my head again. The mask she seems to wear around everyone else slips when she's around me. If pushing her buttons gets her to let out some of her pent-up anger and hurt, I'll be that for her. It's no skin off my back when I get enjoyment out of watching her squirm and the light that flares in her eyes when she's mad.

I nod, letting a wide smile cross my face. "Sooo, can I congratulate you on the baby now?"

Tears well in her eyes as she bites her lip and nods.

"You two will make the most incredible parents. I better be the godfather. Congratulations, Lily."

Thoren comes up behind me, and I wrap him in an embrace. "I am so excited for you guys."

"Just keep it on the down low for another month. We were hoping you could make the crib?"

"Fucking hell, is the goal to make me cry today?" I mutter. "I would be honored."

CHAPTER TWELVE

amber

With the opening of Jake's store today, I was a little busier than the average Monday. It was a welcomed distraction from the man next door. I had to pick my jaw up off the floor when I saw him this morning. The button-up shirt he was wearing fit like a second skin, pulled taut over every muscle. Black ink swirled on his exposed forearms and peeked from the opened buttons on his chest. The mix of broody biker and put-together businessman really does it for me. My brain immediately went to the last time I saw him dressed up, which inevitably led to thoughts of the mind-blowing sex we had.

"Hey, Amber, you okay? You look a little flushed," Lauren asks, plopping her purse behind the counter. I hadn't even heard her come in. Clearly, a busy store isn't cutting it on distraction techniques.

"Yeah, I'm fine." I pick up Socks from where he's scampering behind her and set him in his bed on the counter. "I'm going to run upstairs and make a sandwich and grab my laptop, then I'll be right back down."

She waves me off and clocks in, then gets right to tidying up the displays. I may only have two employees at the moment, but they are hard workers and amazing to me. Upstairs, I make a quick lunch, extra grateful that I live above the store, and head back down. Things have slowed a little, so I take the stool from the back room and set up my laptop on the checkout counter.

"What are you working on?"

Lauren leans against the other side of the counter, playing with Socks. "Doing some branding and marketing for Jake next door."

She stills, glancing over like she can see him through the wall. "That man is fine as hell, but damn if he hasn't been hated on by the rumor mill."

My finger stills over the logo I'm designing. "What do you mean?"

"I'm a bit older, but my younger brother was the grade above him. He said he was always outgoing but that he was picked on a lot, even when he became one of the popular kids. It's messed up, but his mom cleaned houses sometimes, and kids would make comments about making her clean their rooms in a little maid costume and stuff. He was suspended a few times for fighting over it. Kids were harsh about his clothes and stuff too. The bullying stopped in high school, but the fighting didn't. He just stopped doing it on school grounds. He had a reputation where he was feared and loved all at once. Then, when he came home from college, it was like he was this totally different person. Hardly talked to anyone, was shut down, covered in tattoos, and always had a scowl on his face, then came the reputation as a womanizer."

She pauses the conversation to help find another size for a customer, then stands by me as she rings her up. Once we're alone again, she continues. "My brother is a bit of a man whore. Kind of a little kid still despite being thirty, but he doesn't have the reputation, and I guarantee he has slept with more women than Jake. I think it's this whole broody persona people have given him that draws attention when he does go home with someone. Just let the guy live his life, ya know?"

I mull it over but decide to drop it and focus on the task at hand. He's a big boy, he can handle his own reputation. If he doesn't like it, then he could work on changing it. If being teased for your mom having a job is the least of his worries, then he'll be fine. I should know. Even if I still harbor hurt feelings over the way I was treated by my peers, so it would make sense if he did too.

The afternoon flew past as I perfected my three logo options and the possible slogan for him. I have the bare bones of his website designed but can't do much else without a list of what he offers, photos, timelines, and the like.

Lauren's kids have after-school activities today, so she stays to close the store while I tuck the laptop under my arm and head next door. This morning when I rushed over with the gift, my focus stayed on Jake and not the store, but now I take the time to really see it all. Whoever designed the space did an incredible job of staying true to his masculine style with deep moody colors, but the decor has a feminine touch. I make a mental note to take photos of it all to add to the website.

"Can I help you?" a petite woman asks from behind the front desk. Her dark hair and deep-blue eyes look so similar to Jake's, but her bright smile is hers alone.

"Hi, I'm Amber. I own Cedar and Sage next door. Is Jake around?"

Her eyes light up as a deep voice calls from the corner. "So you're the one who drives a hard bargain. My type of woman. He's out getting dinner, would you like to join us?" Turning, I see a man sitting on a couch in the corner. He looks frail for his age, but his smile is warm and his eyes are kind. "I'm Henry, Jacob's dad."

"You two are the only ones who call me Jacob," Jake mutters, strolling through the back door, arms laden with food. "So, are you staying to eat with us?"

His curt invite throws me for a loop. I look from Jake to his parents, all staring expectantly at me. This is the last thing I expected when I came over here. The last meal I had with a family like this was Sunday dinner at the James', and that was my only one. That realization hits hard, but everyone seems oblivious to my thoughts.

"Of course she is," Jake's mom says, moving to lock the door behind me. "I hope you have enough food. I'm Sonja, by the way. It's nice to meet you."

She walks me over to the couch and coffee table in the corner, and pulls up a bench, placing it on the other side of the table. Jake unceremoniously drops the food on the table and starts pulling out containers from the Chinese restaurant across town. Sonja takes a seat next to Henry on the couch, leaving the bench for Jake and me. Setting my laptop down, I take a tentative seat on the edge.

"I really don't have to stay. I didn't realize you were closing. I just wanted to show you what I've done so far and get some input."

Jake doesn't bother looking at me as he talks. "It's fine, there's plenty of food. I'm keeping shorter hours until I can hire another staff member. I don't have time to sit in here unless I can find an apprentice." His mom opens her mouth to speak, but he cuts her off with a sharp look. "You're doing too much already, and I don't like keeping you from the house. These hours are plenty."

I notice the cane at his dad's side and the way Sonja glances at her husband in acknowledgment. She must be his caretaker and, from what he said, also the one working in the store. It shouldn't matter, but I like that he's looking out for her even though she clearly wants to do more to help.

"Everyone help yourself," Jake says when all the containers

are open and paper plates are passed out. His gaze lands on me, and he scoops noodles on a plate. "What input did you need for the website?"

I wait as the three of them load up their plates with food, rubbing my thighs. "Oh, I reworked your logo a few different ways and wanted to see if there were any you liked. I also came up with a possible slogan. Now that I've seen the inside of here, though, I'm going to change up the colors on the website to match."

A plate piled with a little of everything lands on my lap, almost spilling as I rush to catch it. Before I can tell Jake thank you, his dad speaks up. "What's your slogan idea?"

When I was working on it today, I thought it was hilarious. Lauren thought it fit Jake perfectly, even with her opinion of the rumor mills around here. Looking between his parents now, I might be rethinking it a little.

"Umm, well I thought it should be something catchy and funny with a play on what he does …" I stall. "So … I was thinking 'Get a load of this wood.'"

Jake chokes on his bite of food, and Henry's laughter booms around the store. Sonja's face turns pink, and she wipes at her mouth with a napkin. "That is certainly something. I like it."

I'm sure my face is red again. I've been trying to come up with a cute slogan for my shop for years and still have nothing to show for it. This one came so easily, and as ridiculous as it is, I'm proud of it.

"It'll work."

Sonja scowls at her son, then turns to me. "I'm sorry. I swear we raised him better than this." Her words are kind, but his hit their mark, brushing off my hard work like it's nothing.

Jake blanches at his mom's admonishment, giving her a sorry expression. The love in this family is palpable, even sitting with them brings me a sense of the happiness they share. Their banter is easy and kind, and no topic seems off-limits. Henry and Sonja rope me into the conversation as much as possible, making me feel like I'm part of the family. I remember the days I dreamed of this as a kid, wondering what it would be like to not eat every meal alone, if there even was a meal. Warmth spreads through me at seeing this other side of Jake. His softer side that clearly loves his family. Does he even know how lucky he is to have them and their undying support?

Henry's face becomes more sallow as dinner goes on, and his heavy eyes droop. Jake clears the coffee table, tossing all the extra food back into the bag. "Dad, let's get you to the car. Mom, do you want to take the food with you? It will spoil before I get back to the house."

I gather our plates to throw away, trying not to stare at how Jake has to practically carry his dad out the door. Everything inside me wants to ask, but it's not my place. It's not fair to ask others to share when I won't open up to anyone.

Sonja squeezes my arm, grabbing her purse and the bag of food. "It was lovely to meet you, Amber. Thank you for helping him. He's too stubborn to ask most of the time, but this business means everything to him, and he wants it to succeed. I'm also really sorry to hear about Jana. She was such a wonderful woman and loved you fiercely."

I can do nothing but nod and smile politely. The wound is still so fresh, and I haven't taken the time to grieve, so every reminder is like a shot to the heart. The notion that grief comes in waves has not been true for me. I have shoved that shit down so deep, but it's still ever present, trying to bubble out. There's no time to grieve; not when I have a business to run that's success lies wholly on my shoulders. Jana poured her life into that store, and I will not have it fail at my hands.

Jake says goodbye to his mom, so I give them their moment,

not turning until I hear the door shut and lock. "Do you want to look at the website? I need input before I can go any further."

Jake cocks his head to the side, assessing me. "I didn't know about your aunt passing. Is that why you've been upset lately?"

The scoff leaves me before I can stop it. *Upset?* He has to be kidding me. I have so many things I want to say to him. She wasn't just my aunt. She was my best friend, my confidante, the only person who loved me. She held me together when the pain of my past tried to take hold. Upset doesn't even begin to cover it. More like, drowning in pain, searing cuts every time her name is said, bitter loneliness pulling me deeper into depression.

Instead, I say none of it, grabbing my laptop and moving around him to the door. I can't deal with this tonight. I flip the lock, then yank open the door. "Goodnight, Jake."

jake

Amber stomps back over to her store, but that won't do; she can have her attitude, but not with me. I'm not the bad guy she thinks I am, at least not completely. She doesn't get to dismiss me like I'm nothing. As much as I hate to admit it, that strikes a little too close to a painful wound for me. I'm worth more than brush-offs and people not taking a second look.

I close up, turning off all the lights and locking down everything before slipping out the back door. There's still things to do, like inputting orders and going over sales, but it can wait. I have a bottle of champagne in my cabin fridge waiting for me, but dealing with Amber takes precedence. That and the fact that drinking champagne alone is depressing as fuck. The sun is slowly sinking behind the mountain peak, the brisk spring air cooling my overheated skin. There's no way Amber will stay in her store with her anger, so I kick up one leg and lean against the brick, waiting.

Sure enough, not even ten minutes later, the back door to her store slams open and she storms out. Her steps falter when she catches sight of me, but she plays it off. "What do you want,

Jake?" she huffs out. Without waiting for a reply, she moves to the glass door that leads to her apartment and unlocks it.

My train of thought derails at her opening the door without checking her surroundings, having no regard to her safety. Looking around, I notice there are no cameras back here, nor a light. I didn't even consider that when I locked up my shop every night last week. Of their own volition, my feet move until I'm crowding over her soft body. Her flowery scent invades my senses as I put one hand to the door above her head, holding it closed.

"You're being reckless. Anyone could have been back here waiting for you to open this door, and you didn't even look around."

She huffs again, not bothering to turn and look at me. "You were right there. Doubt anyone dangerous would be willing to cross you."

With my free hand, I twirl a piece of her hair around my finger before tugging it hard, forcing her to look up at me. "What if I'm the dangerous one?" The hitch in her breath sends a thrill running through me. "We need to chat about your attitude. I'm tired of you stomping off like a child every time you're mad. When I move my hand, you're going to invite me upstairs to talk about this like grown adults. Understood?"

Her grumbled "Sure thing" grates my nerves, but I let it go and move so she can open the door.

"Thank you," I mock, and step around her to ascend the stairs. At least she has the sense to lock the door behind her, so I don't have to punish her for that too. I leave little space so she has to brush against me to unlock her apartment. Tiny meows greet us as she carefully opens the door, ensuring she doesn't run over the fluffy kitten.

To my horror, he latches onto my jeans and climbs them as I step in. "Ow," I mutter, grabbing his small body and prying him from my pants where his claws are digging into my skin. Putting him back on the ground, I give his butt a pat to encourage him to run away. Standing, I take in her studio. It's a little cramped, but it's clean and bright.

Amber moves to the small kitchen and pours a glass of water. She doesn't offer me one, simply eyes me over her cup as she takes a long sip. Her shoulders are tight, her posture rigid. Lily's words from earlier come back to me, so I know I need to get her talking. Making myself at home on her couch, I kick off my boots and stretch my legs out in front of me. "Before you walked out, I was asking about your aunt. Want to talk about it?"

She blanches but tries playing it off by rolling her eyes. "That's not exactly how the conversation went."

"A conversation implies you actually responded to me. Have you talked to anyone about her?"

I catch the bristle of anger before she changes the subject to me. "What happened to your dad?"

If this is what she needs to talk, I'll give it to her. It's not like it's a secret, just not something I talk about frequently. Tragedies happen every day, my dad's accident isn't special, and it could have ended much worse than it did. I'm still mad at her, but those feelings can be pushed to the side for this.

"He had an accident at work about nine years ago. His harness broke on a jobsite, and he fell two and a half stories onto cement. It's a miracle that he lived, but the recovery has been a long and expensive one. There's good days and bad days for him now, but he has a daily struggle with pain and his body not doing what he wants it to."

Amber crosses the room to take a spot on the other side of the couch. The pitying look in her eyes is the same one I get every time someone hears the story. She doesn't offer empty words though; she nods and focuses her gaze on the kitten batting a toy mouse on the floor.

"Jana took me in when my mom died. She was the only family I had left."

"What about your dad?"

"Never knew him. Not sure my mom even knew who he was."

That gives me a little insight as to who raised her. I shouldn't push further, but I can't help myself. "How'd your mom die?"

The pained look in her eyes is raw and guts me. Her lower lip wobbles as she tries to keep it together. "It doesn't matter, she's dead now. I don't want to talk about this."

If that's the only bit of information she's willing to give me tonight, I'll take it. I won't give her the same pitying look she gave me, or the "Sorry for your loss" everyone else says. They do nothing to ease the ache, and I have nothing to be sorry for. The pain is still written all over her face though, with nowhere to go. If she goes to the gym to work out the hurt, it's not doing a good enough job. Luckily, I know something that works just as well.

"Okay. Then we're going to talk about you. Your little truce was bullshit because I'm still fucking mad. You used me like a means to an end, you spit your little venomous words at me, then go sulking off when I throw them back, and I'm tired of it. Own up to your shit."

Before she can fight me, I cross the couch and bring her into my lap. Her strength as she struggles against my hold shouldn't surprise me, but it does. It's still no match for me, though. I bring her back flush to my chest, wrap my legs over hers, with one arm around her waist pinning her arms, and the other gripping the hair at the back of her neck.

"This what you wanted? What was the goal? To fuck me and forget me? To get a piece of me to mark it off your bucket list? Or are you constantly pissing me off, hoping I'll snap and fuck you into submission again?"

The whimper that leaves her mouth is indecent, but she plays it off, spitting out, "Fuck. You."

I'm pushing boundaries again. I know she's still inexperienced, and this could look really bad, but there isn't an ounce of fear in her eyes. In fact, when I use my grip in her hair to turn her head to the side, the lust in her blown pupils is obvious. Still, even though this position—her plump ass grinding into my growing erection and her restrained and at my mercy—is exactly what I like, I don't want to push too far. There's still a knot in my chest from how aggressively I took her the last time. I never want to be that guy.

"Since neither of us seem particularly good at apologizing, I'll give you two choices as punishment. Afterward, we can wipe the slate clean and start fresh tomorrow. Unless you get bratty again, then I will happily keep doling out punishments. Option one, ten bare-ass spankings, and no, I won't be going easy. Option two, you get down on your knees and wrap those pretty lips around my cock."

Her reply is breathy as she wiggles in my hold, only making my cock harder for her. "Fuck you, Jake."

"That won't be happening this time, Whiskey." The heavy rise and fall of her chest causes her tits to rub against my arm, and my breathing quickly matches hers. I can't deny that I want her. I want her so damn bad it hurts, and I know she feels it too. A few months ago, I confessed to Thoren that I'm tired of the empty fucks. I'm not a loner, but my friend circle is small, and with Thoren married now, my time alone has increased. It's not only on him, but I try to give them time together, especially now that Lily is expecting. A hollow part of me longs for someone to spend my time with.

Before Amber, I hadn't had sex in over six months. My person is out there, and I've been trying to look for her, but with my crazy hours, it's been rough. It doesn't help that no one seems to take me seriously when I say I want to settle down. When I asked a woman at the bar on a date two months ago, she gave me a crazed look and stated I wasn't the "dating kind." Fuck if that didn't sting and may have been part of the reason I was ready to take out my anger on Amber at the wedding. What I hadn't expected was to feel something with her.

"I have all night. I'm not leaving until you decide." I loosen my grip on her hair as she relaxes against me. When it's clear the fight is leaving her body, I let her go completely, and she steps out of my hold.

"If you put your dick anywhere near my face, I will bite it off." She accentuates her statement by snapping her teeth, but that only riles me up more.

I grip her neck and pull her face back down to mine. "I like pain with my pleasure. You're just making this more fun."

She seethes, her hot breath fanning over my lips. I caress them with my tongue, ghosting over her lips, and she shudders. Her eyes close as she takes a deep breath, and when she opens them, the desire in them overwhelms me. "You don't want to feel the pain sitting right below the surface anymore. If you were a good little slut, I would fuck that pain away. Maybe you'll think about that next time you get an attitude. Now, get on your knees and take your punishment."

To my delighted surprise, she sinks to her knees in front of me. "You want me to suck you off? Fine. But this won't get me to respect you or even like you." Her nimble fingers tremble slightly as she undoes my jeans, and I lift my hips so she can pull them and my boxers down. Her eyes go wide at the sight of my cock standing proud under her heated gaze.

I give it a lazy stroke, making a bead of precum leak from the tip. She watches with rapt attention, unconsciously licking her lips. She may not respect me, but I respect her. No part of me wants to force a woman to do anything, the thought alone makes me sick to my stomach. I would never demand this of her if I didn't respect her or if I wasn't positive she wanted this too.

"Michele said it was pierced. I didn't realize there were so many," she whispers.

"You talking about my dick with others?" I ask, spreading the precum down my shaft. "Sorry you didn't get a good look at him last time. Have you ever sucked a cock before?" She shakes her head, and damn, another spark shoots through me.

"Open your mouth wide, and keep your tongue flat." Amber is still staring, so I grab her hand and wrap it around my base. My hand encases hers, encouraging her to stroke with the amount of pressure I like.

Golden eyes hold mine, and she leans forward, wrapping her pink lips around the tip. Her tongue swirls the thick head, licking up the cum and coaxing a groan from me. She pulls back her lips to give me a clear view of her teeth sinking into my flesh around the head. The pain sends a shockwave through me as I grip her throat again, squeezing until she releases her bite. The tenacity of her to bite my dick only turns me on more, and I might have found a new kink.

"Do it again," I grit out, still squeezing her throat. She does, sinking her teeth in until I throw my head back on a deep groan, and she lets go again, running her tongue over the indentations. She opens wider, warming my dick as she slides her mouth over my length. Ever so slowly, she bobs her head up and down, taking me a little deeper each time. Every time she sinks her mouth back down, another barbell disappears.

"That's it. Relax your throat, you can take it all." It takes all my willpower not to grip her hair and maneuver her how I want. The warmth of her mouth feels incredible. Any guy will tell you that the best head is the kind where the woman is eager to give it. Amber is eager to please, breathing through her nose like a pro already and hollowing out her cheeks every time her mouth travels down.

One hand of hers is still gripping my base, the other is digging into my thigh. I don't mind the pain, too mesmerized by the way her eyes spark when she glances up at me. On instinct, my hand moves to her hair, holding it in a fist so I can see everything.

"You're doing so well," I grunt out, and her tongue swirls the tip again, then runs flat down the underside over each rung. She looks up again, a look of pride crossing her face as she doubles her efforts. The hand digging into my thigh moves to cup my balls, squeezing tight. Her hips are subtly rocking, in an attempt to relieve the ache there. Seeing her getting so turned on from my dick in her mouth sets me over the edge.

"*Fuck*, I'm gonna cum."

She doesn't relent, keeping her mouth tight around my length as the first jet of cum releases. Amber struggles for a moment before swallowing down everything I give her. My cock jerks one last time, then she lets it fall from her lips.

Grabbing her chin before she can retreat, I look her in the eye and plaster on an arrogant smirk. "Such a good slut, swallowing me down like that." Her eyes flash with anger and pride. Pushing away from her, I stand to fasten my pants and slip on my boots. "See you around, Whiskey."

My long strides have me out the door in a matter of seconds, and something smacks the door as I pull it shut. Maybe that clean slate won't be happening after all.

SAUSAGE SQUAD GROUP CHAT

RIVER 🏐:

Congrats on the success today, Jakey. Thoren
said there was a line at opening and three sales
in the first hour.

JAKE:

Thanks man.

RIVER:

Well, that's a depressing response.

THOREN:

Yeah, WTF, Jakey.

JAKE:

Sorry, weird night.

THOREN:

Lily and I are heading over.

JAKE:

I have champagne in the fridge for you, I'm not home yet.

RIVER:

I always miss the fun stuff. Getting a celebration lay?

THOREN:

Don't answer that. Lily told me things you didn't. I can't keep secrets from her, so if you're banging someone other than Amber, don't say it.

JAKE:

Don't make me come christen another room in your house, buddy.

amber

Frustration from my alarm interrupting yet another dream of Jake has me kicking my legs around in the silky sheets. Over the last two weeks since he stormed in here and demanded I get on my knees, my nights have been plagued with dreams of him—of his heated stare, dirty mouth, and the way his tattooed hand wrapped around his thick cock.

I've been telling myself I only listened to him because I wanted a clean slate, but that's a lie. Saliva pooled in my mouth at the thought of tasting him. The way he sat on my couch, legs spread wide, so casual while I was on my knees for him had my panties drenched. It felt dirty and depraved, like I was the slut he claimed me to be, and I loved it. The way he held my hair and kept his focus solely on me, the way his Adam's apple bobbed when I swirled my tongue, and the guttural growl he let loose when he came down my throat have haunted me ever since.

My vibrator has been working overtime again, yet I'm a horny, frustrated mess most mornings. All because of that arrogant prick and the way he's able to read and command my body. And the craziest part of it all? I felt lighter after. When he sauntered out of my place and I released my initial frustration by throwing a pillow, I noticed the change in me. My shoulders were loose, the ache in my chest wasn't so present, and my mind was clearer.

A small part of me wanted to thank him for giving me that when I was heading into another night of curling up on the couch alone while trying to fight off the waves of grief. Not only that, but he didn't stick around to witness my confused spiral afterward, which I was grateful for.

His big-dick energy grows tenfold when he's turned on, and seems to put me in a trance. I wanted to drop to my knees and taste him, just like he asked. The power that came from driving him wild went straight to my head. I've overheard Thoren call Lily a good girl, and while I had to fan myself a little, it was nothing like when Jake referred to me as his little slut. It was like I was still pleasing him, just in a more depraved way, and it unlocked something in me.

He stopped in the store last week to take measurements for my shelves, and he wore a smug look on his stupidly hot face the entire time he chatted with Lauren. Even Socks was enamored with him, following after him and snuggling into his chest once he was picked up. I tried to keep the annoyance from my face, but his wink every time Lauren laughed at something he said told me I wasn't doing a good job at it.

That "punishment" was supposed to wipe the slate clean for us, but it did the opposite. As hot as it was, I hate that I succumbed to him so easily. Though, I'll admit it did make me forget all about our painful conversation from before.

Chimes from my snoozed alarm start again, and I finally haul myself out of bed. This used to be my favorite part of the day—my sacred gym time. Now it's filled with thoughts of Jake and his looming presence around the gym. While he may be keeping his distance, I still feel his gaze on my every movement. Men watching me in the gym isn't a new phenomenon, but Jake's gaze never feels leering, just present.

Throwing on a ratty shirt with my bike shorts, and a topknot in my hair, I rush down the stairs with my pre-workout in hand. Along with my summer shipment arriving today, I promised Jake's mom I would pop in so she can help me finalize some things with his website. She has been amazing and so kind, working with me to get photos of all his work and explaining what customization options I needed to add to his online storefront. Despite it being clear I'm avoiding her son, she hasn't asked about it once, much to my relief.

Jake's bike is already out front, the black gleaming in the last of the moonlight, when I park at the gym's entrance. My traitorous body flushes with thoughts of him in tight shorts throwing around heavy weight. So maybe his eyes weren't the only ones that wandered while he worked out. Kyle's smile greets me as I set up a mat in the corner to do an ab set.

"Mind if I join you?" He never does a workout with me, but I smile and sweep my arm to the open space next to me. The hair on my neck rises as I glance around to find the source. Sure enough, Jake is glaring daggers at Kyle from his spot doing deadlifts.

"Any big plans this weekend?" he asks, stretching out his legs.

"Inventory. I have a huge shipment coming today. What about you?"

"Probably hit the bar with some buddies tomorrow night and do some golfing. If you get a chance, you should come out with us."

Finishing my wood chops, I put down the dumbbell and really take him in. He's attractive, but I feel nothing when I look at him. No spark or rush of excitement. To be fair, I've never given him a chance. We've never gone out, and he's never touched me or pressed his lips to mine. Maybe that's what I need to do in order to get those feelings.

"I really won't have time this weekend, but next time?"

His smile falters slightly, but he nods and continues stretching next to me. I've moved onto planks when a pair of worn high-top Chucks steps into my line of sight. Why I find the shoes so attractive is beyond me, but when Jake drops to a squat in front of me, his shorts riding high on his muscled quads and accentuating the bulge in the center, my mouth dries.

His smirk is filled with mirth when he catches where my eyes are glued. "Hey, baby, just wanted to let you know it will be me in the store today. Stop by whenever." He ignores Kyle next to me, which seems to piss him off. Kyle huffs, picking up his mat with a muttered "See you later" to me.

"There isn't a redeeming quality about you, is there?"

He chuckles darkly, pushing a stray hair behind my ear. "You've seen exactly what qualities I have. Just don't like that tool hanging all over you like a lost puppy. He needs to learn you're mine to play with."

Sitting up, I swat at his hand. "Are you tired of hearing me tell you to fuck off, because I'm tired of saying it. I'm not dealing with you today. Why isn't your mom going to be at the store?" His face shuts down, and I know instantly. "Your dad?"

"He had a bad night," he says, the fight leaving his body. "See you later."

I should feel like an ass, but I don't. He's doing the exact same thing he punished me for. Screw him and his attitude and thinking he controls me. There's too much pent-up energy flowing through me, so I deviate from my routine and hop on a treadmill to run this out. A sense of satisfaction hits when Jake walks out of the gym, but I stay and run until my legs give out.

It may only be six in the morning, but I know Sonja's awake if she already told her son she couldn't work. We exchanged numbers earlier this week so she could text me some photos. I shoot off a quick text asking for her address which she gives with no questions. The poor thing must be exhausted. While I wasn't Jana's caretaker since she needed round-the-clock care I couldn't give, I essentially was for my mom. The toll it has on a person can be immense, so I make a quick pit stop at the local bakery and pick up some breakfast sandwiches and muffins, as well as a latte.

Jake's parents live in a small neighborhood that has weathered homes. Some yards are taken care of, while most are sorely overgrown. The houses are all on the small side, but pulling up to Henry and Sonja's, it's clear theirs is taken care of. There's a set of worn rocking chairs on the small porch and pots on the steps teeming with an array of brightly colored flowers.

I don't want to knock and risk waking Henry if he's asleep, so I set it all down and shoot off another message telling her to check the porch as I walk to my car. It may not be much, but I hope it helps take one small thing off her plate today.

Growing up the way I did, I never went out of my way for anyone else. Not that I was selfish, it was simply out of necessity. We had so little, and when we did have things like food or money, I tried to make Mom hide it. My mom wasn't all bad, she just wasn't great either. After I moved in with Jana and saw how involved she was in the community and how she donated her time, money, and items from the store to others, I was terrified. Terrified that I would end up in the same situation I was with my mom: hungry and desperate.

It wasn't until she sat me down and explained she was blessed enough to own her home and run a business that paid her bills, that I understood. She helped me see there was no need for her to live in excess, and she was happy to help people in worse off situations. She gave as much as she could but would never risk us going hungry. What she didn't say at the time was that she was helping people like Mom and me—adults struggling with addiction, and children who weren't cared for. This small community meant so much to her.

When everything happened and Evelyn, Lily, and Michele stepped in to help me, I was reminded how much small acts of kindness can make all the difference. Jake may piss me off, but I'm all too happy to help his parents.

After pulling into my usual parking spot, I rush upstairs to take a shower. My deliveries usually come around eight, and that little stop put me behind schedule. I shower quickly and thank my genius self for grabbing an extra muffin from the bakery.

By the time I make it downstairs, the large FedEx truck is parked in the alley but thankfully, not waiting. The door to my section of the shop is propped open, and the driver is walking his dolly out as I walk up.

"Hey, Frank. Sorry I wasn't here," I say. I know I locked up. Although, if it was unlocked, it wouldn't surprise me if Frank let himself in to drop off. He's been our delivery man for the last six years and knows the routine.

"No problem, Amber. Jake was here and let me in," he says over his shoulder as he walks up the ramp to get more boxes.

Before I realize it, I'm stomping into my shop to find Jake trying to move the new boxes around to empty spaces in the room. He stops when he sees me, crossing his arms over his chest. "Your storage in here sucks. Frank said he has eighty-two boxes for you. Your ten little garment racks and two foldout tables aren't going to work."

His tone drips with condescension. Why the hell does he care, it's not his problem. Still, I find the need to defend myself. "Thanks, Captain Obvious. I had no idea." I mirror his stance and roll my eyes. "It's on my list, but I've been too busy to work on it. You know, doing things like creating your website, even though you've yet to do anything for me except take some measurements."

"Ordering the wood, making them, and sealing them takes time. If you wanted a crap and quick product, you could have ordered something online." He stalks off toward his shop, calling, "You're welcome for the help" over his shoulder before the door slams.

Frank chuckles from behind me, dropping off another stack of boxes. "Oooh, boy, there's a spark between you two. Hope I'm nowhere near you when it detonates." The look of horror on my face must be amusing because he throws his head back in laughter and walks back out again, cackling all the way to his truck.

Fucking great.

jake

My boots kick up a pile of sawdust as I storm over to my laptop. No matter how often I sweep or vacuum, this floor is always a mess. Slumping into the chair at my desk, I open the computer and pull up my latest supply order. How dare she insinuate I'm not holding up my end of our agreement. I have half the shelves sitting on a workspace in the corner. I was simply waiting on the lumber for the rest before I installed them.

My intention was to not make more of a hassle or mess in her store than I had to, but to hell with that. If she wants a fight, she has one. I hope she's ready.

With my mom not coming in today, I'm losing valuable time in my shop. When I open my store, the first thing I do is print out a "Now Hiring" sign and make an ad for an apprentice and a part-time sales associate. It's not fair to either of my parents to have my mom working every day, and with the unpredictability of my dad's pain, I can't risk falling behind on orders to work in the store.

When I called my mom at lunch, she assured me everything was fine and I didn't need to stop by after work. That gives me the ability to wreak some havoc next door since I close at five and Amber doesn't close until seven. Aside from a few sporadic customers, the store remained mostly empty for the day, and I filled that time with drafting some of the custom orders I have in my queue. The crib for Thoren and Lily takes most of my attention because I want it to be perfect.

Right at five, I close the store and head straight next door. The tinkling of bells chimes when I walk in, drawing golden eyes to me. She scowls but goes back to talking with the customer in front of her. However, her stare is on me like a burn as I walk around the edge of the store looking at the shelves I've made replacements for already.

Like the gentleman I am, I wait until it's just us in the store before bombarding her. "Empty these six shelves, I'm tearing them out and replacing them."

"Oh, you suddenly have time to hold up your end of the deal? It's been a busy day, and I have a long night ahead of me, Jake. You can do it next week. Preferably when the store isn't open."

I spin around, piercing her with a glare. Amber has one brow raised in challenge, just waiting for my rebuttal. The tiny stud in her nose glinting under the store lights reminds me of the way it sparkled under Thoren's bathroom lights. Instead of giving in, I start pulling the shoe display from the shelves and setting them on the floor.

"Jesus, okay, okay," she gripes, coming over to move everything out of the way.

I toss her a self-satisfied smirk before heading for the back door. "I'm going to grab my tools and the shelves. I'll buzz twice when I'm back."

All the stores have a door that leads to the back alley, and all come with a buzzer that lets you know someone is waiting to be let in. It's meant for delivery purposes but is helpful here too. Realistically, Cedar Ridge is a safe town, and she could easily leave this door propped open with no issues. Except, I know all too well how quickly a situation can turn dangerous.

Throwing on my leather apron, I fill my pockets with everything I'll need before getting the deep-walnut shelves. Every project I work on is to the best of my ability. I could have bought cheap lumber since I'm technically doing this job for free. No part of me would have been okay with that, though. Walnut is quality, durable, and beautiful wood, so that's what I ordered for her. It's not always the easiest to get in bulk, hence why I'm waiting for my larger shipment to finish the rest of the shelves and tables.

With everything in hand, I kick shut my workshop door and use an elbow to hit her buzzer. It crosses my mind that she could easily ignore me and hope I don't feel like carrying this all to the front of the store. Surprisingly, her keys jingle on the other side, and she lets me back in. Her scowl is still planted firmly in place. Paired with her cardigan, ripped jeans, and pink Vans, she looks cute as fuck, and it hits me again that I like her annoyance with me.

"Can you hurry your ass up? I don't want Socks getting out."

Totally forgot about that little guy. My back brushes against her as I shuffle through the doorway, trying not to scratch her walls, and a zip of awareness shoots south. There's no reason for me to be this aware of her body next to mine. Hell, last week, I ran into someone I slept with—literally *ran into* because my big ass was too focused on my phone—and I didn't even notice until she called me out. One little brush of T-shirt to sweater on Amber, though, and my cock takes notice.

Thankful for the thick leather of my apron hiding the erection trying to make itself known, I set everything down and get out my drill to start removing the old shelves from the wall. They come out easily, only leaving small holes I can patch later. The shelves I built aren't floating shelves like she had before, but they look much better and should last much longer.

Soft meows sound behind me as I mark off where I need to put in anchors. The kitten is growing quickly but is still a little fuzzball. He's jumping around the shelves, batting at my boots every time I get too close to where he's hiding. As much as I hate to admit it, the little shit is growing on me.

It takes me another twenty minutes to get the shelves level and hung. While it's a small thing, it makes a huge difference in how the store looks. The other displays have chipping paint and are sagging, making mine stand out.

"Those look good. Thank you," Amber says from behind me.

"The rest of the wood should be in next week, so I should have all the shelves replaced the week after. The tables may take a bit longer." I put my tools back into my pockets and grab the old displays to throw in the dumpster out back.

"Thanks. Sorry I was rude about it this morning. I'll be working on that shipment all weekend, but then we can get together to finish up your website." She looks sincere in her words, but this morning's interactions play through my head. I was genuinely trying to help her by getting those boxes put away and not in towering stacks right by her door. With her shorter stature, it would have been a recipe for disaster, and I could easily haul the boxes around. Her feisty spirit and attitude keep me on my toes, and as much as I like it, I equally hate it. Blood rushes south every time she fights me, and I have to refrain from doing what I really want, like making her get on her knees for me again.

"Sure thing. Just let me know," I say, putting one extra thing in my pocket when she isn't looking. Making my way out the back, I toss the scraps of wood and head into my shop.

Tonight, I keep the bay doors closed. I can't have my new friend escaping. Socks is nestled nicely in one of my apron pockets and doesn't seem to want to leave when I start putting my tools away.

"Okay, little buddy, I should be working on one of my eight

projects I have going, but I think I want to make you something instead. How does that sound?"

His tiny paws flex against my chest as he purrs. If I'm honest, I don't know the first thing about what cats like, but I'm sure I can figure it out. Pulling him from my pocket, I set him on my desk and open my laptop to do some research. To my surprise, he jumps right back down into my lap when I sit, so I deposit him back into the big pocket on my chest. Stroking his soft fur releases some of the tension from my neck I didn't realize I was carrying.

Finding what I want to build for Socks is easy, and I have plenty of scrap wood around to start on it. He's asleep now, so I go about my business, careful not to bump him into anything. The wall behind Amber's register has a large sign that says Cedar and Sage but is otherwise bare. Some strategically placed shelves for Socks to climb and lounge on would be perfect.

Some will need carpet to give him more traction and something to scratch, so simply making the base of the shelves is easy. I have four complete when I decide to make one into a house for him to hide in. I'm making the cuts for the side pieces when Amber comes yelling through the door that leads to her space.

"Jake! Have you seen Socks? Is it possible he followed you out of my store earlier?" Her eyes are trained on the floor, looking around in every nook. "I searched that place high and low and couldn't find him anywhere! Can you help me search the alleyway for him?" she shouts hysterically over my saw.

I was debating playing dumb, but the look in her eyes stops me in my tracks. She's petrified, hands trembling as her eyes rove around. On instinct, I move in front of her, gripping her shoulders tight. She glances down where we're connected, then up to my face.

"Hey, it's okay. He's okay. I have him." I move one hand to the pocket on my chest and pull it open to reveal a sleeping kitten.

Her shoulders slump, relief relaxing her body. Soft-honey eyes take in her cat before turning hard again as she slaps my shoulder hard.

"What the hell. Why did you take him? And not say anything? I've been frantically looking for him for an hour, Jake!" Her voice wobbles, and tears rim her eyes. Anxiety is pouring off her in waves over the distress of losing her kitten.

I've done nothing but fuck up with this woman. I'm not a selfish jerk, but somehow, she draws that out of me. Her worry didn't even cross my mind when I took Socks. My intention was to do something nice for her and the cat. He's my neighbor too, and his playful manner made me happy when I was in her store earlier.

I live alone, I work alone … I do most things alone, and it sucks. Even my time with Thoren's dog, Shadow, has been limited since Lily works from home. Having Socks's company has been nice, and I wanted more time with him. The tremble of Amber's bottom lip is like a punch to the gut, and I feel like an ass. *Again.*

"I shouldn't have taken him without your permission, I'm sorry. I wanted to spend time with him and make him something." Rocking back on my heels, I palm the back of my neck. "Want to see?"

My question takes her by surprise as much as it does me. She stares at me befuddled, then slowly nods. I lead her over to the little stack of wood I have on the table. Embarrassment floods my body when I look at the little shelves. What if she hates them? This isn't what we do. She hasn't seen a glimpse of the man I am, but that is one hundred percent my fault. I haven't shown her the caring, selfless, protective side of myself.

Pushing through the uncomfortable feeling in my chest, I hold one up. "I was making small shelves for him. I was going to wrap some in carpet so he has something to dig his claws in. This one, I was going to make like a box with a hole in the front and side so he can jump in and peer out. They could go on the wall behind your register, but if you hate that, you can put them anywhere."

Putting the shelf down, I pet the kitten again to give my hands something to do. She's quiet for so long I fear I've broken her. The silence makes my skin itch, so I finally look up from my pocket to meet her eyes. They're soft again and scrutinizing me so intently I have to look away before she sees too deep.

"Thanks, Jake. He will love that. Please don't take him again, though." There's a quiet calm to her voice I haven't heard before. When she reaches for Socks, I step back.

"Will you be working next door for a while?" I ask, nodding to her storage room.

"Yeah, a few hours at least."

"Can I keep him with me until you're done?" I can't have an animal of my own. I work too many hours, and as much as I would love a shop dog, or hell, even a shop cat apparently, it wouldn't be safe for them. The noise, the fumes, the rogue nails and screws always on the floor. It's not fair for me to do that to an animal. For a few hours though, Socks can fill that lonely void in my life tonight.

"Sure," Amber says, retreating to her side of the storage unit. "Bring him to me if you head out before me." The door between our two areas stays open until we both call it quits for the night, and that feels like progress.

amber

Yesterday, I worked seven to seven in the storage space unpacking and organizing all the boxes. Natasha and Lauren agreed to work the weekend so I could focus on this project, and I'm beyond grateful. Jake was holed up in his shop the entire time, and when I finally called it quits for the evening, he was still over there working. He left the door between our areas closed, which kind of annoyed me until I heard his sander going.

The growl from his Harley as he left didn't sound until almost nine, and I promptly passed out after. I slept past my alarm and am moving slowly to get ready this morning. My body aches from all the bending and lifting I did yesterday. It seems I'm not the only one taking it easy this morning, as Jake is rolling in when I pull open my back door.

He's hot all the time, but damn, watching him pull off his helmet and unzip his leather jacket while running his hands through his hair really does it for me. So effortlessly sexy as he slings a long leg over his bike, stepping off, and heads straight for me.

He steps painfully close, nudging my chin with his knuckle

and closing my mouth I didn't realize had popped open. Embarrassment heats my cheeks as Jake winks at me, then moves around me like I'm nothing and opens up his workshop. That would have been the perfect opportunity for him to make a joke at my expense, and it floors me that he didn't take it. I'm half tempted to float after his scent like in a cartoon, the leather he's wearing mixed with something clean that will be overpowered by the smell of wood as soon as he gets in his shop.

Something is subtly changing between us. I don't know if it was the vulnerability behind his eyes when he asked if he could keep Socks with him Friday or the fact he's showing me his softer side, but the hostility isn't so apparent.

Hell, he apologized to me Friday evening. He actually said the words "I'm sorry," which I didn't think he was capable of. Granted, he should have been sorry. Who the hell steals someone's cat? Now he's not taking shots at me when he can, and it makes me feel even more unnerved than when he was rude. At least then I knew what to expect.

After pulling my keys from my pocket, I unlock my side door and head in for another long day. With everything organized-ish within my limited storage options, I get to work on photos, pricing, and uploading the inventory to the website. After thirty minutes, I realize my speaker is upstairs and the quiet is driving me crazy. I rush across the street to get it from my apartment, and decide to bring Socks back with me too. He spent all yesterday alone, and I can't do that to him again.

Sleep Token is calling my name today, so I put Socks on the floor in a cardboard box for him to happily destroy with his tiny claws, and allow myself to get lost in the tasks at hand. I'm so ingrained in the music and steps of putting the garments on my mannequin dress form that I don't hear Jake come in, so my heart leaves my body when I turn around to find him crouched next to Socks's box, petting him.

His deep chuckle rumbles through the space as I glare daggers at him. "Jesus, say something next time."

He slowly stands, eyes raking over every inch of my body. "I knocked, but you must not have heard. Then I didn't want to disrupt your dancing and got distracted by my little friend."

Cheeks heating, I turn back to my project. I wasn't dancing, at least I hope I wasn't. I'm tired of embarrassing myself in front of him. There used to be days when nothing I did or said mattered. No one's opinion of me could have been lower than my own, so I did what I wanted and let the cards lie where they may. That also may have been part of why I had no friends before Lily staked her claim on me.

"What do you want?"

The room is silent as I wait for his reply. Annoyed when he says nothing, I spin on my heels to find him with sights locked on me. His casual stance of leaning against the doorframe with his muscled and tattooed arms holding my cat makes my mouth water. A slow smile spreads over his face as he holds my stare.

"There she is," he mutters with a slight lift of his lips. "I was hoping you could turn up your music or put your speaker in the doorway. It's too much for us both to have music on, and your choice isn't horrible." He's in another tight shirt today, this one gray, with black pants and his signature work boots. His beard is slowly growing back, and his hair looks recently trimmed, giving him a clean but primal look.

"Yeah, okay. You have to leave your bay doors closed then in case Socks wanders to your side."

He nods, pushing off the wall without breaking eye contact. "You look good today. That slutty pinup look is really doing it for me." Turning, he walks back to his shop, Socks still nestled in his arms, and calls over his shoulder, "Oh, and I'm taking my new friend."

My shock doesn't last long and is quickly masked with anger.

His words hit hard, but I'd be lying if I said they didn't send tingles to my core. There's no AC in here, and it gets hot quickly with all the maneuvering I'm doing, so I'm wearing jean shorts, a red tank, and combat boots. Okay, the bandana in my hair might have given that impression, but it keeps my hair out of my face.

My phone vibrates from the table when I move the Bluetooth speaker closer to the open door.

TRIPLE THREAT GROUP CHAT

MICHELE:

How much work do you have left today?

I know she's talking to me since Lily is waiting on her next round of feedback for her novel.

AMBER:

I'll be here half the night. Have over 40 items to photograph, price, inventory, then upload. Have orders to pack too.

LILY:

Cool, we'll be there at noon with lunch. What sounds good?

AMBER:

You guys don't have to do that.

MICHELE:

😊 You know we will anyway, so might as well get the food you want.

AMBER:

Smoothie and salad place down the road?

LILY:

Omg yes, I would kill for a smoothie. See you in 2 hours.

Around noon, they pull up, hands full of food bags. To my surprise, Michele walks right through my space and into Jake's. I help Lily set down the drink tray and grab the salads, when Michele comes sauntering back, closing the door between our spaces.

"Sorry, I picked him up something too. He has your cat asleep on his worktable."

I snort. Of course my traitorous little fuzz bucket is lounging happily over there. "Yeah, they seem to be friends now. I'm sorry, I don't have seating in here besides an old stool."

Neither seem to care as they dig into their lunch standing at my foldout table. Lily wolfs down her food in half the time we do, then starts digging through the mess of clothes. She sneaks some pieces into the corner, claiming them for herself. Hell, for all the help these women have given me, they could each take one of everything for free, and I would still feel like I owe them.

After we finish eating, I dish out projects for everyone. Lily starts packing online orders while I work on inventorying everything onto the website. Michele, our little fashion expert, starts on the photos. My eyes wander to her frequently, always surprised at the things she pairs together on the mannequin that end up looking chic and trendy.

An hour in, Lily gets antsy, looking over at me every other minute. Michele's pointed stares between us don't escape my notice either. With a lighthearted huff, I close my laptop and stare them down.

"Out with it."

Lily flushes, squeezing her fingers together in front of her. "How are you doing?"

Her simple question takes me by surprise. With their behavior, I expected them to demand a play by play of everything that has transpired between Jake and me. "I'm finnne …"

"Oh, bullshit," Michele says, moving to stand next to Lily across the table from me. Their looks mirror each other as they stand like sentries, not backing down. "Talk to us, Amber. You've been running yourself ragged since the funeral, you're always in your head, and you hardly make time for us anymore. You can't keep running from your feelings."

Quieter, Lily adds, "We hate watching you suffer alone. You need to talk to someone. We're your best friends, and we hardly know anything about you. We want to be your support system, but we can't do that if you don't let us in."

Shit, I was not expecting this today. They aren't wrong. For the last five and a half months, I've been moving through each day with the mindset of *if I don't stop moving, my feelings can't catch up*. You can't grieve if you have no time. Every day I miss Jana, and every day, I tell myself today will be the day it hurts a little less.

It never does.

They have done so much for me and continue to despite my brush-offs and closed-off demeanor. I want to let them in. These two would be the last people on earth to judge me, but opening up is hard. Trusting is hard.

"Tell us something about your past. One thing. You can't keep your whole life bottled up. It's not healthy," Michele says.

One thing about my past. That's easier than facing my grief at the moment. "I, uh, it was just me and Mom growing up. She never told me who my dad was, and she never mentioned other family. We struggled; she liked to self-medicate and couldn't hold down a job, so we often moved from one shitty apartment to another." I look to them for any signs of judgment, but they are simply listening, waiting for me to continue.

Looking back down at the table, I clear my throat and keep going. "Food was scarce because my mom spent her money on drugs or she forgot to shop. I had no idea I had an aunt until I was nine and found a photo of Jana and my mom in the closet. Apparently, my grandparents were religiously strict, so when Jana turned eighteen, she moved far from home. My mom was a few years younger and didn't take it well. She was kicked out when she got pregnant with me at seventeen."

Finding out all this was hard. Not hearing it from my own mother was harder. Jana was the one to tell me how they were raised and where things fell apart between them. My mom drunkenly filled in the bits about her getting kicked out when I asked, but that was the extent of her opening up to me.

"My mom spent more time high than not, and when she wasn't, she was out looking for her next fix. That often came with a revolving door of men. I've been handling things alone since way before any child should have had to. Showing emotions or expressing needs was pointless with her. So talking to others, relying on others, is not something I do easily." I hope they understand what I'm saying. That I want to trust them, and I know I can, but it goes against everything in me to do so.

The tears sting my eyes, and my chest gets tight with emotion. Refusing to meet their eyes, I divulge a little more. "Anyway, I tried to find Jana behind my mom's back. I messaged so many women on the internet at the library hoping one was her, until finally, I found her. It was crazy, she was only a few hours away. She had no idea that I existed, or what our situation was like, so she drove over one weekend. It didn't go well, and my mom was livid. She refused help, refused to let my aunt take me, and I begged her not to call CPS. We stayed in contact when I could, and she took me in about a year later when my mom overdosed. She was my savior. The mom I always dreamed of having. She got me through some dark times and loved me through every second of it."

The tears are streaming hot down my cheeks now, but I don't bother wiping them. "So, no, I haven't opened up about the pain, and I haven't talked to anyone about the loss I suffered. I was a child when I lost the mom who made sure I knew I ruined her life, and it took me years to work through. I'm an adult now, and the loss of Jana … That loss is too great. The love was too great. I can't let myself feel that pain. I can't talk about it. I can't face it. I will *never* recover."

I'm not sure who moves first, but both wrap around me in an instant. Neither says anything, Lily's tears falling as quickly as mine, and Michele squeezes my hand tight. They hold me until I pull myself together, suppressing the emotions and shoving down the pain. That was only the tip of the iceberg, the bare minimum I could scrape out without getting dragged under the waves again.

Jake knocks on the door between our spaces before peeking his head in. Michele, the incredible woman that she is, blocks me from his view and greets him. Lily's small hands squeeze mine tight before we let go and wipe away our tears.

"I just wanted to bring Socks back. I have to make some cuts, and I don't want him in there when I have the saw going," Jake says.

"Thanks," Michele says, taking my cat.

I should turn around and say something, anything, but there's no way I'm showing him an ounce of weakness. The amount of times I was made fun of in middle school for having red eyes from crying still haunts me. Lily moves around me, keeping me at her back so I'm covered by her and Michele, even though my back is to them. The small act makes all the difference. They know how I laid myself bare for them and that I'm too raw to do it for anyone else.

"We'll get the gang together next weekend," Lily says, forcing cheer into her tone. "Friend dinner has been put off too long. Saturday night at our house."

"Yeah, sounds good," Jake says, then the silence ensues. Eventually, he clears his throat. "Well, I'll see you all then."

As soon as the door between our shops closes, the girls go back to the work they were doing before I had my breakdown.

My nerves are fried, but I pull the laptop over to me and open it up.

"Thank you. For listening to me. For not pushing for more."

"We're here for you," Michele claims, "whenever you're ready to share the rest. Thank you for trusting us with that."

They stay for another two hours, and Lily helps Michele with the photos once all my orders are packed. Before they leave, I thank them again for giving me the space to work through my thoughts after opening up to them.

"We can do this every time, you know. You give us five minutes of truths and then we go on with our days. No matter what, we will stay by your side after. You're not alone." Lily's hug is tight, and then they're on their way out.

That night, I let myself feel a little bit more.

jake

"Morning, Jake," Frank calls, taking a tentative step into my workshop. The bay doors are open, as they have been all week. With the summer heat rising, I like to take advantage of the breeze it provides and fresh air it lets in.

"Hey, Frank, do I have a delivery today?" I ask, confused. My wood and supplies don't get delivered by him, and I'm not sure I've ordered anything else.

"Actually, yes," he says, handing over a box. "I also wanted to pop in and ask you a question. There's a help wanted sign on your storefront. What are you hiring for?"

It's been up for almost a week now, and no one has responded to it or to my online post. "I need an apprentice and someone to run the store part-time. Do you know of someone?"

Frank rubs a hand over his jaw, looking a little sheepish. "My son needs a job. He graduated earlier this month and has no idea what he wants for his future. Colby's a hard worker, and he's good with his hands. He's been helping me fix things around the house for years."

My last apprentice I hired wasn't bad, but he had a big ego.

Everything I taught him he claimed to already know and excel at from his previous job. It was beyond frustrating, and the quality of the pieces he worked on often weren't up to my standards. Having someone with no training is enticing. Building his skills from the ground up can ensure I teach him the correct and safe way to do everything.

"Send him in, I'm sure we can work something out."

Frank leaves with a wide smile and a promise that Colby will stop by this evening. Apparently, he's been out camping with his high school buddies this week before they go off to college but is heading home today. My type of guy already. I have plans to meet with Amber after she closes her shop today, so hopefully he shows before then.

We've seen each other in passing at the gym all week, and my mom mentioned Amber brought her lunch and ate with her twice this week while she was working. Other than that, she's kept her distance from me. I clearly walked into something on Sunday when she was with the girls, but the sadness in Lily's eyes and the subtle shake of Michele's head told me not to ask or get involved.

Hopefully, she's finally opening up to them. Evelyn's request to keep an eye on her has stayed at the back of my mind. The thought crossed my mind to tell her to call Amber, but I didn't want to push, and the girls seemed to have it handled. When I see her tonight, I can get a better read on how she's doing. Plus, we have friend dinner at Thoren's place in two days.

My mom closes the store at five, poking her head into the shop to say goodbye. She informs me she left a sticky note on the door for Colby, letting him know to come around back. About an hour later, a young man walks into the shop. I thought all day on how to see if he would be a good fit. It dawned on me that since my delivery today, I had a task that was easier with two sets of hands, so I put him to work while I interviewed him.

Together, we installed the motion-activated light and security camera I ordered for the back of the stores. Both are in range of Amber's store and entrance to her apartment. It bothered me knowing she had no protection back here. I don't work late every night, and it's a dark alleyway. There was no way I was leaving her unprotected like that.

Colby is eager to help and doesn't complain once even though I'm extorting free labor out of him. He seems like a good kid and had no problem agreeing to work two days in the store and three in the shop with me. We agree he will start Monday, then I send him on his way. Having his help will make a huge difference for my mom and me. She can be home for Dad more, and I can possibly even take a full day off once in a while. Things are slowly coming together around here.

After putting away my tools, I realize it's after seven thirty, and I was supposed to meet Amber at seven. Surprised she hasn't come to yell at me, I grab the shelves I finished for Socks and ring her buzzer for the back door. She takes a few minutes to answer, but when she pulls the door open, I instantly know something is wrong.

Her usually tan skin is pale and blotchy, with a light sheen of sweat coating her skin. Amber ushers me in before closing the back door, then ambles over to her register where she slumps onto a stool. There are no angry words at being late, not even an annoyed glare.

"I finished your website with your mom this week. I can walk you through everything after you hang the shelves." Her movements are slow, and concern races through me.

"Are you okay?"

"Fine," she grits out, clearly in pain. "You can hang them wherever you think will look best. I'll be right back."

I know better than most that you can't help someone who refuses to acknowledge they need it. Letting her slip into the back, I pull out my pen, level, and drill and start marking off where to put the shelves. It takes me fifteen minutes to install them all, plus the box one for him to hide in. With my mom's help, I lined the bottom of that one with a little foam piece and covered it with a fuzzy material for him to lounge in.

Stepping back, I admire my work, then realize Amber never returned. I figured she was out here folding things or cleaning, but looking around, she's nowhere to be found. The back room is small, mostly filled with extra stock, and a desk, a chair, a microwave, and a mini fridge sit along one wall. She's not there either, which only leaves one place.

I rap my knuckles on the bathroom door and wait for a response. After a minute of nothing, I call out to her, only to be met with a grumble. The door is locked, but that's never stopped me before. Grabbing my drill, I use the small bit to pick the lock, and it swings open.

Amber is sprawled on the floor, her head over the toilet. Crouching, I move to touch her shoulder only to feel the heat radiating from her body.

"Shit, Amber," I say, putting my hand to her forehead. "You're burning up."

Bleary eyes look up at me, widening in horror, then she leans farther into the toilet and hurls. My hands rush for her hair, holding it out of the way. Stroking her head, I tell her it's okay as she continually heaves, even when there's nothing left in her stomach.

When she finally stops and slumps back into the wall beside her, I wet some paper towels. She takes them to wipe her mouth, so I wet more with cold water and run them over her forehead and down her neck.

I keep my voice low and my movements tender. "Do you need to go to the hospital?"

"No," she rasps. "Just to bed."

No part of me likes this. She looked okay at the gym this

morning, but now that I think about it, she didn't stay as long as usual. I jog through the store to ensure everything is locked up. Turning off the lights as I go, I grab her keys from the back desk. My tools will have to stay for now, so I put them off to the side before making my way back to the bathroom.

Amber groans when I lift her off the floor and into my arms, her head tucking into my chest. Careful not to run into anything, I step out of her store, locking the door behind us, and walk the few steps to her apartment entrance. Unlocking that door, I carry her up to her home.

Socks meows at my feet as I move to the couch and set Amber down. She's shivering, though her skin is slick with sweat, and she's radiating heat. Caressing her hair, I tell her to stay there, then kick off my boots and turn on her shower to lukewarm. On my way back to her, I open her kitchen cupboards until I find a glass and fill it with cold water. She's only half lucid as I help her take little sips before carrying her into the bathroom and setting her on the closed toilet lid.

"You need to bring your temperature down, and a shower is the quickest way to do that. I promise not to look, even though I've seen it all already," I muse, trying to ease her discomfort. She hardly cracks a smile, looking at me with agony in her eyes. Together, we strip her of her clothes, and I discard them on the floor. "Can you stand in there or do you need help?"

"I can stand."

Holding her hand, I help her step into the shower, then close the small glass door. While she's in there, I grab her clothes and put them in her hamper. Then I refill her water glass and put it on her bedside table. Socks scampers around my every move, so I rummage through her pantry until I find a bag of kitty food and fill his dish. Lastly, I rifle through her drawers to find sweats and a shirt.

My eyes linger in her panty drawer, but I feel like a creep with the condition she's in, so I grab a random pair and add them to the pile on her bed. I expect her to be done by the time I get back in the bathroom, but find her sitting in a ball on the tile floor. Stripping off my shirt, I open the shower door and poke my head in.

"Did you wash your hair?"

She slowly shakes her head no, so I grab a bottle that says shampoo and do it for her. It's not easy with the water cascading around her, but I manage. As I'm helping her rinse it out, she turns to me.

"Thank you, Jake." Her eyes are filled with defeat and humiliation. Yet, she's looking at me like I hung the fucking moon. Like she's viewing my soul and likes what she sees. I'm not that guy for her, even if I'm thinking I want to be.

So, I do what I do best. "Well, you smelled like puke."

She turns away, hiding her face as I finish up, then I turn off the shower. Her towel is hanging on the wall, so I hand it to her and hold her hand to help her up. Thankfully, her skin isn't as hot to the touch.

With her towel wrapped around her, she walks on shaky legs to her room and sits on her bed. I hand her the clothes, but she's weak, and her hands tremble as she tries to slip on the shirt. Sighing, I pluck it from her hands and slide it over her body, crouching to help her into her underwear and sweats. Avoiding eye contact, I pull the towel from under her and do my best to dry her hair with it. I don't want her to be vulnerable when she has no choice. I want her vulnerability when she is in control and chooses to let me see her at her worst.

"Come lay down, I'm going to get you Tylenol," I say, pulling back the covers for her to get in. She does so without argument while I rifle through her bathroom drawers until I find what I need. There're no complaints from her when I hand over two pills and a glass of water. Her head hits the pillow, and she seems to fall asleep almost instantly.

There's no way I'm leaving her here alone, so I put the bathroom trash can by her bedside, then attempt to get comfortable on her couch. It's way too small for me, but I manage a decent position where I can see her in the bed still. Socks jumps onto my lap, cuddling on my bare chest.

We only last like that for about twenty minutes before Amber rustles around before shooting up. "Next to you," I rasp, lunging off the couch to hand her the small trash can. I'm not quick enough, and she throws up down my jeans right as I get there.

Tears stream from her eyes as she continues to retch, this time in the trash, and I hold her wet hair back. "It's okay," I whisper, stroking her back. When she's done, she slumps back onto the bed, still crying.

Slipping off my soiled pants and socks, I rinse them in her sink before throwing them into the washer with my shirt. With that started, I get her a damp cloth, clean out the trash can, and wipe down the floor. I guess I'm chilling in my boxers for the rest of the night. When everything is taken care of, I slink back to the couch to try and get comfortable again.

I have no idea what the hell I'm doing here, but I can't seem to stay away from her. Knowing she's in pain and suffering is killing me, even with her just fifteen feet from me sleeping peacefully. Settling in, I pet my furry friend and keep focused on Amber's breathing, knowing sleep won't be happening tonight.

CHAPTER EIGHTEEN

amber

There's a persistent ache in my throat, and my body feels like it went five rounds in the ring last night. I'm a sweaty mess, my mouth is dry, and my head is a little woozy. Rolling over, I pry open heavy eyelids to stare at my ceiling. How the hell did I get in bed last night? I was at work when I started feeling sick, then Jake came for our meeting.

Jake.

Oh shit, Jake was here last night. I lull my head to the side, and sure enough, he's awkwardly lying on my small couch fast asleep. My gaze lingers on his body, his mostly naked body with no blankets. He's only in black boxers, and my god, it's a delicious sight. His tattoos run from neck to pecs and down both arms. One leg is tattooed from his ankle all the way to beneath his very tight boxers.

Even in sleep his muscles are prominent, the definition of his abs mouthwatering, and the way his thick arm is cradling Socks to his chest cracks my heart wide open. I'm so busy ogling every inch of his delicious body, it escapes my notice when he wakes.

A throat clearing drags my eyes up, but instead of finding his signature smirk, I'm met with a look of concern. He sits up, places Socks on the cushion next to him, and stretches his neck and back. Before I can figure out what to say, he's across the room and crouching next to my bed.

"How are you feeling this morning?" His calloused fingers brush over my cheek, pushing my wayward hair behind my ear.

My hand flies to my mouth, aware I spent my night puking. "I'm okay. Better than last night."

His hand moves to touch my forehead, lingering for a minute before he runs his fingers through my hair. His eyes are soft and searching, but I don't know what he's looking for. Last night is hazy. I know I had a fever and got sick, but I feel like I was hallucinating for part of it. Did he help me shower? *Oh, God*, I think I puked on his pants.

"Did I vomit on you?" I ask, cringing.

"Yeah, Whiskey, you did. You don't feel like you have a fever anymore. Do you think you can handle some toast?"

This is my worst nightmare. I have so many questions, but all I want is for him to leave so I don't embarrass myself further. Why did he stay last night? Why is he still here? He needs to leave so I can pull myself together and get to work. Work!

"I have to call in one of the girls," I croak, sitting up to reach for my phone. Stars float in my vision at the sudden movement, but strong hands steady me.

"Hey, it's okay. I texted Lily last night, and she's handling it all for you." He hands over a glass of water from my nightstand. "Drink this, rest, and I'll make you toast."

I watch the tattoos on his back shift and flex as he makes his way to the kitchen. With him distracted, I slowly slip out of bed and close myself in the bathroom. Brushing my teeth, I stare at my sullen reflection. My face is pale, but there's some color in my cheeks now. Can't say anything nice about my hair. It's clear I went to bed with it still wet, leaving it a tangled, frizzy, knotted mess.

I'm working my brush through it when Jake taps lightly on the door. "You okay in there? Your breakfast is ready."

Opening the door, I find him standing with a coffee mug in one hand and a plate with my buttered toast in the other. He's still gloriously rocking his underwear, and I realize he may not have any clothes to change into. I have so many questions for him, but before I can ask any of them, he nods toward the bed and tells me to sit.

My body is so exhausted, I comply without complaint. After crawling onto the bed, I sit cross-legged in the middle, and Jake hands over the plate. He watches me cautiously as I take a bite, then sets down his coffee and grabs my discarded brush. Scooting onto the bed behind me, he runs it through my hair, taking extra care when it snags on a knot.

"I didn't know what to do with it last night. Probably should have brushed it." His deep voice is gentle and soothing, as are his subtle touches.

We aren't those type of friends. I'm not even sure we are friends. This is the softer side of him the girls have sworn is there, but I don't like that he's showing it to me now. It feels like he's only doing it because of how he saw me last night. Like he's pitying me in this vulnerable moment, and that feels like absolute shit. I don't want nor need his pity.

"Thank you for helping me last night, but why are you still here?"

He's quiet and continues brushing through my hair. I'm aware I'm being rude, and he's finally showing me kindness, but I'm embarrassed. He helped me shower, dress, and cleaned my vomit when I only made it in the trash and not the bathroom. The correct response is probably overwhelming gratitude to him. My response, however, seems to be anger that he saw me like that, and confusion as to why he cared enough to stay.

When he still says nothing, my anxiety ratchets up a notch.

"No one shows kindness like this without wanting something in return." I have nothing left to give him. I have nothing left for myself.

Finally, he responds, but it's not what I'm expecting. "Why do you say that?"

He's dropped the brush, and his hands have moved to my shoulders, kneading at the knots there. With him out of my sight, I decide to share this one small thing. It feels like it levels our playing field again after he cared for me.

"I had a lot of men come through our place when I was a kid. Not all of them were kind, but they all made sure they got something out of it. The ones that came off as nice were typically the ones that took the most in the end. Or maybe it was that my mom had higher expectations from them, giving them further to fall in her eyes. Thoren was the first man I saw care for a woman with no intention of taking something in return."

Looking back now, I'm still not sure if my mom was having sex for money, drugs, or hoping someone would fall for her and take care of us. Realistically, I think it was a little of each. I was lucky, though. *Lucky.* That fucking word flutters through my head again. The older I got, the more I noticed the wandering eyes of the men, but so did my mom. Not that she stopped anything for my sake. No one took advantage of me, but it scarred me all the same. It was only solidified when a boy in high school saw me struggling with chemistry and offered to help. He was a friend of the one boy I went on an awkward date with. That help quickly turned into flirting, then him pushing my boundaries. When I shut it down, he spread nasty rumors about me, and I went back to being the girl with no friends.

"Were you safe?"

"Safe is relative. Did I have a roof over my head? Yes. Did I have food to eat? Sometimes. Did I have a mother who preferred getting high and forgetting the daughter that ruined her life? Yes. But no man ever touched me, if that's what you're asking."

Heat creeps up my chest with that admission. Even with him at my back, I feel like he's judging me and making assumptions. I hate it. This is why I don't open up to people. My hands feel clammy, and I no longer want the food in front of me. It's like he can feel the self-loathing falling from me in waves.

"Sometimes, people just want to help. Sometimes, that help is laced with selfish intentions. After my dad's accident, I begged my friends that were still living back home to help. People I've known since childhood that I had stood up for, or that claimed to be my friends. My parents refused to let me defer a semester to help with his initial recovery. Everyone had some excuse as to why they couldn't even stop by to check on them. One friend came through, going over once a week to help out. Turns out, he was going over to steal my dad's pain meds. People wonder why I came back from college a changed man. That's one of the reasons." His hands are still rubbing my shoulders, maybe hoping to soothe the pain we're both feeling at being open.

He's trying to tell me he understands not everyone is good, but all I heard was there are always selfish intentions. He's admitting he knows I'm right, that people always want to be rewarded for their actions. It feels like he stayed last night for a reason, to get something for his kindness. "What do you want from me?"

Jake steps off the bed, drains the rest of his coffee, and slips it into the sink on his way to my little stacked washer and dryer in the corner. He pulls his clothes from it and slides them on.

"I already told you, I don't want anything from you, Amber. I'm tired of you only seeing the worst in me. I already own the one part of you no one else can have." He grabs his keys and stuffs them in his pocket. "Don't you dare leave. Your body is screaming for rest, if last night is any indication. Give it rest."

With a scratch on Socks's head, he leaves my apartment. I'm

in a state of shock. Even though I wanted him gone, I don't think I really wanted him to leave. I thought we were over the back-and-forth feelings between us.

I'm left with even more questions than when I woke up. I might have messed up here. He cared for me in ways no one else has, and he did it with empathy. In return, I was ungrateful and rude.

I've never had someone care for me when I was sick. As a kid, I was sick frequently from living in nasty apartments, not having clean clothes or getting bathed enough, eating moldy food because it was all we had. Not one time can I remember my mom stroking my hair, helping me feel better, or even caring I was sick. When I moved in with Jana, it was like night and day, and I was hardly sick again. The few times I succumbed to illness, I refused to let her care for me because I had relied on myself for so long. I was scared to rely on her too much and become the burden my mom always told me I was. Yet, here was Jake, doing it without being asked and with such tenderness.

By this point, I know that he hates when people make assumptions about him, yet here I am doing exactly that. After his blowjob punishment—that wasn't a punishment at all—it's clear he can have anything from me. I owe him an apology, but I'm too damn tired to give it now. I send a thank you text to Lily, with a promise to call when I wake up again, and tuck myself back in bed to recover from whatever illness that was last night.

CHAPTER NINETEEN

SAUSAGE SQUAD GROUP CHAT FRIDAY MORNING

THOREN 🔨:

Jake has a girlfriend.

RIVER ⚾:

WHAT?!

JAKE 🪜:

Yeah …what?

THOREN 🔨:

Lily said she watched you come out of Amber's place this morning.

RIVER ⚾:

My man. She's stunning.

JAKE 🪜:

Watch it. She's not my gf, we didn't even fuck last night.

RIVER ⚾:

Then what the hell were you doing? Also, protective much?

THOREN ⚒:

See! Told you. You don't stay at a girl's place
and not sleep together unless she's your gf.

JAKE 🪜:

She was sick.

RIVER ⚾:

And you took care of her? Goodbye bachelor
life. How the mighty have fallen.

JAKE 🪜:

picture flipping off camera

THOREN ⚒:

I'll get the deets at friend dinner tomorrow night.

RIVER ⚾:

I hate missing all the good shit.

After leaving Amber's place on Friday morning, I rushed home to shower, eat, and change before heading right back to work. I was planning on showering there, but then she had to go and ruin that. I knew she would freak out when her fever broke and she realized I helped her shower and dress, but she surprised me. There was a tenderness to her, and she let me see a small part of her. I tried to stay quiet and out of her line of sight, hoping that would make it easier for her to keep talking.

It was going well, and I got more insight into who she is until she shut down and put me in the same category as the men who used to fuck her mom. In my anger, I lashed out in a cruel way, but what the hell? I opened up to her too and tried to explain that I understood where she was coming from. Trusting that people have good intentions, or even no intentions, is near impossible some days. We were trusting each other with our stories until she gutted me with that question. I might want a lot from her, but none of it in the way she was insinuating.

Then I had to face Lily and her questioning gaze as I picked up my tools from Amber's store. If there's one person I could talk to about this, it would be her. Instead of confiding in her though, I avoided all conversations and hid in my workshop like a pussy. Turns out, it was a very productive day that way, except for checking the new camera's notifications hourly to ensure Amber stayed home.

Now I have to face her at dinner. I left the shop early to come talk with Thoren before the chaos of the women descended onto the house. Lily puts a beer in my hand and points me to the back deck when I show up. I love these two together and have no qualms about telling my best friend that his wife is amazing.

Shadow barks and barrels for me when I slip out the back door and take a seat next to Thoren. "Don't know who was more excited to see me, Lily or Shadow."

He shakes his head, laughing. "Get your own girls."

"According to you, I already have one. Her cat's a boy, though, so it kind of ruins it."

Avoiding his assessing stare, I bask in the warmth of the summer night and take a sip of the cold beer. "You want to talk about it?" I appreciate that there's no beating around the bush with him.

"I don't know, man. I don't know what the hell I'm doing. She's feisty and funny, and I can push her buttons because she pushes mine right back. But she's wound so tight, holding every-thing so close to the chest, I don't think she will ever be able to let someone in."

Thoren hums, bending down to throw Shadow's ball for her again. After another long sip of his beer, he glances back into the house before turning to me. "Can I tell you what I think?"

I feel eyes on the back of my head, and the small smile from him tells me what I already know. "Is this what you think or what Lily thinks? I would trust her opinion more in this matter."

"Oh, screw off." He punches my shoulder. "It's what we both think. Between subtle comments from my mom and what Lily and I have seen, she needs someone. She lost the one person she trusted and doesn't know how to establish that trust with anyone else. Lily said she's working on it, but she will need time and patience. Now, for what I think … Living with you in college showed me you know how to unwind someone. Maybe she needs someone to take control for a bit so she can let things go."

He gives me a meaningful stare, and I know exactly what he's getting at. I saw it happen when I doled out her little punishment. Her body was begging me to take control of the situation at the wedding and again when I followed her into her apartment. It seems she has had to be in control for so long that she's desperate for someone to take on the role, even if it's only for a moment. She may say she doesn't want me, but her body says something different. Her feelings are obvious from the way her eyes trace every ridge of my body, how her breath hitches when I'm near, and the shivers that run down her spine at the sound of my voice.

I've been desperate for another taste of her. The way she's always riling me up stokes the fire inside me, and only she can fan the flames. If she needs to relieve some tension and let go for a while, I'm all too happy to tie her up and give her that release.

Before long, Shadow bounds around the side of the house with her happy woofs and tail wagging. Reluctantly, I leave Thoren outside to start the grill and head inside to see if Lily needs help. Michele greets me first, giving me a quick hug, and my gaze catches on Amber. She looks better, the color back in her cheeks and her eyes bright. She's dressed casually in sweats and a hoodie, but the cozy look suits her. It makes me want to drag her to bed and snuggle her, which is not typical for me. Plus, I know what's hiding beneath it, and I want to see it again.

"Anything I can help with?" I ask, grabbing another beer from the fridge.

"If you want to bring the tray with the burgers out, then come back in and grab plates and condiments? We can bring out drinks and toppings when we come out." Lily smiles over her shoulder, cutting a tomato.

"Absolutely."

The girls join us outside as we settle around the table. Michele pulls out the chair next to me, and Lily takes the one across from her. That leaves the two ends open, and unsurprisingly, Amber takes the one between the girls. The back porch on the cabin I'm living in is nice, but there's a homey vibe to their setup here, with the string lights overhead and the potted flowers scattered around the edges. We always talk about doing more dinners together, but it doesn't happen as often as we would like.

I cherish these times together. There's something about eating dinner alone that's depressing as hell. It's the reason I like to eat in the shop, because then it feels like I have an excuse instead of sitting in my quiet cabin by myself. I've noticed Amber likes to work the closing shift at her store, and I wonder if it's because she feels the same.

"How are you feeling, Amber?" Thoren asks, placing the tray of burgers on the table and taking his seat next to Lily.

"Much better. Seemed to be a twenty-four-hour thing, but it sucked. Thanks for sharing your wife to help in the store."

"She's not the only one who helped," I mutter.

Michele side-eyes me, and I'm guessing this is all news to her. I doubt Amber even told Lily how much I did for her, but I don't mind keeping her secrets. No one deserves to be embarrassed when they need help.

"You know I'm always happy to help," Lily says, mouth full of food. "Did you guys hear Thoren's good news?"

We all turn wide eyes to him, waiting. "Since the department has been having trouble finding someone to take over running the search and rescue (SAR) team, they're combining it with the Task Force Leader Wildfire position to make it more enticing. They've had ten applications come in this week alone."

Thoren is a park ranger, and he loves his job. He's also been volunteering with the SAR team since high school, so when they had a position open to run it, they begged him to take it temporarily. Problem is, that temporary position has been over a year now. There's no doubt he would keep the position because that group saved Lily's life one fateful night, but it takes a lot of his spare time, and I know it's been harder on him since finding out Lily's pregnant.

"That's great. Any good candidates yet?" Michele asks.

Thoren's gaze bores into hers, and something there makes her flinch. It isn't until he glances at me that I realize who they're talking about. Michele's high school boyfriend, Ethan, is a fire-fighter. They were attached at the hip until he moved away with his family when he graduated. If he's applying, there's a good chance he'll get the job. His dad was the fire chief here for a while, and the town loved him.

"They're giving priority to locals, and he's been put in that category. I'll let you know if I hear any more on how the inter-views are going," Thoren adds. Leaning over, I give Chele's hand a squeeze. We loved Ethan in high school. He and River were best friends, and I think they still are. When his dad got a job offer in Colorado, Ethan was eighteen and had just graduated. He could have stayed, but he chose not to, and that broke Michele in a way I'm not sure she's ever recovered from. We will have her back, no matter how this plays out.

Clearing her throat to break the tension, Lily looks lovingly at her husband before sending me a wink. "There's another reason that's good news," she declares. "He's going to need more time off to spend with the baby."

She drops it so casually that the eruption of screams from Amber and Chele are startling. There's a rush of squeals, hugs, and congratulations. I may already know, but I play into it and show my genuine excitement. These two will be the most incredible parents.

When the excitement dies down, we go back to eating our dinner while the girls ask about how Lily has been feeling, her cravings, and all the things that go along with pregnancy.

"Our poor kid will be old by the time you guys get it together and pop out some friends for him or her." Thoren eyes us all speculatively like we're going to volunteer to have kids for him.

"I'm not having kids," I state without shame. "I had a vasectomy four years ago."

I love kids and think they're great, but I have no desire to have any of my own. My business is my baby, and I like the freedom of doing what I want. There's no judgment for working late nights, spending hours at the gym, or riding my bike a little recklessly when I don't have kids in the picture. I've never had to bring it up to a woman yet, but there's a fear that I'll never find someone who shares the same sentiment.

Looking around the table, everyone looks stunned by my revelation. Shocking us all, it's Amber who breaks the awkward silence. "I've never wanted children either. I love them and can't wait to come get baby snuggles and buy them obnoxious toys and cute outfits, but I will not be having any of my own."

"I should clarify. I will be the funkle and will love all the little noisemakers you have."

Amber's heated gaze snags with mine. I'm aware the conversation is continuing around us, but I can't seem to focus on anyone but her. She's the first to look away as I clue back into the discussion. The topic changes again, and we all take our time chatting about life and how boring we've gotten as we age. Chele is the oldest at thirty, but Thoren and I are only a year behind.

"I think I'm going to get my nipples pierced," Michele claims out of nowhere.

Beer flies from my mouth, and Thoren chokes on his bite of cookie that was set out for dessert. "Jesus, Chele, give us some warning," he coughs out.

"What? I need something exciting in my life. Jakey boy has his dick done, why can't I get my tits? They're nice tits."

"They're exceptional tits," Amber comments. "You have the nicest tits at this table, for sure. No offense, Lily."

"None taken. She wore this low-cut top last week, and I've never wanted to motorboat anything so bad in my life." Lily shrugs.

This, right here, is why I love this group of people. You never know what will come out of their mouths, and there's never a dull moment. My soul doesn't feel so heavy with them around. Michele and Thoren know how much I fought in school, hell, even how many bar fights I got in when I moved back after college. They know I can come off as a dick and my asshole persona isn't always a persona. Yet they love me anyway.

When the night starts winding down, and Lily's eyelids start to droop, we help clean up and head for the door. "My place next month," I tell them all. "I'll snag one of my outdoor tables for the evening. Dinner will be whatever lil mama is craving at the time."

"Good man," Lily says, wrapping her arms around me, and I drop a kiss to her head. "Now, everyone get out of my house so I can go to bed."

amber

As we step onto their porch, Michele says goodnight and heads to her car. Steeling my nerves, I grip Jake's arm. "Can I drive you home?"

"I live a thirty-second drive away." He chuckles a deep throaty laugh.

"I know. Please?"

He takes me in, and I try not to fidget under his stare. Without saying a word, he walks to my passenger door and gets in. Okay, then, I guess that's a yes. Following him, I slide into the driver's seat and back out of Lily's driveway and into his. The lane they live on is secluded in the woods outside of town. Thoren and Lily own all three of the cabins on this lane—occupying one, letting Jake stay in one, and the other is empty.

Parking in front of his cabin, I hesitate to get out. My nervous habit takes over, and I run my hands down my thighs, trying to calm my anxiety. Jake's large hand covers mine, halting my movements. When I turn to him, his face is expressionless.

"Come inside, Whiskey."

His voice is pure sex, demanding and smooth. My body listens instantly, my nipples hardening behind my bra. When he steps out of my car, I follow. He leads us up to the cabin and kicks off his boots when he gets inside, so I toe off my sneakers. It smells nice in here, and I recognize the smell when I see one of the small candles I gave him sitting on his kitchen counter. Something about the fact that he brought one home sets off butterflies in my stomach.

I've never been in this cabin, and it's surprisingly charming. There's a discarded pair of socks by the couch, but aside from that, it's clean, if not a little bare. There's nothing on the walls, no artwork or picture frames. No curtains on the windows or decor on his coffee table. It's bigger than my studio but is similar in the way everything is open. His kitchen is to the left, bathroom to the right. Directly ahead is a small dining table and his living room that opens to the back deck. The one and only bedroom is up the stairs.

"Sit," he orders, nodding toward the couch while he moves to the kitchen and pours himself a drink.

I do as he says, and he leans against the kitchen counter. He keeps his eyes pinned on me as he swallows a sip of the amber liquid. This is probably the part where I should apologize, but I'm too entranced by him.

He didn't turn on any lights, the ethereal glow of the moon streaming through the windows the only illumination. Jake looks dangerous with deep shadows hiding half his face. A fierce hunter eyeing his prey.

The longer he stands across the room unmoving, the more turned on I become. His sinister looks are alluring, and his heated and unwavering stare feels like he's seeing every dark and depraved part of me. My pussy clenches when he swirls the drink and licks his lower lip, finally taking a step toward me.

He takes a seat on the coffee table in front of me, his legs bracketing mine. Still not saying a word, he rests his arms on his thighs, making himself eye level with me. The shadows dance over his features, giving his eyes an onyx color. We stay like that, unspeaking. Unmoving. Lifting the glass to his mouth, he takes another sip, keeping his gaze trained on mine.

My heart is beating out of my chest, my breaths coming in quick. The anticipation of what he might do next is soaking my panties. All thoughts of why I wanted to talk to him this evening are long gone and replaced by the visceral need to be devoured by this man.

Slowly, he turns the glass, holding the spot he drank from up to me. "Drink."

I haven't had a drop of alcohol this evening, but I listen, relishing the burn of the last of the liquid. He takes the glass from me and sets it on the table next to him. One hand pulls the tie from my hair, letting the mess of my locks fall around my face and shoulders. Stroking my jaw with his thumb, he tucks some wild strands behind my ear.

"Do you want something from me?" he asks, his usually smooth voice filled with grit.

I'm all too aware I'm a hypocrite. This is the exact reason I need to apologize to him. For thinking he wanted something from me, and here I am *needing* something from him. Because that's what this is, not a want but a need. His jaw tics, waiting for my response.

"Jake, I'm—"

"Stop. Answer me, Amber."

"Yes," I breathe out, looking down at my hands. "I want something from you."

His hands grip under my thighs, lifting me with ease. My hands instinctively wrap around his neck, and he holds me close to him and climbs the stairs. He drops me in the center of the bed, then pulls my sweatshirt over my head. It flies to the side, discarded carelessly on the floor. He sucks in a breath, getting a good look at what I'm wearing underneath. I knew there was a chance I'd get another punishment tonight, so I came prepared in my favorite lacey bra and pantie set under my sweats and sweatshirt.

"The only things that can come out of your mouth are 'Stop' or 'Yes, Jake.' Do you understand?"

"Yes, Jake."

His eyes darken, raking over my body again. I lean back on my elbows, enticing him. He grips the waistband of my sweats and yanks them down my legs to join the rest of my outfit on the floor.

"Fuuuuck, did you wear this for me? My pretty little slut came here wanting to get fucked? Is that what this is?"

My nipples poke through the thin fabric of my bra, and my core is dripping around the skimpy panties. I let my legs fall to the side, opening myself further to him. "Yes, Jake."

His chest puffs, then he moves to the side of the bed, grabbing something from his nightstand. With his other hand, he grasps my wrist and ties a knot around it, then wraps the soft rope around his headboard. He drops one knee to the bed, leaning over me to tie the end around my other wrist.

My heart pounds in anticipation as he moves back to the end of the bed to stare down at me. "You remember the two things you're allowed to say?"

"Yes, Jake."

"Good." Reaching behind his head, he tugs his shirt off and flings it to the floor. Large hands deftly unbutton his jeans and pull down his zipper achingly slowly. With his jeans kicked to the side, he crawls onto the bed, straddling my lap. His face changes from lust to anger as his expression hardens.

"I'm not some lowlife piece of shit, Amber. I would never take something that wasn't mine already or expect anything from anyone." His hands slide up my waist to cup my breasts through my bra. He tweaks my nipples, pinching them hard, making me cry out. "I want to punish you for being so cruel and callous with your words. But you're lucky. I think you're hurting and need to see that someone can care for you simply for your benefit."

Goosebumps erupt over my chest as he lowers his head to bite my nipple through my bra, then lavishes kisses down my stomach until he reaches my panties. With solid pressure, he licks over my center, taking a deep inhale and smiling wickedly up at me. His wink is enough to send a fresh wave of arousal through me, my hands tugging on the restraints to touch him.

His chuckle is sinister before he takes the edge of my panties in his teeth and drags them down my legs to join the pile of discarded clothes. Spreading my legs wider, he settles his broad shoulders between them. Hot, wet kisses trail my inner thighs and all around where I really want him. With one thick finger, he rims my center, then pushes it into my dripping pussy.

He strokes me ever so slowly, moving it in and out of me. His mouth meets my overheated skin again, but still not where I want him. I revel in the delicious torture when he adds a second finger. The pace stays the same, lazily stroking me.

"Please, Jake," I whine after a few more minutes, my arms getting sore from pulling on the rope.

"You beg so sweetly. Say it again, Whiskey."

"Please," I cry, needing something, anything from him.

He growls in approval, diving into my pussy like it holds his dying breath. His fingers curl and pick up their pace as his tongue flicks my clit. I moan, wondering how the hell I went without this for so long. The first time he did this, I was a jumbled mess of nerves and anticipation. I didn't get to focus on the feel of him licking me so thoroughly and the way my body responded to every swirl and suck of his tongue on my clit.

He drives me higher and higher, my body wound so tight tears leak from my eyes. Not once does he let up, until I'm right on the precipice of something great. With a bite to my clit, I fly over the edge. Blinding sensations of warmth and light sear through me as he slows his fingers, stroking me through my orgasm.

As my mind and body connect again, I find Jake leaning over me, untying my wrists. He brings them down, kneading the reddened skin, rubbing up and down my arms, massaging the feeling back into them. Satisfied they're back to normal, he strokes my cheeks with his thumb, wiping the errant tears that had escaped.

I'm not sure what I expect to happen next, but him maneuvering us under the blankets and tucking me into his chest isn't it.

"What are you doing?" I whisper hoarsely. He has my back to his chest, my bra and his boxers still on. It does nothing to hide his raging erection poking into my ass.

His hand splays protectively over my stomach, keeping me in place. It's then I realize how relaxed I am and how safe I feel. As if Jake knew exactly what this would do for me and gave it easily.

"Sleeping," he grumbles into my hair.

"What about you?" I ask, wiggling my hips a little so he gets my point.

"That's not what this is about. Tonight's about you, so shut up and let me hold you."

His growly and grumpy demeanor is at complete odds with the way he just worked my body. I want to apologize and tell him I'm seeing the good man he is. I also desperately want to climb on his dick and see what nonvirgin sex feels like. With the exhaustion from getting sick this week and the endorphins flowing through my body, I don't have the energy to do either. Instead, I close my eyes, nestle further into Jake's warm embrace, and let sleep take me.

jake

My body is too warm, and there's no feeling in my left arm. The blankets feel too heavy, but when I crack an eye open to push them off, I'm met with a mess of blonde hair draped across my chest. *Amber.* Filling my lungs with her lavender scent, I settle back into bed, content to hold her until she wakes. I haven't woken up with a woman in my bed since college. She's also the first girl I've brought back to this cabin.

Everyone I've slept with since moving back has left the minute the deed was done. Not that I complained. There is something about her still being here, though, that fills me with pride. I was a little worried she would run in the middle of the night. She seems like the flighty type to run when things get real.

Yet, here she is, wrapped around me like a koala. At some point, she discarded her bra, her bare tits smashed against my stomach making my cock stir. One of her legs is draped over mine, the heat from her pussy making my morning wood hard as steel. My balls ache from not getting off last night, but I wouldn't change a thing. She needed that release, and she needed to see I'm not trying to take anything from her.

I want to wring every ounce of pleasure from her and show her everything she's been missing. To have her scent marked on my skin, and her pretty cunt dripping with me. For god's sake, she let me tie her up and have my way with her without complaint. It's like she was made for me.

She stirs on my chest, and I hold my breath, anticipating the freak out. Instead, I feel her heart rate increase against me, but she doesn't move. Her lashes flutter against my skin as she awakens. She stays still so long I think she might have fallen back asleep, until her hand moves, tracing the tattoos on my arm draped over my stomach. Her light touch tickles, but I do my best not to move.

I wait patiently as she starts at my elbow, tracing the waterline and the two figures there until she reaches my wrist. That arm has a full sleeve with the top half covered in the mountain peaks and trees, and the bottom is a photo of my dad and me fishing at the river. It was one of our favorite things to do together when I was a kid.

"That was our favorite spot to go," my sleep-soaked voice says.

Amber lets out a small screech and tenses against me. "Jesus, Jake. How long have you been awake?"

I ignore her question and keep going. "We would go every chance we had, spending hours out there enjoying each other's company. My dad's never been a big talker."

"It's nice," she whispers, and her body starts to relax again, her fingers caressing the figures. "What do these ones mean?" She traces over my knuckles where I have ABOVE written across one set and ALL on the middle fingers of the other.

"It's a reminder to always do the right thing, above all else. No matter the consequences, backlash, or fears." That was my hardest tattoo to get, after an incident in college.

"Hmmm" is all she says. She angles her head to finally look at me. "How long have you been awake?" she asks again.

I let out a haughty laugh, caressing her pouty bottom lip with the pad of my thumb. "Longer than you. Mind getting up? I've got a raging hard-on, and I need to get rid of it so I can pee."

Her gaze travels to my boxers, staying glued to said erection. Tentatively, she sits up further, then strokes me through the fabric of my boxers. "Have you had this since last night?"

"I've had it since I was born," I quip back. Angry Amber lets me get out all my anger, but feisty Amber is fun, and means I get to be playful with her.

She scowls at me, but it's quickly taken over by a cute-as-fuck giggle. "You're so stupid. You know what I mean."

I thrust my hips up, winking at her. "I do, and no. It went away, but you're still in my bed, so it came back." Amber smacks my chest but gets off me, dragging the sheet with her. "It's not like I didn't see it all last night, baby. Come downstairs when you're ready. I'll make breakfast."

Her undies fling past my head when I'm almost to the stairs. Bending down, I pick them up and bring them to my nose, then smirk over my shoulder and take them downstairs with me. By the time I've relieved myself and brushed my teeth, Amber is dressed in her clothes from last night and sitting at my small island.

Without a word, she stalks into the bathroom while I start a pot of coffee and gather the ingredients for omelets. I probably should put on shorts, maybe even a shirt, but I like when she gets so distracted by me that she loses her train of thought. When she exits the bathroom, the scowl is back on her face.

"Where are my undies?"

She can't see my smirk with my back to her, but I casually walk around the kitchen, pouring us each a cup of coffee. "No idea, but I like knowing you're bare under there for me." At the fridge, I pull out the milk and pass it over to her. Her nose scrunches, making the little diamond catch the morning sunlight.

"No flavored creamer?" I raise an eyebrow at her, and she shrugs like that's something she expected me to have. Back in her spot at the island, she rubs her hands down her thighs. "Look, I wanted to apologize. I was wrong and out of line. It's hard for me to accept help, and even harder to accept it without worrying how to repay people for said help. Over the last year, I've had no choice but to let people help me with Jana's health, then death, with the business and figuring out her estate and finances with full-time care and then after her passing."

She takes the time to pour some milk into her coffee, and I grab a spoon for her to stir it. "I don't want to sound ungrateful for any of it because I don't know how I would have survived without the help. I just feel like I've been drowning, unable to repay everyone's kindness. When I woke up and you were there caring for me, my fears took over and I panicked. How am I supposed to help others when I can't even hold my head above water most days."

"Amber—"

She holds up her hand. "I know that none of you want anything from me, but that's hard to accept. I'm so incredibly sorry I acted that way. Thank you for all you have done. And thank you for installing the light and camera in the alleyway. I'm assuming that was you, anyway." Her eyes slowly lift from her lap, and I nod. "Well, thank you. I'm not really sure what to say about last night except it was incredible, but I have to get going."

"You can stay for breakfast," I say, not ready for her to leave. She's finally opening up to me. Maybe Thoren was on to something, and I need to keep the orgasms coming. I'll need to change things next time though because my balls are going to fall off if I keep denying them the pleasure of getting off.

Now I know she strikes out when scared, and can navigate things easier with her. I already assumed that when she started lashing out at me. My mom would have smacked me upside the head, knowing I was just as cruel back, but I think Amber needed that. I want her to see I'm a big boy and can take her on. If she needs a safe space to let go of her emotions, I can be that. I'll even dish it right back so she doesn't feel alone and cruel after. And if I really want to be honest with myself, I want someone to do the same for me. It's why this thing between us, whatever it is, works so well.

"I can't. I have to interview a new associate in an hour and really need a shower. Plus, I feel bad leaving Socks alone any longer. We can get together this week so I can finally go over your website with you," she says, moving around me to put her mug in the sink.

This is the running that I was expecting from her. When I found her still in my bed this morning, I hoped she would stay. Maybe I also wanted a repeat of last night. We have unfinished business, aside from the fact that my cock needs to be buried deep inside of her. Every tidbit of insight she gives me makes me want to unravel her further. What other skeletons are in her closet? I'm not always great with my words or explaining how I feel. I don't feel that pressure with Amber to have the right things to say.

Swiping the keys from the counter, she turns toward the door, ready to leave. "See you around, big guy." She smirks, taking one more heated glance down my body.

The laugh that rumbles through me is loud, shaking my chest. Fucking Thoren and his genius thinking. The same spark I missed seeing in her is back. She's playful, funny, and deeply scarred but takes no shit, and it's sucking me in.

SAUSAGE SQUAD GROUP CHAT

JAKE 🪜:

You can have the title of Thor back, your unwind tip worked.

THOREN 🔨:

Lily never stopped calling me Thor. She loves
the way I work my hammer. And you're
welcome. You should have figured that out on
your own, you're supposed to be some
sex god.

RIVER ⚾:

He's not Aphrodite. Did you bone Amber?

JAKE 🪜 :

Who the hell calls it that?

RIVER ⚾:

Fine, did you hit a home run? Plow her pussy?
Plunder her treasure? Fuck her into oblivion?

THOREN 🔨:

Why can't you guys be normal?

JAKE 🪜 :

Next time I'm leaving you out of the chat, Riv.

Jake 🪜 :

I got her to open up and relax. She even stayed
the night.

RIVER ⚾:

I bet she opened up 😉

RIVER ⚾:

Sorry, I can't help myself. This is the first time
you've really talked about a girl. I'm happy for
you, man.

RIVER ⚾:

Guys? Don't cut me out! You love me!

I make my omelet and take it out to the back porch to eat
alone. The gentle breeze and the warmth of the sun's rays do
nothing to quell the bitter feelings I have about Amber leaving.

I'm so lonely out here that last week I looked into how much it would cost to turn the storage room above my storefront into an apartment. At least then I would have Amber next door and could probably snag Socks for some sleepovers. Once I saw the quote from a contractor, I realized I could renovate that or keep paying off the rest of my parents' mortgage. The mortgage won out.

After pulling my phone from my pocket, I snap a picture of my half-eaten breakfast and the view from my spot on the porch and send it to Amber.

JAKE:

This could have been you this morning.

I'm surprised when the three dots pop up right away.

AMBER:

Didn't have time. That view is something, though. Perfect spot for a porch swing.

JAKE:

I never thought of that.

Lily took the outdoor couch when she moved in with Thoren, and I replaced it with a chair. One pathetic chair.

AMBER:

Jana had one on her porch. It's where we had all our best talks. Leaving that swing was one of the hardest parts of having to sell her house.

I was going to take the day off, knowing Colby was starting tomorrow and that hopefully my workload was about to lighten a little. Instead, I scarf down the rest of my breakfast and head inside to shower and get ready for the day.

With a text to Michele, I get the address to Jana's old house and make my way there to get a look at the porch swing Amber was talking about. I take some sneaky photos from my truck, then head to my workshop to draw up some plans. Oh, and go to the pet store to get a litter box and some cat food. Next time, she can bring the cat with her so she has no excuse to leave.

CHAPTER TWENTY-TWO

amber

"So, did you decide to hire her?" Lauren asks after Madison walks out. I wasn't lying to Jake this morning, I did have an interview. It just happened to align nicely since I couldn't stand staying there a moment longer without begging him for a repeat. My body physically revolting to all the hours I've been working and hell I've been putting it through was a wake-up call. While recovering in bed on Friday, I posted about an open position on the town's *Facebook* page. It was my first time posting anything on there, but I had three applications by the end of the day.

"Yep. She's going to start training on Wednesday." Madison is in her mid-thirties and a self-proclaimed bored housewife. She seems ridiculously sweet and has near open availability, which is amazing. Once she's trained, I could actually have whole days off. In the last year, I've had three days off. The day Jana died, the day after, and the day of her funeral. And that was only because I closed the boutique for all those days.

"You could actually take a day off," Lauren says, like she can read my mind.

"I was just thinking that. What would I even do with my free time?" I joke.

"Sleep, go to the spa. Oh, I don't know, maybe go on a date. I heard Jake left your apartment the other morning." Her smirk gives away her casual inquisition.

I don't need people knowing about that. We aren't together. I'm not sure what we are, but I don't want to be part of the rumor mill until I figure it out. There's no denying that he's the perfect male specimen: rugged, pure muscle, good with his hands … and other things. He still gets on my nerves, though, with everything that comes out of his mouth. He probably thinks the same of me since he brings out this need in me to fight.

It's not even that he brings out my worst, more so I feel safe to be my worst around him without fear of judgment. *Holy shit.* I feel safe around Jake. The man who took my virginity and can claim every sexual experience since then. The one who spits my cutting words right back at me every time. He makes me feel like I can be myself.

If that's not the most terrifying thought in the world, I don't know what is. Jake isn't a safe bet, even if he is my type. Jana never married; I hardly even saw her date. She always told me that her satisfaction in life came from running the store and helping to raise me. So the only positive relationship role models I have are Lily and Thoren, and Thoren's parents. Neither of them fight the way Jake and I do. They have a tender love, a quiet love that is felt and not heard.

I refuse to repeat the cycle of my mother's toxic relationships. There was a lot of yelling and fighting growing up. My mom was always upset, drowning her feelings in booze or drugs. No part of me wants that life, so I will wait for someone who is a safe choice.

"Jake and I are friends," I state, not willing to explain that complicated mess.

"Mm-hm," Lauren hums. "You're seeing the good in him finally. Good luck not falling for him now."

Yeah, that is definitely already a problem. Maybe I'll ask Lily about frenemies in her romance books. I'm sure she has good recommendations for me to learn about how to navigate my feelings. Feelings that revolve around his delicious body that sets mine on fire with one look. The bells over the front door jingle as Evelyn sashays through them. She navigates straight to me and wraps me in a hug. "I'm sorry it's been a while since I've been in. How are you doing?"

"I'm doing better. Congratulations, grandma-to-be!"

She squeals in delight, holding me even tighter. "Isn't it the best news? Lily's little baby bump makes my day every time I see it. But I came here to talk about you, dear." Stepping out of the hug, she keeps a grip on my shoulders. "I heard you were sick last week, so I thought I would bring you some casseroles for your freezer to take something off your plate."

A lump forms in my throat at her kindness. From the day she walked into Jana's room at the rehab facility and asked if she could spend some time with her, she's been a pillar of strength and love in my life. I don't have words to express my thanks to her, but she gives my shoulders a tight squeeze in acknowledgment.

"Lauren, honey. Can I snag your boss for a quick lunch?"

With mischief written all over her face, she gives me a wink. "Of course, but only if you get her to spill what's happening with her and Jake."

My cheeks heat at the callout, especially in front of Evelyn. She doesn't seem at all surprised, linking her arm with mine and pulling me toward the front door. "Well, isn't that perfect. We're having lunch next door with his mom."

After a trip up to my apartment to drop off the frozen meals she made, we walk over to Jake's store. As much as I love Sonja, this is the last place I want to be. Her son had me tied to his bed last night, and the image of his round ass in those tight boxers he was flaunting around in this morning hasn't left my mind. I know he intentionally didn't get dressed, and damn, I couldn't even be mad at it. He should never be dressed.

"I'm so glad you could join us," Sonja calls when we walk in the store. "I ordered sausages from Munchen Garten." She sets up to-go boxes by the couch in the corner, and we settle in. Sonja has been nothing but kind since we met and has been so helpful at getting Jake's website and marketing set up. Yet in all those times, we never once talked about her son. I can only hope that my luck hasn't run out.

"Good choice." Evelyn nods, taking a seat on the blue velvet couch. "Amber was just talking about them with her coworker."

I choke on air, spluttering and coughing as Evelyn stares sweetly at me, not an ounce of remorse on her face. When I've gotten myself under control, we all have a seat and dig into the food.

"I stopped by Jana's grave the other day," Evelyn says. "The headstone is finally put in, and it looks beautiful. You did a wonderful job picking it out."

I haven't seen it yet. I received the email Wednesday notifying me of its placement. That was the first time I deviated from my Monday/Thursday schedule of visiting her. I started feeling ill at the gym Thursday morning, so I went straight home after. What I'm not willing to admit to myself is I think the anxiety made me much worse. The thought of seeing her name in stone, seeing the permanence in the reminder that she's gone, makes my stomach roll. My overly exhausted body can't handle more grief on top of it.

"I plan to see it tomorrow morning," I mutter.

She picks up on the shift in my mood and changes the subject quickly. "How was dinner with everyone last night? And when are you coming back to Sunday dinner at the house?"

Evelyn has extended an open invitation to her family Sunday dinners. Thoren and Lily try to make it as often as possible, and I've gone once, but it's been a while. She and David are incredible people, but seeing the love between them and their love for their children and anyone who enters their home is hard. It's a stark reminder of things I never had with my own mother, and things I will always be on the outside of.

"You do Sunday dinner too? We need to have one together. Jake almost never misses one, and I know it's the highlight of Henry's week."

That makes me smile. I love how the big grumbly man cares for his parents. After this last week with him, it doesn't surprise me in the least. He's not always sure in his actions, but it's clear he's a nurturer. The tender way he brushed my hair and the way he snuggles Socks and sticks him in his apron pockets are at odds with his dark hulking frame and intense scowls.

I'm so lost in thoughts of him that I space out on the conversation until Evelyn looks at me. "It's settled, then. Next Sunday, everyone is coming to family dinner for the holiday. You never told us how dinner was last night."

Sonja pipes up with a questioning raise of her eyebrows. "Amber's car wasn't out back when I opened the store this morning."

Evelyn turns to me, and they both stare expectantly. "Does this have anything to do with what Lauren mentioned?"

While I would love to have Jana to talk to about this, sweet Evelyn and Sonja are the last people I'm willing to open up to about where I was last night. Thankfully, Jake walks in the back door of the store. His steps falter as he glances between the three of us finishing our lunch. He raises a brow identical to his mother's.

"Hey, Jake." Evelyn waves him over. She gives me a devious smirk before turning back to him. "Come have a seat. Amber was about to tell us where she was last night."

I choke on my water, trying to cover it with a cough. Jake's cheeks turn pink, which is the cutest thing I've ever seen and does nothing to help this situation. What did I say about her being sweet? I take it all back. She's a mother through and through, meddling with her kids for her own enjoyment. She pats my back, winking when she catches my eye.

Thankfully, Jake is quicker to recover. "Actually, Amber promised she would finish showing me how to manage and make changes on my website."

I could kiss the man for his clever thinking. Plus, it's a legitimate excuse because I do need to do that. Standing, I thank Sonja for lunch and give the women hugs, promising to show up to dinner next Sunday.

As Jake and I head toward the back door, Evelyn not so quietly states we would make the cutest couple. The back of my neck heats with embarrassment as I whisper to Jake that I was *not* going to tell them anything because there was nothing to tell.

"Nothing to tell? Not even how you whimper when I suck on your clit, or how my beard still smells like your sweet pussy and it's kept me half hard for the last few hours?" he asks as soon as we get outside.

"Jacob!"

"Ew, only my parents call me that. Can we do this at your place, I miss my little buddy."

I shake my head at his antics. Lauren was right, I am in trouble with him. There's no way I can trust myself alone in my apartment with him, so I head to my store's back door instead. "Socks is hanging out in here today, and I'm supposed to be working. Bring over your laptop, and I can walk you through it all in between customers."

He leans in too close, gripping the back of my neck in a domineering hold. "Yes, Amber," he practically purrs, with a wink.

Oh, fuck. My panties are so screwed.

CHAPTER TWENTY-THREE

jake

The annoying, overly cheerful jingle of my phone alarm shatters the peace of my dream, a painful awakening for my overtired body. I thought this week would be easier because Colby started, but that has not been the case. He's a hard worker and picks up things quickly, but there's so much I need to teach him. I've been working later into the evenings again to catch up on work after he leaves.

At least it's Friday and I have the weekend to focus on orders. That, and what's wrong with Amber. We've both been busy with work this week training new associates, but something's going on with her. Monday and Thursday she left the gym before me, and like previous weeks, I beat her back to our stores. I've debated following her to see where she goes, except my motorcycle is obnoxiously loud and my truck can't blend in with the three other cars driving around town that early in the morning.

Something is bothering her though. I see it in the way she walks with her shoulders slumped and how her eyes never quite meet mine when we see each other. I've racked my brain for things I could've done or said and came up empty. Everything was fine on Sunday between us, and I was a well-behaved gentleman since Lauren was watching our every interaction.

It shouldn't bother me this much when her mood changes, it shouldn't bother me at all. Learning about her past has made me hyperaware and worried about her. She's been through things no one should have to, and I'm sure we've only scratched the surface. Our friends seemed so surprised when she mentioned she never wanted children, but it made all the sense in the world to me.

Despite how tired I feel, I grab my gym bag and truck keys and head out for the morning. It's the perfect breezy day to take my bike, but I need to bring the wood for the porch swing home. All the pieces are cut, but I can't have them in my workshop for Amber to stumble upon if she walks in. The drive into town passes quickly, with the windows down and the warm summer breeze flowing through the cab. I've always loved the smell of the woods, an earthy scent with fresh flowers and crisp trees. I can point out most trees blindfolded by their scent alone. It's one of the many reasons I love living here and will never leave.

Amber's little Honda is parked out front, so I park next to it and walk inside. A gravitational pull draws my eyes to her. She's in the corner splayed out on a mat doing stretches and ab work, and unsurprisingly, Kyle is sidled up with her again. He gives me bad vibes, and not because I'm jealous. There's something about the way he carries himself with an air of importance and superiority that sets my nerves on edge. I knew someone who acted the same way in college, and that didn't end well.

The longer I watch them in their own little world, the more agitated I feel. After such a busy week, a light stretching routine sounds perfect. Grabbing an extra mat, I plop it on Amber's other side. They startle as I settle on it and lean forward to stretch out my hamstrings.

"Hey, man," Kyle says with a sneer.

Ignoring him completely, I keep my gaze on Amber. "How's the training going this week?"

"It's going. How's Colby? Frank has been gushing about how proud he is of him."

It's interesting that Amber is always saying she's alone and an outsider here when that is so far from the truth. I've been watching her at the gym for weeks now, and aside from Kyle, the other members all make a point of saying hello and giving her encouragement or spotting her when needed. When in her store, I've seen her customers seek her out to chat. All the parents in our friend group are in love with her. Hell, she even has Frank half in love with her. A whole community of people are wanting the best for her.

"He's a quick study. I actually have him working on your shelves this week, and he's doing great. I almost have your tables done, probably can come install it all next week." I switch the leg I'm stretching and look around Amber to the douche canoe still sitting there. "You're still here? You're never going to be a big boy like me when you grow up by sitting around. And I am a big boy, isn't that right, Amber?"

The flush is so pretty as it travels up her neck … until it reaches her face and I see the anger there. If she actually cares what this guy thinks, she has bigger problems than being embarrassed at knowing how big my dick is. Kyle sneers at me but makes the smart choice and gets up to leave us, smiling at Amber as he goes.

"Every fucking time I think things are good between us, you go and ruin it."

"Please, that guy is the worst. I wanted him gone so I could ask how you're doing."

She huffs an indignant laugh and continues with her workout. I stay by her side, going through it with her silently. Asking her isn't going to get her to open up to me, but I know one thing that worked to get her to open up before.

"Come over tonight," I say between sets.

"No."

"Oh, come on. You're clearly wound up over something, and you know what I can do for you. How good I can make you feel. Hell, I'll even cook you dinner first."

She stares at me, and the longer she does, the more her walls drop and the easier I can see the pain etched into her very soul. With a blink, the moment is broken, and her eyes are blank again. "No thanks." Standing, she cleans her mat and puts it away before moving to the treadmills.

I don't want her to open up to me, I need it, and she needs it just as bad. After finishing a set of pushups, I clean my mat but get stopped on my way to putting it back. A small hand wraps around my bicep, but the lack of spark tells me it's not the hands I want on me.

"Excuse me," a shrill voice says, and I turn to the girl touching me. "I could really use a spot, and since you're the biggest man in here, I was hoping you could help."

The woman is dressed in the smallest shorts I have ever seen. She points to the squat rack she has set up with only a bar, and I try not to laugh. Anyone in this gym could spot that bar, but I'm not one to judge someone trying to better their health or fitness, so I agree. Her long pointy nails stay wrapped around my arm as she leads me over, and I repress a shiver.

The Jake of a few years ago would have loved this and would nail this woman in my truck within the hour, but looking down at my crotch, there's not an ounce of interest. It seems my dick is as stuck on Amber as I seem to be.

The girl, Becky, as she made sure to tell me, sets herself up at the rack before looking over her shoulder. "Would you mind putting your hands on my hips while I do this?" The look she gives is meant to be flirty but misses the mark.

I feel eyes on me and know Amber's watching my every movement. Jealousy might be a good thing, or maybe it will bite me in the ass. "How about you do one, and I'll check your form first?"

She does, and her form is awful. There's no way she's ever squatted with a bar before. Her stance is wrong, her back is bowed, and she's placed the bar on her neck instead of her shoulders. Reluctantly, I fix all her mistakes before leaving my hands on her hips while she goes through her "set." Three … she does three squats. Nothing compared to my beautiful and strong woman.

With a quick glance over my shoulder, I see Amber still watching, and the look on her face catches me off guard. She doesn't look upset or jealous, she looks resigned. Like this is what she expected of me. Even worse, Kyle is on the treadmill next to her, vying for her attention.

Becky pulls my attention again, thanking me with a hand on my chest this time. I tell her she needs to work on her form before she hurts herself, which she laughs off and makes a joke about her form never having been a problem before. It falls flat, and I stare at her until she removes her hand and stalks away.

When I look back to Amber, she's focused on Kyle again. As I make my way over to them, I can just make out parts of their conversation.

"I'm busy this weekend, but maybe next?" Amber says.

"Saturday, next weekend? It's a date." He winks at her before smirking at me and walking away.

"What's that about?" I growl in a low voice.

She looks at me with empty eyes, her features schooled into indifference. "It's called a date, Jake. Surely, you've heard of it."

A date? She's going on a fucking date with this guy? God, I'm so stupid for thinking that something was happening between us. Is this my fault for how things started between us? I like our fighting and how we feel safe enough together to express every part of ourselves. Across the gym, Kyle is watching us through the mirrors with a smarmy grin on his face.

By the time I turn around, Amber is gone and I feel like I just sealed my fate.

—

I don't see Amber the rest of the day, and since she refused my offer of dinner, I grill a steak alone and work on the porch swing in the garage. I'm not sure what's more pathetic, me making a sentimental item for a woman who seems to hate me most of the time, or the fact that I'm beyond used to spending my weekends working and alone.

Sleep is rough, so I rise with the sun and go to the shop to start another project. The feeling of watching Amber accept a date with that prick sits heavy in my stomach, and I need to do something to make it better. Something to show her I'm not a bad guy and if she gives us a chance, I can be the man for her.

She has captivated me, making me crave her body as much as her soul. It grates on me that she's willing to give me her body but still won't fully open up to me. The more I get to know her, the more I can see something really blossoming between us. We have the same drive and desires, the same fire in our bones and hurt in our heart.

My skills lie in making things beautiful, so that's what I rely on to make her see there's more to me than meets the eye. That I'm a man worthy of her trust. The planter boxes come together easily, and I decide to stain them a dark mocha color to really help the flowers stand out.

They are all completed before it's even time to open the store.

I gave my mom the day off to spend time with my dad. Turns out, he's having a good day, so they stopped by the store on their way to the farmers' market. When I told them about the planter boxes for outside Amber's store, they took over for me. Four hours later, they show back up with a trunk full of little pink flowers and bags of dirt.

With one look at Dad, I know he's done for the day, so I send them home and promise to video call my mom after I plant them so she can ensure I did it correctly. We made a plan for me to work on it after the store closed so I can do it when Amber won't see.

I really hate working in the store when I have fun projects I could be working on. Colby has been doing so well in the workshop that I'm not sure I want to spare him for the store too, which means I need to hire another part-time associate. When I text Amber to ask how she hired someone so quickly, she only sends me a screenshot of her *Facebook* post and nothing more. I guess she's still upset about the gym thing, but that's what the planters are for. I make a similar post and move on to printing a sign for tomorrow.

I kind of forgot it was a holiday until the mass text came through from Evelyn saying Sunday dinner was turning into Sunday barbeque and everyone is expected at three. Fourth of July has never been my favorite holiday, but I won't complain about good friends and free food. My simple sign that says "Closed Sunday the 4th" looks a little sad, but it gets the point across. I'm sure Cedar and Sage has some flowery shit that looks nice stating the same, and I'm half tempted to check, but I don't want to push Amber.

Finding the balance of pushing her enough to get a reaction and bring out her feisty fun side but not pushing too much and pissing her off, is hard. I still haven't found that sweet spot. After closing up the store and having dinner at the local burger joint, I bring all the planters to the front of Amber's store. Being only upstairs, I'm not sure how she doesn't catch me as I drill them underneath her windows, or how she doesn't hear my video chat with my mom as my meaty fingers try not to crush the delicate petals.

It's almost nine by the time I get home, happy with my secret mission. Spending a few more hours working on her swing gives me something to do with my hands besides stroking my cock to thoughts of the beautiful blonde with golden eyes.

All the pieces of the swing have been sanded, and the first layer of stain is on when I decide to call it a night. The little projects I have going on for Amber are at the forefront of my mind as I shower. If this isn't the way to get her to truly see me, I'm not sure what is. Climbing into bed, I drift off easily, dreaming of seeing my girl tomorrow.

jake

The distinct sound of wood being clawed pulls me from sleep. Sitting up, I look around the dark room, then heavy thumps come bounding up the stairs to my room. Shadow jumps onto my bed, all but tackling me before I can even think to move. Her tail is wagging a mile a minute as she presses her cold nose to my bare chest.

It takes a moment to right my mind and realize she shouldn't be here. My heart pounds hard in my chest at the thought of her coming to get me because something's wrong with Thoren and Lily. I jump up from bed and race down the stairs on a mission to rush to their house but am stopped short in the kitchen.

Lily is in her pajamas and a robe, digging in my freezer. I wipe my bleary eyes and blink a few times to make sure I'm not dreaming, but sure enough, she's still there. A quick glance at the clock shows it's just after one in the morning.

"Where's your ice cream? I know you have some," Lily asks, not bothering to turn around.

"Under the frozen broccoli. What are you doing here? You scared the hell out of me. Are you okay?"

"Found it!" she hollers, holding it above her head. When she finally turns, her nose scrunches and she puts her back to me again. "Can you put clothes on? I don't need to see all that." Her hand waves haphazardly over her head at me.

Bemused, I scratch the back of my neck and look between Shadow making herself at home on my couch and Lily again. *Okay, then.* I trudge back up the stairs and throw on some shorts and a shirt. She's lucky I at least had boxers on, but I'm not telling her that. Pregnant women scare me.

When I make my way back downstairs, Lily is sitting on my couch next to Shadow, eating my ice cream straight from the tub. I take a tentative seat across from her, and she picks up a spoon from her lap, handing it to me. "Want some?" she asks, holding the tub out to me.

Shaking my head, exasperated, I take a scoop, then she pulls it back to eat more. "Want to tell me what you're doing here?"

"The baby wanted ice cream, and we were out. Thor's been so tired, so I figured instead of making him run to town, I would just raid your stash. And before you yell at me, I used a flashlight and brought Shadow for safety."

Jesus, this woman is something else. While she's not the woman I wish was here with me tonight, she's definitely a close second. Lily has this sweet nature about her that you can't help but love and admire. I give Shadow a belly rub, then sit back and kick my feet up onto the coffee table.

"I was going to talk about boundaries, but I appreciate your safety measures, and so will your overprotective husband. You know he's going to flip when he finds out about this." She shrugs and takes another bite. Yeah, I've heard them together once and once only, but it was enough to know maybe Lily doesn't mind getting in trouble. It makes me think of the punishments I like to dole out to Amber. *Fuck, focus.* "We agreed when you moved in with Thoren I wasn't allowed to just walk into your house anymore, so you can't walk into mine either. What if I had a woman over?"

"Oh, please, you don't bring girls here." I hold my tongue about the fact I indeed had a woman here last weekend and she would have been scarred for life seeing her other bestie tied to my bed.

We sit in silence, passing the quickly emptying tub back and forth and taking spoonfuls. Eventually, Lily turns to me with a serious face, and I feel like I'm about to be scolded. "Can I ask you something?" I nod apprehensively. "What did you tell Tyler? The day he showed up here."

She's asked me this question before, but I wasn't ready to share that with her because we were still waiting to find out his fate. Tyler's her ex who lied about being married and used her, then got her fired from their company. Despite a restraining order, he showed up here and tried to attack Lily. Thankfully, Thoren and I were on our way, and Thoren beat him to a pulp. I would have preferred it to be me, but I was a few minutes behind. I did get the last word in with him though.

I smile, recalling all the shit I told him. It may have been a year ago, but I remember it like it was yesterday. "I told him that despite his best efforts, he didn't break you. That his pathetic life would never mean anything, and once the trial was done, you would never think of him again. That he's lucky Thoren barely broke him, but me?" I chuckle, but it's dark, and Lily shudders. "I would break him. Every prickle of awareness he feels will be me watching him, every freak coincidence, lost job, and case of bad luck; I'll be behind it. And one day when I get tired of the cat-and-mouse game, I'll finally strike. I'll relish in the snap of every bone and his pleas for help."

Lily surprises me by not balking or staring at me like I'm crazy. Instead, she takes me in with a thoughtful look on her face. "Did you mean it?"

"That's not the point. The point is that for the rest of his meaningless life after prison, he will be looking over his shoulder, wondering if this is the day karma comes for him."

I did mean it. Lily's lawyer has my contact information and promised to keep me updated on when his release will be. A quick beating and some prison time isn't enough for someone who fucks with my family. I will stop at nothing to keep those I love protected. So yeah, when the time comes, he'll find himself at my mercy, and I will make no apologies about it.

"That's good enough for me. Thanks, Jake. Don't tell the girls, but I love you as much as them." She pats my hand, then takes my spoon and the now empty ice cream tub to the kitchen. I get up and follow her over, slipping my feet into my boots. "You don't have to come with me. I have Shadow."

I give her a stern look, and she relents, looping her arm through mine. Our feet crunch over the gravel drive as Shadow bounds ahead of us. "What's going on with you and Amber?"

Well, if that isn't a loaded question. I would like to know the answer to that as well. I'm not sure what she's told her friends. She didn't tell Lily she was a virgin, so I doubt she told her about anything else that's happened between us. I'm already on thin ice, and I don't want to divulge more than I should and make it worse.

"Nothing. We're friends, and I'm looking out for her."

The words taste like hot garbage coming out, but they aren't wrong. I am looking out for her, even when she refuses to let me help.

"Be careful with her. She's an awful lot like you. Her hard exterior is a defense mechanism to keep her from getting hurt further. Under all that, she has this bright and caring center despite the crap in her life. I think she has spent so much of her life suffocating in the shadows that she's scared to live in the sun. Maybe you both can learn to stand in the sun together."

I mull over her words the rest of the walk to her house. She gives me a squeeze and tells me she'll see me tomorrow, and I make sure she's safely inside with the door locked before heading back home.

The defense mechanism was a given and one I pegged early on. It's the fact Lily thinks Amber doesn't know how to live her life outside of loneliness, depression, and hardship, that's sticking with me. It makes sense. When you're forced to swim against the current for so long, your body doesn't know what to do when it has the opportunity to relax. You're always waiting for the current to come back, bracing for that first impact, unable to accept that things can be easier from now on.

I need to show her the current isn't lying in wait to sweep her out to sea again. With time, I can make her see even though the tides may change, she has people around to pull her to shore. I'm hoping she will let one of those people be me.

After sleeping in, I wake to a warning message from Lily saying Thoren caught her sneaking back in the house and another from Thoren thanking me for taking care of Lily before telling me off for not immediately notifying him she needed something. His poor kids; he's going to be a total helicopter dad.

With the rest of the morning to kill, I stain all the back sides of the wood in my garage. That only takes forty minutes, so I call my mom and ask her what's needed for the barbeque. She ensures me that her and Evelyn have all the sides covered and that David, Thoren's dad, is grilling. I ask if I can invite Michele, to which she insists I do, and then tell her I will bring dessert.

BBQ GANG GROUP CHAT

JAKE:

My mom said to bring desserts. I've got pie.
Also, Michele, this is your invite. 3 PM at the OG
James house. Be there.

MICHELE:

Wow, I feel so special …

AMBER:

I'll make cookies.

LILY:

That better be the berry pie, Jake.

JAKE:

Yes mom.

MICHELE:

😂 Can I bring liquor?

*THOREN HAS ADDED RIVER TO THE GROUP CHAT

THOREN:

Big bro is surprising the parents by driving over
for the night.

RIVER:

What's up party people?! Michele, I'll double
your liquor budget.

LILY:

It sucks not being able to drink with you guys.

THOREN:

Suck it up, princess, you're growing our baby.

MICHELE:

I'll make you a mocktail.

RIVER:

Why does everyone always ignore my texts??

LILY:

You don't live here, you can't sit with us.

MICHELE:

she doesn't even go here GIF

With that settled, I run into town and get the ingredients for Lily's favorite mixed berry pie. I cheat and buy the crust, but I'm hoping she won't notice. The simplicity of baking makes me happy. If you follow the measurements, you are rewarded with a delicious dessert. It's so similar to woodworking in that way, and it calms my anxious mind. While I'm a master of creativity with wood, it turns out I'm not with pie crusts. I cut a smiley face onto the top that ends up looking like a terrifying demon that's bleeding from all of its orifices when it comes out of the oven.

Shoving some tinfoil over top to hide the monstrosity, I leave it on the counter and take a shower. My beard is perfectly trimmed into a light stubble, I've manscaped, and my nails are clipped in the odd chance I can convince Amber to let me in her bed tonight. If not, at least my mom won't complain about how scruffy I look.

I throw on black shorts and a navy-blue T-shirt, to be festive, and slip on my Chucks before grabbing my pie and keys and heading out the door. It's still early, but I'm picking up Amber. She doesn't know that, so we shall see how this goes. I park my truck right outside her door in the alleyway before letting myself in. Owning the building next door has come in handy for so many things, but having the keys up to her apartment is one of my favorites.

There's a startled yelp when I knock and realize I probably should have given her a heads-up. Even though I'm the only other person who can get up here, it's probably scary getting a random knock on the door. "It's me, Whiskey."

She unlocks the door and slowly pulls it open, but that doesn't stop Socks from skittering out and meowing at my feet. "What are you doing here?" she asks, looking confused.

I pick up the fuzzbucket that's looking more like a cat and less like a kitten every day and step into her place. "I'm driving you," I state, taking a seat on her couch and snuggling with Socks. "Go finish what you need to do, I'll be here hanging with my buddy."

amber

The nerve of this man to show up at my front door and barge inside, demanding he's my ride. Especially after letting that girl paw all over him at the gym. If I'm being honest, she's the biggest reason I said yes to the date with Kyle. Well, that and I want to see if what I feel with Jake is something I will feel with other guys. With one more backward glance, I close myself in my bathroom and slump against the door. What is it about him snuggling with my cat that looks tiny in his big arms that does it for me? Don't even get me started on the shorts that hug his tree-trunk thighs. Thighs I have dreamed of having between mine. He's had his head between my legs, me on my knees, and he's fucked me on a vanity, but I have yet to have this man in a bed, our bodies writhing together, with his heavy weight pounding me into the mattress. God, I want that.

The bell on Socks's collar jingles from outside the door, and pictures of him playing with the cat fill my head. Trying to focus, I finish curling my hair and swipe on some mascara and eyeliner. I'm in ripped-jean shorts and a cute red tank top, so I swipe on a red lipstick to match.

With everything ready, I step from the bathroom to find Jake lying on the floor, playing with Socks. It's so stupidly adorable I stay rooted to the spot watching him swirl a feather around the floor while the cat chases and bats at it. When he finally looks up, his eyes widen as he takes his time moving from my feet up to my face.

He lets out a low whistle, pupils blown wide, and sucks in his bottom lip. "Damn, Whiskey. You look hot, but that red lipstick just makes me want to have it smeared on my cock later." He lies there for another minute, taking me in with a mix of reverence and lust before he shakes his head and pulls himself out of it. Pushing off the ground, he moves to the small kitchen island to grab the tray of my cookies, then brushes past me. His lips meet my ear, and he whispers, "It'll be the second time you've left red on my cock."

A shiver skates down my spine, and I gape at his retreating back. The arrogant asshole—an arrogant asshole I wouldn't mind smearing my lipstick for. Shaking my head clear of the wayward thoughts, I grab my purse, give Socks a pet, and follow Jake out my door. He's waiting at the passenger door of his truck, holding it open for me. I get a whiff of his cologne as I pass him and have to bite back a moan. He smells so good, that earthy clean and masculine scent.

When he shuts me inside, it only makes it worse, being surrounded by all things *him*. The ride to the James' is silent, but I catch his subtle glances in my direction. It's hard to sit still when all I can seem to focus on is the way his shorts have ridden up, leaving his tattooed thigh on display and his bulge held tight. Pair that with his forearm flexing every time he makes a turn, and I'm done for.

My panties are undoubtedly soaked, and I'm rethinking every boundary I set for myself with him. While there's no way we could work in a relationship, maybe we don't need one. Who says we can't just sleep together? I'm sure he could teach me some things … or a lot of things. I would happily learn anything from this man. I've been a good girl for so damn long, why can't I have fun, mind-blowing sex simply for the sake of having sex?

Right as I'm about to ask him if that's something he would consider, we pull into Evelyn's driveway. Jake glares when I open my own door, but I snag my tray of cookies, and he grabs a pie and a baseball hat from the backseat, slipping it backward on his head. Holy mother of God, he has to know what he's doing. He's wearing a cocky smirk as we walk around the side of the house to the back where there are tables and chairs all set out.

Shadow races over to get her obligatory pets, then runs back to Lily's side where they're sharing a plate of snacks. Lily already has the whole mom thing down, knowing she will never be able to enjoy food alone again. Evelyn rushes over to give us hugs and shows us where we can put our desserts.

There's one cushioned chair mixed in with all the random camping chairs and Adirondacks, so I immediately know it has to be for Jake's dad. The care this whole group has for each other is astounding and makes me miss Jana extra. She would love this. Jake seems able to read me well because he gives my hand a quick squeeze before abandoning me to go check on his parents inside.

I make my way over to Lily and take a seat at her side, snagging a grape from her plate. "Where is everyone?" I ask, realizing it's only us and David out here.

"The moms are taking their time finishing up the sides so Henry can sit on the couch a little longer. Thoren and Riv are off planning something special for later. Michele's on her way, and you"—she turns to me with eyebrows raised— "came with Jake."

Uhhh, yeah. How do I explain that when I don't even know why he picked me up? "I'm happy for you. Whatever is or isn't going on." I give her a small smile and steal another grape.

"Okay, I might be happy for you, but I'll still cut you if you keep stealing my food."

"Don't poke the bear!" River yells from across the yard as he strides over. "I asked to touch her belly earlier, and I had to borrow my mom's frozen peas. They're now nut peas."

Thoren slaps him over the head before taking a seat on Lily's other side with a fresh plate of snacks for her. "No, your exact words were, 'so can anyone just touch your belly now like a free-for-all buffet of touches?' I would say the ninja kick to your nuts was well deserved."

"Same thing," River gripes, moving to take the seat next to me. As he goes to sit, Jake comes out of nowhere and snags the seat out from under him. River's ass hits the ground with an audible thud, and Michele cackles from where she walked around the side of the house. "This day is the worst," River mumbles, lying in defeat.

Jake leaves the chair he stole to help Michele, who is carrying a box filled with clinking bottles. "You owe me two hundred dollars," she hollers to Riv, pulling out bottles of wine, tequila, whiskey, and mixers.

"Jesus, woman, you're lucky I love you."

"Love you more. Now, who needs a drink?"

After pouring us each a drink, Michele plops herself on the grass in front of Lily and me, snuggling into Shadow. She picks a small dandelion, and it reminds me of what I discovered when I walked to the bakery this morning. Those little pink flowers spilling from window boxes, that definitely weren't there yester-day, match the pink of the Cedar and Sage logo and make the whole boutique look more inviting and pretty.

"Thank you, girls, for my surprise. I almost cried when I saw it this morning."

They both wear a mask of confusion as they stare at me. "What surprise?"

"The planter boxes on the storefront? The ones that appeared out of thin air last night?" Again, they stare at me like they have no idea what I'm talking about.

"That was me," Jake says, taking a seat with an almost shy smile. "Thought you might like them."

"Whipped," River coughs into his hand, only to be smacked by Michele this time. They get into a slap fight, bringing in a whole round of laughter from everyone. Yet I can't take my eyes off Jake. What am I going to do with this man?

Three hours later, everyone is sitting around enjoying burgers and drinks. I love everything about this get together: the people, the food, the love between us all. When Henry came outside earlier, I died with laughter. He had on a T-shirt with Anderson's Fine Furnishings new logo on front, and across the back was his bold "Get a load of this wood!" slogan. Sonja was proudly telling everyone she ordered a few shirts to test out designs, and they would be distributed as Christmas gifts this year.

Jake has hovered, always taking a seat next to me, his gaze following me wherever I go. While all these conversations have gone on around me, all I can focus on is the fact I want Jake. He's wearing me down, and I don't want to fight our attraction anymore. The man made me flower boxes after he heard me agree to go on a date with someone else, for god's sake.

Our differences of opinions translate to explosive sexual chemistry, and I want to experience more of it. I want to feel him inside me, beyond a rushed and slightly painful fuck in a bathroom. I want to watch his piercings slowly disappear inside of me as he marks me as his again.

"Is it dessert time yet?" Lily asks, rubbing the smallest bump under her shirt. "I want some of the pie Jake made."

"I got you, sis." River jumps up from his seat, and I see Jake flinch out of the corner of my eye. He lowers his head, and I'm about to ask what's wrong when River yells, "What in the nightmare-inducing hell is this?!"

We all turn, seeing River holding up the pie, with the horrifying red face cut onto it. "Look, I tried to make a smiley face," Jake says, rubbing at the back of his neck. "It didn't turn out."

"Never cut a face in a pie with red filling. It's baking one-oh-one," Sonja chimes in.

"Or at least make the mouth a circle," Michele mutters.

"Oh, you sick fuck, I love it." River laughs, having clearly heard her too.

"No! No one is sticking their dick in that pie, I've been craving it all day," Lily huffs.

"But you already had my dick this morning, babe." Thoren elbows her, and David chokes on his beer. Evelyn and David put their hands over their ears and yell, "Lalalala."

Watching this all unfold is hilarious, so I rest back in my chair to enjoy it all … until Jake leans over and brushes my hair from my ear. "Don't worry, the only place I intend to stick my dick is in you." I try to hide the goosebumps that scatter down my arm. Getting up, I make my way over to the table and get a piece of pie as well. As terrifying as it looks, it tastes amazing, and I discovered another thing Jake is humbly good at.

When Lily is happy with her dessert, River stands and whistles to get everyone's attention. "I have exciting news. Lily and Thor have given me the honor of knowing their baby's gender first. This is honestly the second-best honor they've given me, and I can't tell you how much it means to me to be a part of this with you guys. Thoren left it up to me how to tell you all, but I figured it's the Fourth of July, what better way than with fireworks? Are you guys ready?"

He moves to the edge of the yard and pulls out a lighter and firework. When the fuse lights, he rushes back toward us, and it shoots into the sky. An array of brilliant-blue sparks light up the sky above us, and everyone loses their mind. Thoren jumps from his seat, pulling Lily into his arms, Evelyn is crying, and David wraps her in a hug, and Shadow, the devious little devil, is eating Lily's discarded piece of pie, oblivious to the fact she's getting a little brother.

"Congratulations, you guys!" I hug them both, then move to congratulate the very excited grandparents. It's such a joyous moment, and I want to be present and part of it, but it feels heavy. No matter how much I love these people, they aren't my family. There's no one left for me to celebrate my wins with or to cry over my losses. Everyone here is on loan to me, but they aren't mine.

I try not to get stuck in my emotional spiral and enjoy the rest of the evening with everyone. More drinks are poured, fireworks are set off, and conversations flow. Eventually, the evening starts to calm down, and the night air settles around us. "You ready to go?" Jake asks with a hand on my shoulder.

"I am," I admit. I was ready hours ago so I wouldn't bring down the mood, but I don't think anyone noticed. We say our goodbyes and congratulations again before Jake leads me to his truck. He opens the passenger door, like earlier, before slipping around the truck. After backing out of the driveway, he glances over at me.

"Want to tell me what's wrong?"

How does he always know? I'm not sure what to say. That being around happy families makes me feel resentful that I don't have one? That I want to use him like every other woman and sleep with him without any attachment? I'm buzzed enough I decide to go with the latter.

"I have a proposition for you." When he doesn't respond, I continue. "Look, I don't know how else to say this. Can we have sex?" He still doesn't answer. "I don't want a relationship, and I don't want anyone else to know, but there's obviously chemistry between us. We can help each other out."

His jaw works, but he says nothing. The cab of the truck is eerily silent, and it puts me on edge. I couldn't have read this all wrong; he literally told me tonight he wants to fuck me. Jake doesn't say a single word as he drives me home, but instead of pulling up to my door, he parks his truck in the little lot.

Taking the keys from the ignition, he finally turns to look at me. "Let me get this right. You like me enough to fuck me but not enough to be with me?"

Anger and embarrassment heat my cheeks. "You don't date, Jake. Plus, we would be terrible together. Couples shouldn't fight as much as we do. And you said they sleep with you to claim they did. It's not the same."

His eyes narrow, and his voice drops as he growls out, "So I'll just be your dirty little secret, then?" His hand shoots out and wraps around my throat, then brings my face an inch from his. "That's what you want?" His warm breath skates over my skin as I struggle to nod.

"Get inside." He releases me, and I slump back into my seat, disappointed. When I grip the handle and step from his truck, so does he, and my adrenaline shoots back up. Does this mean he's agreeing, or is he walking me to my door? I pull my keys from my purse but turn to face him when I get to the door.

He raises an eyebrow at me before looking around the alleyway. "If you don't want people to know, then I suggest you turn around and unlock that door because I will fuck you right here against this wall and make you scream loud enough for everyone to hear. When I said get inside, Amber, I meant it."

CHAPTER TWENTY-SIX

amber

With trembling hands, I fumble with getting the key in the lock. I poked the bear and am now equal parts terrified and excited to see what he will do next. Our footfalls thunder up the small stairwell as I all but race to my apartment. I get the door opened in record time, practically stumbling in.

Socks's tinkling bell gets louder as he comes running for us, but Jake scoops him up and deposits him in the bathroom and shuts the door. When he turns to me, his eyes are molten and there's a large tent in his shorts. "I've been waiting all afternoon to have those pretty red lips around my cock, and I'm not waiting a second longer."

Clothes fly as we strip ourselves naked, and Jake stalks toward me. He runs his thumb across my bottom lip before shoving his thumb in my mouth. I suck on it, his eyes zeroing in on it, and his cock twitches. He withdraws his thumb, spits into his hand, then coats his erection with it.

He commands me to my knees with his eyes, so I do. Opening my mouth, I wait for him to drop his tip to my tongue. I wrap my hand around his at the base of his cock and lick the underside of him. My tongue caresses each barbell as it moves over them, causing Jake to grip my hair with his other hand and groan. He tips my head back to look me in the eyes. "Open."

I obey, and he leans over and spits in my mouth. "Good fucking girl, now suck my cock."

Happily, and with fervor, I wrap my lips around him and swallow him as deep as I can. Holding myself in place, I try to relax my throat and lower myself on him even further.

"Fuuuck," he groans. He releases his base and spears his hands in my hair at the sides of my head, guiding me off his cock. Continuing to hold me like that, he thrusts in and out of my mouth. Saliva drips from the corners of my mouth, and his pace becomes merciless. With every grind of his hips, the tip of his dick hits the back of my throat.

"I don't want to come in your mouth tonight," he says, bringing his hips back. In one swoop he bends and picks me up, carrying me over to the bed. With me still in his arms, he scoots back to lean against the headboard. When he's settled, he moves me to straddle his lap, lining his erection perfectly with my slit. "My little slut with her lipstick on my dick."

I really shouldn't, but I preen at his words. He makes me feel wanted, even when he calls me names. His hands grip my hips, rocking me over him achingly slowly. The way his barbells roll over my clit is unholy, so I moan in response. He doesn't have to guide me any longer as my body moves of its own accord, chasing the feel of his hard length between my legs. Being used by him turns me on beyond belief, but him letting me use him right back sends shivers of delight through me. The head of his dick gliding over me with ease because of how wet he's made me is something that will live rent free in my mind.

I adjust my knees, sinking further into his lap, and continue grinding over him when one of his hands leaves my hip and grasps my chin, guiding my eyes to his. He presses a light kiss to my lips, whispering, "That's it, Whiskey. Take what you need from me." He kisses along my jawline, nipping at the sensitive spot below my ear.

It feels so good—his hands, mouth, and cock all working over my body. I'm so close to coming, I just can't get over that edge. "I need more," I rasp out, grinding faster over him.

"I know what you need." He grips my throat again, squeezing enough to make my head spin. I whimper when he rocks me over him while slightly spreading his thighs, widening mine further and driving his cock harder against my clit. "So pretty when you make those little sounds for me. Now, come for me."

His mouth latches to my nipple, sucking it hard, and he cuts off my air supply, and I shatter, my body becoming weightless at the lack of oxygen. My mouth opens on a silent scream as euphoria rushes through my body. Every nerve feels alive, like I might float away. Jake keeps slowly rolling my hips over him until it becomes too much.

He kisses me with such a fiery passion, his tongue hot against mine. His lips devour me, the soft stubble adding the most delicious friction. With a swift move, he flips us over so I'm beneath him, his hard body covering mine. His kisses are endless, like he's pouring himself into me, and I can't take it. This has to be just sex, or it won't work.

"Please, Jake, just fuck me," I beg.

He sits up, taking his time to look at every inch of my exposed body. Biting his lip, he trails a finger over my stomach, causing goosebumps to follow. Out of nowhere, he slaps my tit. "On your stomach."

Without an ounce of grace, I roll onto my stomach, settling my legs around his large body again. He lifts my hips, placing me on my knees. "I'm going to fuck you bare. I'm going to fuck you so hard and so deep that you'll be choking on my cum. I want you dripping with me for days. That means the only one who gets this pretty pussy is me, do you understand?"

Unable to form a coherent thought after that claim, I mumble a "Yes, Jake."

He slides over my slick pussy a few times, coating himself in my release before pushing into me slowly. "Christ, you're still so tight. Relax for me, baby." Rubbing my back, he keeps his thrusts gentle and shallow until my muscles loosen and he can slide in with ease.

I feel so full, and he only has one piercing in. "I'm going to go slow, okay?" he says, still massaging my muscles. With each thrust, he pushes farther and farther in until the second piercing slides in. They rub against my inner walls, creating an incredible feeling. When we did this the first time, I was so focused on trying to stay relaxed so it wouldn't hurt worse. Now I get to focus on each new sensation as he pushes in again, driving a third barbell in. "Fuck, you're taking me so well. Almost there, baby, just two more."

"Two more?" I shriek, and he squeezes my hips.

"You can do it. Relax and let me in." After three more thrusts, I feel impossibly full, and he stills his hips as he rubs from my neck to my ass. "You did so good, baby. I'm all the way in. I'm going to fuck you now, Whiskey. There're no neighbors, so you scream as loud as you need."

I don't have time to respond before he pulls out and slams back in. My back bows, and I scream out in pleasure. With no condom, I can feel everything. He pushes one hand in the center of my back, holding me in place, the other gripping my hip as he pounds into me. His hips piston, smacking against my ass with every thrust.

He feels so deep, like he's in my stomach, but the slight pain turns to pleasure when he changes his thrusts to rolls of his hips. Keeping a steady rhythm, he fucks me, groaning when he hits a spot that makes me cry out and clench around him. My body is coated in sweat as he continues to work me over, building me higher but never enough.

He reaches under me and hauls me up until I'm on my hands and knees. His hand delves into my hair, tugging. "Tell me what was wrong earlier," he says through gritted teeth.

What the hell, that's not what I was expecting. I don't want to think about that now. "No."

He grabs me by my throat and brings me flush against him, my back to his front. His hips never stop moving, his thrusts becoming lazy, making my pending orgasm fade. Squeezing a little tighter on my neck, he growls in my ear, "Tell me or I won't let you come again."

I could cry from how close he had me, slight tremors racking through me. "Seeing everyone together reminded me I have no family left."

The hand around my throat loosens, and his other wraps around my stomach, hauling me into an embrace. "Family doesn't just mean blood, Amber. You are not alone."

His hot breath skates over my ear, and the tender way he holds me brings on too many emotions. It's all too much, and he seems to pick up on it. A rogue tear slips from me, and he picks up his pace, moving the hand around me to my clit as he angles my head to lick the tear from my cheek.

With small circles on my clit and kisses along my shoulder, he works me up again, quickly getting me to the edge. "You're squeezing me so tight, baby. Give me one more so I can mark this sweet cunt as mine."

With a matching pinch to my clit and a squeeze on my neck, I tip over the edge for the second time tonight. This time, my cry is audible as my exhausted body sinks into Jake's. He lets me slump forward onto the bed, pistoning his hips twice more before he stills, burying himself deep inside me. Jake comes with a roar that

I feel in my bones before lying on top of me and rolling us over together.

Our sweat-soaked skin sticks together, and my hair clings to the side of my face. His heartbeat against my back is racing as fast as mine. That was incredible. I want to punch him in the balls for the emotional roller coaster, but it was amazing, nonetheless. There's no way sex always feels like that. Socks meows from the bathroom, making Jake let out a low chuckle, but my legs feel like Jell-O and I'm too tired to move.

"Go to sleep, I'll get you cleaned up and take care of him." He presses a kiss to my forehead before sliding out of me. I wince. *Definitely going to be feeling that in the morning again.* I vaguely hear him moving around, then feel something warm between my legs before I let sleep take over.

jake

Last time I was here and watched Amber sleep, it was under very different circumstances. I very much prefer this time around where I'm lying in bed with her tucked into one side of me with Socks sleeping in the crook of my neck on the other. It's the cutest combination, but now I can't move for fear of waking either of them.

While being snuggled in her bed is much better than the couch like before, I still can't seem to fall asleep. My mind is racing from the events of today. My dad stayed pain free most the day, which in of itself was a gift. Finding out I'm getting a nephew was the greatest news. I can't wait to teach the little man how to build things and buy him his first real tool kit. I may not be a real uncle, but I will be one in every way that counts.

Getting to end the night with Amber is the cherry on top. The minute everyone celebrated tonight, I watched the light drain from her eyes. She tried so hard to keep that smile plastered on her face, but I saw the pain she tried to hide. It bothered me for hours, watching her shut down while everyone else stayed engaged.

I thought she was rethinking her stance on having children or maybe thinking about how her mother felt when she found out she was having a little girl. Hearing her admit she felt she had no family made me irrationally angry. Did she not see the group of people gathered today? That family is as much hers as they are mine. Evelyn and David love her like a daughter, my parents think she's an absolute sweetheart, and Michele and Lily love her like a sister.

I understand they aren't blood, but can't she see she has a family right here if she wants it? I guess I can understand why she felt that, but it still took everything in me to not bend her back over and spank her ass raw. I don't want to have to fuck her into submission to get her to open up to me, but I will if that's what it takes.

When she asked me to be her secret tonight, that stung. The pain struck deep in my chest, bleeding me out as she kept on explaining why I wasn't the man for her outside of a good fuck. What's so wrong with me that women don't want to be with me? Maybe a few years ago I could have believed the he-sleeps-around-too-much excuse, but that's not the case anymore. I know I can be an ass, but I thought that was part of our charm. Can't she see that I care for her? Without even trying, she's burrowed herself under my skin, and at first, I wanted to get her out, but now I hate the idea of her not being a part of me.

She's beautiful, funny, and feisty but also stubborn, hurting, and stuck in fight-or-flight mode. Amber is everything I didn't know I needed and everything I see for myself. Her fire and drive match mine. I don't see her past trauma and darkness as shameful things that need to be hidden, only beauty that shows her strength and perseverance.

I've always worn my anger and hurt in the palm of my hands, unafraid of the judgments of the world. My parents didn't love the fact I fought so much, but I see it as passion. They instilled good morals in me and showed me how to treat others and how not to. When I saw kids get bullied or guys getting aggressive with girls, I put a stop to it. That behavior shouldn't be tolerated, and I had no problem enforcing that when the school didn't. I silently carried that burden because it was the right thing to do.

Thoren once asked why I stuck up for others but never fought people when they bullied me. The answer was simple: his parents gave me the same walnut speech they gave to him and Riv. Be hard on the outside, creating that barrier where actions and words bounce off us, especially while standing up for others who are missing a hard shell of their own. Like a walnut, we need a soft inside with empathy, compassion, and love. I have that soft center, but very few have seen it.

It didn't use to be that way. I had no problem letting people in, even with that hard shell, but over time, my outside hardened and closed off. Every time a "friend" made fun of my mom, every time a girl flirted with me to turn around and laugh at my hand-me-down clothes, when not one of my "friends" back home checked on me after my dad's accident, even though it was the talk of the town. The final nail in the coffin was when someone I considered a good friend in college assaulted one of my favorite customers and tried to blame it on me. No one knows that story though, not even Thoren and River.

At some point in the night, I must have drifted off, because I wake to an empty bed. Well, almost empty. There's a black furball sleeping above my head that sounds like a mini motorcycle with all his racket. Amber slips out of the bathroom and slinks around her kitchen, grabbing a shaker bottle and tub from her cabinets. She looks more relaxed than last night, the shadows in her eyes hidden behind her walls again.

"You sneaking off to the gym without me?" My voice is gruff with sleep as I sit up in bed, careful not to disturb Socks.

Her hand flies to her chest, and she jumps. "What is it with you and scaring me? I wasn't sneaking, I always go to the gym on weekdays."

I run a hand over my hair with a yawn. Pretty sure I was only asleep for three hours, but it'll have to do. Slipping from the bed, I head into the bathroom, all while my morning wood bobs between my legs. "Will you make me one of those? I'll be ready in five." I point to the pre-workout she's shaking before closing myself in the bathroom.

Thankfully, I always keep a bag of workout clothes in my truck. Honestly, I kind of forgot today was Monday, so I'll have to run home after the gym to change. I had hopes of talking to Amber this morning about what she said last night, but it'll have to be put on hold. Maybe I can finally figure out where she goes after the gym sometimes. With a quick rinse of her mouthwash and taking care of business, I step from the bathroom in search of my clothes.

Part of me expected Amber to be gone already, but she's waiting at the counter with a second shaker for me. Her gaze lingers on my body, so I take my time pulling on my outfit from yesterday. After a quick pet to the still-sleeping cat, I stalk into her space, brushing against her. I love the full body shivers she gets whenever I'm near.

"You ready?"

"Oh, I'm driving myself," she says, grabbing up her shaker, keys, and a single pink rose.

"No, I'll drive us." I pluck her car keys from her and grab everything else I need before heading for the door.

"Jacob." She full-names me, which she never does.

"Amber."

She hesitates only a second before following me out the door. I lock her apartment and the main door at the bottom, then click the locks on my truck. She stops between our cars, looking nervously between them, then down at her rose. The pink hue of the beginnings of sunrise gives her an ethereal glow as she chews on her bottom lip.

"Can I please drive myself?"

Instead of going to the driver's side, I stop in front of her and release her lip from her teeth. "Tell me why."

"It's Jana's day. Every Monday and Thursday, I stop by her grave on my way home." Her eyes stay glued to the ground even when I lift her chin. This is something she clearly wants to do alone, and I can respect that. At least it's not her wanting to hide our little thing from Kyle like I suspected.

"Okay, baby." Her lips look soft, so I lean down, placing a gentle kiss on them. She melts into the kiss, leaning against my chest, and opens for me. My tongue sweeps in her mouth, tasting a mix of minty toothpaste and cherry pre-workout. When I pull back, she lets out a soft whimper that shoots straight to my dick. I'm so gone for this girl; how the hell did I not see it before?

"Let's go." I spank her ass and plop her keys into her hands. "You aren't too sore, are you?" She winces a little as she unlocks her car and lowers herself into it.

"Just say the word, and I'll lick it better." With a wink, I shut her door and jog around my truck to get in and follow her there.

After we parted ways on Monday, I've only sporadically seen her. She's in her little section of my shop most mornings, and it takes everything in me not to sneak over and kiss her pouty lips. Kissing has never really been my thing. I kissed women before we fucked for foreplay but never during sex and certainly not after—until Amber. I could kiss her soft lips for hours and still not have enough.

Instead of acting on my desires, I've been a good boy and stayed in my side of the shop. Colby has been amazing and asked if he could come in earlier when he realized I was starting a few hours before him. I was hesitant at first because that was my catch-up time, but he's been doing more helping than learning this week. He picks things up after one demonstration, making him invaluable. That's the only thing keeping me from firing him for being too damn helpful and ruining my chances of getting some alone time with Amber.

Her stupid rule of keeping us a secret is killing me, but I respect her enough to follow it. I doubt Colby would care or say anything to anyone except his dad. Hell, maybe I could teach the kid a thing or two about women … Although, then again, maybe I'm not the best to be teaching him.

I want to know if she's still sore or if she thinks of me at night too. Seeing her in the gym every morning though, I would say she's still sore. It hits me with a sense of pride but also regret that I wasn't gentler.

When I see her chatting with Kyle on Friday talking about what time they're meeting this weekend, my blood boils. I thought when she asked to fuck me in private that at least meant we were exclusive. There's no way in hell I'm letting her go on that date. If she wants to date, it'll be with me.

Fuck. I can't be here. I'm going to demand Amber cancel her stupid excuse of a date, or I will deck that guy. Walking away from her is hard, but I need to clear my head. After a quick stop at the locker room to change and grab my helmet, I head out of there. Starting up my Harley, I feel eyes on me and catch Amber's gaze as she watches me from the front stoop of the gym. With a shake of my head, I flip down my visor and speed off.

I need a moment to not feel. The early morning breeze flows through my sweatshirt as I change gears and turn to go farther up the mountain. The rumble of my engine reverberates through the thick forest with the early morning sun peeking through, lighting my way. There's no wrong time to ride, but I love early mornings when the weather is mild, the roads are empty, and my thoughts can fly right out of my head with the wind.

I've never felt this way about a woman before. It's terrifying, falling knowing she barely has one foot on the ledge. There's no guide on how to navigate this. Amber's beauty goes beyond her soft hair, golden eyes that sparkle like the little diamond in her nose, and thighs strong enough to crush my head. She's beautiful in the way she fights for every good day, her dedication to everything she loves, in her stubborn ways, and how she encourages and supports everyone even though she won't accept it in return.

In a world colored by shadows and echoes of pain, she stands out with her dark past, a tapestry woven with threads of anger and sadness that seem to envelop her like a shroud. Despite the weight of her emotions, there is a magnetic pull in the way she expresses herself, drawing me into the depths of her being, begging for understanding and connection.

I'm captivated by the challenge of unraveling her past. I can make her see that her pain isn't something to hide. The very depths of our hearts have been dancing around each other, we've shared experiences of hurt and desire for love. Beneath the surface, we both carry scars and wounds that have shaped us into who we are today. By allowing ourselves to truly see each other, we open the door to a deeper connection, where empathy and understanding pave the way for healing and growth.

I want to unravel our black souls and make her see the beauty in her darkness, just as I have. Together, we can navigate the shadows and the light, learning to embrace it all.

After an hour of riding around, the grip on my chest loosens as I work through all my feelings, so on the next inlet, I turn around and head back home. I make a quick stop at my house to shower, then set out for the shop to figure out how I'm going to stop Amber's date tomorrow.

amber

This week has been so busy I haven't had too much time to dwell on the two conflicting things happening in my life. Like how I'm falling for Jake, even after I told him last weekend that things between us need to remain strictly platonic. Or how I'm supposed to go on a date with Kyle tonight and my initial excitement about it is turning into slight dread.

Kyle's feelings for me have been a little more clear lately with the way he follows me around the gym. It's only started since Jake swapped to morning workouts with us, and it almost seems territorial more than anything. I need to give him this shot though because I have to know if my feelings for Jake are normal or if that's how I can feel with any man. Will there be a spark on this date, or will I spend the whole time comparing him to Jake?

I've always tried to hide the darker parts of myself from the world, but Jake sees it so easily and makes me feel like it's okay. Like struggling not to see the worst in people and taking my anger out on him when I'm hurting are normal things. If I show a glimpse of that to someone so cheery and bright like Kyle, will he be as accepting? I always thought I needed someone light to balance out my dark, but maybe I've been wrong. Maybe I need someone who isn't afraid to seek me out in the overwhelming depths. A steady presence to hold my hand until I'm ready to face the light again.

Jana used to say things like that. She was always trying to get me to see that while I saw hardships and felt pain as a child, my blackened soul was the coal waiting to meet the right person who would spark my fire back to life. Only someone who had a soul made of coal like mine would know how to care for the embers of my burned past and treat them with care until together, we would burn brighter than either of us ever imagined.

I owe it to her, and to myself, to find that person. I've never put real effort into dating, and it's about time. I told Natasha about my date with Kyle this week, and while she seemed surprised, she asked if she could pick out my outfit. I'm only six years older than her, but apparently, she sees me as a decrepit old maid who needs help securing a man. It's possible she's not wrong.

So, that's how I find myself sitting on my bed petting Socks on Saturday evening while Natasha rummages through my drawers and small closet trying to find the perfect outfit. "How is it that you own a boutique and know all the perfect styles to order, yet half your wardrobe is jeans and leggings?"

I roll my eyes, my fingers splaying through Socks's fur, his purr the only other sound in my apartment aside from her rustling around. "They're comfy. I have a few dresses somewhere in there."

"Try this on," she says, laying a little black dress on the bed. "Where are your heels?"

Begrudgingly, I grab it and make my way to the bathroom. "Top shelf in the closet. You know we're just going to get drinks, right? I know you can't do that yet, but I don't think people normally wear heels."

Her reply is muted through the bathroom door, but it sounds like she says, "Beauty is pain." More like beauty is awkward being the only one overdressed to grab a beer. With the dress on, which I have to admit looks great, I step out. It's my favorite little black dress, essentially a tight T-shirt that extends to my mid-thigh. It's not overly sexy, but it hugs my curves perfectly and is easy to pair with anything.

Natasha whistles when I step out, looking me over. "Hot. Okay, this jacket and these shoes," she says, handing me a light-weight jean jacket and black combat boots. I have to admit, it gives sexy and badass vibes while still looking effortless. I'm glad she didn't go with heels because I was planning on walking to the bar, and heels aren't really my thing. "Jake would love this whole look, and can you imagine yourself on the back of his bike in this? So hot." She fans herself, then picks up Socks to cuddle.

"I'm going out with Kyle from the gym, remember?"

She rolls her eyes, lying back on the bed. I'm curling my hair in the bathroom with the door open so I can still hear her. "Whatever, you're missing out with the big guy. Colby said he's really cool."

"Ohhh, what else did Colby say?"

Her cheeks tinge pink, and she tries to hide from my gaze through the mirror. "I say this apartment is badass. I need something like this. My parents are driving me crazy."

We continue talking while I finish getting ready until it's time for me to head out. Natasha is like the little sister I never had, so I love having her around. I can't hide in my apartment with her forever though, so I grab my purse, and we head out. With her car parked out back, I make sure she gets to it safe, noticing Jake's bike is still here. Trying to avoid an awkward interaction, I jog past his shop even though he has the bay doors closed.

The walk to the bar is nice in the warm summer evening, and I can't help but preen over the front of my store. Our street is clean, and all the stores have quaint fronts, but with my new flower boxes, Cedar and Sage stands out among them. I'm still secretly swooning over the fact that Jake did that for me for no reason other than he could.

There are two bars in Cedar Ridge: The Burnt Barrel and Loggers. I know, real original with the names around here. Loggers is a little more gritty, geared toward the locals and is the place to go for decent cheap drinks. The Burnt Barrel, where Kyle is meeting me, is newer and a little classier. The music isn't as loud, the decor is rustic but nice, and the drinks are drastically overpriced. It's a nicer joint for a date, so I don't mind the spot.

When I pull open the heavy wooden door, the sounds and smells of a rowdy bar assault my senses. There's a live band playing in the corner and clinking glasses coming from the bar. With a quick glance around, I see Kyle sitting at a small table made from a whiskey barrel near the back of the bar. His eyes raking over my form widen in appreciation. It feels different than when Jake does it, but I brush that thought off.

He doesn't stand when I get to the table, so I take the open seat across from him. "Hey, Kyle," I say plastering on a smile. "Have you been here long?"

"Just long enough to have a beer to calm my nerves." He winks. "I've never seen you out of gym attire. You look great."

"Thanks, you clean up nice as well." He's clean shaven like always, his hair buzzed short. His khakis and T-shirt look dressy but not fancy, which I can appreciate. There's a boy-next-door charm about him that fits with his easygoing demeanor. "I'm going to grab a drink, would you like another beer?"

"I'll get them. What would you like?"

When he comes back to the table, he sets down my pale ale in front of me, and I take a sip. The cold beer slides down easier than the whiskey I've been enjoying more frequently with Jake around. "I'm glad we were able to finally do this. I've wanted to ask you out for a long time, but I knew you had a lot going on with Jana's health. I wanted to give you time to get over that." He must miss my flinch at the reminder of her and the harsh way he said that because he keeps talking. "Then I saw you around with that shady asshole, and I thought it was time." I wish he wouldn't have continued speaking, as that sentence is another slap to the face.

He has to be talking about Jake, and I don't like his assumption of him. Before I can stand up for him, Kyle keeps going. "I'm sorry about her passing. I wish you would have let me be there for you more."

I hum in acknowledgment, then take another sip of my beer. While I've known Kyle for a few years, it's been surface level. A few quick conversations here and there between sets or stretches hardly makes us close enough for him to help me through her death. Plus, he didn't really try except for some nice words here and there. I try to think of something to move the conversation along.

"This place is pretty nice. I've only been here once, but it's not a far walk from my place, so maybe I'll have to come more often. Have you been here much?"

He leans forward, running his tongue over his bottom lip. "Talking about walking to your place already? Buy me a drink first, Amber." His hand lands on mine, and he winks. It's meant to be flirty, but it sends shivers of disgust through me. The sparks I get from Jake every time he's near are missing, and his touch feels all sorts of wrong.

I subtly try to pull my hand away, but he turns my palm over and draws on my open palm with his finger. "So what do you do for fun?"

An uncomfortable chuckle leaves my lips. "I don't even know what fun is anymore. Most of my time is spent working, but I enjoy spending time with my friends as often as I can. What about you?"

"I can show you fun." He winks again, and I fight the urge to cringe. This is not the same man from the gym. Kyle can be a little forward, but this is off-putting. When he sees the look on my face, he laughs like that was a hilarious joke. It wasn't. "My buddies and I like to golf. There's a nice course a few towns over we try to frequent. It's attached to a five-star hotel we often stay at, if you ever need a getaway."

Are all guys this creepy on dates? He said he was nervous, and maybe he gets verbal diarrhea when he's like that. Either way, I'm growing more uncomfortable by the moment. Jake called him a douche, and I thought it was a jealousy thing, but boy, was I wrong. I didn't even tell the girls to call twenty minutes into the date for a bailout because I knew Kyle. Never in my wildest dreams did I think the quiet and kind guy from the gym would turn into *this*.

I'm debating escaping to the bathroom to text one of them when I feel *him*. I've had Kyle's eyes on me all night and would have never known if I wasn't staring at him, yet Jake's gaze is like a heated caress across my skin. I'm instantly put at ease knowing he's here. I've been fighting my growing feelings for him and the fact he gives me a sense of safety, but now I'm sinking into the feeling.

Kyle must spot him as well because his smile instantly sours. His fingers grip around my wrist in a claim as he glances between me and somewhere behind me. "Do you want to go somewhere else? I know you said your place isn't far."

The one downside of never having dated is having no experience with letting a guy down easy. I like Kyle at the gym and don't want to ruin the friendship we have, but that is where things need to end with us. He hasn't tried to get to know me at all, and it seems like he's only here to get laid, which was never on the table for me. He also answered the one question I've been asking myself all week. The way I feel with Jake is not a normal occurrence.

"I don't, actually. Look, I think you're a great guy, but I'm not feeling a connection between us. You're a good friend, and I hope this doesn't make things weird when we see each other around." I slip my wrist from his grasp and head straight for the door. I'm uncomfortable and want to crawl into bed and forget about this mess. When I pass the bar, Jake's eyes connect with mine, and he stands to follow me out but so does Kyle.

I'm two steps out of the door when his arrogant laugh follows me. It sounds downright wicked as he shows a side of him I've never seen. Kyle grabs my shoulder, spinning me around to face him. "You're just like every other bitch out there. Flaunting around, stringing along every guy you can. It's because of him, isn't it?" he spits. "I'm so fucking tired of nice guys finishing last. You want me to be an asshole like him? Is that what girls like you need? I can be an asshole, sweetheart."

Hot tears sting my eyes, and I try to pull away from him again. "Let me go, Kyle. This isn't who you are."

His body presses closer to mine, the smell of stale beer coating his breath. "But it's who you want, right? You need to be pushed around and controlled. Someone to tell you what you need?" His fingers dig tighter into my shoulder as I wince with pain.

I'm frozen, afraid of this man. I do want those things, but I want them with Jake, who knows what I want and need and gives them freely. Jake, who would never put his hands on me in anger. Jake, who gives me the space to explore myself and knows how to put my mind and body at ease.

"Please, Kyle. Let me go." My words come out in a scared cry.

In an instant, Jake has his hand wrapped around Kyle's throat. "She said let go," he says with a deadly calm.

CHAPTER TWENTY-NINE

jake

This night has gone from bad to worse. I had every intention of following Amber on her date, not a care in the world to how either of them would feel about it. I was going to sit near them and make sure they were aware of my presence, but then my mom called, and I missed Amber leaving. Her car never left, but Natasha's did, so I knew she had to be within walking distance. The two bars were the first places I checked. I had no luck at Loggers, but I saw her beautiful figure the moment I stepped into The Burnt Barrel. Even from the back, sitting in a corner, I would know her anywhere.

Anger poured off me seeing them together, with his hand on her wrist. I was making my way over to them when she stood and walked straight for the door. My feet were following her before I could register what was happening. Kyle was hot on her heels, and for a moment, I thought they might be leaving together, until I stepped outside and heard the words come out of his mouth.

My hands clenched at my sides, trying to hold back, but when Amber's voice shook as she asked him to let go, I lost it.

"She said let go." My hand easily wraps around his throat, and

I squeeze past the point of pain, not letting up until his grip loosens and Amber steps back. It isn't enough, so I pick him up by his throat until his toes barely graze the cement.

"Nice guys don't talk to women like that, and they certainly don't lay hands on them when one says no." My voice comes out low and deadly. I may not have saved my friend in college, but I will die before anyone puts their hands on Amber again. "Apologize."

His feet are kicking, trying to gain purchase, and his hands are scratching at my arm to make me break my hold. *Pathetic.* When he makes no move to say anything, I slam him into the concrete wall of the bar. "I said apologize."

Soft hands wrap around my bicep. "Jake, don't. It's okay. He's not worth it." Her eyes are red and her lip quivers like she's holding back tears, and my rage hits an all-time high.

"He's not. But you are."

Amber's eyes pierce mine, and she steps back, so I let my fist fly. Blood sprays from his nose, the crimson color bringing a smile to my face. It's my new favorite, after all. We struggle when he lunges for me, but I invite the fight. He gets in one decent punch before I hit him again, splitting his lip and my knuckles as I rain down blow after blow. With a punch to his kidneys, he slumps to the ground, but I follow him down. He deserves to suffer.

I will feel this in my hand tomorrow, but I won't regret it. With a satisfying crunch, I hit him again. There's a voice in the back of my head telling me to cool it, but I can't. He had his hands on Amber. No one hurts my girl.

I feel hands pulling at me, and when I realize Kyle is a limp form beneath me, I let them drag me off. The random bystanders look from me to Kyle, but I pay them no mind. Turning, I immediately seek out Amber. She's only a few feet away, hand to her mouth and glassy eyes barely holding back tears. "Leave him," I say to the guys leaning over the knocked-out douche, then take my girl's hand and lead her over to my bike. They don't try to stop me. The cops know where to find me if he comes to and tattles. Small town and all, and it's not like I'm new to fighting.

As soon as we get to my bike, I pull her into my chest. She's shaking, and her tears soak my shirt. I wrap one hand around her back and spear the other through her soft blonde hair, holding her tight to me. "Are you okay?" Her head nods against my chest, but it feels wooden.

I'm not okay. My heart is racing, and anger is flowing hot through my veins. He landed a decent punch, and I can feel the cut inside my cheek where he clocked me. It's the least I've been hurt from a fight in a long time, and I would laugh at the wimp he ended up being if I wasn't so furious. He put his hands on my girl, and that won't stand. No matter the outcome from here, I'm finding him again.

Pushing her from my embrace, I use my thumbs to wipe her tears, but it only smears some of the blood from my hands on her. *Fuck.* I grab the bottom of my shirt and clean her up while she stares at me in a daze, then slip my helmet over her head. It's a short ride, but I'm taking her home. I slide my leg over my bike, then grab her hand to help her get on behind me.

A flash of pink panties has my gut clenching when her legs wrap around mine, and she giggles. It's such a bittersweet sound after hearing her scared and dejected voice a moment ago. If I think about what he said to her anymore, I'll go back and finish the job.

"What are you laughing about?" I ask, grazing my hands down her thighs to her knees and drawing her flush against my back.

"This is exactly what Natasha wanted. She said my outfit was perfect for the back of your bike, and now here I am."

There's mirth in her tone, but it turns quiet again. "Did I cause that?"

I don't like the wavering in her voice or the insecurity he put there. She didn't do a damn thing wrong except give the wrong guy a chance. I want her laughter again or the anger she should be feeling.

After sliding my phone from my pocket, I open the camera while hooking two fingers under her helmet and angling her head to snap a selfie of us. "She deserves photo proof for picking that outfit for me. You look stunning in it."

She snatches my phone from my hand to get a better look at the picture. "There's blood on your face. You know what, leave it. She'll love it. Now take me home, big guy, before you get arrested."

That, I will happily do. Her hands squeeze tight around my stomach when I start the bike. She giggles again, snuggling impossibly closer as the bike rumbles to life beneath us, and I can't hold back my cheesy grin. I'm careful navigating us out of the parking lot but speed up a little, and we fly down Main Street back to her place. Thank God it's such a short ride. My knuckles are swelling by the time I park behind her apartment.

She hops off easily, pulling my helmet from her head to reveal a dazzling smile. "That was fun. Can you take me on a real ride some time?"

Hell, if all it took was a two-minute ride on a Harley to have her forget about her night, I can't imagine the joy an afternoon ride through the mountains will bring her. "Anytime, Whiskey."

My leg swings over the bike, and I pluck the helmet from her and follow her up the stairs. "Where do you think you're going?" Amber asks without turning around.

"If you think I'm leaving you alone tonight after that, you're dead wrong. And you owe me frozen broccoli or something for my knuckles. Anything but nut peas, really."

She huffs another small laugh as we ascend the stairs, and I feel like I'm on cloud nine. If I can bring a smile to her face this many times after her night, there's nothing I can't do. When we get into her place, she dumps her purse and shoes and heads for the freezer while I kick off my boots and go in search of my buddy. His tinkling collar gives him away when he tries to attack my feet from under the couch. Cute little fucker. I let the fingers of my left hand trail along the bottom edge so he can bat at them.

"Let me see," Amber says, grabbing my right hand and sitting next to me. "Shit, Jake. This might be broken."

I look down at my swollen knuckles, flexing them slowly. The tears in my skin stretch and bleed further when I close my fist, but nothing feels broken. It will, however, be a bitch to work with the next few days. "Nah, just a little tattered."

Her delicate hands wipe the blood clear with a damp paper towel, then she places a bag of peas over top. When I give her an accusing look, she rolls her eyes and smacks my chest. "These have not been placed on any nuts. I bought them last week to make stir fry."

My mind can't fully focus on what she's saying because all I can do is check over every inch of her to ensure she's okay. I'm cataloging every little thing about her. The way her curly hair looks freshly fucked from my helmet, her makeup lightly smudged where I tried to wipe her tears, the little freckles dotted over her nose, and the tiny gold ring she has there instead of her usual stud. She's so beautiful it hurts.

"I'm sorry," she whispers, avoiding looking at me.

"For what?"

"Agreeing to go out with him. Not seeing earlier there was nothing between him and me. Hurting you. Getting you hurt"— she runs her fingers over my wrist—"all of it."

There's a lot I could say. A lot I want to say, but she keeps going. "I was scared."

"What were you scared of, baby?"

She smiles, her fingers tickling up my arm now. "You. My feelings toward you. The way I come alive when you're around. I wanted to know if those feelings were exclusive to you."

"And what's the verdict?"

Finally, those beautiful golden eyes meet mine, and a small smirk lifts the corner of her mouth. "They are."

jake

There's no stopping myself. I know we need to talk, but words can come later. My lips crash into hers, and there's a slight sting where I got decked, but I don't care. Her lips are soft and warm and feel like heaven against mine. There's a time for soft and slow, but the way she pours herself into this kiss tells me it isn't now.

I slide her jacket off her shoulders and toss it to the floor along with the peas, pulling back from the kiss to really take her in. The way this dress hugs every inch of her body makes my brain short-circuit. With my good hand, I slip my shirt over my head, wiping at my face in case there's still some of the douche's blood there, then discard that too.

Amber's hooded gaze rakes over every inch of my chest and arms, her tongue sneaking out of her mouth to lick at her bottom lip, and my last shred of control flies out the window. I scoop her off the couch and carry her to the bed, kissing her the entire way. When I set her down, my fingers glide up the hem of her dress and bring it over her head. Those cute as fuck pink panties match her pink bra, and goddamn, that makes me angry. Did she wear this for him?

Pushing her back to lie on the bed, I lean over her. "Did you put on this set for him?" I caress her inner thigh until I get to the pink satin, then press into the wet spot in the center. "Because it's getting wet for me."

"Only you," she whimpers as I stroke over the panties.

"I'm going to fucking ruin them anyway," I grunt out, tugging until I hear the fabric tear. "Now you won't have to look at them and remember the time you made a mistake."

With her glistening pussy so close to my face, I need to have a taste. My tongue glides over her, cleaning the mess she made. A growl sounds from deep in my throat, and I dive deeper, licking every inch of her I can reach, but it's still not enough. I trail open-mouth kisses over her thighs as I undo my jeans and slide them down. Standing, I kick them off, then lie on her bed, summoning her over. "Grab the headboard and sit on my face."

"What?"

"You heard me. Get your ass over here and sit on my fucking face."

She tentatively crawls over to me, so I grab her thighs and help situate her on me. It's such a pretty view, her dripping cunt spread open over my mouth. When she hovers, I pull her down onto me until I'm smothered between her strong thighs exactly how I want.

I might be mad still, but this is my personal heaven. I'm a man starved, and she's the only meal on earth that can satisfy me. My tongue spears into her like my cock is dying to. Even with an aching hand, I grip her hips and grind her over my face, encouraging her to take over.

"Jake, oh, god, Jake," she cries, writhing over me. I know the moment she grabs the headboard because her hips move with purpose, allowing me to lick from her ass to her clit and back. I swallow down every drop of her essence, savoring the tangy taste. My cock is rock hard and aching to be inside of her.

"I'm, mmmm, close," she moans out, so I double my efforts, sucking her clit every time it passes my lips. Her little whimpers whenever my tongue reaches her ass have me on the edge. My hands grip her ass, holding her in place so I can suck her clit. I'm rewarded when her pussy gushes, soaking my face with her release. "Mmm, fuuuck," she cries, shuddering above me and riding out the last of her orgasm before slumping beside me.

I wipe my beard, then lick those fingers clean, Amber watching with rapt attention. "Such a good little slut, doing what you're told. I'm going to erase his touch from your skin and remind you who you belong to."

Taking her wrist, I tenderly place kisses along the inside of her forearm while kicking down my boxers. I settle between her thighs, lightly grinding my thick erection over her swollen pussy. When she whimpers, I reach under her head and lift it so she has to watch me take her.

"This cunt is mine. You are mine," I say through clenched teeth, pushing my thick length into her wet heat. "See how good we look together?" I let my forehead fall to hers, and we both watch me slide out, covered in her release, and push back in.

"Yours," she repeats, and something inside my heart cracks.

No one has ever been mine before. The fact this incredible woman is, is almost more than I can bear. Her presence is a revelation, a beacon of light in a world that has always been blanketed in darkness. The mere thought of her choosing me fills me with a sense of wonder and gratitude that I struggle to put into words. I find myself on the brink of a new chapter, one where I'm no longer alone and get to share my life with one woman who needs me just as much as I crave her.

I lift her hips, place a pillow under them, and continue rocking into her. The frenzied feeling of needing to pound her from before is gone, replaced with the need to see her. To see everything she normally tries to hide as I fill her.

She reaches back and undoes her bra, then tosses it, my hands exploring her body, from her cute little toes up to her slender neck. Her skin is soft, so delicate and pretty. So different from the war always raging behind her eyes. The golden eyes looking at me with such a soft and broken expression are threatening to gut me.

When she tries to look away, I lean down to take her lips in a passionate kiss. Our tongues tangle, and I pour out all the hurt she has caused me over the last few weeks, and she takes it without complaint. My hips never stop rocking into hers, building us both up higher and higher. Her heart is pounding against her chest, and her breath quickens as she gets closer to the precipice of orgasm again.

When I back away, she looks down, so I slide my hand up her neck, angling her head to face me. My fingers stay over her pulse point, feeling the fluttering there. "Eyes on me, baby."

Honey-colored eyes bore into mine, setting off my orgasm as pulse after pulse of release spills into her. I growl out her name, and she crests over that edge with me. Her hot cunt grips me tight, spasming around my spent cock. Our bodies are slick with sweat, and she looks wrecked beneath me. "Stay here," I whisper, and drop a kiss to her nose.

As gently as I can, I pull out from her and make my way to the bathroom to grab a washcloth to wet with warm water. She's still splayed out on the bed as my release slowly spills out of her. Seeing my mark on her is so satisfying, and suddenly, I don't want to wipe it away. With two fingers, I push the cum back in, then lick the rest of her pussy clean as she mewls in protest. Tasting our combined cum makes my cock thicken again, so I pull back and wipe the rest before tossing the rag into her hamper. As if the floor of her place isn't littered with our clothes.

I draw the blankets back on her bed and scooch her over to get under them before sliding in on the other side. She curls into my side, placing her head on my chest. "I really am sorry. How're you feeling?"

"Don't worry about me, pretty girl. He hits like a bitch, and my hand will heal. How are you?"

A hot tear hits my skin, and I squeeze her tighter to me. "I never should have gone. It all just felt wrong. I've never had a relationship. I wasn't sure the way I feel around you wasn't just because it was new. I just needed to know, you know?"

I don't know. I knew what we had was special. No woman has ever made me feel the way Amber has. No woman has let me fully be myself before. No woman has been able to make me hard with only a look or had me thinking of all the things I could build to make her fall for me. Only Amber.

"Now you know. Next time you want to go on a date, you get sick, you need something from the store, anything. You call me. I'm your man."

"Yes, Jake." Her sultry voice flows over me, like she knows exactly what those words will do to me. With one finger, I lift her chin, pressing my lips to hers, and start our night all over again.

SAUSAGE SQUAD GROUP CHAT

JAKE :

I got the girl.

THOREN :

Finally

RIVER :

Does this mean we're no longer the sausage squad?

THOREN :

No, idiot. We will always be the sausage squad.

JAKE:

Does your girl have a sausage we don't know about?

RIVER:

I'M TELLING LILY YOU SAID THAT. The nut peas will be yours next, fucker.

THORΞN:

Speaking of peas, did you hear Jake mauled a guy?

JAKE:

What does that have to do with peas? And how did you know?

THORΞN:

Once a cop, always a cop. My dad hears everything.

RIVER:

Whoop whoop, that's the sound of the police!

RIVER:

Did you get arrested? Why do I miss all the fights? Do I need to fight someone now? Is he dead? Is that how you got the girl??

CHAPTER THIRTY-ONE

amber

Hazy light shines through my living room window, barely making its way to the corner of my room. After two rounds of passionate sex, Jake and I fell asleep, only to wake up in the night for him to shove my head in the mattress and fuck me hard and fast from behind. A smile crawls over my lips at the ache between my legs with its own heartbeat. Sex with Jake is unbelievable, but sex with Jake where he tells me I'm his, tips the scales.

His body is warm and hard against mine, his little snores tickling the hairs on my neck. It feels good being in the safety of his embrace. He proved last night how safe I am with him. I'm a little worried the cops will come and take him away, but he said it was fine. I don't know if that means he knows Kyle won't say anything or if he just doesn't care if he presses charges.

I think I've been falling for Jake a lot harder than I realized. Trying to avoid my feelings has done nothing except make them come forward tenfold after acknowledging them. He said I was worth it before he beat the hell out of Kyle. When he saw me crying after, he probably thought I was upset about what Kyle had said or the fight, but that wasn't it. Those were the first words

Jana said when she came to pick me up after my mom died. I remember a caseworker telling her she would have months of costly court cases before the state awarded her full custody and I would probably have mental health issues and was at risk of being a troubled youth. Jana simply looked at me over her shoulder with the softest smile and said, "She's worth it."

When Jake parroted those words, I lost it. Spending eleven years with my mom broke down my sense of self-worth, but Jana did her best to build it back up. I didn't realize how much I needed to hear it from someone else until he said it. Then he fought for me. *Literally.*

Violence shouldn't turn me on, it really shouldn't. Yet, there I was, falling for the guy as blood sprayed across his face when he broke Kyle's nose. It confirmed my original thought that I indeed had a type, and that type was Jacob Anderson.

"Good morning." Jake's rough sleep voice skitters over my neck, and his arm tightens around me. He winces, and I look down to see I should have bandaged his knuckles last night. They're not as swollen, but they look angry, and the cuts need antiseptic.

I roll in his embrace so I can see his handsome face. There's a slight bruise forming along his jaw, barely peeking out from his stubble. "How are you feeling?"

His smile is filled with mirth, and he gently cups my pussy, watching for my reaction. "The real question is, how are you feeling?"

"A little sore," I admit, kissing his chest.

"I can kiss it better," he says, tucking my hair behind my ear before tilting my chin to look at him. "No freaking out this morning. It killed me to walk out of here every other morning, but I did it because I saw the panic in your eyes. No more of that, Whiskey. No running. I'm staying, no matter what, you understand?"

My lips lift of their own accord. "Yes, Jake."

With a deep chuckle, he leans forward, pressing an achingly soft kiss to my lips. "I love when you do what you're told. Don't let that fire burn out though, baby. It gets me hard when you fight with me."

That makes me freeze. This is the whole reason I've been running from him. Jake is amazing and he cares deeply, but that doesn't mean we would be good together, even if I'm getting in deep. Couples shouldn't fight like cats and dogs. They shouldn't enjoy trading barbs. "Jake, I—" I don't even know what to say. How to get this out.

He scoots back and sits up against the headboard, his biceps bulging as he crosses his arms and scowls at me. "Don't stop now. Say what you need to say so I can tell you it is utter shit."

He's mad again, and it's all my fault. I keep hurting him, and that's the last thing I want. Wiping my hands down my thighs, I try to start again. "This isn't what a relationship should look like. Two people together shouldn't find joy in fighting and taking their anger out on each other. It isn't normal and it isn't healthy. It's part of the reason I went out with Kyle." Jake's eyes darken and he clenches his jaw. "You and I, we aren't the safe choice."

"That's all you got?" I nod, feeling even worse now. "You don't want a safe bet, Amber. You want passion and fire and a love that burns so hot you get warm just being around it. You need someone who matches your fight, your darkness, and your anger. Someone who lets you explode when you feel over-whelmed and loves you even deeper after. You think this isn't how two people should treat each other? With love and respect, and a safe place to land when their emotions get too big?"

He runs his hands down his face, and a knot sits heavy in my throat. "I'm tired of fighting."

"Baby, fighting is all you know how to do. You've spent your childhood fighting for yourself, then fighting to keep yourself together, and now fighting to keep everyone out. But instead of fighting to not let people in, how about you fight for love? For the life you want? For something real? Fight with me, fight for me, let me take over the fight, Amber, I don't care. Just … just don't push me away anymore." His eyes are imploring me to hear the words he's saying and take them to heart.

Every word out of his mouth rings true. It makes no sense that he's as inexperienced in relationships as I am yet can see things so clearly. Maybe it's just me he sees clearly. It's what I told myself when I first met him, that I needed someone who could sit in the dark with me on days I couldn't handle the sun.

Jake has been living in the shadows as long as me, but even in the shadows, his presence ignites a warmth that chases away the chill and loneliness I've always known. He's been holding my hand and leading me back into the sun little by little, with every kindness he's shown and every project he's done. Every time, he ignited my spark when it felt like it might be going out. He's been drawing me closer to the shore's edge and out of the depths I couldn't handle alone.

"Is this why you're always pushing my buttons?"

A small smile graces his lips. "I hate that desolate look in your eyes. The look you get when you start to spiral is just as bad. If I push the right nerve, your eyes spark to life and I see the fight come back to you. I've been low before, Amber, and I've been trying to keep you from hitting the bottom."

Holy shit, Jake has been helping me fight my depression in the only way I would let him. Sneakily, behind my back because I was too stupid to see that every interaction was intentional to bring us closer and show me I could fight for myself. But now I don't have to.

"Thank you." My voice breaks as I whisper out the words. I crawl across the bed to him, and he pulls me into his lap, threading his fingers through my hair.

"You're welcome," he whispers into my hair, placing a kiss

there. "Sooo, do you remember the IOU I made you promise me when I agreed to let you keep your storage space?"

Well, I had forgotten, but I remember now. "Y-yes …"

"Being the generous man that I am," he states, "I've decided to give you a choice. You can go on a date of my choosing with me, or you can let Socks have a sleepover with me for one whole weekend."

I bark out a laugh, not expecting that. "You would need a litter box, a kitty carrier, food—"

"I have it all but the carrier. Also have some mouse and feather toys. I bought them after you rushed from my place last time, claiming you couldn't leave Socks alone. Now you can just bring him with." He tightens his arms around me, sounding a little sheepish.

That was *weeks* ago. I can't believe he did that. The friendship between him and my cat is something I never saw coming but is stupidly cute. I'm about to tell him he can take him any weekend he wants and choose the date, but he opens his mouth again.

With his lips pressed to my ear, he whispers, "I also still have your panties. The only way you're getting them back is covered in my cum for you to wear all day."

That should not be hot, that really, really should not be hot. "Just for that, I'm choosing the date."

I feel his smile against my cheek. "It was a win either way, baby."

CHAPTER THIRTY-TWO

JAKE:

Your shelves are done, and your tables will be
finished by Friday. Install this weekend?

AMBER:

Could you do Friday after closing?

JAKE:

Trying to get me alone?

AMBER:

No, I just anticipate a busy weekend. Plus I
have Natasha working Saturday morning, and
she's great with the displays.

JAKE:

…but we will be alone, right?

AMBER:

Yes.

JAKE:

I need you to spell it out for me. You trying to
smash?

AMBER:

You're annoying.

JAKE:

I'll see you Friday at seven with dinner in hand.
Wear something red, it's my new favorite color.

This week has been surprisingly amazing. Evelyn's freezer meals have kept me from having to make dinner, I hit a new PR for deadlifts yesterday, and Madison has been the greatest addition to the store. Lauren and Natasha love her as much as I do, which is great for being able to schedule anyone together. Natasha is hoping to take online business classes and asked for more responsibility to prepare herself. I had her take over displays and helping to pack and ship online orders. Those two things alone have taken so much off my plate, and I was able to give her a small raise for her help.

I'm finally feeling like the death grip my depression has had on me is slowly loosening. On Monday, I actually enjoyed the smell and color of the vibrant pink rose before I placed it on Jana's headstone. Wednesday, I enjoyed a book before bed, thanks to Lily's vast collection, and found myself feeling the emotions of the characters. Neither thing would have happened even a few weeks ago.

If I were to really look into it, I can see the correlation to those being the days I had the most contact with Jake. The store is quiet tonight, but it always seems to be on rainy evenings. Socks has a new hammock perch that suctions to the front window which he refused to sit in until the rain started. He's been in love with the shelves Jake made him, especially the one that acts as a little house. When I lock the front door for closing, he rolls his head over the side of the little hammock to watch me. I give his little chin a scratch and tell him his best friend will be here soon.

Right on cue, the buzzer for the back door rings, and I rush to let Jake in. His hands are full as he shakes off his hood and drops all the shelves near the register.

When he turns to me, I see he's soaked from head to toe, and he looks defeated. "I'm so sorry, my mom's car was having trouble, so I had to take her home, and my dad was in a lot of pain, so I helped get him in bed. My mom was having a rough go of it, so I stayed with her for a bit and then I forgot to pick up dinner, and I don't know how I'll get the tables over here without help."

He looks to be falling apart at the seams, and I can't stand it. With a reassuring touch, I give his arm a light squeeze. "Hey, take a breath." When he does, I encourage him to take another. "Good. Now, first, I have a frozen lasagna from Evelyn upstairs I can throw in the oven. Second, your parents should always be a priority, and I would have understood if you couldn't have made it. Third, I can help move the tables."

He stares at me, and there's a struggle to read the look in his eyes. His heavy shoulders deflate, and I get the feeling there's more going on. "Is that all?"

Jake takes an unsteady inhale, his gaze fixed on the floor, before shaking his head no. I've had hard days and days that start hard but by the end of it feel impossible because things keep piling on. It seems like he's having one of those days.

"I'm going to run upstairs and turn on the oven. Are there more shelves?"

"Yeah, I have another two trips, at least."

"Well, good thing you're already soaked," I joke, and he placates me with a halfhearted laugh. I threw him a softball with that one, and he just let it fall flat. Trying to ignore his missing spark, I grab my keys, prop the back door open, and rush around to my apartment to turn on the oven and throw the frozen lasagna in.

Normal people might make smaller portions for someone living alone, but not Evelyn. It's a full nine-by-thirteen pan of cheesy, saucy goodness. I set a timer on my phone, grab a towel from the bathroom, and rush back downstairs in time to see Jake run across the alley into my shop.

"This is the last of the shelves. Do you want to do the tables now or later?"

I look at the downpour outside and Jake dripping wet in front of me. "We can get those another time." Shutting the back door, I edge around him and pull one of the men's tees off a back shelf. "We just started venturing into men's clothes, so all I have is a shirt. I grabbed a towel from upstairs, though, that might help a little."

He takes both from me with a small smirk. "Trying to get me to strip for you?"

I shrug, not taking my eyes off him. "Well, I'm not going to turn around if that's what you're asking."

His laugh is deep and sends a chill down my spine. "Would you be offended if I worked in my boxers? Wet jeans are the worst."

Raising an eyebrow, I trail my gaze down him, then slowly back up. "Be my guest." If he needs this flirty banter to get back to the Jake I know, I'm all but happy to give it to him. Without hesitation, he undoes his button and zipper, then yanks his pants down. He kicks them off with his boots, then pulls his shirt over his head. Using the towel, he dries his arms and stomach, his heated gaze locked on mine. He finally breaks our stare down when he throws the towel over his shaggy hair and rubs it vigorously.

It's sticking up in all directions when he takes the towel off, causing a giggle to escape me. Him standing in my store in boxers and socks with his hair a mess makes him look ridiculous and so stupidly attractive I can't stand it. He chucks the towel at me, then drags the fresh shirt over his head.

"Thanks. Now, let's get to work, I'm starving."

We work in tandem, me removing everything from the old shelves, and him taking them down and putting up the new ones. We make quick work of it, and I put things back as he finishes. Natasha will help make them pretty in the morning.

"I'll come fill all the holes next week when I get Colby to help me bring the tables over."

I've heard them working in the shop while I was working on inventory out there, and they seem like the perfect duo. Jake is softer with him, always taking the time to educate and never yelling when he makes a mistake. He calmly explains how it can be avoided next time and has him try again. I don't want to admit how often I've listened through the doorway instead of doing my actual work. Colby seems like a really good kid too, and I know he has to have his head on straight after being raised by Frank.

"You guys should come Tuesday morning. Natasha will be here again, and they seem to have hit it off."

"You playing matchmaker, Whiskey?" There's a lightness to him that wasn't there earlier, but shadows of pain still linger in his eyes.

The timer on my phone dings, startling me. Shit, I forgot about the food. "I'm going to go turn the oven off. Want me to run to your parents while you finish up and drop some off for them?"

His head whips up, surprise written all over his face. "You know where my parents live?"

I run my hands down my thighs. "Yeah. I'll just call your mom. I'll be right back down." Grabbing my keys, I run into the rain and back over to my apartment. I dial Sonja on speaker as I pull the pan from the oven. She ensures me they don't need dinner but thanks me for checking. Before hanging up, she asks if I can run some food over to Jake because he seemed off when he was there. He told her he was heading back to work for a bit, clearly lying for my benefit. It must be a true mother's intuition to be able to tell when something is wrong with your kid even when you're in crisis mode yourself.

I promise to check on him and make sure he eats. Before I can make my way downstairs, footsteps sound from the stairwell. With the realization Socks is still down in my store, I fling the door open to see Jake standing on my doorstep. He has Socks wrapped in the towel in one arm, and his jeans and soaked shirt in the other.

My shoulders slump in relief, but Jake scowls at me. "Did you open this door without checking if it was me? I could have been anyone."

"You're the only other one with keys to the downstairs door. Do you really want to have this argument while you're standing in boots and boxers?" I raise an eyebrow at him, and he lightly shoves me out of the way, kicking off his boots as he steps inside. He sets Socks down first, then opens my small laundry closet and throws his clothes in the dryer.

When he turns around, he stalks toward me, and I step back until my back hits the island. He twirls a rogue strand of hair around his finger and tugs. "I will spank your ass for your blatant disregard for your safety. But after dinner, I'm starving."

He's quick to push off me, but when I think he's going to take a seat at the island, he surprises me and moves to my small pantry to feed Socks. As he refills his bowl, he talks to him in hushed tones and pets his furry butt. Everything he's doing tonight is getting to me: the way he walks around my spaces like he knows them well, how he cares for my cat, the way his boxers cling to his thighs and the bulge in front.

Turning from the temptation, I grab plates and silverware and serve us. "What would you like to drink?"

"Water's fine. Mind if we eat on your couch?"

I shake my head, so he gets our plates, and I fill two cups with water for us. He settles on one side of the couch, so I take the other, tucking one leg underneath me and facing him. A groan escapes when he takes his first bite. "Evelyn makes the best lasagna."

Chuckling, I nod. "She said she's famous for it. You can take some home, otherwise I'll be eating it for days."

Jake hums around his next bite, staring around my space and avoiding eye contact. "Or we could eat dinner together sometimes. We're both here in the evenings, eating alone. I wouldn't mind coming over for leftovers."

This tender version of him is what's making me fall. He's too raw underneath it all, too kind, too willing to fight for himself. He is the exact person I strive to be, hardened to the things that don't matter but willing and open to love and protect those that do. I'm not to that point yet. I'm fighting every day to try and let love in, even though all it has ever brought me is pain. I can't fall for a man who will push me to face my demons before I'm ready. I'm still trying to reconcile falling for a man who sees my demons.

Jana would smack me upside the head for thinking that, but if she was still here, maybe I wouldn't be so broken. She would tell me if love isn't soul-wrenching, heart-mending, and doesn't have the power to break you with a simple word, it isn't a love worth fighting for. So, for her, I will try to fight.

"I think that's something we can do."

He hums again, his eyes boring into my soul, but I can't pull my gaze away. The hardened edge of him fades, and a tender look takes over his face. I can't blink, I can't breathe, all I can do is let him see every fear he's searching for in my gaze. We stay locked in on each other for so long a knot forms in my chest and my eyes burn. Every emotion floats through his gaze as he lets me truly see him. A single hot tear escapes, and I finally break the trance to brush it away.

I take another bite of lasagna when Jake breaks the silence again. "Did you call my mom?"

"I did. She assured me she didn't need dinner but asked me to feed you instead. For what it's worth, she sounded okay when I talked to her."

He rests his fork on the edge of his plate, watching it balance. "How do you know where they live?"

"I've brought your mom breakfast a time or two. Evelyn used to bring me coffee when we crossed paths visiting Jana at the rehab facility, and that small act made all the difference on the hard days. I wanted to do the same for your mom."

Jake stares at me blankly, setting down his plate, then takes mine and places it on the coffee table next to his. I'm hauled into his arms, and he holds me like I'm his most-prized possession.

jake

mber's stiff for a moment before melting into my embrace. She wraps her arms around my neck and settles into my lap. Her hair smells like her signature lavender, and I bury my head in her, inhaling deep. My parents are the most precious people in my life. I owe them everything, and I work hard to give them the love and care they have unconditionally given me. No one has ever cared for them the way I do. Hearing Amber admit she's silently helped my mom, broke something in me. I'm a broken man, I know that, but some of the things in me need breaking. As my dad always says, you have to cut the tree down to build something beautiful from the wood.

My voice breaks as I whisper a hoarse "Thank you."

She runs her hands through my hair, scratching my scalp with her nails and sending chills down my body. It feels good, soothing, and exactly what I need today.

"What's going on tonight, Jake?"

That's a loaded question. What isn't going on tonight? "I don't know where to start."

"From the beginning?"

That, I can do. I readjust her so she's straddling me and keep my forehead pressed to her chest while she continues scratching the back of my head and down my back. It's fitting that it's raining today, the bleary dark and cold outside matching the way I always feel on this day. "We're going way back, then. If you've been to my parents' place, you've seen where I grew up. It's not a bad place, just small and a little rundown. My pops worked really hard so that my mom could stay home and raise me. We had enough having each other, you know? They've always been very involved and present in my life. They taught me right from wrong, and my dad especially instilled a sense of being a protector and a good man. He treated everyone with respect, fought for what was right, and loved my mom fiercely, always treating her like a queen."

A memory takes over of my dad coming home after a long day at work and pulling my mom into his arms as soon as he walked through the door. He danced with her right then and there in the living room—no music, no reason other than he missed her.

"I took that all to heart, so when I saw peers getting picked on, I stood up against it. Sometimes, the only thing to stop a bully is a bigger bully. I was a big kid and used it to my advantage, but I did it for the greater good. The first time I was suspended for fighting, I explained that I tried to get the guy to stop first, but that I was doing what he told me to do and making sure everyone was treated the same. That night, my dad taught me how to throw a proper punch. My knuckles were so swollen."

She chuckles with me. "How old were you?"

"Ten. My dad thought sports would help, so I joined the base-ball team with River, then the football team as well in middle school. Since it's a small town, the sports programs don't have much money, so we had to pay for all our equipment ourselves. My mom started taking on odd jobs to help cover those costs. Never once did they tell me no for anything, they just always found a way to make it work. I owe them everything. Who I am, what I have is all thanks to them.

"Seeing my mom crying in the kitchen today after I got my dad into bed, broke me. She's a full-time caretaker, and I know she wouldn't have it any other way, but it's hard on her. It eats at them both. Not being able to work and provide for his family is devastating for my dad. When I moved back home after college, I found out my parents borrowed against their home to pay off medical bills that disability and insurance didn't cover. I've been paying off their mortgage since I graduated because the disability checks were leaving them with nothing after bills were paid. With their car breaking down, I can either keep paying off the last of the mortgage or get them a new car. My mom doesn't want me doing either, but I want to do both. I could get them a decent used car if I traded in my bike."

Amber tugs on the hair at the back of my head until I lift my head and look at her. "Jacob."

"Whiskey."

"You don't have to take this all on. I mean, I commend you and I get it, because there's nothing I wouldn't have done for Jana. But your parents would hate it if you sold your bike for them."

My laugh is deep and makes her bounce against my chest. "They would be thrilled if I sold it. My mom gets scared every time I ride it. There's just something so … freeing about being on it. It's a feeling like you can take on the world, and yet everything around you fades away."

"That sounds nice." She's so pretty in this light, the street-lights from outside streaming in and making her eyes shine a golden hue. She strokes my shoulders, keeping me calm while admitting this all to her. Maybe I can stop here and not admit what truly has me shaken up today. I'm not ashamed of my past or that I help my parents, in fact, I'm proud that I'm able to. It doesn't make it easy to open myself up though. I want her to see all of me, to know all of me, but I want more than her scraps. I want every tattered piece of her soul. If I have to keep pushing her and telling her my truths to get there, then I will.

"I'll take you sometime."

She hums, her eyes searching mine. "Are we at the part of the story when you tell me what's really going on?"

"Do you like me?" I have to ask because she may not like me in a minute. I know what I didn't do, and it was proven, but I also know what I did, and for that, I don't have an ounce of remorse or regret. This story paints me in a bad light, and it's one of the deeper cuts on my soul. The only part I regret is not seeing something sooner and not doing more to stop it. I'm not to blame, but the scar still sits ready to be ripped open again.

"Yes," she answers honestly but hesitantly.

"You might not after this." I take a steadying breath and let myself go back to that broken place inside me. "I shared an apartment with Riv and Thoren in Seattle for college. River paid the rent and bills, but I needed to help out and pitch in for myself. It was hard enough relying on him for housing." I clear my throat, trying to push past the discomfort. I know it's okay to get help when you need it, but being friends with the James family was hard at times. They had so much we didn't, and fighting the feelings of being less than was hard.

"I started Anderson's Fine Furnishings small time using the university's wood shop. It paid for the necessities, but then my dad's accident happened. Driving back home as often as I could, plus trying to help them out, wasn't cheap, so I took on a construction gig part-time. Everything going on with my dad took its toll on me, and I found myself at the bar more often than I should have been. One night, I saw a help wanted sign and saw it as a way to stop myself from drinking so much. It worked better around school, the tips were good, and seeing people get plastered night after night actually helped me cut down on my own drinking."

Those nights are still so clear in my head. The chaos of drunk college kids, heavy bass music, and sticky surfaces everywhere. "I met a lot of people there, we were in a location near a lot of college apartments, so it was a big hang out place. One guy was in one of my business classes, and he always sat at the bar with me. He seemed like a good dude, and we talked a lot. We both had eyes for this one girl that came in. She was a bundle of energy and life, always happy and kind, and a great tipper. She came in twice a week for months and became a good friend, just like I thought he was."

I swallow down the uncomfortable knot in my throat. I'm still angry over it all. Angry for Clara, angry at Isaac, hurt by how everything was handled. "One night, the bar was packed. Way beyond what capacity should have been. I was slinging drinks left and right, and I saw both of them there, but just for a moment. When I saw Clara, though, her eyes were glassy, and she seemed out of it." I scrub my hands over my face, the words not wanting to come out. "I tried to get her attention to check on her, but she was quickly lost in the crowd. On my break, I walked all through the bar looking for her, but she was gone. Isaac said he thought he saw her leave with me, but I had been behind the bar all night. I should have known then something was up."

"Do you have alcohol?" I need something to get through this next part. To get this image out of my head. The image that still haunts my nightmares on occasion.

Amber climbs off my lap and rummages through her kitchen. She comes back with a bottle of tequila and whiskey, offering up both. I take the whiskey, uncapping it and swallowing a few gulps. Her soft hands take it from me and put the cork back in before setting it on the table. When she tries to sit across from me,

I bring her back into my lap. Trying to hide my trembling hands, I wrap them tight around her.

"I was one of the closers that night," I continue, my voice cracking. "When I went to the back alley to take out the trash, I found Clara. She was passed out, her clothes ripped and dirty, her face a mess of cuts and bruises." The whiskey churns in my stomach, and I squeeze my eyes shut, willing the images away. "It was clear exactly what had happened to her, and seeing her there, tossed aside like trash after what someone took from her … Amber, it broke a part of me that will never be repaired.

"I carried her back into the bar and had my coworker call 911. I covered her with my shirt, and just held her, scared out of my mind. Scared that she would wake up and freak out at my touch, scared that she wouldn't wake up at all, scared that she would never be the same. It was stupid, of course she wouldn't." Fuck, this is so hard to get out. To explain the pain and the fear and the heartbreak I felt in those moments. Those feelings that came crashing back when I walked out of the bar and saw Kyle's hands on Amber.

"The rest of the night was a blur, the ambulance took her away, and I was questioned. As soon as they left, I remember rushing to the bathroom and losing my stomach. When I woke up the next morning, it was to two officers at my door. Luckily, Thoren and Riv were at the gym, but they took me in for more questioning. Apparently, a *good samaritan* said they saw me spike her drink. The bar's cameras were crappy at best and there was no proof otherwise. My coworker said I disappeared for my break, and my DNA was on her."

A hot tear slips down my cheek, and Amber wipes it away. "Long story short, I spent some time behind bars because I refused to call anyone for help. I was too embarrassed and angry. They let me go five days later when her rape kit came back and didn't match my DNA. The only reason my DNA was on her was because I held her. In her worst moments, I held her, and they tried to blame me." Another tear slips out, and then another. "It was Isaac. He drugged her, assaulted her, left her, and then kept drinking and partying and tried to pin it on me."

"Oh, Jake," she whispers hoarsely, then I realize she's crying too.

"A few weeks later, I talked to Clara and asked what she would do to him, if she could. Then I planned and waited and did exactly that." I let the words sit between us, willing Amber to look me in the eyes and see the truth in what I'm trying to say. Her whiskey eyes meet mine, but they aren't filled with fear or disgust. They hold the same weight mine do. The weight that a bad man did a bad thing, and I made sure he was punished for it.

"Is he …"

"He attacked her nine years ago today. He won't be hurting anyone again."

Every year on this date, I live the nightmare of finding her out there over and over again. Her bruised and battered body haunts my thoughts, but they're soothed by the sounds Isaac made when I found him. It turns out, hammers are useful for more than just building things. They can also smash all twenty-seven bones in the human hand. I didn't kill him, but I did break into his home and shatter every bone in both of his hands, and then I cut off his most-prized possession. I'm sure he knows it was me, but there was no proof since Clara and I were together that night.

I've never claimed to be a good man, but I try to be one I can look at in the mirror. I like to think that if my family or friends ever found out the truth or about any of the events around then, they would understand. Riv and Thor think I went to visit my parents for an extended weekend while I was in a holding cell, and that's the way I like it. I'm not a good man, but I'm not a bad one either.

Amber's still looking deep in my eyes when she finally nods. "Good. Would you like to stay the night?"

With my demons out in the open, she accepts me. I help her clean up from dinner, then we take turns showering and crawl into bed with her. Tonight, she holds me as much as I cling to her, and for the first time in nine years, I feel like everything might be okay.

amber

The natural light in my apartment isn't great since I only have one window facing the front street and a small one in the kitchen facing the alley, but on mornings like this, I'm grateful for it. Despite the rising sun, Jake is sleeping soundly, stretched out beneath me, his warm body taking up most of my bed. I don't even mind because snuggling up next to him brings me a sense of peace and safety.

It's probably the last thing I should be feeling around him since he confessed to harming a man last night. If I read him right, he didn't kill him, but I don't doubt he wishes he was dead. I'm glad he hurt Isaac, he deserved it. I also think he would have killed him if that's what Clara had wanted, and that wouldn't have changed my opinion of him.

He bared his soul last night and let me see the dark and broken pieces of him. They are beautiful in their own way, like him. What you see is what you get. His love for those he cares about is beyond what most people realize. Jake is his own avenging dark knight, silently fighting for those who can't fight for themselves. It's commendable and hot, and most people don't even see it. They don't take the time to look beyond the scowl and the tattoos to the man beneath.

It must have killed him to have been thought of as Clara's attacker, even if it was only for a few days. To have people believing he could be capable of such a thing. Lauren said he came home from college a changed man, and between that and his dad's accident, I don't doubt it. Those things change you down to your very soul. To come home and have women throw themselves at him, the same ones who didn't show up for his dad, probably shut him down even more. Yet here he is, still looking out for others.

The camera and light he installed for me in the alleyway, the way he gets angry when I don't take extra safety precautions like checking who is at my door, the visceral rage toward Kyle when he put his hands on me. It all makes sense. He's seen the worst that can happen and wants to do what he can to prevent it. The look of horror on his face when he realized he took my virginity flashes through my mind, and it all starts piecing together. No wonder he was so angry at me. What we did was one hundred percent consensual, but I can see where the fear came from.

This broken side of Jake makes me realize two things. One, he will never balk at my trauma or the things I went through. And two, I like everything about the stupid man. Our pasts, our hurt, our broken souls could either mend so beautifully together or tear each other apart. Hurt people, hurt people. There are no two greater hurting people than him and me. It's a recipe for disaster, as our tumultuous relationship so far has shown. He is the best man I have ever known, even with his stubborn attitude and desire to dole out punishment. It would be so easy to give him my heart.

The first time we were in bed together, he caught me tracing the tattoos on his arms, but now I get to study the ones on his chest. There's a skull on one side surrounded by a snake with flowers growing from its eyes, and on the other is the face of a bear with its teeth bared, and intricate designs connect the two. They're beautiful, if not a little terrifying. Perfect symbols of him.

The tinkling of Socks's collar sounds from the couch as Jake's eyes flutter open. He takes a moment to take in his surroundings before glancing at me. The smile that spreads over his face warms me down to my toes.

"You're still here."

"Well, it's my bed. So …"

He chuckles, running a hand over his hair and sitting up a little. "I meant you're still here in bed with me. After last night …" The silence lingers a moment, then he adds, "And last time, you tried to sneak out and leave me for the gym."

"I did not," I say, trying to sit up and move off the bed, but he grabs my wrist and hauls me back to him. He leans down, placing an achingly soft kiss on my lips. "I haven't brushed my teeth."

"I don't care." He deepens the kiss, sweeping his tongue against mine. "Good morning."

My body melts for him, and I know this whole resisting him thing will be the death of me. It would be so much easier to give in, but how do I reconcile our head-butting with the moments that make me feel like he's the only one who truly sees me. As soon as he lets me go, I slip out of bed. It would be so easy to sink into his embrace and let him hold me. To feel protected and cared for, like I'm not so alone in the world.

"Thank you for trusting me with your secrets last night. You know I will keep them safe. I'm just scared, Jake. We're good at the sex stuff, but neither of us know what to do in a relationship." I keep my back to him while rummaging through my dresser so I don't have to see the hurt that I know is on his face.

I'm so busy trying to distract myself I don't hear him slip out of bed, and his warm breath on my neck sends shivers down my spine as his hand slips around my waist and straight into my panties. "If you needed to get off, all you had to do was ask," he says, his rough fingers circling my clit, then they slide lower and plunge into me. I'm embarrassingly wet already from tracing the lines of his body this morning. "Is all this for me? We both know this pussy is mine, but you need to start admitting that heart of yours belongs to me too."

Keeping himself at my back, he pulses one finger in and out of me, dropping kisses along my neck. His other hand wraps around my waist, slowly moving to cup my breasts through the flimsy night shirt I have on. A moan escapes when he swirls around my clit again before adding a second finger. He curls his fingers and strokes while his other hand pinches and plucks at my nipples. Whimpers fall from my lips as he gives just enough pressure. His kisses on my neck turn to little bites and hot open-mouthed kisses, adding to the sensations.

Jake's experience speaks for itself as he drives me higher, picking up the pace with his fingers while using his palm to rub my clit. "Such pretty noises, baby," he growls in my ear, tweaking my nipples and grinding his thick cock against my ass. My hands fall to the dresser in front of me, holding me up as my knees go weak. My eyes lift, taking in the sight of him in the mirror in front of me. His large body plays mine like a puppet all while his stormy-blue eyes stay locked on me. All the position does is make it easier for him to grind on me.

The hand on my breasts leaves, then I hear him rustle behind me. He shucks his boxers down and lifts my shirt while continuing to finger me. I'm so close, and his corded muscles exposed behind me in the mirror are only driving me closer. Jake ruts his cock faster against my ass, the barbells no doubt leaving red marks. His fingers match the pace his hips set, and before I know it, I'm coming. My muscles clench around him, holding him in place as he grunts behind me. Hot spurts of cum spray over my back when Jake finds his own release.

His breath is hot on my neck as he recovers. There's a rasp in his voice when he stands back up and rubs his cum into my skin. "You can keep pushing me away all you want, but you're mine, Amber. I'll make you see that. I told you I'd take over your fight, and I meant every word."

With his fingers covered in his release, he rubs my clit again, combining our cum before spinning me around to look at him. He sucks those fingers into his mouth, then places a light kiss on my lips. Without saying a word, he moves to pull his clothes from my dryer, gets dressed, and heads to the door. "I'm not leaving, Whiskey. I'll be right here waiting," he says with a wink and his signature cocky smirk before leaving my apartment.

I feel the loss of him the minute the front door shuts. My back is sticky with his cum, and a sick part of me doesn't want to wash it off. I like being marked as his. I stare at myself long and hard in the mirror. Why does this keep happening like that? I know he doesn't want to leave, yet he always does, for me. Every morning I wake up with him here, I have an internal freakout that we're getting too close. Nothing I'm doing is fair to him, but I don't know how to fix it. He agreed to sex only, but that's not the case anymore and hasn't been for a while. There are real emotions involved, and damn it, I can say this won't work until I'm blue in the face. The truth of the matter is, it works. It's been working between us for weeks now. We show up for each other, we've been opening our hearts and our past, and have been building this steady foundation.

After hopping in the shower, I scrub myself down and get ready for the day. Natasha is opening, and I have no idea what state Jake left the store in last night in the downpour. Maybe he left some tools in there that will need to be returned. I wonder if he went home or straight to work. Did he get to eat breakfast? The least I can do is feed the man or make him coffee after he gives me an orgasm, yet here I am freaking out and chasing him off. He's been doing so much for me, little things like moving boxes in my storage room, to big things like making planter boxes and keeping me safe. It's time I start doing the same for him.

I need to get off this crazy carousel I put myself on and give Jake a fighting chance. Giving him a real chance means opening myself up to him. With his scars, I know he would accept all of mine, but maybe that's what scares me the most. That someone will truly see me and accept me, but I'll still get hurt in the end. I can't take another loss.

CHAPTER THIRTY-FIVE

SAUSAGE SQUAD GROUP CHAT

RIVER ⚾:

I'm coming up next Friday and we're having a boys weekend.

THOREN 🔨:

I'll have to talk to Lily.

RIVER ⚾:

Already did. We're going camping.

JAKE 🪜:

I'm in. We haven't had one in years.

THOREN 🔨:

So the girls can't come?

RIVER ⚾:

You're so pussy whipped.

JAKE 🪜:

What girls?

THOREN 🔨:

I thought you got the girl. Are we pretending you and Amber aren't fucking? Right, my bad.

RIVER ⚾:

Oh they're fucking alright.

JAKE 🪜:

I'll bring the tents.

RIVER ⚾:

I thought people getting laid were supposed to
be happy?

THOREN ⚒:

I'm happy. He must be bad at sex. The sparkly
peen just isn't cutting it.

JAKE 🪜:

I'm not coming anymore.

RIVER ⚾:

Maybe that's his problem, bro. He can't make
her come either.

Working on a custom project used to be the highlight of my week. Taking it from an idea to a beautiful piece of furniture that will be kept and cherished for years to come, is so fulfilling. Now, the highlight of my week is finding ways to see Amber.

I hated leaving her place Saturday morning, but I saw her starting to spiral again. She has real feelings for me. Maybe not as deep as mine are for her, but there's something big between us, and she just needs to be brave enough to accept it. There must be something I'm doing right because she brought leftover lasagna down to me Saturday evening. She didn't stick around to eat it with me, but it's a start. Sunday, I saw her through her kitchen window. Yes, I might be a little stalkerish now, but that's not anything new. I've stalked my prey before.

Monday, I left a coffee and muffin on her doorstep when I beat her back from the gym. Turns out, I don't want to do that again because I couldn't see her face when she found it. Still worth it, though. It's finally Tuesday, and I get to spend time with her again. Since she hinted at Colby and Natasha hitting it off, I set myself up for a win-win. I let Colby know I'm crazy about Amber, which at this point is probably obvious to everyone except Amber, and asked if he could wingman me by working with Natasha so I can work with my girl.

I press the buzzer on the back door at seven like we planned and am met with Amber's beautiful face. Even though I saw her thirty minutes ago at the gym, seeing her again puts a stupid grin on my face. "Hi," I sputter out like an idiot. "You look really nice today."

She looks down at her leggings, floral Vans, and graphic tee, then back at me with a raised eyebrow. I nudge Colby forward. "He bought us all coffees, can he put them inside?"

Amber moves to the side and thanks him as he scoots past her with the tray. When he's out of earshot, I lean down and whisper in her ear, "You look absolutely fuckable, just like always. But you also look really pretty, and I thought you should know."

I leave her standing in the doorway and step into her shop where Natasha is pointing out where she wants the new tables placed. "If you guys can get them in here, we can take over," she says.

"Actually, I was thinking Colby can help you organize and set up. Amber and I have to work on filling the holes from the old shelves, anyway."

Natasha nods with a small smile and blushed cheeks as she eyes Colby. "Sounds good."

Colby and I carry in the four tables I made and place them where Natasha and Amber instruct. The old folding tables are easily broken down for me and Amber to carry over to her storage space. Following her lead, I set them up against a side wall and move some boxes onto them. When she bends to lift a box, I have to bite back a groan. I slink up behind her, grabbing her hips and inhaling her lavender scent. Having her in my arms feels right.

"What are you doing?" she asks, trying to sound annoyed as she leans into me.

"Holding my girl. And don't you dare say you aren't mine." I feel her wanting to argue, but she sighs and lets me hold her. Looking around, I see she has most of her inventory in big see-through bins, but they are still strewn around or stacked danger-ously high. "You still need better storage in here."

"I know." She sighs, pulling from my embrace. "Let's go, I need that coffee."

When we step back into her store, the sound of laughter rings out. Amber whispers a "Told you" as we watch our associates flirting while organizing a display. So there's a romantic in Amber after all, she just hasn't figured out how to fight for herself in that department. I pull out the putty and scrapers from my pocket and teach her how to cover the holes in the wall.

"I'll have to come back in two days to sand this down, then you can paint it," I say, and we work in tandem.

"I can do that. Sanding is easy." It's obvious she can do it, anyone can grab a small sanding block and wipe it over a wall a few times. The point is, I don't want her to have to, I want to have an excuse to come back here and be in her space. If she won't let me help out here, there's another project I can do for her.

When all the holes are filled—no pun intended because it has been way too long since I've filled Amber—Colby and I head over to the shop to get to work. With his help, it's becoming easier to get caught up on orders. I was about three-to-five months behind on custom orders, but now I'm closer to two-to-three months, which isn't terrible. He's asked for more hours, and I've happily given them. My mom also asked to work at the store more to help save for their new car since she's been using my truck and I've been riding my bike everywhere.

I don't love my mom working more, even though I know it's a little reprieve for her. We compromised, and I decided to keep the store closed Monday and Tuesday, she works Wednesday through Saturday, and Colby is working Sunday. It's a win-win for all because it gives her time off and Colby more time in the workshop with me.

Colby and I have even gotten into a routine I never had before. We work different machines on different days, and it seems to be flowing smoothly. Best of all, the website Amber designed is working beautifully. Everything is organized and I know exactly what projects are next and all their specifications. She set up some marketing and advertising with it, and the amount of inquiries I've gotten has been wild.

This week has flown by between watching Amber, making changes to my business, and working longer hours so I can take the weekend off to camp with the boys. Even with these things going right, I feel off. It's still not clear exactly where I stand with Amber. She's on my mind night and day but is still holding back. I'm not giving up, though.

When she held me as I ripped out my heart and handed it to her, I knew she was the one for me. That girl is mine through and through, and slowly, I'll make her see I can be her safe space. The broken parts in her can find their home in the darkest parts of me. I might not be the light she's looking for, but I will burn myself to start her fire again. Her fire is coming back, and I see the light returning to her eyes.

I've watched her smile in the gym every day this week, and it warms something in my chest every time I see it. Her real smile, not the empty one she throws on to mask her pain. She hums while working in the storeroom next door, and has been leaving her store doors open for the summer breeze. Normally, I would be worried for her safety, but I can hear her warm laughter float out to my shop, and hell if it doesn't make my day. My girl deserves to be happy no matter what.

I want that happiness to be because of me. *With me.* Thank God for having a weekend with the boys. I know Thoren fell for Lily long before she was all in with him. Hopefully, he can give me some advice on how to make her jump into this with me. The boys will be waiting for me when I get home later, but I have things to take care of at work first.

I verified with Lauren that Amber was working in her store all day so I can put together the storage shelves I made for her. The door between our two rooms is always unlocked, so when I arrive at work, I make sure Colby is fine, then sneak into her space and get to work. By midday, I have shelving built for all of her tote boxes along one wall. I replaced the table in the center of the room with a much larger one that has drawers and shelves underneath for her to store all her shipping material.

Despite my protests, Lauren even pops in to help me organize it, and she painted little chalkboard signs so all the shelves can be labeled by size and what's in the totes on them. It's not perfect, but it's better and much less of a hazard without boxes stored five-to-ten high. I hated that safety risk, and I'll do anything to protect Amber. With the final boxes squared away, I thank Lauren for her help and check in with Colby one more time. He's almost complete, but I know the boys are waiting for me, so I hand him a spare key and entrust him to lock up when he's done. The look of pride and excitement on his face makes me chuckle. With a slap on his shoulder, I grab my helmet, and climb on my bike, ready to get this boys' weekend started.

JAKE:

I need a favor.

LILY:

Anything.

JAKE:

Make her see. Show her that she has a family here. That she has people who love her.

LILY:

People ... or you?

JAKE:

Both.

amber

I'm locking the front door to the store, when a blaring horn makes me jump out of my skin. I look up to find Michele parked out front, cackling in her driver's seat. She gets out, and I let her inside before locking up again. "I almost had a heart attack," I say, swatting at her arm that she wraps over my shoulder.

"But you didn't," she singsongs. "What do you have left to do before we can go?"

Since the guys are all camping, Lily invited us over for a girls' weekend. We plan to do our nails, watch chick flicks, and eat our weight in snacks while they rough it in the woods. It's exactly what I need with everything going on. My coworkers swore they had the store taken care of and made me promise I wouldn't check in even once.

"Just need to put the money in the safe and text Lauren where I'm putting my apartment key so she can check on Socks." Michele hums as she flicks through the racks of new summer dresses we recently put out. I have no doubt the girls will have him down in the store with them most of the day. When I slip my phone from my pocket, there's already a text from Lauren.

LAUREN:

Before you leave tonight, go peek in your
storeroom. Say what you want, but if there's
nothing between you two … there should be.

My heart beats faster in my chest as I read it again. "Hey, Chele, I need to check in the shop out back, grab my bags, then I'll be ready."

She links her arm through mine. "Lead the way."

I kind of wanted to see this alone. This weekend, I was going to tell the girls the truth about everything with Jake and me and what happened with Kyle but needed time to think on how to bring it up. Whatever Jake did, Michele will know right away there's something between us.

The back light kicks on when we enter the alley, and Michele smiles up at it. She must know Jake installed it for me, and clearly approves. No matter the feelings between us, Jake takes care of me. He's shown it over and over in the things he does. When I open the door to my section of the workshop and turn on the lights, I see the difference immediately. A large square table is set up in the center with storage on all sides underneath. All my packing, shipping, and organization supplies are neatly squared away instead of laying in random piles. The shelving unit to the side is to the ceiling and houses each tub of clothes and supplies as if he made them specifically for me, which he obviously did. I spin in a circle, taking it all in, and try to keep my emotions from bubbling over.

It isn't until I see a lone pink rose in the center of the table with a card that the first tear slips free. With trembling hands, I pick up the note to read his chicken scratch.

Whiskey,
Just wanted to do something to make your life

a little easier and safer. I may not have known Jana, but I know she would be so proud of all you have done, not only with the store but with how you have handled everything with grace and tenacity. I hope this helps you keep kicking ass. - Jake

My fingers trace over the rose that I now see isn't a real rose but one carved from wood, with the petals painted pink. Like the ones I bring to Jana's grave. Tears fall freely, and I turn to Michele with desperation. I don't know what I'm asking from her, but I know I can't handle this alone. She instantly understands and wraps me in a hug, holding me tight.

"Let's go get your things. Lily has alcohol and snacks, and we are filled with terrible advice. We'll help you figure this out."

I don't know what I would do without these women. Their love and support are top tier, and they never judge. Michele plays with Socks while I feed him dinner and grab my bag, then we're off to Lily's for the weekend. Following her SUV, I think on all the feelings running through me until we pull up to the cabin.

I've always loved it out here. As much as I enjoy being so close to work, the seclusion and peace out here calls to me. To be surrounded by the woods, the only light streaming through your windows from the stars, and no sounds of cars or people would be heavenly. Lily has offered to rent out the third cabin to me since Thoren's parents have said they aren't ready to get rid of their place, but it's too much space, and I don't know how I feel about renting out my apartment. It was the first place I've ever had as my own, and Jana and I worked hard on it together. The biggest reason though is I'm not sure I'm ready to give up one lonely space for another.

Lily greets us at the front door, Shadow at her side with her tail wagging and barking happy woofs. "I'm so glad you guys are here! Why haven't we done this sooner?"

"I don't know but it's needed now. Amber is in crisis mode." Dropping my bag inside the door, I give Shadow some love and glare at Michele. "What?" she shrugs. "I'm not wrong."

We all settle in the living room with our girl dinner of a charcuterie board and wine for Michele and me before they make me spill the beans. "I don't have all night," Lily whines. "I'm growing a baby, and I get tired easily. Tell us what's going on."

"I don't even know. I'm kind of seeing Jake, but I'm screwing up left and right. My heart is fully invested, but my head isn't. I'm hurting him, and above it all, I'm scared."

Michele wears a look of understanding, and Lily seems sad. "Can you start from the beginning? What do you mean you're only kind of seeing him?"

I chug my glass of wine, then take a steadying breath. "We were kind of messing around sometimes and then I convinced him to be friends with benefits," I admit, embarrassed. "I like him *a lot*, and he's a good man, but he knows exactly how to push my buttons, and he does it all the time. He makes me so angry, then the next minute he's doing these sweet things. Like taking care of me when I'm sick, bringing me coffee, and he built shelves and a worktable for the storage space."

Shadow moves from her spot next to Lily and rests her head on my lap, making me chuckle. Maybe I am in crisis mode if she can sense it. "I don't exactly have role models for healthy relationships. You and Thoren and his parents are the extent of my knowledge. The way you speak to each other, it's nothing like the way Jake and I talk. I watched my mom go through so many toxic relationships, and I won't subject myself to that."

"So you're not going all in with Jake because you argue?" Michele asks without an ounce of judgment.

"I guess. I've had too much pain in my life already, I want a normal and easy love. One like you and Thoren," I say to Lily. "When Jake does these sweet things for me, I can almost see it, you know? A future with him. I see that soft side, that big teddy bear you guys are always talking about. But how am I supposed to overlook the fact that we fight like cats and dogs? What if I'm too much for him, or worse, not enough? Besides bouts with depression, a slew of familial trauma, and a habit of overworking, I don't have anything to offer."

Michele looks to Lily, a silent conversation passing between them before Lily speaks. "There is no normal love, Amber. Everyone's love is different because we all need something different. You and Jake are two of the most hardworking and passionate people I've met. When you feel something, you feel it deeply. So yeah, you clash sometimes, but that's part of your draw. I love Jake like a brother, but he needs the fight. He's bullheaded and has a prick side to him, and he needs someone who will go toe to toe with him. You're stubborn and have a tendency to shut down. You need someone who will put the wind back in your sails, even if it means getting you riled up."

"You have to remember, Jake's never had a girlfriend. He's new to this. He's in uncharted waters, and I can tell you he's doing his best. His way of showing that is through his actions. He's always been better with actions than words, and his actions show that he is beyond smitten with you. You being too much for him is laughable because if there is a man that can handle anything thrown at him, it's Jake," Michele adds.

"You are everything, Amber. You're his everything," Lily whispers.

I know what his actions say, that's why I can't seem to stay away from him. Even though he's on the opposite side of the spectrum with sexual experience, we're on even footing with relationship knowledge. Not that I'm complaining about the first part, how he learned to be a beast in the bedroom doesn't matter because I'm the one reaping the benefits. I'm starting to see what they're saying. When they first told me we could be good for each other, I didn't see it. After seeing the trust and shock in his eyes when I was still with him the morning after he told me about Clara, I'm starting to.

"Can we take a moment to talk about why the hell you went on a date with that fuckwit from the gym if you're kind of seeing Jake?"

My cheeks heat; I never should have done that. "He was everything I'm not: stable, bright, and happy all the time. I thought I needed someone light to balance out my dark. Someone who hasn't seen the hardships I have, who still views the world as a good place."

In true Michele fashion, she scoffs at me. "I'm saying this out of love, but you're an idiot. So you've been through hard shit. That's what made you who you are. The strong woman who will claw her way out of the darkest depths when life kicks her down. The woman that cherishes each moment because she knows how precious they are, and who uses her past to try to make a difference for others' futures." She leans across to take my hand, tears in her eyes. "We see you, Amber. We see the way you guard yourself. We saw your books when Lily was helping with your finances. We saw that you cover school lunches for kids, and Evelyn has divulged how many boxes of new items you donate to the women's shelter every season. You say you don't view the world as a good place anymore, but can't you see that it's people like you who make it good?"

The tears sliding down her cheeks are mirrored on mine. I do those things for the little boys and girls like me who need someone looking out for them. And for the women in situations like my mother who refuse to continue the cycle and do everything they can to better their futures. They deserve a Jana, and while I can't be that for everyone, I do my best to help where I can.

"And while we're on the subject of you, I'm going to tell you exactly what Thoren has said to me because I know you need to hear it too," Lily adds. "Family is not just blood. Family is who you choose to love and who chooses to love you back. Who shows up for you, no matter what. I know I still have my parents, but they suck. I haven't heard from them since before the wedding, and they have no idea I'm pregnant." She caresses her growing bump with hurt-filled eyes. "Borrowed family, found family, best friend family ... they're all still family. It just looks a little different. We're your family, sweet girl. You are loved." She looks up then, hope shining in her blue eyes.

"You also need to accept that you have the perfect man falling head over heels for you. I heard how badly he beat that guy, and I saw firsthand tonight the things he's doing to show you his love," Michele adds.

I choke on my drink. "Love?"

Both girls nod vigorously. Lily clears her throat. "One last thing, then we'll drop it and move on. You said your only view of love is me and Evelyn. If there's one thing you need to know about us both, we have a once-in-a-lifetime love. A love that has the power to break but only heals. A love that is burrowed so deep in our souls that it changed who we are. That type of love isn't normal, or safe, or without risks. It's a gift. Whether it's said or not, Jake loves you, and based on the look in your eyes, you're close to those feelings too. Take the risk. Take the gift."

They let me ruminate on that, and I know I'll need to go visit Jana's grave after this weekend. Being there with her always feels like she's with me, and I swear I can still hear her telling me what she thinks. Sitting here watching rom-coms with the girls, I already know what Jana will say. The same thing she told me the week before she passed. *"Be brave, and find the thing that sets your soul on fire. For me, that was my store. I can already see that yours will be a person. Don't let your past dictate your future, and don't settle for less than you know I would demand."*

I think she could sense that her time was coming to an end, and she was ready for it. She was brave to the very end, and now it's my turn.

CHAPTER THIRTY-SEVEN

When I get home from work, Riv's new Land Rover is parked next to Thoren's truck outside my house. Neither are in them, which means they're somewhere in my house. Parking my bike in the garage for the weekend, I'm surprised to find my gear already in the bed of Thor's truck when I walk past.

They're walking out my front door, snacks from my pantry in hand, when I step onto the porch. "Hey, buddy," River says, hauling me in for a hug. "Want to ride with me?" Thoren slaps me on the shoulder as he passes while tossing trail mix into his mouth.

"You break into a man's home, steal his snacks, and still want to be friends?"

"Yep, get in the car." He smacks the back of my head before hopping in the driver's seat. About fifteen minutes up the mountain, he turns onto a dirt road.

"Are you sure we're supposed to be here?" I ask. This is the second private-property sign we've passed.

"Yes," River says. He swore he had the perfect spot for us and made Thoren follow in his truck behind us. I really need to get my mom a new car so I can get my truck back.

River beams at me, proud as punch as he finally pulls into a grassy clearing. It's a nice spot, a big enough clearing for the cars, our tents, and to build a firepit, while still being far from the main road and in the middle of the forest.

"This is my land," River says when we're all out of the cars.

"What?!" Thoren and I shout at the same time.

"I bought it a few months back. Put Michele through the ringer making her stomp through the woods for me. You can't say she isn't dedicated to her job. I want to build a home on it for when I retire. Figured this was a good chance to get a feel for the land and what I'm working with."

"So this boys weekend has nothing to do with you wanting to spend time with us?" I ask with mock hurt in my voice. River rolls his eyes and shoves me, and Thoren opens his tailgate and pulls out our gear.

"He didn't even put plumbing in before he made us come out here. Straight savage," Thoren gripes. Out of all of us, he's the one who spends the most time in the woods. I'm not sure the last time River went camping, but it's probably been longer than me, and mine was two years ago on a backpacking trip with Thor.

We unpack everything and put River's dainty hands on tent duty while Thoren and I collect firewood and dig out a spot to safely start one. Riv griped the whole time he was in better shape than us, but his contract with the league prevents him from taking risks on injuring his hands. He'd be fine cutting up some fallen trees, but it's more fun to make him feel like a delicate flower.

As secluded as this place is, there's thankfully still service. I planned to not check my phone this weekend, but the incessant buzzing from it is testing my willpower. Focusing on the task at hand, I get the firepit dug and a fire started while the brothers finish setting up the camp and chairs.

Out of the corner of my eye, I catch Thoren incessantly

checking his phone. "Are you going to survive two nights without your girl?"

He flips me off and keeps texting. "She's growing my kid, fuck off. She said you have news for us too."

I groan, even knowing I had plans to talk to them. If Amber's talking about me to the girls, that's a good thing. I'm desperate to get their advice. I've never been in this situation, and I don't want to screw it up. As tough and stubborn as Amber can be, she's a broken girl on the inside, wanting someone to love her. I don't know how deep her hurt with her mom goes, but I know that. There has to be a right way to navigate this all with her.

River pulls out the cooler and places it between our chairs around the fire. He cracks a beer and takes a seat, spreading his legs out in front of him. "Alright, you have an hour before I get hungry again. What's going on?"

"You're worse than a pregnant Lily," Thoren says, taking the chair on the other side of him and nudging him to pass a beer. As soon as he opens it, he's resting his arms on his knees, both of them focused on me.

"Well, fuck, this is intimidating." I crack a beer of my own before settling into my seat, watching the bubbles fizzle from the beer instead of looking at them. "I'm in love with Amber."

They stare at me deadpan. "Okayyy, don't all jump at once." Running my free hand down my face, I take a deep breath. "I don't know where we stand. She asked me to be her fuck buddy a while ago but agreed to a date last weekend, so I think we're past that, but I'm not certain."

River scratches at the back of his neck while Thoren scratches at his stubble. Yeah, that's how I expected them to act. "At least now you know you're not shit in the sack."

"The hell." Thoren glares at him. "If it makes you feel better, Lily said she's crying in a good way because of something you did."

That sends a rush of warmth though my chest. Lauren said she would make sure she saw the storage room, but I ducked and ran so I wouldn't have to see if she hated it. The rose might have been too much. Since I started stalking—I mean, paying attention to her, I've noticed that same pink rose in her passenger seat every time she visits Jana. I've never whittled anything like that before, but it turned out nice, and my mom was all too happy to paint it for me. I wonder when she will see what I left at Jana's gravesite.

I'm doing too much, I know that. I can't help it, though. She said she felt like she only had family on loan and no one left for the good or the bad. I need to show her she's not alone and I'll be there for both.

"I need help deciding on a date idea. I only have one shot, and I cannot fuck it up."

"Tie her to your bed and eat her pussy until she can't form words anymore," River says with a shrug. "That's your thing, isn't it?"

While Thoren and I have had a few locker room chats, River and I haven't. My accusing stare bounces between them when River cackles. "Saw rope in your bedside table. In college and your cabin." He shrugs like it's no big thing that he's been snooping in my room, and I'm tempted to chuck him into the fire. Not like I can judge though, Thoren and I snooped through his room so many times in high school … and maybe in college a time or two also.

Thoren nods, reclining in his chair. "Sex is an awfully good way to lock someone down. But you need a real date. You can't do something boring like dinner or movies."

"Oooh, take her on a bike ride. She's a little wild, right? I bet she would love that."

"Finally, a decent idea." Thoren slaps Riv on the chest. "Pack a picnic."

Well, color me surprised. That's actually a great idea. When my phone buzzes in my pocket again, I finally give in and pull it out. The first few are from Colby ensuring he locked up the shop and was grateful for the chance to prove himself and to earn my trust. He's a good kid, and I'm lucky to have him.

The next is from Michele with a bunch of emoji hearts.

MICHELE:

I always knew you were a big softie. It was fun making the wedding pact with you, but it's going to be even better watching you crumble when Amber walks down the aisle to you.

I chuckle, wearing a stupid grin. My God, Amber would be stunning in a white gown. The last is from Amber, and even though it's simple, it means the most.

AMBER:

Thank you, Jake. Just ...thank you.

It's followed by another that makes my heart beat through my chest.

AMBER:

You can take Socks for a sleepover any weekend you want as long as I'm invited too.

Things are finally falling into place with her. Maybe I didn't do too much but just the right amount. "I like that plan. Going to take her to the lookout and show her she's mine."

"Great, you and Thoren are twins now. All demanding and shit with your girls. I brought sausages to grill for dinner," River gripes, heading to the truck bed to get the food cooler.

"He just doesn't get it because his girl walks all over him, and he doesn't have the balls to do anything about it." Thor leans over and tips his can to clink it with mine.

"I heard that, asshole."

We burst out laughing, only laughing harder when River throws a raw sausage at Thoren's head. This is what has been missing from my life. Laughter and time spent with friends and people I love. I've been making an effort to spend more time with my friends and family, and it has made such a difference for my happiness. I hope Amber is feeling the same this weekend with the girls.

jake

This was the perfect getaway that we all needed. We spent all of yesterday morning exploring the property and talking about where the best place to build is, how big he wants it, and all the custom touches he will have me make. He has a creek through the back of the property that would be stunning as his backyard, and if he clears one section of trees, his sunset will be filled with views of the mountain. It's a beautiful piece of property. Then we got drunk around the fire while shooting the shit. It was all fun and games until we woke up this morning to a downpour.

Rain in Washington is nothing new, but an absolute monsoon is. To make matters worse, we set up the tents in the grassy area with no coverage and a slew of dirt beneath us, which quickly turned to mud. We hauled ass trying to pack up camp and get everything into the cars. We didn't even put away the tents since they will need to be hosed down. Rookie moves on our part to not put tarps down, but we were being cocky and lazy.

By the time we have everything packed up, I'm caked in mud, so I hop in Thoren's truck to avoid messing up Riv's fancy car. He calls Lily on the way back to the house, and I can only hear his side of the conversation, but I already know what she will say.

"She's making breakfast for all of us. Her and the girls were already making waffles."

I want to see Amber, but I'm not sure I want an audience. Can I wrap her in my arms, or do I have to give her space? Maybe I should skip breakfast and ask her to come over after. Looking down at my muddy pants, I see the perfect excuse.

"Don't you dare. I'll drop you off at your place to shower and change, but if you aren't at my house in twenty minutes, I'm sending Lily over to get you."

I suppress a shiver. "Please don't. I love her, but she's scary right now."

The bastard grins like he knows and is proud of that. "She can make my balls shrivel up with a glare. But she's Lily, so ten seconds later, she's making my favorite dessert and trying to do too much. I love that girl."

"Bleh …" I mime vomiting, and he smacks the back of my head. "Just drop me at home, I'll be there."

I've enjoyed spending time with my friends too much this weekend to skip out on breakfast with them. My shower is quick, and as I dry off with the fuzzy purple towel Lily intentionally left here, it makes me want to head over there even more. It's a small luxury, and I know she did it because she thought it was funny, but the towels are incredible, and just one more kind thing my friend has done. Upstairs, I pull on a pair of sweats and a sweatshirt, throwing on my hood to tromp over to their place.

I'm soaked through by the time I get to their front porch, so I toe off my boots out here to not get anything muddy. When I push open their door, Shadow comes barreling for me with barks of joy as her tail swats at everything in reach. Surprisingly, she's not even the loudest thing in here. Laughter and voices talking over each other echo through the front hall, and Shadow races me back to them.

The kitchen's a mess, plates and mugs everywhere, but it's exactly what I expected to walk into. Lily, Michele, and Thoren are sitting at the island, and River has taken over the cooking and feeding everyone, but Amber surprises me. She's right next to Riv, dishing up plates. She's actually allowing herself to be part of it all instead of standing on the edges watching everyone else experience it.

"Perfect timing," Riv calls, sliding me a plate. "Just finished the last batch."

Amber looks up, a small smile lifting her pouty lips as she takes me in. My feet move on instinct, eating up the distance so I can pull her soft body into my arms. Her signature lavender scent wafts from her wet hair in a bun on her head. Her presence causes a visceral reaction in me, calming me to my core and heating my blood, sending it all south. Small arms wrap around me, and she settles into the hug, not caring that the kitchen has grown quiet, with our friends staring at us. With a kiss to her forehead, I let her go and take the offered plate of food, leaning against the counter so we're still side by side.

"Well, slap me on the ass and pinch my pierced tits! Is this finally official, or are we supposed to pretend like we didn't see that and spent the weekend talking about you two?" Michele asks, breaking the silence.

"He put a guy in the hospital for her, I thought that made it official?" River adds.

Thoren turns red with how hard he's trying to hold in his laughter, and Lily has her eyes glued to Michele's tits. Amber looks up at me, shocked.

"I don't know where to start. The fact I'm offended Michele didn't immediately show us her new boob jewelry, or that no one told me Kyle was in the hospital," she grumbles.

"Yeah!" River shouts, slamming the counter. "Where was the titty show and tell?"

Thoren loses it, and they all start arguing over whether they should have gotten to see Michele's new jewelry, but I pull Amber's body back against mine. With my lips to her ear, I whisper, "That's not the last time I will put him in the hospital. You can decide his ultimate fate, but if you don't want to, know that he hasn't felt anything yet."

A shiver racks down her spine as she looks over her shoulder at me. Her eyes search mine before she smirks and joins the conversation again. No explanation, no fear. She knows I mean what I say, and I won't ever let anyone hurt her. She's perfect.

Breakfast continues as we all stuff ourselves and catch up like old times. Thoren and River start on cleanup duty when the conversation takes a serious turn.

River clears his throat and looks uncomfortably at Michele. "Ethan called me on Thursday. He was passed up for the job here. Since they're combining two positions essentially, the committee wasn't looking for a field firefighter. The official position is Task Force Leader, and he didn't have enough leadership experience they were looking for."

Thoren reaches over, squeezing Michele's shoulder. She's looking down at her hands, refusing to meet anyone's eyes. "Is it normal to feel equally crushed and relieved?"

My heart breaks for her. She deserves the greatest love, and I've never seen her face light up the way it did around Ethan. If he came back, I truly believe they could fix their past pain and work things out. "Yeah, Chele, it is. We have you for all your feelings, okay?" My voice sounds like gravel, but I need her to really hear it. I also want Amber to understand that within this group, we're family.

"It doesn't matter. He didn't get it, and he's not coming back," she says, with hurt evident in her tone. Slipping my phone out, I pull up Ethan's contact and shoot off a text. We will absolutely be having a talk later.

Lily moves the conversation along, talking about all the foods she threw up last week, and has us all rolling with her dramatics. She's come out of her shell and really stepped into her own since we first met her. It's the magic of our group.

River is the first to depart, wanting to see his parents before he has to head back to Seattle. Michele isn't far behind, with air hugs because "sore tits," and a comment about being the only single one left. Instead of flinching, Amber giggles and promises her she will find her own dark knight one day.

Lily gives me a pointed look across the room as I mouth a *Thank you*. I know she talked some sense into my girl this weekend. I've had enough of sharing her. I need her in my home, in my bed, and I need to hear her say she's mine for real.

Plucking up Amber's bag and keys from by the door, I tell her to get her ass in her car so I can drive her home. She gives me a puzzled look but doesn't argue and follows me outside, climbing into the passenger seat.

Amber's laughter echoes through the small car as I try to squeeze my big ass behind the wheel. Even with the seat all the way back, my knees are hitting the steering column. Why I decided to drive, I don't know, but at least it's a thirty-second trip.

When I pull up in front of my cabin, Amber turns to me. "I thought you were taking me home?"

Unfolding myself from that hell, I step out and rush to her side, taking her hand as she climbs out. "I did."

amber

"This is my home?" I ask, eyebrow raised in challenge.

"It should be." His eyes stay locked on mine, not an ounce of fear or humor written there. The words don't scare me nearly as much as they should, but my heart beats faster in my chest anyway. I follow him into the house, his large hand still wrapped tenderly around mine.

After kicking off our shoes, he leads me straight up the stairs to his room, his steps sure and his pace determined. The room is clean, only his black silky sheets sleep rumpled. It smells like him up here, like leather and wood, purely masculine. He slips his sweatshirt over his head and tosses it to the floor, then climbs onto the bed and leans against the headboard, rubbing his socked feet together and holding a hand out to me. "Come here, baby."

It's his second three-word sentence in as many minutes that has me feeling like a melted puddle. How have I convinced myself I don't want this man for so long? From day one he has wormed his way into my brain, and with each kind gesture and tender way he cared despite my snarky attitude, he moved from my head to my heart. Fear or not, I shouldn't have run from this for so long. The feelings I had when Jana took me in, of being wanted, valued as a person, and accepted through it all, are the same feelings I get when I'm with Jake.

Crawling up the bed, I drape my body over his, and he wraps me in his arms, pulling me tighter to him. My head rises and falls with his every breath, as he plays with my hair while lightly scratching over my back.

I don't know how long we lie like that, holding onto each other like we can't bear to be apart. When my eyelids get heavy and start to droop, I try to keep myself awake. "What are we doing?"

"Cuddling."

I let out a small chuckle at his obvious answer. "Why?"

"Because I missed you."

It hits me that I missed him too. I saw him not even two full days ago and had a fun-filled weekend with my girls, and yet, on a bone-deep level, I missed him. Jake has been slowly inter-twining our lives and our bodies to where the only time I feel whole anymore is when I'm in his arms. He turns me into a pile of mush with hands that never stop touching me, soothing me, and making me feel like this is exactly where I belong.

"Thank you. For the storage makeover, the rose, and note. I can't put into words how much that means to me. Thank you isn't enough, but I don't know what is."

"Say you're mine."

There's no hesitation on my part. I think from the day I bled on his cock, I've been his. "I'm yours."

He sucks in a sharp breath, then flips us over so his warm chest is on mine. The smile on his face is brighter than any I've seen on him before. Running his nose over mine, he whispers, "Say it again."

I run my fingers through his scratchy beard, looking into his piercing blue eyes. "I'm you—"

His mouth is on mine before I can finish the thought—hot and demanding, searing my very soul. My fingers move up from his beard and into his hair, pulling him tighter against me. It's more than a clashing of lips and tongues, it's a claiming. "You're mine, Whiskey. You're mine and I'm yours." His gruff voice reverberates against my lips between kisses.

I am his and he is mine.

Sitting back, he hauls me up with him, only letting our mouths part when he strips my sweater and tank top over my head. His nimble fingers unhook my bra, discarding that too as he lays me back down. Hot, open-mouthed kisses are trailed down my stomach, and he nips at my flesh along the way. He licks a line from my navel down to my legging-clad pussy before shoving his face between my thighs and inhaling. When he looks up at me with hooded eyes, my whole body trembles beneath him.

"You always smell so damn delicious," he growls, his fingers hooking into my leggings, before he pulls them down with my panties.

Settling his body back between my legs, he grips my thighs, pushing them out and down onto the mattress, splaying me for him. "Such a pretty pussy." His tongue flattens against me, licking from my ass all the way to my clit, circling there. "And all mine. Only ever mine."

Zips of pleasure erupt from my core as Jake spears his tongue into me, licking me deep and swallowing every drop of my arousal. My thighs quiver, and his fingers dig into the flesh, the slight bite of pain adding to the heat of the moment. Watching his large body easily hold me in place while he draws out my moans and works me right to the edge over and over is a sight to behold. This wild and dangerous man who turns soft just for me.

His lips suction to my clit as he uses his middle finger to rim my pussy, slowly pushing it in and coating it in my wetness. Pulling it out, he stares at me, his finger tracing me until he's rimming my asshole. He waits a beat, our gazes locked, before slowly pushing in.

My back arches, an unholy whimper leaving my mouth. A slow, sexy grin spreads over Jake's wet lips. "You like that? Of course my good little slut wants all her holes filled by me." He thrusts his finger in and out of me, diving his tongue back into my pussy, matching the rhythm of his finger. The sensations are over-whelming in the best way.

"More," I cry out, rocking my hips against him.

Approval rumbles through Jake's chest, and he lifts his head to watch his finger disappear into me. In a move that should not be as filthy hot as it is, he spits on my hole, working it into my ass with a second finger.

"Oh, fuck, oh god, Jake," I'm not even sure what I'm saying as he stretches me, and I try not to focus on the slight burn.

"Give me what's mine," he grits out, his mouth latching back to my clit with a hard suck, and I fly off the cliff. My orgasm hits me like a freight train, barreling through me, and I cry out, holding his head down on me. His fevered movements turn slow as he gently licks up my release and pulls his fingers from me.

"I'm going to fuck that tight little hole one day. I won't even give your sweet pussy a break, leaving you dripping from both holes. My perfect little slut."

I want that. I want everything he gives me. He doesn't let me respond before shoving off his sweats and impaling me in one hard thrust. The groan that he lets out reverberates around the room. With a hand on the headboard and the other shoving up my thigh, he ruts into me, eyes locked on mine. It's deep at this angle and so … intimate. Even without his weight settled on me, I feel surrounded by him. From this position, I can see every inch of him and the way his tattooed body should look daunting over mine. Instead, all I see is a man who wears his heart in every mark on his skin. If anyone were to take the time to really look, they would see the protector, the warrior, and the proud son.

There's a vulnerability in his eyes, and it causes a knot to form in my chest as he looks at me with longing. Like I'm something so precious in his arms. His movements slow, drawing out each piercing before he rolls his hips and pushes them back in. He stays like that, glancing from my mouth to my eyes and back again.

"You're everything, Amber."

A tear slips out, and Jake tracks it rolling down my cheek. Letting go of my thigh and the headboard, he wraps his arms around me, changing the angle again. This time, his pelvis hits my clit with each rock of his hips, and he presses soft kisses to every inch of my face. Between each one, he whispers something he loves about me: my drive, my strength, the bite of my nails against his skin. Finally, he presses his lips to mine, sweeping his tongue into my mouth.

Tangled around one another, we come together, and I finally feel like I'm home.

JAKE:

When's your next afternoon off?

AMBER:

Saturday.

JAKE:

Great. I'm taking you on our date. I'll pick you up at 2.

AMBER:

Where are we going?

JAKE:

Wear jeans and those hot as fuck combat
boots.

AMBER:

That doesn't help.

JAKE:

And that light blue panty set I took your virginity
in. I'm not fucking you, it's a proper date, but I
like thinking you'll be wearing that for me
anyway.

AMBER:

photo in red panties I thought red was your
new favorite color.

JAKE:

Don't fucking move. I'll be there in 2 minutes.

amber

Wednesday morning, when I was supposed to be doing inventory in the storage room, I was sitting on a stool in Jake's shop instead. Colby is covering for Sonja in the store today, so I'm taking advantage and watching him work. It's not often I see him in his leather apron, and I don't know why it's so sexy, but it is.

"I think I'm going to take Michele some lunch and check on her before I have to work in the store today."

Jake looks up from where he's leaning over his workstation measuring things. Soulful blue eyes travel down my body in a heated caress before meeting me head-on. "Funny you should say that, because I talked to Ethan yesterday."

That has my interest piqued. "Really? What did you talk about?"

"This doesn't get relayed to Michele," he says with a stern look, and I hold up my pinky in a promise. Chuckling, he shakes his head and returns to measuring while talking. "I asked him if he ever got over Michele."

"Aaaand?" I drag out.

"He said no, and that his answer will always be no. Based on past conversations, I can safely assume Michele feels the same. I told him that if he intends to find a way to come back here, he needs to make sure it's for good, and if he intends to pursue her, he better mean it for a lifetime." Jake leans against the table, crossing his arms, and I have a feeling he used intimidation tactics, even through the phone.

"So what did he say to that?"

He shrugs, his piercing gaze locked on me. "That's his exact intention, but it will take time. He needs more experience under his belt and to find an open position. You can't tell Michele. I have no idea how long he means, and worse, he's broken her before. If she holds out hope and he never comes back … you can't tell her."

I nod. I can't knowingly put my friend in any more pain. Two hours later, I pick up lunch and drive to Michele's office. I'm relieved to see her car parked out front because she's always busy with something.

She's behind the desk in her office when I walk through the french doors. Her whole face lights up when she sees me, and I hold up the bag of takeout. "I brought lunch."

I realize this is the first time I've ever shown up unannounced for her, and I feel like a terrible friend. From the first dinner out with her and Lily, they have consistently checked up on me, stopping by randomly, often with food in tow. It's then I vow to be better, to be the friend her and Lily have been for me.

She rounds her desk and pulls me in for a hug. "I see that. What are you doing here?" We move to the couch and chairs in the corner, and I unload the burgers and fries onto the coffee table.

"I missed you and wanted to see how you're doing. There was a small bomb dropped on you at breakfast this weekend." Everyone seemed to know more about Ethan and Michele than me. She's made little comments about him here or there, but I didn't know the story until I asked Jake about it later that day. I get the feeling the only people who know the full story are Michele and Ethan.

Michele steals a fry, taking her time to chew it. Her lower lip wobbles as she turns to me, tears rimming her eyes. "I'm crushed." A shuddered inhale heaves her chest before she continues. "They say your first love is an idealistic love, the one that seems like a fairy tale until we learn what we really want in life. But what if all I learned was that he really was what I wanted for my life. My mom thinks I'm romanticizing what we had, but I know I'm not."

I scoot closer to her on the couch and use the back of my knuckles to wipe her falling tears, feeling a burn in my throat. Loving and losing so early in life had to have been excruciating.

"I can't even tell you what it is about him, except when we were together, all felt right in the world. The sun felt warm, the rain felt cold, and my heart was whole. Nothing has been the same since." Her words come out choked and full of hurt.

An errant tear escapes, and realization dawns on me that she's been living with ghosts as long as I have. She hid her pain and her quiet suffering from all of us, mourning the man she thought would be her forever. How awful it must have been to have the hope he was coming back, maybe even coming back for her, only to have that hope crushed again. My chest squeezes at the knowledge that could happen again. "I'm so sorry, Michele" is all I can manage.

"I was lucky enough to get that love at all. I've accepted that the only choices from here are to settle for less or to be alone. I'm coming to terms with the latter." She is filled with defeat, but what can I say to that? A once-in-a-lifetime love can be out there a second time? Give it time because he told Jake he was still trying to come back for you? I know better than that. So instead, I unwrap our burgers and slide hers closer to her.

"I have those same five minutes anytime you need to talk about him, okay? Five minutes to not feel that pain alone and then I won't bring it up again." She places her hand on mine, giving it a grateful squeeze before we dig into our lunch.

When the air around us feels less heavy, we talk about my upcoming date with Jake, and she talks about the garden she's planting for her latest clients. It's so clear now, the family and love that surround me. These people mean everything to me, and I will be better at showing them how much that love is appreciated.

jake

This has been the best week of my life. It might seem a little pathetic saying that, but it's true. After I made love to Amber on Sunday, I wrapped her in my sheets and sat on the little balcony outside my bedroom with her snuggled in my arms. We laughed about the fact that I make furniture for a living yet have none out there. I don't care though. Bare ass on the old wood wasn't going to stop me from enjoying a quiet moment with my girl, even if I got a horribly placed splinter.

She told me how much she loves the woods and the quiet of the cabin. How if she ever leaves her apartment, she wants it to be for a little cabin like this, filled with love. I love that about her; the fact the things she wants aren't things at all. She wants friends that feel like family, to bring Socks with her everywhere she goes, to love someone the way her aunt loved her store.

The minute she left that afternoon, I ran over to Thoren and Lily's and asked if I could buy the cabin from them. Lily squealed and said it was mine as long as I promised to move Amber into it with me. Michele dropped the papers off to me the next day, with a bill of sale for twenty dollars. *Twenty fucking dollars*. Apparently, they were always planning to give me the place, Thoren just wanted to buy a case of beer out of the deal since I'm always stealing his. I love that prick.

To top it off, Amber and I have been spending every free moment we have together. We eat dinner together nightly, bring each other coffee, and have been alternating whose house we stay at every night. Socks, of course, made himself right at home when she brought him over Tuesday. I felt a weird sense of pride when he climbed right into the little cat tree I bought for him. The two of them fit so seamlessly into my life, but I feel Amber is still holding back. I don't know what it is, but I'm determined to figure it out.

All this has only elevated my excitement for our date. I have everything planned out, and thank God the weather has decided to cooperate. August can be miserably hot, but when the weather app said a warm seventy-two, I felt like Jana was giving me her approval.

Like promised, I pull my bike into the alleyway right at two, catching Amber bounding down the stairs through the glass door. Her eyes light up when she sees me, eyeing up my bike.

"Are you taking me for a real ride?" she asks, a huge smile on her face.

"Yeah, baby, I am. But I need you to put these on first." From my backpack, I take out the leather jacket, hoping it fits. I guessed her size when I picked it up on Monday. She's practically vibrating with excitement as she slips it on. It hugs her curves perfectly, and she runs her hands down the front of it, grinning.

"What's this?"

Her fingers splay over the little emblem I had my mom sew over her heart. It's a small x, one line made from a cedar leaf, and the other a simple plank of cedar wood. I thought it was fitting, but seeing her quizzical gaze now, I'm a little embarrassed. "Something to make you think of me. The cedar leaf from your store logo, and the cedar wood for my company."

The heat in my cheeks spreads as her eyes soften, and she places both hands over it. "I love it, Jake."

"Good." My voice cracks, so I clear my throat, pulling her closer by the flaps of the jacket so I can put my helmet on her head. I want her to pick out her own, so for now, she gets to wear mine.

"It's going to mess up my hair," she pouts. When I tug the buckle under her chin tight, she lets out a small squeak.

"Too tight?"

"No, I just prefer your hand choking me."

My forehead drops forward and thunks on the helmet as I let out a groan. Taking a deep breath, I try to will the blood away from my quickly thickening cock. "And I'm wearing the blue," she says, giggling when my fingers fist in her jacket.

Without my help, she grabs my shoulder and hops onto the back of my bike. One time on this thing and she thinks she's a pro. It's so fucking cute. "Closer, baby." Her chest hits my backpack, and I hate that barrier between us.

"Give me your backpack. It's in my way." I preen at the thought that she doesn't want it between us either. It's not like it's heavy; only filled with some snacks, water, and a small blanket. She tightens it on her shoulders, then presses herself to me, her small hands wrapping tight around my waist.

"Hold on and lean with me. If you need to get my attention, tap my leg twice." I turn to look over my shoulder to see the smile still plastered on her face under the visor of the helmet. "You ready?"

With a nod, she squeezes tighter, and the bike rumbles to life beneath us. I love this feeling, the power thrumming through me, the wind blowing past me. It's freeing and grounding all at once. With Amber on the back, I'm more cautious than normal, making this a leisure ride farther up the mountain.

On every straight stretch of road, my hands find a way to her thighs, holding them tighter, rubbing over them. Knowing she's here with me, safe with me, brings on a sense of peace. The longer we ride, the more relaxed she feels against me. Her hands wander from their spot on my stomach, rubbing up and down my chest, even down my thighs. Her nails scratch over my jeans, wandering closer to my dick with every upward stroke.

When her soft hands finally connect with my now throbbing cock, I rev the engine, causing her to grip it tight. Her laughter rumbles against my back as I let loose a chuckle. With an extra squeeze, she lets it go, throwing her hands out to the side.

Her little whoop of delight as the warm summer wind flows around her outstretched arms fills me with satisfaction. She remains that way for a few moments, and I don't have to look behind me to know what I'll see—her arms out wide, her face tilted up to the bright sun, eyes shut as she just feels. Truly feels.

Thirty minutes later, I pull off to the lookout spot. It's not a well-known spot, but it's magical all the same, with a field of wildflowers leading to a drop-off overlooking our small town. The perfect spot for a quiet picnic with my girl. Amber hops off the back, heading straight for the cliff edge. She removes the helmet as she walks, and I'm rooted to the spot, still straddling my bike.

The early afternoon sun reflects off her leather jacket, her hair an adorable rumpled mess from the helmet, and that damn little stud in her nose sparkling. But the look on her face truly has me stuck. It's calm, relaxed, and dare I say, happy. Truly happy.

Kicking the stand out, I step off my bike and join her. After taking the backpack and helmet from her, I drop them to the ground and pull her back to my chest, resting my chin on her head. She places her arms around mine, hugging her waist, and we stand there, taking in the sights below us. I will never take this for granted, being able to hold her in the way she deserves.

"It's perfect." Her voice is subdued, almost reverent. "This place. The ride up here. Being with you. The way it all makes me feel alive after months of feeling nothing."

I have a lot of things I'm proud of. My business I've built from the ground up. Taking care of my parents. Being a man I can look at in the mirror every day. None of it compares to knowing I had a hand in helping her heal. With two fingers under her chin, I tip it to the side, giving me access. Her lips are soft and warm against mine, the intended quick kiss turning into more as she turns in my arms. Like most times we kiss, my hand spears into her hair at the base of her neck, needing that hold to know I have her. That she's mine, and she's right where she's meant to be.

My cock swells again, and I pull back. This is supposed to be a proper date, not a fuck in the woods … not that I would complain about that. I wonder how she would feel about a little primal play. *Shut it down, Jake, shut it down.*

"I brought food. I thought we could sit out here and watch the sunset," I say, picking up our discarded things. There's a thin blanket folded in the backpack that I spread out in a grassy spot where we won't crush too many flowers.

Amber's watching it all with an amused and awed expression. "I didn't know you were a romantic," she says, biting her bottom lip before climbing onto the blanket. She undoes her boots, setting them at the end, and stretches her legs out in front of her, so I do the same.

"There's a lot you still don't know about me," I admit. "I would like to change that."

amber

"Tell me something, then. What did you want to be when you were a kid?"

He chuckles, grabbing my hips and bringing me closer to his side. "I wanted to be a logger. Thoren and I have always loved the woods. Everything about it. The sights, the smells, the animals, the activities. One weekend, David took the three of us boys to a Seattle Rainiers game. On the drive over, we passed a huge chunk of land that had been completely stripped of trees, and I hated it. I wanted to learn how to do that without ruining the forest."

That is totally something I could picture him doing. His powerful arms swinging as he chops down trees while wearing tight suspenders. "What changed your mind?"

"My dad. One Spring, we had to cut down a tree in our yard because its branches were getting too close to the house. He asked if we should cut it down for firewood or send it to get stripped into planks to use to build something. I chose to build and found my passion." The whole time he talks, he finds a way to touch me. His rough, calloused fingers playing with mine or moving a piece of hair behind my ear.

Every touch makes me feel special. Cherished. Not liking the little space between us, I climb into his lap, settling my butt between his thighs and leaning against his chest. He lets out a contented sigh that soothes my cracked soul.

"What did you want to be?"

"I didn't really have any idea when I was little. I just knew I wanted to be proud of what I had."

His chest vibrates as he hums. "Are you proud now?"

That was an easy question. It's why I worked so hard, not only for Jana's legacy but to expand on it and make it my own. To feel like I could do something for myself and for others. "I am."

"Good. I wish you could see yourself through the eyes of everyone around you. When I look at you, I see strength personified. I've seen the bins filled with orders you send out every week and the growth you've brought to that store. You bring joy to those around you and help others when it isn't asked. I'm so damn proud of you, Amber, and I'm so glad you feel it for yourself."

His words are an echo of what the girls said last weekend. Letting people in, allowing them to see who I am and being a part of their lives is such a new concept to me. Being surrounded by them and seeing I can bring something other than pain and heartache into their lives is the greatest blessing. People who look below the surface and see what I hope to portray and not what I've been fighting to leave behind. I don't want to say thank you because it doesn't seem like enough. Nothing I can do or say feels like it's enough after all the things he's done for me.

"Are we dating?" I ask instead.

"It feels like more than that."

His hand runs up and down my arm, and I see the a-l-l written across his fingers. I know the tattoo means a lot more than that, but that one word represents him so well. He has it all. The protector, the nurturer, the lover, and fighter. He has a heart of gold, the body of a god, a humble take on his success, and a deep love for those in his circle. Jacob Anderson is the type of man a girl like me could only ever dream of loving one day. And here he is, holding me in the most romantic of settings and telling me I feel like more to him.

"Okay." I don't know what else to say. It seems like more to me too. I might have thought I hated him a few weeks ago, but I never did. I hated the way he could make me feel. Hated the fear and longing that came along with it. Hate and love have such a fine line, and I can feel myself tipping over the other side.

"Okay," he repeats.

Jake pulls out some containers of fruit, nuts, cut-up meats, and edamame. When I raise a brow, he shrugs, placing them in front of me. "I'm a big boy, I need protein."

"Big boy indeed," I say, rubbing my butt further into his lap before moving off him so we can snack. I don't make it far before he grabs my hips, grinding me over his lap, and a moan slips from his lips. I try to keep it going, but he places me next to him, settling my legs over his lap.

"This is supposed to be a proper first date," he grumbles, adjusting his hard length, then grabs a handful of nuts and throws them in his mouth. I try to stifle a chuckle as he aggressively chews while looking out over the town below. As if he hasn't commanded my body how he pleases many times before this date.

I grab some blueberries, plopping one at a time in my mouth, and he groans, shaking his head. "Stop it, Whiskey. Everything you do is sexy, and I'm trying to be good."

I chuckle again, leaning on his shoulder. "I've never been good on dates. Probably why they never go past the first one. I revert to manager mode and ask questions like, where do you see yourself in five years?"

"That's a valid question." He's quiet for a minute, then answers, voice full of gravel. "I see myself here, still taking you on dates like this. Finding moments where we can reset and unwind together between the craziness of our schedules. I see Socks still batting at our toes from under the couch, and waking you with my tongue between your thighs before we head to the gym. Dinners on our back porch on the nights we have off together and in our shops on the nights we don't. I see exhausting days as we push to expand our businesses and epic fights when we get overwhelmed, followed by an explosion of feelings as I fuck the fight right out of you. It doesn't matter if it's five days, five years, or five decades, all I see is you."

The tears are falling before I can stop them, but Jake is there, scooping me back into his arms. My safe space, my harbor from the dark waters. By his side feels exactly where I'm meant to be.

"I want to build that life with you." I cry into his chest, and he caresses my back.

"I'm really good at building, baby. I can take all our hurt and ugly pieces and make something beautiful with them. We can have whatever life you want, just build it with me."

This whole time I've been trying to resist Jake, I've been doing it with the thought that broken people shouldn't be together. I was wrong. I see it so clearly now, the most broken people are actually the best ones to repair. They know what's important to save and how to hold things together when everything seems to be falling apart.

My tears slow, and I sink further into him, into his heady scent that calms me. His hands never leave me, soothing and comforting in the way only he can. He lies down, bringing me with him, and places soft, sweet kisses on my lips, and I feel it. The love Jana swore I would find is right here, with him.

We stay like that, kissing, cuddling, and talking about our hopes and dreams. Dreams that suddenly don't seem so out of reach for either of us. And when the sun sinks down, painting the sky in an array of pinks and purples before draping us in the darkness that I've grown accustomed to, Jake lowers his lips to my ear and whispers how I'm everything to him. How I'm the best thing to walk into his life; and for the first time in forever, I shut out the words of the past and believe him.

CHAPTER FORTY-THREE

jake

Heaven and hell. Two places I have lived between for most of my life, floating in that subspace leaning more toward one. It's empty in the space between, and I've spent so long there I almost forgot what either side could feel like.

Until Amber told me she wanted to build her life with me. Heaven. Pure fucking heaven.

Driving her home last night, I rode as slow as I could, reveling in the feel of her body against mine. No part of me wanted to take her home, but I had a plan, and that plan involved walking her to her door and kissing her goodnight.

That plan also involved finally hanging the porch swing because the cushion I ordered for it was delivered Saturday while we were enjoying our picnic. I've been dying to show it to her, to help her feel at home in the cabin I'm trying to make ours, but I want it to be perfect. She deserves that.

When I helped Thoren build a cover for his deck, I did the same to half of mine. Who knew it would come in handy to hang the swing under. It looks inviting and cozy, the perfect addition to the space out here. The cushion fits nicely on it, and I add pillows my mom made recently at the store.

Taking a seat on it, I kick my legs, letting it rock gently in the summer breeze, and gaze out at the woods. I hope Amber loves it as much as she did the old one. That she feels she can finally open up to me on it, and we can spend our nights curled on it together.

When I asked Amber last night what time she was working today, she said she had the whole day off. I was surprised, especially since she took last weekend off as well, but it works well for me. I'm bringing her here tonight, bringing her home, with every intention of convincing her to move in with me.

As I'm putting chicken in the fridge to marinate for dinner, my phone pings from the counter. Hoping it's from my girl, I rush to get it, when it starts ringing. Seeing Lily's name, I swipe to answer.

"Jake," she says in a hoarse voice before I can even get a word out. "Evelyn collapsed and is in the hospital." I can hear the panic in her voice and the rev of an engine. "Thoren and I are on the way, and Riv is coming too. Can you, uh, can you come too? I think Thoren needs you."

I hear what she doesn't want to say. She doesn't know how bad it is, but I've been in that waiting room waiting to see if today is the day I lose a parent. I know what's going through his head and can support him in the way he needs. The thing is, showing up is all he needs. That's all you can do, and knowing you have people, your parents have people, makes all the difference.

"On my way."

Not bothering to turn off lights or do anything other than throw on my boots, I rush out the door and hop on my bike. I fly down the country roads and into town, making it to the local hospital on the outskirts in record time. Parking on the sidewalk without a care, I slam the kickstand down and rush through the front doors.

It's a smaller hospital and easy to navigate, plus I know these halls well. My dad's visits are frequent, and I join every chance I get. It only takes a few minutes to find the waiting room the James' are in, and when I do, I hate the looks on their faces. Thoren stands to give me a hug, then immediately sits back down, his face is pale and withdrawn. I give Lily a squeeze on the shoulder, then move to David.

"How is she?"

"We don't know yet," David says, wringing his hands. "She was fine, then out of nowhere she started slurring her words, her movements turned slow and wobbly, then it was like her legs gave out and she collapsed. We haven't heard anything since they took her."

Evelyn has been in the hospital before. She has a heart condition she was managing well, but sometimes, the body does what it wants. "How far out is River?"

"He's driving, so maybe another two hours."

"I'll get us some of the good coffee from the café. Decaf?" I ask Lily.

She nods, and I head down to give myself something to do. For as much time as I've spent here, I hate it. It makes my skin crawl thinking of the days I spent here and the weeks my dad had to stay. Slipping my phone out, I text my mom to let her know what's going on, then call Amber, but when she doesn't answer, I text to let her know too. She reads my text but doesn't reply. I'm debating calling her again, but then it's my turn to order.

With a tray full of drinks, I make my way back to the waiting room and distribute the drinks so everyone else has something to do with their hands too. The air is tense, but I try to keep it light, talking about baby names and my ideas for the crib. Not too long after, a doctor finally comes in to talk to us.

"Mrs. James's CT results show a pulmonary embolism. We have her on a few medications to see if we can get it to resolve without surgery, but that may be a possibility in the future. There were some other concerning findings on the CT, but we will address that after we get this resolved. Would you like to see her?"

Everyone stands at the doctor's question, and he chuckles, waving us with him. "She said everyone would fight to come. If you can stay calm and quiet, I can let you all in."

We follow him down the hall, Thoren holding Lily's hand so tight his knuckles are white. All I can think of as I watch them is how Amber had to do this alone, and the outcome was much worse for her aunt. She will never have to face anything alone again.

Evelyn's room is small but private as we all shuffle in. David wraps her in a hug first, wiping his eyes as he moves back so Thoren can hug his mom. They talk in hushed tones until Evelyn spots me, and her lips purse.

"What are you doing here, Jacob?"

Stunned at her response, I palm the back of my neck awkwardly, glancing between the others. She's like a mother to me and has been there for me almost as much as my own. When she reads my confused and hurt expression, she softens. "It's Amber's birthday, honey, and a really hard day for her. You should be with her."

"What?" I croak, then shoot an accusatory glare at Lily.

"I didn't know either." She looks back to Evelyn, a question on her face.

"It's the day her real mom died. Thank you for coming, but go, Jacob." I lurch forward to give her a gentle hug, then sprint out the door as quickly as I ran in.

Why didn't Amber say anything to me? I had no idea her birthday was even coming up. I'm about to pull out my phone to call her when the warmth of the summer sun hits my back and the heat of it seeps into my bones.

I don't need to call. I know where she is.

amber

The low growl of Jake's Harley cuts through the quiet air of the cemetery. My body wars with itself to run or break down. I knew he would come for me eventually, and as much as I want him here, *need him here*, I don't want him to see me like this, fighting these demons. My day was already hard, then he texted me that Evelyn was in the hospital, and I lost it. The woman has been a literal godsend for me, and I couldn't get myself off this bench to go be with her. Couldn't make myself step into that hospital today.

Birthdays are supposed to be spent celebrating your life, but my mom ruined that for me a long time ago. My earliest memories of my birthday are all the same. Anger, fear, hurt. I've never had a cake or candles. Jana asked once if I wanted them, but I told her this wasn't a day for happiness. The feelings were always too heavy. My mom made sure of that.

I'll never understand why she had me or why she kept me. Part of me fears it's because I was a weapon she was keeping for later. Someone she could use to get money from the state and later try to get money out of me. She never hid her disdain for me, and on this day, it always hit a nerve for her. Reminding her of the day I entered the world and entered her life, putting the nail in her coffin, as she often said.

Jake's presence causes a visceral reaction like it always does, relaxing me and threatening to make the tears I've been holding back all morning fall. His footsteps stop behind me, but he doesn't make a move to touch me.

"Whiskey." His voice is low and filled with emotion. It tips me over the edge, the first tear breaking loose, quickly followed by another and another.

He's around the bench and kneeling in front of me in an instant. His rough hands gently cup my jaw. The look in his eyes is pure agony, and I cry harder, fearing the reason. "Is she …?" I croak out between sobs.

I'm scooped into Jake's arms, where he sits on the bench with me in his lap. "She's okay. I'm so sorry, I should have said that. Evelyn's okay." He shushes my cries, and I breathe in the warmth of his scent. "She, uh—" He clears his throat as his fingers brush through my hair. "She told me it's your birthday. Why didn't you say anything, baby?"

I try to control my ragged breaths with that knowledge. Sucking in lungfuls of the humid air, each inhale a desperate attempt to quell the storm brewing. I didn't lose one more person, and Jake is here. The relief I feel doesn't last long because he's here. He's here and I have to tell him the ugly truth I've been hiding. The stain on my soul I can't scrub off. The tears I was getting under control dry up completely as the numbness I always feel on this day takes over once again.

"My mom died on this day, and I'm the reason she's dead."

His hands still, and my body tenses, waiting for his reaction. "Why do you think that?"

"I don't think, I know. We never celebrated my birthday, but it was always commemorated. In her words, it was the day that ruined her life. *I* ruined her life." I press myself farther into Jake's chest, and he holds me tighter, his hands moving up and down my back now. "On my eleventh birthday, she woke up yelling that she needed to be high to forget the worst day of her life. She died trying to forget me."

"Baby," he whispers with so much pain, but I'm not done.

"I loved my mom. Even as shitty as she was toward me and hating me for merely existing, I still loved her, and it's my fault she's dead." I nestle into him to soak up his strength to help me continue through the pain spearing through my heart. "It's taken years of therapy to come to terms with the fact that I won't ruin everyone's life. I hid from people for so long because I thought it was me. That there was something wrong with me and I was going to ruin everyone the way I did her. Even learning that's not the truth, I still have to live with the guilt that I'm the reason she's dead."

The same guilt I've been battling for fifteen years now claws at me, fighting to take hold. My chest squeezes, my lungs fighting for air as images from that day float through my mind. Hiding under my tattered covers while Mom yells from the other room, each word making me flinch as something shatters against my bedroom door. The silence that followed where I knew she was injecting something into her veins. The hours I spent there, hungry and needing to pee but too scared to face her wrath when the high wore off. Then, finally, the fear when the sun streaking through my window moved across the wall before sinking down and shrouding me in darkness without a sound from outside. How, with shaking hands, I slipped out of the room to find my mom on the living room floor covered in a puddle of her own vomit, her eyes unseeing and her skin a pale gray.

"It's not your fault." The deep timbre rumbling through Jake's chest as he repeats those four words over and over, pulls me further from the memory and back to reality. Lightly pinching my chin, he brings my gaze to his, his deep-blue eyes hard and determined as he repeats it again. "Damnit, Amber, I need you to really hear me. It. Is. Not. Your. Fault."

The sincerity in his eyes has me focusing on the here and now. On the beautiful man in front of me who gives me every reassurance in the world. One tear slips down my cheek that he quickly wipes away.

"I didn't want you to see my demons."

"I think there was some confusion, baby. You're mine, which means you get me for the good, the bad, and the devastating. I'm yours through it all."

The tears fall in earnest as I look him in the eyes and spill the last tiny bit of truth. "I'm fucked up, Jake. I like when you call me your slut, when you dole out punishments that use me like an object." Working through the shudders that rack my body, I put my hands to his chest, needing to feel his heartbeat to steady my words. "About a year before my mom died, she started noticing the men that came through our place would … linger when I was around. It was then she started calling me those names. Slut. Whore. Greedy little skank. She would say them with such venom, often followed by things like 'I see you trying to steal my man' or 'You're lucky I don't let them have you. I'd get more money.'"

"Fuck," he growls out, but I splay my fingers over his shirt, keeping that grounding presence.

"The first time you said it, it was derogatory, sure, but you had this desire and grit in your voice. So different from the way it was used before. It felt freeing. The next time you said it, there wasn't hate in your heart the way it was with her, and hell if it didn't light me up from within. How fucked up is that? That I feel pride from the words that cut me down as a kid."

Gripping my hair at the roots, he leans down and kisses me

hard. "If that's the most fucked-up thing about you, what does it say about me that I want to drive to where she's buried and fuck my little slut on her grave?"

My body trembles for a whole new reason when he kisses me again, his lips prying mine open as he explores my mouth, salty tears and all. The kiss holds all the things neither of us have said, but I know we both feel. Trust, understanding, acceptance … love. We kiss for what feels like hours before he pulls back, placing soft kisses on my cheeks.

"I feel like I should apologize to Jana for being so crass in front of her resting place, but I warned her I wasn't a good man."

A startled laugh bubbles out of me, and I look up at him. "You what? When?"

"When I dropped off this bench. We had a chat and came to an understanding. She's okay with my lesser qualities because I promised I'd be the man you deserve."

Poof. There goes that last little brick protecting my heart. Shattered and turned to rubble at the hands of this man. On one of my hardest days, he makes me laugh, cry, and melt at the way he cares for me.

"Thank you for the bench. It's much nicer than sitting on the ground." Moving off his lap and taking a seat next to him, I let my fingers trail over the little J&A engraved in the center. "You're pretty sure of us, huh?"

He laughs, a deep and throaty sound, and shakes his head at me. "I am, but that was meant for Jana and Amber. I love that your mind went to me though."

My cheeks heat, and I slap his arm. "Don't make fun of me, it's my birthday."

"I know, baby. I'm still mad you didn't tell me. What do you normally do on this day?"

My hands rub down my thighs as I look down at the headstone before us. The reason I'm here today. "Eat brownies on the porch swing with her."

He hums, then stands and takes my hand. "Can I take you somewhere?"

jake

Amber looks up at me, her golden eyes still shining from the tears she shed, before slipping her hand in mine. I love her blind trust in me and hope I can make this day a little better for her. This might be tricky with everything going on, but with a plan in mind, I shoot off a group text as we walk to my bike.

"Where are we going?" she asks, when I slip my helmet on her head, buckling it under her chin.

"I have a surprise. It wasn't intended as a birthday gift, but it will have to work since you didn't give me time to do anything else," I say, giving her a stern look. She's getting punished for that later.

"What about my car?"

"Leave the keys in the console, and I'll have it taken care of."

She gives me a skeptical look, so I kiss her nose before closing the visor. Sitting on my Harley, I hold my hand out to help her climb on the back, and she clings to me, wrapping her arms and legs tight around me. Maybe I don't need my truck back. Too much space between our bodies in that thing.

The bike roars to life beneath us, and it's the balm to my

nerves I'm in desperate need of. I knew through the bits and pieces Amber shared in the past that her mom wasn't great, but I didn't expect all that.

Cruising through the downtown streets toward home, I let the wind whipping through my hair take the anger coursing through my veins. Amber deserves a birthday. A real fucking birthday, and while I can only do so much last minute, I'll do everything I can to make it amazing. She better buckle up for next year, though, because it's on.

By the time my wheels hit the gravel of my drive, my body is relaxed, the anger replaced by a wave of nerves. This surprise for her will hit extra hard today, and I hope it's a good thing. She slips off my bike, handing me the helmet and running her fingers through her tousled hair. There's a lighter feel to the moment, her eyes clearer and her body at ease. I love that a ride on my Harley gives her the same sense of clarity it does for me.

My hand trembles as I take hers, and the reality of this moment hits me hard. I'm steady—steady hands, steady in my roots and beliefs—but right now, I'm shaking like a leaf, letting the wind dictate where I go. It's not an unpleasant thought, letting go of the rigid roots that have always held me back and following my heart. Even if that heart means leaving the safety of my tree and following Amber to the ends of the earth.

Instead of going through the house, I walk her around the side, needing the smell of the pine trees and the lilacs that Lily and Thoren planted here. "Where are we going?" Amber asks, squeezing my trembling fingers.

As soon as we round the back of the house, she stops dead in her tracks. Her face is stricken, but I can't tell if it's a good thing or not. Tugging her gently, I bring her onto the deck and set her down on the swing. She's rigid, but her fingers ghost over the edges of the wood as tears form on her lashes.

Taking a seat next to her, I tip her chin to face me. "I've been building this for a while. I was going to show it to you today, for a completely different reason, but this works too. Happy birthday, Whiskey."

"H … how?"

"I drove by Jana's old place and did my best to replicate it. When you said that leaving it was the hardest part of leaving that house, I knew I had to build one here for you."

"Jake, I—" she whispers, sucking in a deep breath to hold back her tears, then shakes her head. "I'm a mess."

My trembling hands still as the sun peeks through the trees, lighting up her face, and I see it all so clearly. Our lives together in this cabin. Our lives free from the burdens of our past. Our lives loving and laughing, bickering and caring.

"I love you, Amber Wright. You don't have to be perfect or have it all figured out to be deeply loved by me. You already are, as you are, in this moment. And every moment. I will love you softly on your hardest days and fiercely when you need strength. But always. Without question. I love you."

I was unsure how she would react, but slamming her lips on mine wasn't it. Her pillowy-soft lips mold to mine, sucking the breath from my lungs. It's demanding and claiming and every-thing I've wanted to feel from her. Her nails spear through my hair, scratching down my scalp and sending shudders through my body.

"I love you too, Jake," she breathes over my lips before placing one more kiss there. Still holding my head in place, her piercing golden eyes sparkle as she smiles at me. "I see you. I see your soul that you willingly burned to help others. Your heart that you pour into every single piece of your work. Your strength that you use to keep those you love safe. Every dark part of you fits with every broken piece of me. Together, we can stop wandering in the dark and step into the sun. I love every part of you, Jake. Thank you for bringing light back to my life."

Sitting back on the swing, I haul her into my side, placing a soft kiss on her forehead. She snuggles into me, curling her feet up on the cushion and letting me rock us gently as the warm sun skates over us. "Thank you for seeing me and loving me all the same."

Her head tilts up, gaze locking on mine. "Thank you for making this. Sitting here, hearing those words leave your mouth, it's the best gift I've ever received." Amber lays her head back on my chest, her hand trailing up and down my thigh. "Jana would have loved this. And you."

I have to swallow past the lump in my throat. She's come so far, from walking away every time her aunt was brought up, to willingly talking about her with me. When I saw her at Thoren and Lily's wedding, she held in every emotion, and here she is, displaying it all for me today. She's incredible, and I wish I could make her see what I do. How I've watched her fight to get her life back, to pull herself from the darkness.

"I'm sorry I never got to meet her, because I have so much to thank her for."

She smiles and lowers herself to lay across my lap, looking out at the forest behind the house. I trail my fingers through her hair as her eyes slowly close. Everything about this moment is perfect, and sliding my phone from my pocket, I know it will only get better from here.

JAKE:

I know this is the worst day for this, but I need help.

THOREN:

We're in. Mom is okay and has dad with her.
What are you thinking?

MICHELE:

Wait, what's going on?

LILY:

Today is Amber's birthday and the day her mom
died. We just found out.

RIVER:

Fuck.

MICHELE:

I make a mean chocolate cake. Where are we
meeting?

JAKE:

Can you make it brownies? Pick up dinner on
the way to my place? And can someone get her
car from the cemetery?

LILY:

I'll get it. Is she moving in with you?

RIVER:

SHE'S MOVING IN WITH YOU? I need to put
eyes on Mom, then I'll be there. I'll grab the
food.

JAKE:

I'm asking soon, but I want her staying here
tonight. Can you grab Socks from her place?

MICHELE:

I'll be there in two hours with brownies and gifts
in tow.

THOREN:

We will be right behind with the cat.

JAKE:

I love you guys.

LILY:

What a sap. I'm so happy to see you happy.

CHAPTER FORTY-SIX

Amber napped on me for over an hour, and my legs went numb, but I didn't care. I enjoyed the soft strands of her hair flowing through my fingers and the feeling of this little cabin finally being a home. Knowing our friends would be on their way soon, I rubbed my thumb over her cheek until those stunning whiskey eyes fluttered open and looked up at me.

"Sorry." She yawns.

"Don't be. I'm a lucky man to have you here with me and am honored to be the place you find rest."

She sits up, letting her feet dangle over the edge for a moment before turning to me. "I used to hate that word. Lucky. I can see now how lucky I truly am to have found someone who loves me enough to fight with me, burn with me, and build a life with me."

"I do love fighting with you," I say, pulling her up as I hear the gravel crunch from out front. "But if you fight me about this, know that it's been a while since I've punished you and I am aching for it, baby."

She tries to gape at me, but an audible whimper leaves her lips, and damn if I don't want to drag her upstairs right now and fuck her with everyone listening. "Later," I growl, opening the back door right as my front door swings open.

Thoren, Lily, Michele, and River all walk in, chatting with arms full of bags and trays. Amber's gaze ping-pongs from them to me, then she mutters, "There's always the bathroom again." She saunters past me, clearly having picked up on what I've set in motion here.

All my blood rushes south at the reminder of our first time together, and I have to adjust myself as everyone pours into my small kitchen. Before I can haul Amber back to me and make her pay for that comment, River is pulling her into a hug.

"Amber, baby, happy birthday!"

A growl rumbles low in my throat, which only makes Riv chuckle and hold her tighter. Amber glances over her shoulder at me and winks as she wraps her arms around him too. Thoren is laughing, watching it all go down, and Lily reappears in the doorway, this time with Socks in hand. "You're going to need nut peas again in a second, Riv," she states, plopping the cat on the floor.

I'm momentarily distracted as Socks comes pouncing over to me, running between my legs while letting out a loud purr. "There's my boy," I say, picking him up and cuddling him to my chest as he rubs his soft head against my beard.

"How the mighty have fallen," River says, and lets go of Amber, only for her to be pulled into an embrace by Michele.

"You're about to get kicked out of my house." I scowl at him.

"Not yours, Jakey-poo. My girl Lily will let me stay."

Lily smacks him on the back of his head before moving to hug Amber. "It's his, and I may be your sister-in-law, but he's my best friend, so I'm taking his side."

I grin like an idiot, raising a brow at River. Amber's gaze bounces between all of us, and she opens her mouth, probably to ask about that, but Michele cuts her off.

"First, I want to say that if anyone else hides any important dates from us, I will throat punch them. But since you're new to learning how this family works," she says, narrowing her gaze on Amber, "we will let it slide this one time. Second, happy birthday. Here's to you and to never spending a birthday or holiday alone again."

The look on Amber's face transforms from confusion to joy. Her cheeks tinge pink and her eyes turn glassy as she takes us all in. All of us are here to celebrate her because this group right here is family. When her watery eyes meet mine, I nod, giving her the reassurance that this is her life now. A life filled with family, love, and joyous moments. A life she deserves.

"Happy birthday," we all echo.

Sensing her emotions being on edge, Lily claps, and I set Socks back down. "Food, then presents."

Everyone shuffles around my tiny island, where Thoren has been spreading out the containers of grilled meats, coleslaw, macaroni, and cornbread. As cramped as it is, I love this. My house filled with laughter and joy, and not feeling like the odd man out. Amber says I gave her a safe space to be herself, but she doesn't see she's done the same for me tenfold. I no longer feel like the freak who doesn't want kids. Or the one they invite because they feel bad I'm alone.

Amber has given me a home with her. She calms me when I feel panicked, fights with me when I need an outlet, stays by my side when the darkness threatens, and loves me through it all. There's no judgment for my past, my dirty work clothes, or my long hours at work. Only support and encouragement to love what I do.

When she gets a plate full of food, I draw her into my side, dropping a kiss to her soft lips. "I love you," she breathes against them, and my chest swells with pride. "Thank you."

She turns to everyone as the room goes quiet. "Thank you, guys. For sticking by my side through the last few months and not letting me pull away. And for dropping everything to be with me today, especially with everything going on." Her gaze lingers on Thor and Riv, and they nod, eyes filled with understanding. "Thank you for showing me that the family I've always wanted has been right beside me all along."

"Thanks for being brave enough to take on this asshole and embracing the love you both deserve." I'm more than a little surprised to hear Lily swear, but she looks at us with such a fondness and rubs her little belly.

"And thanks for making this work between you two because he was getting needy there for a bit," Thoren adds, bringing my scowl back as Amber softly chuckles beside me.

"Yeah, thanks for making me the odd one out." Michele holds up a beer in cheers. "Forever alone."

"You're all a bunch of sad sacks. I'm not saying thanks for shit until you guys start allowing me in all the group chats and secrets," River grumbles. Collectively, we clear our throats and cough uncomfortably as we take our plates of food to the porch. "Oh, come on," Riv whines behind us.

Bending down, I put my lips to Amber's ear. "Thanks for climbing my ladder and making a home in my heart, Whiskey."

She chokes on a laugh as Michele gets outside and starts squealing about how sweet the porch swing turned out and how she wants one on her porch next. It quickly turns into an argument as Lily claims she should get one next because it would be the perfect spot to rock the baby outside.

Amber shakes her head, taking a seat on the deck, not caring about chairs as she watches everyone get comfortable. Her golden eyes lock on mine again, and she lets out a contented sigh.

"I know, baby," I say, understanding it all completely. "I know."

amber

"Whiskey," Jake breathes against my neck, as his arm wraps tighter around me. I rock my hips again, grinding my ass against his morning wood.

"Yes, Jake?" I say coyly.

His sleepy growl shoots straight through me, making heat pool at my core. His hand moves down to my hip, gripping it tight and eliminating the tiny bit of space between us. Open-mouthed kisses trail my neck, causing me to groan into the darkness. This is my favorite way to wake up.

Things have been so good between us. Better than I could have ever imagined. Last week, we were fairly even between the nights we spent at my apartment and here. He thought I would be more comfortable there, and while I love my connection to Jana there, I'm learning it's not the place that matters. I feel her with me always.

His cabin brings a sense of peace and happiness to me. The serenity of the woods around us, the cozy feel of having enough space but still choosing to stay plastered to Jake's side. It feels like home. Ever since I told him that, we've spent every night here, and this has become Socks's second favorite place, after being at work with us. I died laughing when Frank dropped off a package two days ago containing little cat booties, but Socks loves them, and he can safely pounce around Jake's shop with them.

"Where's that head at, pretty girl?"

His hands trace little lines from my hip to my stomach, dipping just below my panties. Humming at the warm feel of him, I admit, "I really love waking up in your bed with you."

"Our bed." His pinky slips farther into my panties.

"I like the sound of that."

"Good." His pinky brushes against my clit, sending my hips rocking against him again. "Because I want you to move in."

I freeze, unsure of how to respond. Am I ready for that? So much has changed for me this year, so much has happened, but through it all, one thing has stuck out. I've grown, I've learned to lean on others, and I've healed through Jake's care and love. So yeah, I'm ready for that.

He takes my silence as hesitation and pushes me so I'm flat on my back. His pinky is still slowly making passes over my clit as he leans over my body. "I want you here, baby. I want this place to be ours. I want to go to bed by your side and wake up with your body pressed to mine. Be my forever, Amber, and move in with me."

Those deep-blue eyes pierce me with intensity, and I melt at his words. I've never wanted forever so badly before now. I never thought I could have a man like Jake. Someone who can shine bright in the darkest of depths. He's my equal in all things, taking my sharp edges and building something beautiful with them instead of sanding them down.

Lifting my head, I brush my lips over his. "Yes, Jake."

His lips lift into a smile against mine, and he lets out a low chuckle. "Forever?"

"Forever."

Jake's mouth is on mine, hot and heavy. Demanding and sure. His hand slips farther down, two fingers gliding through my slit before shoving in. Our moans echo through the room, the feel of his thick fingers filling me the way I like, but it's not enough. They slide in and out, matching the tempo of his tongue in my mouth, but I need more. I need it all.

My hands smooth over the ridges of his stomach, tugging his boxers down when I get to them. He lifts his hips, helping me as a third finger pushes into me. His cock is heavy in my hand, each little metal ball cool against my fingers as I grip him.

Precum leaks from the head, coating my fingers as I rub it back down his length. Going from inexperienced to sharing a bed with Jake means I've gotten a crash course in pleasure. Both giving and receiving. Last week, he let me tie him to the headboard and told me to explore. I felt awkward at first, but being able to take my time touching, tasting, and learning every inch of his body with no judgment was exactly what I needed. It gave me a confidence I never thought I would have with him.

My thumb circles the small opening before I drag his slick precum down, coating it over every rung as Jake's hips buck. His groan is so deep it sends shivers through my body. "Need to be inside you, Whiskey."

"Please," I beg, kicking off my panties, and he rolls between my legs.

Strong fingers grip the back of my neck, molten blue eyes locked on mine, as he pushes in. Each inch, each barbell, sliding in with ease, filling me in the way I've come to crave.

"So fucking perfect," he rasps when he's fully in. "So fucking mine."

Then he's moving, grinding into me slowly, evenly. Stretching my pussy around his thick cock. It's heaven being loved by this man. Being taken care of by him, being his partner, his support as much as he is mine. It's everything Jana used to say was out there for me. How right she was.

Jake's thumb runs over my cheek, wiping the tear I didn't realize had fallen. His eyes shine in the early morning light, seeing everything I'm feeling. And he takes it on, like he always does. Letting me feel all my emotions and meeting them head-on. It's too much, his soft touches, his searching eyes, his promise of forever. I need the pain, the anger, to even out these overwhelming feelings, threatening to take me under.

Jake sees it all, a smirk lifting his lips. "I love you, Amber. But I'm going to fuck you like I don't."

In one swift move, he pulls out and flips me over. He's back inside of me in one hard thrust, his hips slapping against my ass. One hand grips my hair, lifting my head so I don't suffocate in the pillows as he plows into me. My back is arched, my pussy stretched, and the sting of my scalp while he tugs on my hair is exactly what I need to keep me in this moment.

I moan in a mix of pleasure and pain as he slams into me again. My fingers grip into the silky material of the sheets, scrunching it.

"There she is," Jake growls into my ear, leaning over me and pulling my head closer to him. "My little slut needs the fight, doesn't she? Needs it so she can feel safe to let it all out?"

He lifts my hips slightly, changing the angle so every rough thrust lights up that spot inside of me. "Come on, baby. Fight for it. Scream it out for me."

His raspy voice skates over my skin, and with one more slam of his hips, I explode, crying out into the quiet as lights flash behind my eyes. Waves of pleasure roll through my body, and Jake pumps into me four more times before spilling in me with a roar of his own. Our sweat-soaked bodies sink into the mattress before Jake groans and rolls us slightly so he isn't squishing me.

His calloused fingers stroke my hair back from my face and run down my arm. "I love you, baby. Forever."

"It's only forever if you promise to keep waking me like that," my now sleepy voice mumbles.

Jake pinches my nipples until I squeal. "Brat."

I wince when he pulls out of me, unsure if that will ever change. Before I can huddle down in the blanket, he rips them off and pulls me into his arms. "No you don't. It's shower and gym time."

He laughs at my pouty face but carries me down the stairs anyway, his half-hard dick slapping against my ass with every step. After setting me down on the cold counter and turning on the shower, he folds his arms over his broad chest and turns to me with a serious look.

"What?"

"Speaking of the gym … Kyle won't be back." When I raise an eyebrow at him, he doubles down on his scowl. "You said you didn't want to decide his fate, so I did. He won't be back to Cedar Ridge. And no, I didn't kill him."

"Not killing him leaves a lot of wiggle room."

The asshole just smirks. "Yeah, Whiskey, it does." Pulling me down from the counter, he steps into the shower with me, putting us both under the hot spray of water. His kiss is light. Comforting. "Black soul to black soul, I'll do whatever it takes to keep you protected. To love you the only way I know how. Forever, Amber. Forever."

bonus scene — amber

"I get it now."

Looking up at Jake, I cock an eyebrow. "What?"

"Thoren said coffee back here with Lily used to be the highlight of his day. Sitting here with you snuggled into my side, I get it. These evenings are mine too."

My heart melts at the sweet things Jake says so openly now. We still fight. Oh God, do we still fight, but I look forward to it. His punishments usually push me to the edge of what I'm not sure I can handle, only to make me crave whatever depraved thing he introduces me to. Like the spanking bench he made me last week. He even added hooks on the bottom to cuff my hands in place. Who knew I would like being tied up so much.

Living here with him, though, is everything I dreamed of and more. Natasha is also a huge fan, since she now rents out my studio space above the store. We've caught Colby slipping out of there a few mornings, which always leads to a sneaky fist bump from Jake. Silly boys.

The temperatures are dropping rapidly in the crisp fall evenings, but we still love to spend time on the swing after work. I've never taken advantage of the beautiful colors and woods surrounding me before, but I never appreciated them like now. Every breath I used to have to fight so hard for comes easy out here. There's no clawing to get out of the dark anymore, no waves trying to pull me under.

Jake has shown me how to sit at the edge, seeing the beauty in the struggle and appreciating the fight, all while knowing I have the calm shores to surround me now, with the people I love.

"Are you expecting someone?" Jake asks at the sound of a car door slamming and the crunch of gravel. I shake my head as we both get up and head inside to see who's here.

To my surprise, it's Evelyn's sweet face that smiles at us when we open the door. "Hey, you two. Mind if I come in for a minute?"

I've been doing my best to check in on her. Between Jake's parents, Evelyn, and visiting Jana's grave, our days are filled. Since her hospitalization, she's been as active as ever despite David giving us all clear signs he's worried. The blood clot cleared with medication, but Thoren swears there's more going on with her health she's not made us privy to. "Of course. What's going on?"

She follows us into the living room, taking a seat on the couch. "I have something for you. I wasn't sure when the right time to give it was, but as I was watering my garden tonight, something happened. The clouds parted for just a moment, letting the sun break through, and wouldn't you know, it was directly on my rose bush. As I walked over to see, I noticed this." Evelyn reaches into her large purse, pulling out a pink rose. It's beautiful, and upon closer inspection, it has a rare two blooms on the same stem. "The rest of the bush is dead already, but this one here is perfect, and I knew it was Jana telling me it was time."

My head snaps up to her, and Jake grips my thigh. "What?" I manage to squeak out.

Evelyn's gaze is soft as she pulls out two envelopes and sets them on the coffee table, gently setting the rose on top. "About a month before she passed, she asked me to write out these two letters for her. One for you, Amber, and one for the love of your life. It's been the sweetest honor watching your love story unfold. I know this is the time, and Jake is the man."

She gets up, squeezing Jake's shoulder before dropping a kiss to my head. "Read them when you're ready. She loved you so much, honey. Jana saw this future for you, she hoped and prayed she would get to see it, and I know she is looking down on you two with the biggest smile. I love you both."

My hands are trembling and my heart is racing as I stare at the last words I have from my aunt. I don't even realize Jake has gotten up to walk Evelyn to the door until he is squatting down in front of me, brushing my hair behind my ear.

"How are you doing, baby?"

"I, uh—" Choking on the words, I clear my throat before trying again. "I would like to read it now."

"Okay. Would you like to take a blanket to the swing and read it out there? I can read mine in here, and when you're done, you can tell me what you want to do."

Not trusting my voice again, I nod, shaky fingers grabbing for the envelope with my name. On unsteady legs, I make my way back outside, curling onto the porch swing. Taking a deep breath, I open the letter.

My darling Amber,
You did it. You let someone in and found your passion in the person you were meant to be with, and I am so PROUD of you. The strength, trust, and effort it takes to allow someone in after so

much trauma is no small feat. Yet here you are, doing it again.

How I wish I could have saved you from some of the hurt in your life. Instead, I know I am only adding to it. I love you. I love you like you're my own, always have and always will. I'm so sorry I had to leave you before either of us were ready. But you're strong. So damn strong, my beautiful girl.

I hope you're following your dreams. If the store isn't your dream, that's okay. All I ask is that you find what is. And let those friends of yours in. I don't know if you know this, but Michele and Lily visit me. About twice a month, they sneak me in treats on days they know you can't make it in. They love you, baby girl, so let them.

Now onto the love of your life. Show them that heart inside of you and let them see the scars. I know your mom gave you plenty of them, but they are what make you a beautiful warrior. A phoenix rising from the ashes. Let him see that side of you. Let him see everything. Sharing the burdens of our hurt and trauma helps to lighten the load.

You deserve the very best in life, and I just know you have found it. A man that loves you through everything. Who makes you feel like the most important person in their life. Who supports and encourages you and pulls you out of your head when you need it.

I never married, so I don't have much advice to give except this. Give him the love you only showed to me. Put your time and effort into loving the man that stands by your side through it all. You have a huge heart hidden down deep inside, and I hope you give it all to him.

I'm so proud of you. Of the woman you've become. Of the battles you have fought and overcome. Of the kindness you continue to show through it all. And of the life I know you are building. I am missing you, just know that I am by your side always. Cheering you on for the good days and sitting on the swing with you on the bad ones.

I know you will have the best life, filled with love and laughter, and a joy like you've never known. The world made you hard, let this man make you soft again, baby girl. Love hard and deep, and keep fighting for the beautiful future I know you will have.

With all my love,
Mom

jake

I watch through the living room window as Amber carefully opens her letter. Every emotion crosses her face: pain, happiness, sorrow, love. Tears slip down her pretty pink cheeks as she reads through Jana's last words to her.

This seems silly, but the fact she wrote one for me almost took me out at the knees. Jana raised that beautiful woman out there. She took her in with open arms and did everything her mother should have. It's a hollow feeling knowing I'll never be able to thank her for that. And now this? She wrote a letter *for me*. With shaky hands, I open the letter.

To the love of her life,

First, I would like to say I'm sorry I'm not here to meet you. Then I want to say thank you. Thank you for taking the time to love my girl. I know she has walls up, and not just any walls. Her walls are forged over years of trauma, hurt, and feelings of being unworthy and incapable of love. Breaking them down would have taken time, attention, and care that I'm sure was sometimes forced onto her. The fact you stuck through and did it, means you see her heart under it all, and seeing that heart still beating so strong after everything is truly a gift.

Thank you for seeing the light hidden within. Her quiet and sometimes snarky exterior was like a comfort blanket for her for so long. I worked tirelessly to get her to show her amazing light to the world, but she was so selective with it. Standing in Amber's light is the closest you will ever get to standing in the midst of a wildfire. It burns hot, all-consuming, all powerful. When she loves someone and shines that light on them, she does it with her whole being. Relish in that warmth.

Helping raise Amber is the greatest thing I have ever done with my life. I hope loving her is the greatest thing you do with yours. I'm passing on the role of protector, supporter, confidant, and friend. She's your girl now.

Some helpful hints for loving your girl.

When she's overwhelmed, let her fight it out. I was too quiet for her to get her anger out with, so she utilized the gym. Something tells me you can take her fire though, so let her yell. Let her go for a run, let her scream into the void, just let her get it out. It's when she goes quiet that her mom's voice breaks through.

When she's sad, bring her brownies. They're her favorite treat and are best eaten on a porch. She pretends she isn't big on physical affection, but wrap her in a hug, and her whole body relaxes. So hold your girl every chance you get. Show her the affection she never received as a child.

She's a workaholic. Let her be one. It's her safety. Growing up with nothing, she works twice as hard to make sure she never returns there. Force her to rest when necessary, but don't take away her ability to support herself. Help her find ways to do it while finding balance.

Support her in her habits. Allow her to keep your things tidy, it helps bring her peace. Her hands run down her thighs when she's anxious. Try holding her hand when she does it. Find a way to give back to the community and those who need it. Doing that always brings her joy.

Don't feel the need to buy her things, she doesn't want or need material items. Just love her, and love her hard. I promise she will love you back with everything she has.

Have the best life with our girl.

Jana

Folding the letter, I let my body sink into the couch to process everything she said. Caring for and protecting Amber's heart has been my priority, but with the knowledge that Jana passed that responsibility onto me knowing what a treasure it was, heals deeply scarred parts of my soul. Amber is the greatest treasure I will ever hold in my hands, and I'm so grateful Jana felt the same. That she helped to raise and shape the beautiful woman I get to call mine.

The fading light of the afternoon sun is highlighting the halo of hair around Amber's beautiful face, the tears on her cheeks catching the light, giving her an ethereal glow. She looks like an angel, and I know she's feeling the warmth of her own personal angel in this moment.

Dragging my hands down my face, I wipe the heavy emotions from my eyes and watch as she processes Jana's last words to her. When her shoulders finally relax and a small smile stretches on those pouty pink lips, I get up and join her on the swing outside.

Without a word, we cling to each other while watching the last of the fading light. We don't need to talk to know we are equally grateful and heartbroken. It feels like acceptance, and the start of the rest of our lives.

This book was a hard one, covering a lot of emotional topics. I hope I gave them the respect that they deserve. These two fought hard for their love, and for the life they wanted, and that really resonated with me. I love them dearly, and I hope you felt their struggles, their pain and their happy ending the way I did.

Thank you to my alpha readers: Ashley, Emily, and Alyssa. You three helped me work through all my issues in the book and fell for these two the way I did. Your encouragement, feedback, and support was unending and I appreciate you more than words can say!

My beta readers: Lazarra and Sarah, thank you for taking the time to read this and give me feedback. Sarah, thank you for the call, and Lazarra, thank you for feeling the emotions of this book and reminding me how much of an impact reading and writing can have. Your excitement and love for this story fueled my soul.

These two groups of amazing women mean the world to me for taking a chance on me and believing in me on the days I didn't believe in myself.

To my husband and daughter, thank you for your ongoing support. B, I love your excitement over every little win that I have. You're the hype girl everyone needs in their corner and I'm glad you're in mine. I love you both dearly.

To Kristin, my cover artist, you did it again! Your skill is unmatched and you are a true joy to work with.

To Deidre, my editor, THANK YOU. Thank you for fixing

my many repeated words and phrases, as well as my 1000 'as' sentences. Yes I did it once more just for you.

To you, my readers, I am eternally grateful. This dream of mine could never be a reality without your support. I hope to continually bring you swoon worthy stories that touch your heart.

FUCK CANCER. If the emotions felt heavy in this book, it's because my emotions from losing loved ones to cancer were heavy while writing this book. For those of you badasses still fighting, I hope it's a battle you win. For those loving and losing people to this awful disease, I'm sending you my love.

Coming next in the Wanderland Series:
Michele and Ethan's story

about the author

Etta Lane is a married mother who loves to read spicy romance as much as she loves to write it. She loves the outdoors, adventures, and game nights with friends. When she isn't reading or writing, you can find her spending time with her family, gardening, or Facetiming her sister.

connect with etta

Instagram: @ettalane.author
Facebook: Etta Lane
TikTok: @etta.lane.author
Facebook Reader Group: Etta Lane's Reader Group
Email: ettalanewrites@gmail.com